Also by Marc Graham

Of Ashes and Dust
Song of Songs: A Novel of the Queen of Sheba

SON OF THE SEA, DAUGHTER OF THE SUN

A Novel

SON OF THE SEA, DAUGHTER OF THE SUN

A Novel

Marc Graham

Blank Slate Press | Saint Louis, MO 63116

Blank Slate Press
Saint Louis, MO 63116
Copyright © 2019 Marc Graham
All rights reserved.
Blank Slate Press is an imprint of Amphorae Publishing Group, LLC
a woman- and veteran owned company
www.amphoraepublishing.com

For information, contact:
Blank Slate Press
4168 Hartford Street, Saint Louis, MO 63116

Manufactured in the United States of America

Cover photography and graphics: Shutterstock
Set in Adobe Caslon Pro and Avenir Light

Library of Congress Control Number: 2019936759
ISBN: 9781943075638

For Bill Murphy,
teacher of literature and
liberator of minds.

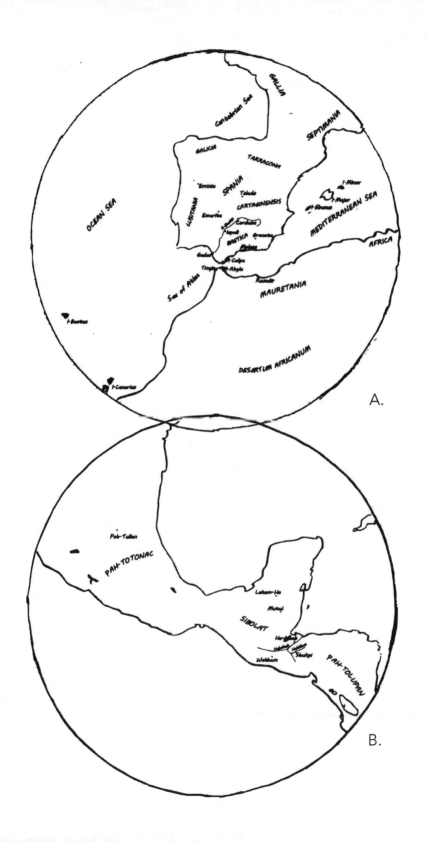

A.

B.

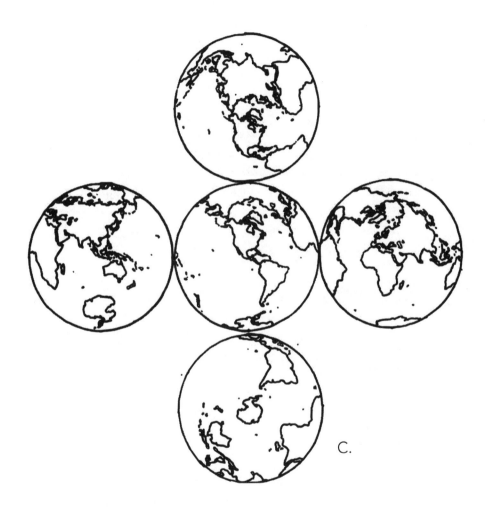

A. Map of Spania
B. Map of Sibolat
C. Map of Pah-Tullan

The Fortunate Isles signify by their name that they produce all kinds of good things, as if they were happy and blessed with an abundance of fruit... Hence the mistake of pagans and the poems by worldly poets, who believed that these isles were Paradise because of the fertility of their soil. They are situated in the Ocean, against the left side of Mauretania, closest to where the sun sets, and they are separated from each other by the intervening sea.

— Isidore of Seville, *The Etymologies*, Book XIV, Part vi, 625 CE

PART 1

MEDITERRANEAN SEA, THE COAST OF SPANIA

610 C.E.

1

THE BOY SHOUTED and pounded on the door of the ship's hold. "Claudia! Anyone!"

His cries went unanswered, but still he beat his fists against the oak as blood-orange flames licked at the timbers overhead. In the dancing half-light, the knotted planks of the door formed a leering demon's face, and he reeled back, slipped and fell into the rising water. Rotten food and human waste floated about him, and he scrambled to his feet and spat out the tainted seawater.

Something tugged on his long hair. He reached back and screamed as he untangled a rat, its screech matching his. The rat's eyes shone red as Iudila shuddered and flung it against the bulkhead.

Above him, the shouts and clang of weapons that had followed the crash of ship's timbers were now quiet. That silence chilled him, but whatever it meant had to be better than the death that would claim him if he couldn't get out. He slogged through water now up to his thighs, and again attacked the door.

The ship lurched to one side. Iudila slipped and his head struck the corner of a thick timber rib. Water cascaded through ruptured deck planks and quenched the flames.

"Saint Gabriel, save me," Iudila prayed into the darkness with a choke and a splutter.

He ducked under the surface, holding his breath as he stroked to the bulkhead and slapped against the door. The water dampened his blows until they fell with no more strength than an infant's. He bobbed to the surface to steal from the sliver of air that yet survived beneath the scorched deck. He beat at the water to stay afloat while he filled his lungs then, as the sea closed around him, made yet another attempt.

The water resounded with the beat of Iudila's heart. The tinkle of distant splashes. A rumble of men's voices. Then, footfalls on the ship's ladder.

Iudila gripped the doorjamb to hold himself in place, pounding with his other hand. He shouted his last breath, and the life-bearing bubbles raced to the surface.

A slap sounded from outside the door. A muffled voice sifted through the oak followed by the scrape of the door's bar. Iudila offered a second prayer, of thanks this time. Before he could manage *Amen*, the door burst outward under the weight of water and the ship groaned as the flood expelled him from the hold. His foot caught on a rope and he slammed into a crate. His head spun and his sight faded. Before the world went black, his vision was filled by a dark giant, bald-headed, broad-faced and flat-nosed. The man moved his thick lips but Iudila heard only the ringing in his ears as he slid into nothingness.

He came back to his senses in open air, the fresh sea breeze tainted by the tang of blood in his nose. A ship's deck rocked beneath him. The sky swayed to a more playful cadence than under the lazy rhythm of the merchant vessel to which he'd become accustomed.

"You'll be all right," a voice grunted in rough-accented Greek as dark-skinned fingers pounded a sponge against Iudila's bruised forehead.

Iudila looked up to see the face of his rescuer, less monstrous-looking in the full light of day. The man's dark eyes shone with kindness and the corners of his mouth arced upward. Iudila returned a tentative smile before the sponge again battered his face.

"Let him be, Dingha," another voice said. "He's been through enough without your bludgeoning him. Can you sit?"

Iudila nodded.

Strong hands gripped him under each arm and hoisted him against the ship's rail. As he came upright, the world twisted into a blur of light and noise. Iudila vomited down the front of his sodden tunic, and the sting of brine and bile brought him fully to his senses.

He squinted against the Mediterranean sun and examined the score of weather-beaten faces surrounding him. Some of the men looked back at him with the same slack curiosity of the rustici that worked his lands. Others stared with raw hunger. As Iudila shrank back from their leers. The men laughed, and he blushed for shame as tears again stung his eyes. Summoning all his dignity, he stiffened his spine and teetered to his feet.

"That's a lad," the second voice encouraged him.

Iudila turned to see a shaven face marred by neither sun nor disease, framed by lank yellow hair.

"I am Milhma," the man said with a small bow, "captain of the *Mari-Nadris*." He looked at Iudila expectantly then added, "And you are...?"

Iudila started to speak but his voice cracked. He cleared his throat and spat a gob of bile over the side. He feigned confidence, using the tone that generally got him his way at home.

"I am Iudila af Goiswinth, Count of Corduba, Duke of Baetica and Prince of Goths." He drew himself to his full height but, at only twelve years of age, his name was more imposing than his stature.

The titles were his by right. Though an orphan, he descended from the Balthi, noblest clan of the Goths. Grandson of a past king, nephew of the present one, he took pride in the royal blood that filled his veins. His lineage earned him the fealty of the slaves and freedmen who worked his lands, the gratitude of the townsfolk whose trade those lands made possible, and the deference of the priests who grew fat off his fields and drunk from his vineyards.

At his villa in Corduba or the cathedral school at Ispali, he was treated with the respect befitting a future king. But here—far from home, alone among strangers, soaked by the sea, and stinking of ash and blood and vomit—here, the royal veins of this noblest of nobles ran with ice water. He wanted nothing more than to curl onto the lap of his nursemaid.

Milhma nodded grimly at the young prince before the captain's face cracked into a smirk. The smirk spread into a grin, then exploded with laughter. The other men followed Milhma's lead and burst into jeers. All except Dingha, who stood mute on Iudila's other side.

"How's that for a day's catch, lads?" Milhma called to his crew. "Not only a hold full of silver, but two princes as well."

Iudila looked up at that. "Two?"

"For the moment." Milhma signaled his men to stand aside so the boy could see.

Sisenanth of Tarracona was six years older than Iudila, already a sturdy young man and a promising warrior. His flowing blond hair and blue eyes contrasted with Iudila's copper and green, but the two shared the solid jaw and aquiline nose of the Goth nobles.

At the moment, though, Sisenanth's nose bore a noticeable bend. It streamed blood that dampened the gag in his mouth, stained his thin beard, and dripped onto the ropes wrapped around his arms and chest. He knelt on naked knees, his richly embroidered tunic having been stripped away, leaving him with only his breechclout. Two men held him fast as his muscles strained against the ropes.

Iudila had once looked up to Sisenanth. That respect was now replaced by fear and confusion, for it was Sisenanth who had stolen Iudila from his comfortable sea cabin and locked him in the hold that had nearly become his coffin.

"He's no prince," Iudila muttered.

"What's that?" Milhma asked.

Iudila shook his head in dismissal then turned on Milhma. "I thank you for rescuing us, Captain, but I demand to know why this man is in bonds."

"You demand?" Milhma said, his face a blend of amusement and anger. "You demand?" he repeated, and the amusement drained away. Milhma lashed out with a backhanded blow that stunned Iudila and drew blood from his fast-swelling lip. "What I would have you know is that your fellow princeling killed one of my men as we saved you from that sinking hulk." He pointed past Sisenanth, beyond the bow of the *Mari-Nadris*.

Iudila turned to look where the captain pointed. What had been a merchant ship was now a floating pyre that poured thick smoke into the azure sky. Iudila gaped at the holocaust then staggered toward the bow. The *Euangelion* rode low upon the sea. An occasional wave penetrated a scupper or leapt over the side, only to be consumed in the flames as fire and water fought over the scraps from Death's table.

Scorched bodies littered the ship's deck. One had its arms thrown over the railing, the blackened head resting on the gunnel as yellow teeth grinned through shrunken lips. Iudila looked away only to find even more bodies floating in the waves. Most were mercifully facedown but a few looked with dead eyes upon the empty sky.

Among the drifting bodies Iudila recognized Claudia, the nurse who had raised him, been a mother to him. Her raven hair formed a halo about her fair face that looked serenely heavenward. Her slit throat, however, gleamed angry and red.

Iudila's mouth flooded with horror and his eyes filled with tears. He cried out when Claudia jerked and other bodies swayed and bobbed in a macabre dance. Some of Milhma's men crossed themselves, others made pagan signs against evil. The calm sea erupted in foam, and a grey fin broke the water's surface to announce the arrival of the scavengers of the deep.

Iudila tore his eyes from the carnage of man and shark. He fell against the stem post with its thick, ironclad spur. The metal was nicked and scarred where it had been driven over the bows of the *Euangelion* and, doubtless, many other ships.

In an instant, all became clear. The collision that had thrown him from his bunk. Angry shouts. The short-lived clash of blades. Frightful screams from both men and women. Then the ominous silence.

"You're pirates," Iudila said, his voice drained of emotion.

"He sees at last," Milhma said. "Perhaps he isn't completely daft. Well, lads, we've a bench to fill and a choice to make. Stand him up," he ordered the sailors that held Sisenanth.

The men hoisted the bound and red-faced Goth to his feet then leaned him against the low-swept bow rail next to Iudila.

"Here," the captain continued, "we a have a strapping lad who should bend to the oar right well. Of course, he'll do no good trussed up, and I dare not cut him loose just yet. Over here"—he stroked Iudila's cheek—"we've a fair scrap of a boy who'll be of little use outside my cabin. Worthless on an oar, but I doubt he'd give us much trouble. Which to choose, which to choose?"

Milhma slid his dagger from its sheath and twisted the blade to splash sunlight in the eyes of the captives. He dragged the blade across Sisenanth's bared chest. "You might have been a joy to tame," he said wistfully as a trail of blood followed in the dagger's wake, "but I've not the time to break you properly." He brushed his lips against Sisenanth's cheek and stepped back.

"No," Iudila screamed as Milhma swept the dagger through the air.

Milhma stilled the blade as it touched Sisenanth's throat, then glared at Iudila. His face slowly softened and he pulled the dagger away.

"Perhaps you're right," the pirate said. "It'll take longer this way."

Milhma kicked Sisenanth's chest, and the Goth tumbled over the rail. The milling fins drew closer. Sisenanth bobbed up once before his head disappeared beneath the waves. Milhma gripped Iudila by the shoulders and led him aft toward his cabin.

"To your oars, lads. We're finished here."

Most of the sailors hustled through the open center of the deck to take their places at the rowing benches. A smaller crewman sat behind a wooden drum and started beating out the strokes while the one called Dingha climbed to his post at the steering oar.

Iudila shot a pleading glance at him, but the big man turned his eyes away and lowered his head. Even the western sun darkened in sympathy as the captain swung open the door to his cabin and ushered the boy inside.

"Welcome to your new home," Milhma said as he stepped in behind Iudila and closed the door.

2

IUDILA STIRRED AND SAT UP in bed. A full moon filtered through chinks in the sea cabin's walls, bathing the space in blue-tinged twilight. Nestled in the crook of bed and bulkhead, Milhma breathed deeply beside Iudila. The captain lay naked, like Iudila, uncovered in the warm Mediterranean night.

A shadow flitted at the cabin's threshold, followed by a faint scratching on the door. Iudila glanced at Milhma, then slid off the bed and crept to the door. He put his ear to the planks and tapped with one finger. The shadow retreated with a whisper of bare feet. A creak of wood told of someone climbing the ladder to the steering deck. Iudila lifted the latch, careful against making any sound. He eased the door open just enough to slip through.

The moon hung in a cloudless sky over quiet seas, and lit Iudila's way up the ladder. A massive doorway was out of place on the steering deck, but Iudila pushed on one of the leaves and both doors slowly swung open.

Iudila stepped through the opening onto flagstones that sent a chill from sole to scalp. The doors closed silently behind him, shutting out the moon's light. A great hall stretched above and before him. The stone floor and wooden beams echoed with the sound of his breathing.

A single candle glowed at the far end of the hall. Iudila cautiously walked that way. As he came closer, the candlelight revealed a throne set upon a dais.

Above the throne hung a banner of scarlet emblazoned with a gold hexagram surrounded by a wreath of olive branches. Unlike the Jews' Star of David with its two overlapping triangles, this hexagram was composed of six lines drawn end-to-end—the sign of Iudila's family, the Balthi. Together with the olive branches, the symbol was Iudila's as Duke of Baetica.

"The scarlet belongs to the king." The voice rang in the darkness.

Iudila looked back to the throne to see a figure seated there. Auburn hair framed a face of sculpted ivory whose emerald eyes fixed Iudila with a playful gleam. He had not seen his cousin Keinan since their betrothal ceremony, before he'd been dispatched to Constantinople. Before Milhma had taken him.

If she had been lovely then, she was positively radiant now, dressed only in a diaphanous blue gown that reached from her shoulders to her calves. Bare feet with ringed toes rested on a scarlet cushion. Iudila felt a strain in his loins as his eyes drifted upward.

"The scarlet belongs to the king," Keinan said again.

"To which king?" Iudila forced his eyes to meet hers.

"Do you not recognize the seal?"

"It is mine, the seal of the Lords of Baetica. But my banner is blue."

"The scarlet belongs to the king."

Iudila was silent for a time as the meaning of the words sank in. "I am to be King?"

In reply, Keinan stood. The gown clung to her body, and even in the dim light Iudila could see the dark triangle of womanhood between her thighs and the twin rubies that crowned her breasts. His longing grew more insistent as Keinan took his hands, turned him around and seated him upon the throne.

"You know the ancient custom?"

Iudila nodded. "Only a daughter of the Scarlet Thread may crown the King."

Keinan ran her hands down his chest and legs and knelt before him.

The doors crashed open and three men entered the hall. An armor-clad warrior with long, flowing hair raced, sword drawn, toward the dais. A tonsured, white-robed priest chased after him, while a black-cowled figure glided slowly up the hall. As the men approached, Keinan rose and stood to the side.

"You dare sit upon the throne, stripling?" the warrior demanded.

"I didn't—I don't—"

The warrior pointed his sword at Iudila's breast. "Only the worthy may rise to the seat of our fathers. Down."

Iudila slid off the throne and down the steps of the dais. By this time, the black-robed man had crossed the great hall and stood across from the warrior, the priest between them.

Iudila studied the warrior. The man's features reminded him of his father, but in place of Goiswinth's blond hair was Iudila's own copper. He shifted his gaze from his older self to the figure in black but could see nothing behind the shadowed cowl.

The warrior looked from man to man, then to Keinan. "Make your choice."

The young woman stepped down from the dais and circled the group. She ran a hand across Iudila's naked back, sending a wave of desire through his body. Keinan placed her hand upon the chest of the cowled figure then dropped her head in sadness. At last she looked the warrior up and down, went to his side and wrapped her arm about his. The warrior smiled victoriously then nodded to the priest.

The cleric pressed Keinan's and the warrior's hands between his own. "*In nomine Patris, et Filii, et Spiritus Sancti. Amen.*" He released their hands, made the sign of the cross then led the couple up to the dais.

The warrior climbed the steps but Keinan lingered a moment. She leaned toward Iudila, brushing his cheeks with her lips. "The princess awaits her warrior-king," she whispered. "Come to me when you are worthy. Until then, I leave you with this."

Iudila closed his eyes and gasped as Keinan's hands surrounded his groin with warmth. He convulsed with the pleasure of her touch then opened his eyes to find a moonlit cabin at sea, where a red-faced Milhma glowered at him from the corner of the bed.

"You faithless bitch," the pirate screamed. "You whoreson whelp."

Iudila huddled in a corner as Milhma whipped a reed cane at him. The pirate had taken his pleasure with the boy for months. In recent weeks, he had sought to return to Iudila the favors he'd taken from him. He often managed to arouse the boy, but Iudila was too young for his body to respond in full.

Until this night. It had taken the Succuba—the demon-temptress that haunted men's dreams—to succeed where Milhma had so often failed.

The captain's wrath matched the injury to his pride. Milhma threw Iudila from the bed. He wrenched open the cabin door, grabbed the boy by the hair and flung him through the opening. Iudila's head struck the jamb and he tumbled, dazed, into the ship's hold. Sailors grunted and cursed at the rude awakening. Coarse hands lifted Iudila to his feet only for the captain to take him again by the hair and drag him toward the bow.

"I've fed you," Milhma screamed, his words punctuated by a lash of the reed across Iudila's cheek. "I've clothed you." He struck the other cheek, and blood bathed Iudila's tongue. "I've kept you warm and this is how you repay my kindness, taking pleasure of yourself? No more. I'll send you to Egyr's feast as I should have done in the first place."

Iudila was too stunned to resist as Milhma flung him against the stem post. He could only envision the long, cold journey to the sea's bottom where the giant Egyr hosted the souls of the drowned in his great hall.

"No," said a voice behind Milhma.

The captain's face twisted with rage, his eyes darting about to see who dared to defy him.

"No," Dingha repeated gently as he climbed up from the hold, his shaved head shining in the moonlight. "You will not do this."

"Won't I?" Milhma spat. "He is my property to use and dispose of as I see fit. If I want to drop him over the side like last night's dinner, who are you to say otherwise?"

The big man cocked his head. "I am Dingha."

Milhma snorted at that and bent Iudila over the rail.

"I will buy him," Dingha blurted. "I will pay. I will buy him from you."

The captain stopped and turned around. "You would buy this rot?"

Dingha nodded.

"Rot or no, he's still a prince, worthy of a royal ransom. You've not enough silver to redeem him."

Dingha's mouth dropped open helplessly.

"Then I will help." Brehanu, a giant of an oarsman from Aksum, stepped to Dingha's side.

"And I," said Eneko, the nimble Cantabrian lookout.

One by one, the crewmen stepped forward.

"It will take all of you to ransom him." Milhma sneered as a pair of sailors hung back.

Dingha glared at the men. A growl rumbled deep in his chest, and they reluctantly stepped forward to join the crew.

"We will all pay," Dingha said.

Milhma glowered at his crew. "You want him, you can have him. But it's as a slave he comes to you." The captain forced Iudila to his knees and pressed the boy's head against the deck rail. "Bring me a ring," he said to Eneko.

The Cantabrian hesitated, but nodded and dropped to the lower deck.

"Your blade." Milhma held his hand out to Dingha. He snapped his fingers and shook his hand when the man was slow to respond.

Dingha pulled the dagger from his belt, studied it in the moonlight then looked at the captain from beneath heavy brows.

Milhma slipped his hand to Iudila's throat. "Don't be a bigger fool than you already are."

Dingha relaxed his gaze. He flipped the dagger in the air, caught it by its blade and gave it hilt-first to his captain.

Milhma twisted Iudila's head until one ear lay flat against the rail. He slowly brought the knife toward Iudila's face, and the boy's knees buckled.

Iudila looked frantically to Dingha, but the big man just hardened his features and gave a curt nod. Iudila swallowed, the blood from his torn cheeks burning his throat. He clenched his teeth and raised his chin as much as Milhma's grip would allow. His eyes filled with tears as the blade stabbed through his ear and into the rail, but he made no sound beyond a small grunt.

There came a tugging sensation as Milhma twisted the blade to round out the hole. He slipped the dagger between his teeth and held out his hand as Eneko returned. A split copper ring glinted in the moonlight. Milhma threaded one end of the metal through Iudila's pierced ear then pinched the ends together.

In the next instant, the blade was again in the captain's hands.

"No," Iudila screamed as Milhma yanked his hair and sawed through the thick locks.

Like Samson of old, the Goth nobles reckoned their hair a symbol of potency. A man might lose his wealth, lose his lands and women and slaves, and he would simply be considered unlucky. To lose his hair, however—to be shorn as a sheep or slave or priest—was to be unmanned. The shame of it crushed Iudila more than all the abuses of the past several months.

Milhma scraped the blade across Iudila's scalp, shaving his head clean and leaving streams of blood to trickle down the boy's face and neck. "What's this?" he demanded, probing the base of Iudila's skull, which was tattooed with an Egyptian eye centered on a six-pointed star.

"It's my sigil," Iudila said, struggling to keep his voice steady. "My father had it made when I was born."

"It's witchcraft." Milhma spat and made a sign against evil. He jerked Iudila to his feet then pushed him toward the crew. "He's your trouble now. But if he brings ill luck to this ship, it's over the side he goes. One more thing."

Dingha stepped in front of Iudila. "He is ours now. You do not touch him."

"Oh, he's yours all right," the captain said. "But this belongs to me."

Faster than Dingha could react, Milhma kneed him in the groin. Dingha grunted and doubled over. Milhma grabbed the man's tongue, stretched it from his mouth and sliced the blade through the flesh. Blood spewed from Dingha's mouth as he screamed and sank to his knees.

"No one tells me *no* on my own ship." Milhma stabbed the dagger through the bit of tongue and into the rail. "Thanks for the use of your blade," he said, then turned on his heels and stalked back to his cabin.

3

LIKE THE SEA SERPENT for which she was named, the *Mari-Nadris* rocked on lazy swells as the heavens wheeled slowly overhead. After Milhma had exiled Iudila from his cabin, the boy feared some of the crew might wish to take up where the captain had left off.

Dingha and Brehanu—the largest men aboard—made it clear, though, that Iudila was not to be touched. All the same, the boy had taken to sleeping topside during mild weather, the better to escape the snoring, belching, farting seamen who slept by their oars.

He missed the comfort of Milhma's bed, but it was a small price to pay for his freedom from the man's attentions. The Succuba that caused Iudila's expulsion from the cabin had yet to return, try as he might to conjure her image before falling asleep.

Keinan, his cousin and betrothed, was already becoming a distant memory, and he feared he might forget all he had known of Spania—his villa in Corduba, the cathedral school at Ispali, the rolling hills, mighty rivers, and ragged mountains that defined his province of Baetica.

Eneko, the lookout from the wild reaches of Galicia in Spania's far north, often joined Iudila on the deck, and the Goth welcomed the lad's company. He was closest to Iudila's age among all the crew. Though his Latin was laced with a thick accent that made him sound as if he were speaking underwater, though his corner of Spania was as far removed from Baetica as could be, though his people had for generations fought Iudila's to resist Gothic dominion over their lands—despite all these things, the pair had somehow become friends.

"Are you really a prince?" Eneko asked one night as he and Iudila watched the stars in their slow trek across the night sky.

"Yes," Iudila said. "King Witteric is my uncle, and Athanagild was my grandfather. Are you truly a king?"

"I am," Eneko said, his voice solemn, "and when I return home, I will take my rightful place and lead my people to victory over the turd-sucking Goths."

Iudila smiled. "And when I return home, I shall take my forces north to show who is truly master of Galicia. If I am elected king."

"Elected?" Eneko nearly choked on the word. "Your kings are elected?"

"Well, yes, by the Council of Nobles. How are your kings chosen?"

"We are not chosen, we just are. My people live from the sea. He who knows the best fishing grounds and commands the most boats is king by right."

"And that's you?"

Eneko cleared his throat and spat over the side. "My father was king. He taught me the paths through the western sea to where the great schools of fish live. They are so many that a single cast of a net would be enough to swamp *Mari-Nadris*. Our boats were twice the size of this one, and we had seven, the best fishing fleet in the Cantabrian Sea."

"So why aren't you with your fleet?"

Eneko's tone turned sullen. "My father died during one of our long fishing trips. Koldo, the master of one of his other boats, led our fleet home then claimed the catch and the boats for himself."

"Did no one try to stop him?"

Eneko shook his head. "My father had no kinsmen, and I was his only son. The people did not care, so long as their men had work and their families had food. Koldo claimed my home, my mother and my sisters, as our law allows. He even set aside my betrothal in favor of his son."

"What did you do?"

"The one thing I could do. The only way to redeem my family was to trade my life, my freedom for theirs. Koldo made me a slave and sold me to Milhma. I was twelve years old."

"Like me," Iudila said. "Did he…?"

14

Eneko nodded. "Until he tired of me and decided I was a better lookout than a plaything." A distant look clouded the Cantabrian's eyes. He drew his knife and studied its slender, curving blade in the moonlight. "I was but a boy when I left home and knew only the sea and the nets. I will return a man—a man who has learned to fight. To kill. And when I do, I will be king in Cantabria."

"And I will help you," Iudila said earnestly. "And one day, when I am king, our people shall be friends."

The Cantabrian laughed. "Eneko and Iudila, kings of all Iberia. Why not?" He drew his blade across his palm. Blood rose shiny and black in the pale light. "We make a pact," he explained to Iudila, and handed him the knife.

Iudila took it, hesitated for a moment, then took a deep breath and dragged the blade across his palm. He blinked back tears, forced a smile and clasped Eneko's outstretched hand.

"I, Eneko, son of Arrano, rightful King of Cantabria, swear friendship to Iudila the Goth, that peace may govern our peoples and guarantee our borders."

Iudila stammered a bit but gave his own oath. "And I, Iudila, son of Goiswinth, future King of Goths, swear friendship to Eneko, King of Cantabria, that peace may govern our peoples and secure our borders."

Eneko smiled, white teeth gleaming from his sun-darkened face. "And may our bellies be cut open and our entrails made into bait for the fishes, should we fail to be true."

Iudila's eyes widened at the pronouncement of the penalty, but he managed a nod.

"So be it."

Eneko released his grip and slapped Iudila's shoulder. He tucked an arm behind his head, lay back against the deck, and pointed toward a cluster of stars.

"That is the Dragon's Head." He traced the dagger's blade along a serpentine trail in the sky. "Follow the curve of his body all the way to his tail, and from the middle of his body to his wingtip. The Dragon circles the sky throughout the year, but the point between his tail and wingtip will always be in the north."

Iudila repeated the words in his mind, absorbing the lessons of sky and sea, as the stars—the heavenly guides and weavers of men's fates—made their slow, inexorable night-walk through the heavens.

4

"SAIL OFF THE STEERBOARD BOW."

Eneko gripped the top of the mast with one hand and pointed at the target with the other. Crewmen ran along the split deck toward the bow, hands shielding their eyes as they scanned the blue-grey sea. As one, a half-dozen hands jerked excitedly at the billowing white sails that peeked over the horizon.

"Prepare to drop sail and ship oars," Dingha bellowed from his station at the steering oar.

"She's a fat one, yeah?" he observed, tugging on one earring as he stretched over the rail to see around the men that crowded the bows.

"Step to, now. She's not the first tub you've ever seen. To your lines."

Iudila repeated Dingha's orders, and the pirates laughed at the lad's cracked voice that echoed the man's deep boom. Since Milhma had taken off the better part of Dingha's tongue, only Iudila—who spent nearly every waking moment by the helmsman's side—could make sense of his mutilated speech.

The men ambled to their stations, but Eneko remained at his high post to track the merchantman and to keep an eye out for possible threats. Dingha caressed the steering oar to drive the pirate dromon ahead of the wind and down on her quarry.

The helmsman hailed from the Mandé, the tribes that inhabited the mysterious lands south of the great African desert. Though his people were landlocked, Dingha's skills were such that he might have been born upon the waves. Iudila watched him carefully to glean whatever knowledge he could.

"They act like they've never seen a galley before," the big man said.

The distant vessel was the first the crew had seen in weeks, and the raid would be Iudila's first. He would be fifteen soon, and Dingha had wrung a promise from Milhma that the lad could join the next boarding party. "How long 'til we reach them?" Iudila asked.

Dingha scanned the waves, gauged the scattered clouds and cupped his hand to the wind. "Time enough to piss now, while you can do it on purpose."

Iudila rolled his eyes, then ran clammy hands through his hair, grown once more to its full length. He thought for a moment, saw the wisdom in going into his first foray with an empty bladder, and stepped to the aft rail. Dingha loosed a hearty laugh that was quickly picked up by the rest of the crew.

"What's so funny?" Milhma demanded as he stepped through his cabin door, one hand shielding his eyes from the harsh sun.

"Ship ahead, Captain," Eneko called down from his post. "The men are just eager for a spoil."

The captain sneered and squinted at the distant sail. "Tell me when you're ready to ship oars."

"Aye, sir," Dingha said as Milhma ducked back into his cabin.

The murmur of the captain's voice rose through the oak planks, followed by a pair of high-pitched giggles.

Iudila felt a twinge of jealousy then fumed at himself for the weakness. He loathed Milhma, despised him for the months of abuse in that cabin. Despite himself, he still sometimes longed for the moments of affection that punctuated the vile acts, affection that was now lost to him as Milhma had filled Iudila's place in his bed with a set of twins—a boy and a girl about nine years old—bought in the slave market of Rusadir on the Mauretanian coast. The captain's new toys had hair as yellow as his own and might have passed for his children. Milhma doted over them like an indulgent father.

To a man, the crew hated the brats. The only bright spot was the fact that Milhma generally confined himself with the twins in his cabin, thus out of his men's way. The crew tolerated the captain's predilections and fell into the habit of following Dingha's commands issued in Iudila's voice.

And Iudila was happy.

He had quickly picked up the crew's pidgin language of Berber, Germanic, Latin and Greek. By day, they taught him the pirate's tools of wind and current, knife and sword, knots and curses. By night—drifting under a reefed sail or at anchor in a hidden cove—the half-pagan crew reacquainted him with the old gods of Europe and Africa, gods the Church had left for dead. They told him the stories of the stars and taught him to track the seasons by their rising and setting.

Eneko told Iudila more and more of the great fishing grounds in the distant parts of the Ocean Sea. The pair crafted their schemes to reclaim their titles and lands and fell asleep to thoughts of glory. Iudila dreamed of fish and sails and plumed sea serpents, and occasionally the Succuba returned to pleasure his sleep.

"Take the steering oar," Dingha said.

Iudila finished watering the sea, cinched up his trousers and stepped to the helm.

"Don't aim straight for her," Dingha advised him. "See how she tracks? Trace a line along her course and aim for the point where we'll meet her."

Iudila nodded as he steered *Mari-Nadris* toward an empty spot of sea. Their target rode the current that swept from the Sea of Atlas, through the Pillars of Hercules into the Mediterranean. As the ship tacked against the eastern winds, Iudila noted how she lumbered through the waves. His mind reeled with the thought of the riches weighing her down.

"Fatter than a pregnant sow, that one," Dingha said, and nudged Iudila's hand on the steering oar a hair to larboard.

The merchantman must be from Tingis, Iudila reasoned, on her way to Rusadir. Perhaps she was even heading for Malaca. The thought of that port city on the south coast of Spania reminded Iudila that—were he back home—he would soon be old enough to hold the title of Duke of Baetica in his own right. A share of all the cargo brought into Malaca was his as Lord and Protector of the province. That thought let him consider the merchantman as his own. He was not a pirate, not a plunderer—merely a displaced nobleman seeking to reclaim what was his by birth.

If the ship was making for Malaca.

But *if* was close enough, and Iudila tweaked the steering oar as he drove *Mari-Nadris* down on her prey. The captain of the merchantman must have sensed the danger then, for the other ship's sails luffed as she changed her tack from northeast to southeast, away from open sea and toward the Mauretanian coast.

"Damn," Iudila muttered, unable to think of a more potent curse.

"Naught there but rocks and gulls," Dingha said. "She'll make herself a bed on some shoal, and we'll just have to pry her legs a bit. Ship oars."

Iudila repeated Dingha's command as the merchantman slid behind a cape and then pushed the steering oar away to drive *Mari-Nadris* after her. "Bring her down, Eneko." The lookout nodded and waited for another crewman to release a sheet knot, then leapt from his post into the billows of the sail. The heavy canvas cushioned his fall as the breath of Eurus, the eastern wind, escaped from the lateen.

"Drum or steer?" Dingha asked Iudila as the crew extended the oars like wings from either side of the ship.

"I told you to call me," Milhma shouted, storming from his cabin.

"I'll drum," Iudila said, then leapt from the steering deck to the main and down into the half-covered rowing deck.

"Just about to call you, Captain," Dingha said as Iudila picked up the pair of cushioned mallets and beat the goatskin drum.

Using the beat of his heart to set the tempo, Iudila pounded out the fourfold cadence of catch-pull-raise-sweep that propelled *Mari-Nadris* through the gentle swells. Iudila caught the looks from the two strokes—the crewmen who set the rowing pace—and realized the excitement of the coming raid made him set too rapid a pace. He took a deep breath and slowed the rhythm to a sustainable pursuit.

"Faster, you dogs," Milhma shouted.

Iudila shrugged and picked up the tempo. The strokes grinned affably, seeming to excuse the awkward pacing for the chance once more to be about their trade. Iudila swept his eyes over the twenty-oar crew, from the strokes, to Brehanu and Tesfa—the twins from Aksum whose bulk filled the beamy midship—to Eneko and the Greek Thanos who now wriggled into their places on the narrow, foremost bench.

Mari-Nadris heeled over and Iudila braced himself as Dingha bent the steering oar against the current to bring the ship around the cape where the merchantman had fled. Iudila peeked up from the rowing deck, but the high bow blocked his view. He swallowed his anticipation and kept on with the rhythm of the drum while the oarsmen grinned and grunted as each stroke brought them nearer to their prize.

"Ramming speed." Milhma finally called the order.

Iudila's stomach tightened as he stepped up the tempo and the men bit their oars deeper into the sea. He scarcely felt the roll of the ship as Dingha brought *Mari-Nadris's* bow in line with the merchantman.

"Lashers ready," the captain called. The fore- and aft-most pairs of men secured their oars and climbed onto the deck to prepare the grapnels and ropes that would bind together predator and prey.

"Clear oars. Brace for impact." Iudila repeated Dingha's warning, and the men raised their oars, locked the handles into notched beams that ran the length of the ship, and prepared for the collision. Iudila kept up his nervous beat, though the oarsmen had ceased to row. He tumbled forward as *Mari-Nadris's* ironclad spar rode over the merchantman's bow.

"Back paddle," Dingha shouted as Iudila picked himself up from between the rowing benches.

Iudila's nose poured blood and his head ached from where he'd struck one of the oars. The men heaved against their handles, pushing against the mass of the ship to clear the ram, while the lashers tossed their grapnels over the sides of the merchantman.

By the time Iudila was back on his feet, the pirates had secured their oars and scrambled topside, arming themselves for battle. He wiped his nose on his arm, sniffed and swallowed a gobbet of blood. He hauled himself onto the deck, waving off a concerned look from Dingha.

Eneko handed Iudila a cudgel and short sword as he joined the men at the boarding rails. They shouted eagerly as the lashers drew the ships together, then—when the distance had closed enough—leapt aboard the merchantman.

Iudila hopped up to the rail and sprang across the gap, landing lightly on his feet. He crouched and watched for repellers. Seeing none, he stood and ran across the deck.

Three men slipped over the side of the merchantman as Iudila reached the far rail. He was surprised they offered not even a token resistance. Even more surprising was the fact that the ships lay in the shallows of a small island. The retreating crewmen splashed through the waves, up the rocky beach and along a dusty inland trail. Most of the pirates had disappeared into the merchantman's hold, but Iudila caught the eye of Eneko who jeered after the fleeing sailors.

"The tide," Iudila said, repeating himself when the Cantabrian seemed not to understand. Iudila pointed at the wide beach where a line of foam crept down the shoreline, chasing after the receding waves. Tides at the inlet of the Mediterranean could vary by more than a Roman pace, nearly the height of a man and more than enough to ground the *Mari-Nadris*.

"Dingha," Iudila shouted when Eneko shrugged his shoulders and dropped into the hold. "The tide," he said again as the helmsman climbed up to the deck.

"Naught but rocks," Dingha grunted and chucked one over the side where it made a feeble splash. "She made her bed all right, but her cunny's stone dry."

"The tide's going out," Iudila said, this time grabbing Dingha by the elbow and leading him to the shore-side rail. The sun glinted silver off the tips of rocks that now peeked above the water's surface.

"Going fast," Dingha said, his observation confirmed as the merchantman shuddered and the keel grated along the beach. "Why don't we drift out?"

Iudila followed Dingha's gaze along the bow line to where the ship's anchor lodged among some stones. A second line stretched from the stern of the ship as well, binding it and the pirate vessel to the expanding shore. As they watched, a dirty column of smoke rose from the island, behind the bluff where the fleeing crew had disappeared.

"Signal fire." Dingha turned Iudila by the shoulders and pushed him across the deck. "Back to the ship. Up, you rascals," he shouted to the crewmen below. "The bitch lured us in. To your oars."

"Where's my prize?" Milhma said, his voice dripping venom as Iudila scrambled back over *Mari-Nadris's* rail.

"She's grounded on the rocks. Nothing but stones in the hold. It's a trap."

"A trap," Milhma repeated, a sneer twisting his thin lips. The expression faded as a rumble shook through *Mari-Nadris's* deck.

"She's anchored," Iudila said, pointing toward the foundering merchantman, "and her crew set a signal fire."

"Eneko, up top," Dingha shouted as he clambered aboard *Mari-Nadris*, followed by the grumbling crew.

"Tesfa, Brehanu—axes. To your oars and push off as soon as we're free," Iudila relayed Dingha's orders to the others.

Milhma's fair skin flashed red as the crew abandoned the merchantman without so much as a pisspot in hand. "Was I sleeping when the crew made you captain?" he demanded of Dingha.

"Pardon, sir," the helmsman answered with his clumsy tongue. "The hold was full of rocks, and her crew threw out the anchors before they abandoned her. She's grounded and holding us fast. Cut those lines," he shouted at the Aksumite brothers, then turned back to his captain. "Pardon, sir."

"Who hauls rocks through the Pillars?" Milhma said, his voice daring Dingha to reply.

"Sail ahead," Eneko called from his lookout post. "Sail abaft."

"Which is it, you fool?" Milhma demanded.

"Both."

The crewmen froze as the word fell across the deck.

The keel scraped along the shallow rocks, an oar snapped and *Mari-Nadris* groaned in agony. The trio of noises broke the spell of inertia and sent the crew into action.

Men dropped to the rowing deck, shipped the steerboard oars and loosed the larboard oars, their handles bowed between the securing straps and the blades pressed against the merchantman's hull.

"Go," Brehanu called as he chopped through the thick boarding rope at the stern, Tesfa having already cut the bow line.

"Wait," Iudila ordered as men braced themselves, ready to push the dromon away from the pirate-trap.

"They're bearing down on us," Dingha said with a warning glance at the lad.

"Wait," Iudila repeated more softly as he gazed seaward. "Wait," he said again, his hand raised in expectation. "Now," he shouted, and dropped his hand.

"Push off, you rogues," Dingha called, then leapt down to the rowing deck to add his muscle to the effort.

The wave Iudila had anticipated rolled under the keel and lifted *Mari-Nadris* from the rocks. Men heaved against the oars to separate the ships, then cheered as the wave rolled back out, carrying *Mari-Nadris* away from the grounded merchantman.

The motion caught Milhma off guard and he lurched over the edge of the steering deck, his arms flailing as he tried to catch his balance. He might have saved himself, but in that moment Dingha ordered the steerboard oarsmen to back-paddle, turning the stern toward the beach and giving *Mari-Nadris* a straight shot to deeper water. Milhma fell to the main deck and his head struck the gunnel.

"Papa," the twins screamed, and ran from the doorway of the cabin where they had been peeking at the flurry of activity. They clung to the captain, pressing pudgy hands to his cheeks.

Iudila was about to climb down to help when Dingha shouted from the rowing deck.

"Steer, boy. Steer."

Iudila ran to the steering oar that dragged in the ship's wake, his palms sweaty as he gripped the handle. He glanced behind him on either side to gauge the approach of the pursuers. Only then did he recognize the banner that flew from their masts.

The lower golden-yellow stripe was the color of ripe wheat, while the purple band at the top represented the mountains of Lusitania. Together, they made up the banner of Suinthila, Count of Eminio, who had been his father's friend.

Iudila's hand froze on the steering oar. If these were Suinthila's ships, he was as good as rescued. He could turn *Mari-Nadris* toward them and let the pirates row him to freedom. Home was within Iudila's reach, needing only the tug of his hand.

Just then, Dingha gave the order to stroke. His eyes drifted up to Iudila's, and his face cracked into a broad grin.

Having spent the morning chasing an empty promise, now fleeing for their lives, Dingha and the rest of the crew pulled on their oars not in fear, but for love of their ship, of the sea. They served Milhma not from any respect of the captain, but out of passionate devotion to *Mari-Nadris*, at once mother and lover to her crew.

In that instant, Iudila knew he belonged to *Mari-Nadris*, that in her was his life and his freedom, kings and dukes be damned. He pushed against the oar and drove the ship toward the point where Abyla, the southern pillar, rose from the sea. Waves crashed white against the stark cliffs as the current from the Ocean Sea squeezed into the narrow straits. "Niord and Gabriel, save us." he whispered the prayer to the old god of the sea and his Christian counterpart as his vision blurred and a wave of vertigo rushed over him. He squeezed his eyes shut and staggered against the steering oar.

When he opened his eyes again, the world was changed. Land and sea and sky were still there, but where the latter two had previously been trackless voids, Iudila now sensed the currents that passed through them as clearly as rivers through a landscape.

He saw Eurus, the eastern wind, as though he were a living being, his breezes cutting through the sky like the feathers of his wings. Beneath *Mari-Nadris*, Oceanus revealed his course in billowing plumes like the folds of his cloak.

Iudila glanced behind and saw how the pursuing ships rode the seas. The northern ship cut across the inlet between island and mainland, fighting the current as she tried to intercept the pirates. The southern ship, however, rode her current like a cork in a stream, the water's course bringing her nearer and nearer to *Mari-Nadris*.

The pirate vessel's wake angled across the natural flow, so Iudila adjusted the steering oar to bring her in line with the current. The chaser's gain dwindled to nothing, and Iudila turned forward to see the bulk of Abyla looming ahead of him, the streams of current compressed as they wrapped around the point. The prudent course was to angle away from the cliff, toward open sea where they might have a chance at escape, but Iudila saw how the current ran stronger, nearer to the great rock.

Therein lay their salvation.

Mari-Nadris, driven by the strokes of her crew, flew along the current and stripped ahead of her pursuers. Iudila guided her into the flow, along the edge of the great Pillar, around the point and into the open expanse of sea.

Where disaster awaited.

Barring their way was a third ship, flying the same standard as the others. By her twin banks of oars, Iudila knew this giant was the hunter. The other ships were merely hounds and they had done their jobs well. They had driven *Mari-Nadris* into the net.

Iudila scanned the seas, searched the sky and found only one hope.

"Prepare to hoist sail."

Dingha blinked up at him. "The winds are contrary."

"Cruiser ahead, and she's a brute. There's no way around her."

Dingha nodded.

"Eneko, Thanos—to the lines," Iudila ordered.

The pair unshipped their oars, scrambled onto the deck and readied the dromon's lateen sail.

"On my mark," Iudila said as he centered *Mari-Nadris* in the current that drove them toward the hulking bireme.

Cantabrian and Greek looked wide-eyed from Iudila to the cruiser and back, watching with dread as their ship drove ever closer to her fate.

"Now."

Iudila leaned hard against the steering oar while the sailors hauled on their lines to raise the sail. *Mari-Nadris* turned, the sea foamed white in her wake, and the pirate ship passed so close to her hunter that Iudila could see the astonished faces of the Goth rowers who peered through their oar holes. He eased the pressure on the steering oar to broaden the turn but kept bending the dromon's course until she came full about. "Secure the lines, then back to your oars," he ordered as the sail bulged in the eastern wind.

Mari-Nadris now sailed with the wind and against the current, but the sea was weakest in the deep mouth of the straits where the wind was steadiest. His oarsmen's strokes easily overcame the sea's resistance, and the ship raced away from her pursuers who scrambled to renew the futile chase.

The ships passed once more between the Pillars, Abyla in the south and Calpe to the north. A fleeting dread told Iudila he would never pass through them again. Such a show of force from the Goth fleet could well mean the end of the pirates' free hand in the Mediterranean. Despite that fear, Iudila was exhilarated by his communion with the wind and the sea.

He had been Count of Corduba, Duke of Baetica and Prince of Goths. Now he was Flota, Matrose, Nauticus.

Now, he was a sailor.

5

THE PORT CITY OF TINGIS BUZZED. The harbor and marketplace teemed with people speaking a Babel of tongues. Latin and Greek and Berber. Germanic dialects belonging to Franks, Lombards, and Goths. These mingled with a smattering of other languages Iudila had yet to learn.

A canvas bag slung over one shoulder, he walked up from the wharf where *Mari-Nadris* lay at rest. The Mediterranean might be closed to the pirate ship, but this Roman enclave on the west coast of Mauretania was open to all, as long as they paid the harbor toll.

Iudila's sack bulged with his share of plunder from the past few months. The crew had assured him that, though the Tingis merchants were tighter than Jewess virgins, they rarely asked about the origins of the items they bought. Iudila followed on Dingha's heels to make his first trade in the bounty of the seas.

Past the harbor, the streets had a pulse of their own. Iudila struggled to take it all in as Dingha led him through the crush of humanity and the garish displays of colored awnings, gowns and robes. Most of the city was whitewashed, the better to reflect the sun's harsh glare. Around the marketplace, however, walls of blue and green, yellow and red and myriad other hues were everywhere to be seen.

Underscoring the sights and sounds was the familiar stink of a port town. Brine, pitch, and rotting fish faded from dockside to marketplace, where roasted duck and lamb and goat, spices from India and Seres, and the fragrant nectar of desert flowers mixed in a heady combination. Suffusing it all was the familiar tang of unwashed bodies and the stench of open sewers, the buried Roman system having long since been abandoned.

Only the alleyways gave respite to the senses. Narrow and packed with bales of goods and heaps of rubbish, they were shaded and quiet and relatively empty of people on this busy market day. The dark, viscid streams that flowed from each alley to join the gutters of the main street suggested that the nose would be given no haven, but Iudila—so long unaccustomed to the bustle of city life—longed to lose himself in the dim, quiet desolation.

From one of those alleys, a flash of red hair caught his attention. Iudila's mind filled in Keinan's features on the face of the girl who leered at him through large, painted eyes. Her bodice was loose, exposing most of her dusky-skinned breasts as she swayed her hips and raised her skirts to display her wares.

Iudila's eyes followed the hem with rapt attention, from ringed toes, past the delicate ankles and shapely calves. Beyond the sculpted knees, prurience turned to revulsion at the pocked and scabby thighs that marked the entrance to her trading house. Any remaining illusion was shattered by the tangle of black at the junction of her legs that gave the lie to her red hair.

A jerk on his arm broke his gaze.

"If you want to feed your cock, find a brothel, not an alley tramp," Dingha said. "You'll pay more, but at least you know what you're getting."

He steered Iudila around a corner, under an arch, and into a smaller plaza only slightly less bright than its neighbor. Iudila glanced back to see the girl give him a rueful parting wave. He bounced against Dingha's backside as the bigger man paused, scratched his stubbly scalp, then found his bearings and pressed on. Iudila followed, but his attention was continually drawn to one gaudy booth or another.

"The teeth of Jasconius," he heard in clumsy, brogued Latin, as he slowed to a stop before one such booth. "From the frozen seas beyond Hibernia."

"Jasconius?" Iudila shot a glance toward Dingha then gave his attention to the vendor.

"The living island discovered by the Blessed Breandan," the fair-skinned merchant explained. "By the grace of God, Father Breandan subdued the beast and, with his own hands, pulled its teeth."

Iudila examined the pieces, which looked like ivory. The longest were yellow-white curved tusks as long as his forearm, nearly as thick as his wrist at the base, then tapering to a deadly point. Some of these were carved with runes, while smaller pieces had been sculpted into figures of fur-clad warriors, strange-looking birds, and beasts that seemed the offspring of a dog and a fish. Iudila picked up a piece carved in the shape of a woman and absently stroked the massive breasts with his thumb.

"A special one, that," the merchant said. Iudila set the piece back down, his face growing warm. "Such a piece would normally go for a solidus, but for you, twelve folles."

"No, thank you," Iudila mumbled as he backed away from the stand and looked around to find Dingha.

"Seven folles, but I cannot go lower," the vendor called after him. "And I'll throw in a velvet carrying bag. Five?"

Iudila ignored the man as he searched for Dingha, who had vanished into the crowd. A bench sat near the entrance to an alley. Iudila climbed atop it for a better view, but found no sign of Dingha. He shouted, but his voice was swallowed by the din of the marketplace. He looked for a shop sign that might suggest a likely buyer of plunder, but the shop fronts were universally anonymous. Fear clawed at his stomach and began to creep up his throat, until he silently chided himself.

He was no child. He had no need of a tutor or nursemaid, someone to hold his hand and wipe his backside. No, he was a man, a sailor. If he found Dingha, well and good. If not, he would simply make his way back to the harbor and sell his bounty another time.

That resolved, Iudila took a deep breath and nearly choked on the pungent smoke from an incense dealer's stand. A giggle burst from inside the booth. Iudila turned to see a girl of no more than ten years. She cupped one hand over her mouth, the other arm wrapped about her middle as she laughed.

Iudila drew himself up to his full height, now taller than most men. His chest, shoulders and arms had been thickened at the oars, the muscles straining against skin burnished by sun and wind. His copper hair, sun-streaked with gold, was tied back in a clubbed braid so the sinews of his shoulders and the rings of his ears—one his enforced bond to Milhma, the other his willing bond to his crew—were visible to all.

His eyes were cold as the Ocean Sea and narrowed by salt spray, and the scars on his cheeks were matched by the thin line of his lips. In short, his was a visage to strike fear in the hearts of men, let alone little girls.

The child's laughter stopped as she shrank back a step and looked up at Iudila through almond-shaped, coal-black eyes. Iudila suppressed a grin at having put the brat in her place, then doubled over as his lungs rebelled against the incense smoke and forced a cough through his nose and tightly clamped lips. The girl doubled over too, in a fit of laughter.

"Fatima," a man snapped, followed by a sharp command in a tongue which was not quite Hebrew, and which Iudila took to mean, *Mind yourself and come away.* "Forgive my daughter's impertinence," the man said in smooth-accented Greek, as he gently swatted the girl and swept her toward the rear of the booth. "She is young and has not yet learned the ways of propriety." He said this last bit in a raised voice, more as a reproof to the girl than as explanation to Iudila.

"It is all right," Iudila said, his Greek coarse and unrefined compared with the merchant's. "I am sure she meant no harm." He looked to the girl, who peeked out from behind her father's billowing robes, and offered her a reassuring smile.

"She can be a djinn," the merchant allowed, "but she has a tender heart." The man's eyes sparkled with pride, though they flicked about as though he expected an attack at any moment.

His nervous eyes softened as they fell on Iudila, and the close-knit eyebrows relaxed. He offered a kindly smile that revealed straight, white teeth.

"Since her poor behavior has brought you to us, however, I cannot be angry with her. Feel free to examine our wares. We have perfumes and incense—as you have already discovered—along with gems and ivories from deepest Africa."

"Thank you, but no," Iudila said, and turned away.

"We also buy or trade," the merchant persisted.

Iudila stopped, turned, and stepped back to the booth. He swung his pack off his shoulder and onto the counter. He had separated out the coins, but the bits of jewelry, pins, cups, dishes and a few small weapons clattered inside the bag.

"Could you use any of these?"

The merchant studied Iudila for a moment, then hefted the bag and shook it. He squeezed his eyes shut and cocked his head, as though to judge the quality of the rattle. Apparently satisfied, he nodded and set the bag down inside the booth.

"Ali," he called, and a young boy—not much older than Fatima—came forward, picked up the bag and retreated to the back of the booth. "Three solidi," the merchant offered, then placed two gold coins on the counter and began counting out a mix of silver and bronze.

Iudila blinked at him a time or two before finding his tongue. "But you did not see what I have."

The merchant gestured him to silence as he stacked whole coins and swept slivers and wedges of others into manageable piles, the whole time moving his lips as he silently counted.

"The coins, you should sew into the hem of your clothes," the merchant suggested when he had finished. He pushed the pile of money toward Iudila.

To a prince, it was a piddling sum—about what a farmhand might earn in two or three months. To the young sailor, however, it was a fortune, the first fruits of his life at sea. Iudila swept the coins into his pouch, carefully so as not to spill any of the pieces, but hurriedly lest the merchant come to his senses.

"You do not wish to examine the bag?" Conscience forced the question on Iudila even as he pulled the drawstring on his pouch.

"Is the amount fair?" The merchant clawed long fingers through his dark beard.

"It is generous."

The man appraised him with deep brown eyes, sharp as a hawk's, and Iudila shrank under the scrutiny. At last, the merchant grinned.

"A generous man will himself be blessed. Let it never be said that Abul-Ghasem failed to help a stranger."

He thrust out a hand toward Iudila, who took a step backward at the strange gesture. At first he thought the man wanted his money back, but he held his hand sideways, the fleshy palm open, fingers together and thumb pointed skyward. The merchant jerked his open hand, and nodded his chin toward Iudila, who slowly reached out his own hand. The man clasped Iudila's hand in both of his and shook it up and down. "*As salaamu alaikum,*" he said with a smile.

Iudila searched his memory to find an appropriate response to the man's blessing.

"*Aleichem shalom*," was the best he could do, and the merchant nodded, patted his hand, then turned to attend his other customers.

Iudila slid away from the booth then pushed through the crowd and beneath the archway that led to the larger marketplace. Not halfway to the harbor gate, he again spied that flash of red hair dancing in the breeze. Painted eyes turned toward him and the full lips curved up in a grin of recognition. The girl pushed herself off the wall and slipped into the alley, throwing an inviting glance toward Iudila before she disappeared.

Iudila followed her, as though entering another world. The cacophony of the marketplace faded to a dull rumble, and the stink of humanity was replaced by the stench of their leavings. The girl had vanished around a corner, but a trace of rose oil on the foul air led the way. Ignoring the sewage and kitchen middens, Iudila took a few deep breaths and followed his nose, guided only by the scent of passion.

After countless turns, he heard a scuffle from around yet another corner. Heavy breathing suggested the nature of the sounds. Iudila thought to pass by until a cry for help rose above the bestial noises, stopping him in his tracks. His head spun toward the sounds and his body followed. Without a thought, Iudila rushed toward the cries, shouting in fury.

A large man in Berber robes pressed the red-haired girl against a wall. With one massive hand he pinioned her wrists over her head. With his other hand he hoisted his robes, eager to drive home the assault. At Iudila's shout, both heads turned toward him, one with a look of pleading and hope, the other with irritation.

"Pass on, boy," the man grunted. "Find your own or take this one after, but she's mine for now."

Iudila wavered, but the girl's eyes pleaded with him. He reached down to pick a broken ewer from a nearby rubbish heap, raised the makeshift mace over his head and raced toward the man.

The Berber's eyes went wide. He released the girl and fled into the mazelike alley. Iudila hurled the pottery after him, but it smashed harmlessly against a wall as the man disappeared around a bend.

The girl's dress had covered little before, and even less now. The low neck was torn all the way to the hem, where only a thread or two held the piece together.

She made no effort to cover her nakedness as she rushed to Iudila, threw her arms about his neck and lavished him with kisses and thanks in her Moorish tongue.

Iudila's instinct was to lead the girl out of the alley, away from danger, but the feel of her hands, the taste of her lips and the press of her body let desire check reason. He wrapped his arms around her waist, losing himself in passion as he returned her kisses, then ran his lips down her neck.

It could have been a tensing of her body, or maybe the way she shifted her hands. Whatever the cause, Iudila's instinct reasserted itself, though the trap was sprung before he realized he'd been snared. He pushed the girl away and spun around even as a club swung toward him.

The man had returned from the alley. The blow should have crushed Iudila's skull, but his sudden turn threw off the man's aim. The club landed in the crook of shoulder and neck, and—even with the spoiled aim—drove Iudila to his knees. He managed to duck away from another swipe at his head, but could not dodge the kick to his belly that forced the air from his lungs.

Iudila rolled into the sludge-encrusted gutter as the man drove after him. A booted foot dropped toward his face, but Iudila blocked it with both hands, twisted it from heel to toe, and threw the man off balance. Iudila struggled to his feet, gasping for breath. The man was faster and rushed him again, the club raised over his head for a fatal, two-handed blow.

Iudila caught the club in his oar-hardened hands and tore it from his attacker's grip. He hadn't the air in his lungs to roar a battle cry, but his eyes burned with rage as he raised the club over his head with one hand and gripped the man's throat with the other. Iudila lifted him off the ground, and the Berber's face turned red then purple. His feet kicked wildly and he rained impotent blows on Iudila's head and shoulders.

The girl screamed at Iudila. She beat his shoulders and leapt on his back, wrapping an arm about his neck. Iudila held his grip on the man's throat but dropped the club. He reached back to grab the girl by her whorish dyed hair and flung her across the alley.

The man's blows fell weaker and weaker, and Iudila tightened his grip, ignoring the burn in his fingers and the distant call of conscience. The Berber's lips were blue now, his eyes bulging. Still Iudila squeezed. He sensed the girl rise behind him and he spun around to meet her rush, using the man's body to parry her attack.

A loud crack filled the narrow alley with its echo. Iudila looked around for the source of the noise, then saw the man's head loll to one side as his arms and feet went slack. The girl's scream brought Iudila to his senses, and he loosed his grip. The man's body splashed in a puddle of filth as he fell to the ground.

"Murder," the girl cried. "Rape. Murder." She clawed at her face and breasts, bringing bright stripes of blood to the surface. "Murderer," she cried as, eyes wild, she tore at her hair with one hand and signed a curse with the other. Even as she stepped fearlessly toward Iudila, shouts and heavy steps sounded from the alley behind her.

Iudila spun around and ran deeper into the labyrinth. He tried to gauge the distance of the voices behind him but dared not look back. He took one blind turn after another, past doors and windows barred against intruders and the midday sun, until he spied the black maw of an open doorway. Without a thought, Iudila dove across the threshold where an old woman sat with spindle and distaff. She made no sound as he leapt past her.

The cries drew near and Iudila pressed himself into the shadows behind the door. Through the gap at the hinge he watched the mob pause, their faces dark with vengeance. The crone responded to their angry questions with a sideways nod of her head that sent the men racing farther along the alley. Iudila stayed where he was, his breath a ragged pant as he tried to slow his racing heart.

Only after the shouts faded and the dust settled in the dingy alleyway did the woman rise. She silently gathered up her spinning, stepped into the room and closed the door behind her.

Iudila was blinded as light fled from the space, only a few beams daring to peek through the cracks at door and shutter. He expected the woman to light a lamp, but she set again to her spindle, humming in the dark. Only when she reached for a fresh bundle of wool did she lean across a shaft of light to reveal the milky film that clouded her eyes.

Iudila eased off the wall and felt for the door's latch. If the woman thought he truly had raced by, he might be able to leave without notice.

"There will be one or two yet watching." The crone's voice was rough as a keel on shingle, but Iudila stayed his hand. "Come, sit a while."

With no choice but to obey, Iudila sat opposite the woman, a bundle of wool between them.

"Set to. Have a hand at the combs."

Iudila's eyes adjusted to the gloom and he spied the bits of tortoise shell. As he reached for them, his hand crossed a beam of sunlight and his throat closed on a sob.

"Holy Gabriel, what have I done?"

He turned his palm to the light to reveal a spot of purple where the Berber's Adam's apple had bruised him. He clenched his fist to hide the mark, but still felt the flesh of the man's neck under his fingers.

"Christ, have mercy."

"So it's murder, is it?" the old woman said. "See to the combs. Guilt cards no wool."

Too dazed to resist, Iudila took up the combs and scratched them through the fleece.

"Artemis shrivel that Eddo's bollocks. 'No, mistress, 'tis clean wool,' says he. 'Nary clod nor thistle nor broom to foul the weave.' By randy Oedipus's eyes, I'll be twice blinded if ever I buy again from that rake. Your first kill?"

It took Iudila a moment to realize she was addressing him. His reply was not spoken, not whispered, only a bending of his breath.

"Yes."

He had seen death aplenty during the *Mari-Nadris's* raids but had always managed to be a step or two behind the swinging blades.

"Well, I suspect you'll have more ere someone returns the favor. Give me your hands."

Iudila obeyed, presenting them palm-up. The crone groped for his hands, grasping them with hers, gnarled and spotted. She turned his palms toward each other then began spooling the spun thread across them.

"Did you get much loot off the poor bastard?" A smile puckered around her three teeth, and a laugh clawed its way up her throat.

"No."

"Take his woman?" She raised a scraggly brow.

"No."

"Then why, by Heracles's farts, did you kill him?"

"He attacked me."

The woman stopped spooling and locked her sightless eyes on Iudila.

"Are you stupid, boy, or just daft? The Spinners use you to trim a thread, and you moan over it like a lioness in season."

"The Spinners?"

She shook her head. "Stupid it is. Yes, boy, the Spinners. The Moirae. The Fates. Were you born under a rock, or do your parents not talk to you?"

"My parents are dead."

Her expression softened. "So that's the way of it, hmm? Widows and orphans are the Spinners' favorite patterns. Here." She took the wound thread from his hands. "The three Sisters. Clotho spins the threads of different color and coarseness. Lachesis measures the weave, while Atropos cuts the threads to length. Before you drew breath, the pattern of your life was set. As it was for the fool who thought to cut your threads short."

"But what if it was meant to be the other way? What if he was supposed to cut my threads?"

"Then your corpse would be rotting in a trash heap while he used your silver to buy wine for that mob out there. The Sisters will not be denied, try though some will. You may work hard or little, chase peace or war, but the final pattern will still be the same."

"Then what's the point of trying?"

The crone shrugged. "The pattern is set, but its beauty stems from its use. See here." She reached into a basket and pulled out a strip of fabric. "This scrap can be used to bind a wound, bathe a lover, swathe an infant or wash your backside. It is the same piece of cloth, but the pleasure you take in it and the good it does for others are determined by how you use it."

She took his right hand and traced a fingernail along the grooves of his palm, humming to herself as she did so. Her expression changed from curiosity to amusement to concern. At last, she lowered her blind eyes, folded Iudila's hand closed, and patted his fist.

"A great path lies before you. Embrace it and chase the sun to glory." She handed the cloth to him. "The way is clear now. You may rejoin your crew."

Iudila looked from the cloth to the door, then to the woman. "I don't know the way."

She smiled. "Turn right out the door, then left at the alley's end."

"Then what?"

"Then you walk down the pier to your ship."

He blinked at her. "I'm that close?"

"Your path is ever only one step ahead of you, if you but have the courage to follow it." She rose and led him to the door. "Go now. Go to your destiny, Iudila of the Sea."

He opened the door, scanned the alley, then followed the crone's directions. In a few minutes he was dockside, helping his crew load provisions. Only after the bales and barrels and baskets were stowed, only after they pushed the dromon away from the pier and Dingha set the steering oar for the harbor's mouth—only then did it dawn on him.

He'd never told the crone his name.

6

SEAGULLS WHEELED AND DOVE around the observation post high atop the mast. Iudila sat on one arm of the narrow crosspiece, with Eneko on the other side. The pair tossed bits of dried fish and hard bread into the void, enjoying the aerial acrobatics as the birds maneuvered for the scraps.

"How far do your fishermen sail?" Iudila gestured toward the dark western horizon.

Eneko's thick eyebrows pinched together as he considered the question and flung a bit of fish toward the waves. A gull screeched in protest, rolled onto its wingtip then pitched over in pursuit of the morsel.

"Far," he said, after the bird had snatched the scrap of food and flared out just above the wave crests. "It could be two months, maybe three. It depends on the winds."

Iudila frowned at that. Even in the predawn calm, the breeze blew strong in his face and made *Mari-Nadris's* bowlines strain against the sea anchor. "I doubt they'd get very far against this wind, even in that time."

Eneko glanced at the men who lazed on the deck below, then leaned closer to Iudila and spoke softly.

"They come back from there," he said, indicating the west, "but they head out that way." He made a small gesture northward.

"Toward Britannia?"

"Shh."

The Cantabrian looked nervously toward the deck, but no one stirred, save to stifle a yawn or scratch at a louse. Eneko had often told Iudila of the great western fishing grounds but had never revealed the secret to reaching them.

"Past Britannia," he now explained in a low voice, "past Hibernia, and into a wilderness of frozen sea." He described floating ice mountains and the strange creatures that inhabited the waters.

Iudila was reminded of the fish-dog carvings he'd seen in Tingis but could hardly imagine the offspring of a dolphin and unicorn.

"Two months out," Eneko continued, "a month or two to fill the holds and dry the catch, then another month back."

"They have drying racks on board?"

Eneko looked about once more before quietly saying, "Camps."

Iudila blinked at his friend. "On the sea?"

Eneko's eyes glinted, then changed before he could answer Iudila's question. Where a young man had been looking into a far distant time and place, a pirate now looked upon a much nearer target.

"Sail ahead."

The lazing crew sprang to their feet. With practiced chaos, men leapt to prepare oars, others to ready lines, haul in the anchor or ship the spar on the dromon's prow. Iudila and Eneko stood on their tenuous perch and peered into the western gloom.

"How many?" Milhma called up from the deck.

Eneko paused briefly before answering. "Five. One ahead, three behind, and a straggler."

Iudila squinted. He could make out no more than a blur of sails that might only be sea mist.

"How will they pass?"

"Well to larboard," Eneko said after a moment's consideration. "The lead boat will likely carry the treasure."

"The men are poorly armed?" Milhma said.

"Gaffs and hooks, usually. Shouldn't be more than six men to a boat—maybe a boy or two."

Iudila noted a wistful tone to the lookout's voice, remembering that Eneko had once been one of those boys. It had been seven years since the Cantabrian had traded his freedom for his family's. Now the lost son was returning home, no longer a fisherman but a pirate, coming to take much from those who had taken all.

"Which way are the currents?" Dingha called from the steering deck.

Iudila studied the seas and the sky. "The wind is toward us, but the current is shifting around. If we sweep south a bit, the sea will be to our back. The wind should bring them straight to us."

"Like a whore to a rich man's bed."

"You're certain they're loaded?" Milhma asked Eneko, then stroked the long golden hair of his pet boy.

The Cantabrian nodded. "Ivory and silver, gold and rubies and sapphires. From Solomon's storehouse, I tell you."

"It'd better be," the captain said, his avarice for once tempered by caution. "I don't like these waters."

The waters were fine—little different than *Mari-Nadris's* usual haunts—but Iudila understood Milhma's apprehension. The crew had sailed north around the bulge of Spania and into the Cantabrian Sea, the gulf shared by the Goths and Franks. Not that either group had much presence in these waters.

The northern lands claimed by the Goths were, in actuality, barely civilized. The cities—little more than settlements, really—were inhabited by tribes of unruly Galicians and Cantabrians and Asturians. What few ships the Goths had were concentrated in the Mediterranean and the southwestern ocean coast. The Franks, on the other hand, seemed to have no interest in the sea at all, so busy were they fighting their own brothers and cousins.

All this made the Cantabrian a deserted waste, the stalking grounds of fishermen. Some trading vessels hugged the coast en route from Britannia to Spania or Mauretania, but the experienced traders stuck to the secret tracks of the open sea, the better to avoid the likes of Milhma and his crew. With few targets, strange winds and currents, and the rumors of marauding Saxons from the north, it had taken all of Eneko's persuasion and promises of exotic treasures to convince the pirate captain to venture to these far shores.

"How long?" Milhma demanded as he gnawed on a fingernail.

Eneko studied the waves, cocked his head to feel the breeze, then shouted down. "Soon."

When the fishing vessels drew near enough for Iudila to distinguish between the sails, Eneko grabbed a line and leapt from the mast. With practiced flair he spun round the mast, the line slowing his descent but speeding his hurtle around the oak. On releasing the line, his momentum carried him from amidships to his post on the upper bow deck.

Iudila scuttled down the mast, using Eneko's tightly coiled line for foot- and handholds. Still several feet above the deck, he leapt down as the other crewmen hefted the mast from its step and lowered it into the cradle between the rowing benches.

Milhma hustled the twins into his cabin while Dingha climbed to the steering deck and the rest of the crew took to the benches. Iudila shipped and feathered his oar, feeling the familiar bite of ash wood against his palms as he readied himself for the first stroke.

The wait was short, as Milhma climbed up to join Dingha on the steering deck then gave the order to row. As one, twenty oars bit into the waves, gnashing the water into foam that quickly fell behind as *Mari-Nadris* sprang toward her prey. Iudila worked his oar in time with the others to the beat of Eneko's drum. The contrary motions of oars, wind and sea jostled *Mari-Nadris*, but Dingha kept her true.

The oarsmen chewed up the distance to their prey with strong, steady strokes until—after what seemed mere moments, though must actually have been several minutes—Milhma called out from his post.

"Ramming speed."

Eneko's beat changed, and the oarsmen fell into the practiced quick-stroke. If the ship were gliding before, she positively flew now. Like a hawk stooping after its prey, she redoubled her speed. Over the wind and waves and grunts of his crewmates, Iudila now heard the shouts of the men on the fishing boat. He braced himself for the impact, careful not to foul his stroke.

"First wave, ready," Milhma ordered. The foremost six banks of men stilled their oars, feathered the blades and hauled in the shafts. Swords and knives and axes lay at hand, and the men now snatched these up. While Brehanu, Tesfa and a half-dozen others kept the ship flying forward, Iudila and the rest of the first wave of boarders huddled in the bow, awaiting the impact. Unable to see out, Iudila took his cues from Eneko.

When the Cantabrian secured his drum, Iudila tightened a sweaty grip on the handle of his seax, the short, double-edged sword he favored in close combat. When Eneko grabbed the bow rail, Iudila braced himself against the shoulders of the man in front of him.

With a jolt Iudila would never get used to, *Mari-Nadris* crashed into the fishing boat. Her spar rode over the bow of the other vessel, locking the two together. Without even a moment to catch breath, Iudila was carried along in the press of men that stormed over the bow and onto the other ship. Once aboard, the crush lessened as the men spread out, and Iudila—again able to see and to move under his own power—stopped in surprise.

It wasn't so much that Eneko—normally the last man in the first wave—had taken the lead. It was the fact that the blade of his axe was already bloodied, the stain matched by the ragged gash across the throat of a full-bellied fisherman. The man fell to his knees, clutched at his throat and locked his eyes on Eneko. His expression changed from fear to confusion, then to recognition as Eneko stepped up to him, bent over him and whispered something in his ear. Before the man could respond, Eneko swung again with his axe, cutting across the wide belly and loosing entrails to spill onto the deck.

He kicked the man's chest and sent him sprawling, then spat on the fresh corpse. Without missing a stride, he stalked to a second man who—though more than a head taller than Eneko—turned sail-white with fear. The man dropped his gaff, fell to his knees and clasped his hands in front of him.

"Eneko, is it you?" he started to say, but the words were cut off, along with most of his head. A similar fate befell a third fisherman before Milhma led the redundant second wave aboard. Other than Eneko, none of the first wave had so much as swung a weapon, and the boat was already taken.

"Search the hold," Milhma ordered Dingha, who led Thanos and another man to the nearest hatch and dropped below the deck. The captain called to Eneko, who turned to him, face red with battle rage and other men's blood. A figure leapt up from behind a pile of netting with a great fishing hook over his head, ready to cleave it deep into Eneko's skull. Iudila tried to cry a warning, but his breath would not come. Instead, he hurled his seax at the fisherman.

Eneko's eyes went wide as the sword flew in his direction, then wider still when it buried itself in the fisherman's chest.

The hook still raised over his head, the man looked with surprise at the hilt protruding from his rough-woven shirt. His eyes floated up to meet Eneko's, and his head cocked in recognition. He parted his lips to speak, but instead of words, blood gushed from his mouth, spattering pirate and deck alike. The hook dropped silently onto the nets, followed a moment later by the fisherman's body.

The pirates stared at Eneko in shock. Few would call him eager for the fray—some had even called him cowardly. None would ever have thought him capable of the slaughter he had wrought. Eneko returned the men's looks with detached eyes that at last settled on Iudila, blinked twice, then returned to their usual cheerfulness.

He grinned at Iudila, turned back to the last fisherman and tugged on the sword. The man's flesh had closed around the blade, and Eneko had to stand on the corpse's stomach and throat to wrench the sword free with both hands. He wiped the blade on his shirt, but each was so covered in blood the gesture was useless. He handed the stained steel to Iudila, then pulled him into a fierce hug.

"I owe you a life, my friend, and I will never forget."

"Well?" Milhma demanded as Dingha and the others emerged from below.

"Fish," Thanos said, then glared at Eneko. "Nothing but fish."

"You searched everywhere? You looked under the fish?"

"Mika was down to his ankles in the slimy bastards."

"I'd hardly call that a thorough search," Milhma said, casting an accusing eye on the lanky Egyptian.

"Head first," Thanos clarified, and the others roared with laughter as Mika picked bits of flesh and scale and bone from his hair.

Milhma stalked over to Eneko. "Where's my treasure, you son of a godless whore?" He snatched up a gaff and swung it at the Cantabrian.

Eneko caught the blow on his forearm, tore the gaff away from the captain and flung it over the rail. "The hoard must be on one of the others," he said calmly, with a nod toward the boats that had sailed past without daring to stop. "And if you ever strike me again," he added in a low voice, "I'll tear off your shriveled bollocks and shove them down your rancid throat."

Milhma staggered a couple of paces back, as if he'd been struck.

"To shore, lads," Eneko told his crewmates, then tossed the fishing boat's anchor in the sea and leapt across the bows.

The rest of the crew stood rooted to the deck, awaiting orders from the cowed Milhma. The captain was still stunned by Eneko's boldness, so Dingha filled the silence. Anger and excitement muddled his words, and Iudila translated for him.

"We didn't come all the way to this empty stretch of sea for a load of fish. Now haul your sorry asses back to your posts, and let's get some real treasure."

The men smiled and nodded their approval. It wasn't the cheer with which they'd started the day, but they filed to their posts and once more took up their oars. Dingha paused as he passed Iudila's bench. Iudila couldn't meet his eyes, for he had lied. Dingha's instructions were to make sail for more familiar waters, but Iudila had replaced the words with his own.

The helmsman laid a heavy hand on Iudila's shoulder, and the lad at last looked up. Instead of recrimination, laughter shone in Dingha's eyes. He raised an eyebrow, crooked a grin, and winked before climbing to the steering deck.

By the time the crew had settled at their posts, Milhma was back aboard *Mari-Nadris*. His face purple with rage, he went straight to his cabin. The crew tried to ignore the cries and pleas of the children as he took out on them his fury at Eneko's defiance.

"To shore," Iudila called, and Eneko took up the beat while the crew eased into the rhythm that set them in pursuit of their bounty.

7

THE JEW RAN THROUGH the early-morning gloom, tears and blood mingling on his face. The air was cold on his cheeks and chin, which until this day had been covered by a thick beard. He stumbled over a tree root and sprawled onto the ground, crying out in fear and pain. He strained an ear for sounds of pursuit and clapped a hand to his bleeding scalp only to be rewarded by searing pain. He pulled himself to his feet and started running again.

Satan take the Christians, he cursed in his heart, and spat into the brush as he ran. Why they would want half-hearted converts to their perverted religion was beyond him, but Gothic law required all Jews to convert to the Roman faith or have their property seized and their children enslaved. He had no children and few enough possessions, but rather than submit, Lemuel ben Iudah fled to the lands of the wild Cantabrians of the north. Their fierce resistance had long vexed the Goths, and the Jew thought he might find refuge there.

The Cantabrians, however, were far older in the Roman faith than their would-be masters. The Goths had, until a mere twenty-five years earlier, followed the Arian heresy and left the Jews and pagans to their own devices. Despite the zeal of their recent conversion, though, not even the Goths could muster the religious fervor Lemuel had found among the northern rebels.

After enduring several beatings and having his head held under water, he had relented, confessed Iesu as his Lord, and accepted the bloody sacrament. When he objected that he had already been baptized, his new brethren in

Christ simply laughed. Contrary to their usual custom, they applied the triple baptism, with each immersion accompanied by a foot on Lemuel's chest to give the Holy Spirit time to fill his soul completely.

"Satan take the Christians and drag them into the Pit," he cried aloud, the words choked with pain.

He had settled uneasily into his new creed, attending the Mass—performed in wretched Latin—and matching the genuflections and pious nonsense of his neighbors. He blamed dietary intolerance for his refusal to eat shellfish and vanity over a prematurely balding scalp for keeping his head covered. When he was discovered at Sabbath prayers the previous evening, however—shawl around his shoulders, phylacteries strapped to his forehead and left arm—apostasy could no longer be passed off as eccentricity. The men of the town—those who were not at sea fishing or in the mountains harassing the Goths—had stripped Lemuel in front of the shrine of Saints Emeterius and Celedonius, exposing his shame to the laughter and ridicule of the women. They then dragged him into the nearby woods, tied him to a tree, and spent the night urinating on him and forcing shrimp, clams and oysters—the unclean fruit of the sea—down his throat.

As daylight approached, the men had tired of the torture. Their ringleader, the town's baker, scraped off Lemuel's beard—untrimmed since puberty—then began the punishment prescribed for all heretics and apostates. He grabbed the Jew's forelocks, pulled the scalp tight, and dragged his knife just below the hair line.

The sounds of tearing flesh and Lemuel's screams filled the woodland, but the baker took his time. When the other men began shouting, Lemuel assumed they were trying to urge the baker to a faster finish. The blade had just passed the line of his ears when the man withdrew his knife, cursed, then threw the Jew to the ground.

Lemuel had looked up to see his persecutors running deeper into the trees, blades drawn, shouting in their incomprehensible tribal tongue.

"Goths" was the only word he could make out of the jabber, and he struggled to his feet and ran. He knew he would find no shelter among the attacking Goths, who would more than likely finish the job the Cantabrians had begun. Instead, he ran back toward town with the hope that, in the predawn hours, he might be able to replace his clothes, recover his belongings and escape.

A few dogs barked, but no one stirred as Lemuel skirted through the shadows and alleys to his rented room behind the baker's shop. He wondered if Esti—the baker's daughter who had discovered him at prayer—would be at her place, preparing the day's bread.

With her father off scalping Jews and chasing Goths, he thought it more likely she would still be abed. As he lifted the latch to his door, he decided to pay a visit to the black-haired, fair-skinned, big-titted girl who was the cause of his suffering.

He stepped toward the inner door—still naked and bleeding—but before he could lift the latch, shouts erupted from outside. He hurriedly pulled on trousers and a tunic and wrapped a belt around his waist. His few possessions had already been plundered, but on lifting a floorboard behind the bed, he found his purse and dagger still there. Mindful of the chinking coins, he pulled out the bag and tucked it beneath his tunic. He retrieved the sheathed blade, shoved it into the back of his belt, then inched open the door.

To his surprise, the shouts came not from the woods, but from the direction of the harbor. Women called out to their men as they rushed toward the landing, and he saw Esti chasing after them, breasts jostling beneath a thin cotton shift as she tugged a shawl around her shoulders.

Against his better judgment, Lemuel chased after her. No one heard the brief cry as he clapped a hand over her mouth. None saw him put his naked blade to her throat or drag her back to the bakery.

He kicked open the door and threw the girl hard against the brick oven. Her head cracked against the masonry, but she charged him, screaming in fury. The Jew sidestepped her and swatted the back of her head so that she stumbled and fell. He stalked toward her, straddled her legs, then dropped atop her thighs before she could raise a knee to his groin.

"You've shamed me, bitch," he growled, then slapped her hard across the face. He pinned her wrists together with one hand and slit the front of her gown with his dagger. Esti struggled beneath him, but he kept his weight hard on her thighs, and squeezed her wrists until she let out a whimper. "By all means, keep struggling," he said, as her breasts spilled from the torn linen.

Shouts and screams rose from outside, and Lemuel checked that he'd closed the door.

"You laughed at this earlier," he snarled as he fumbled one-handed at the flap of his trousers. "Let's see how funny you think it now."

He tore the shift the rest of the way to expose the tight dark curls at the root of her thighs, then squeezed his knees between hers and forced her legs apart.

Esti screamed, and the door burst open even as Lemuel prodded her. A crazed-looking, sun-darkened young man stood in the doorway, a blood-stained axe in his hand. He paused a moment to take in the scene, and his face filled with rage. Before the Jew could react, the man raced across the room and buried a foot in Lemuel's belly, sending him rolling across the floor.

The girl screamed again, pulled her ruined gown about her as best she could, and scuttled into a corner.

More women screamed outside. Men shouted as they ran past the door, weapons gleaming in the dawning light. The men were all weather-battered and dressed in the cotton trousers and loose shirts of seamen.

Another man—younger than the first—filled the doorway, a short sword in his hand. Even as the axe-wielding man stalked toward Lemuel with murder in his eyes, the Jew gave an ironic laugh, for the raiders' arrival meant either his salvation or his doom.

Pirates had come to Cantabria.

8

IUDILA CHASED AFTER ENEKO, following him to a small building that, with its massive brick oven, had to be the bakery. He stepped through the doorway and tried to make sense of the scene. A half-naked young woman huddled in the corner trying to cover herself with a torn shift, while a man of about forty was backed against the oven. Eneko stood looking from the man to the girl. He raised his axe and pointed it at the man.

"You, stay right there and don't move. And put that thing away before I take care of it for you." He gestured with his axe, and the other man hastily tucked himself back into his trousers. Eneko went to the girl who let out a mewling sound and tried to sink deeper into the corner. She cried out as Eneko reached a trembling hand toward her face.

"Esti, it's me," he said, and stroked her cheek.

She blinked and looked at him for a few moments before the light of recognition sparked in her large blue eyes. "Eneko?"

"Yes, it's me. Are you hurt?"

Tears welled up, but she shook her head. "I'm fine. You got here before he—" She broke off the words and covered her face with her hands.

Eneko's muscles tightened, but he spoke calmly. "Your husband should be pleased at that."

The girl looked up through shimmering eyes and fixed Eneko with a look that a mother might give to her slow child.

"I'm not married, Eneko. Father tried to give me to Koldo, but I refused. I told him my true husband was at sea, and if he tried to force another upon me, I'd join the sisters in the convent."

Eneko's shoulders drooped. "Your true husband?"

Esti smiled, and it was her turn to stretch a comforting hand to his cheek. "You, you fool. And now my man's come back from sea, and we can finally make our home."

She clasped his face in both hands and drew his lips to hers. Eneko fell into her embrace, their tears and kisses intermingling.

The other man, seeing his would-be victim and her avenger thus preoccupied, sidled toward the door.

"He told you to stay put," Iudila reminded him, raising the point of his sword level with the man's chest.

The man stopped and Iudila studied his face. He had narrow eyes that sat too close to his long, pointed nose. His thin lips were tight with fear, and streaks of dark, dried blood ran from his scalp to his jaw. Iudila realized the man's fear was of more than Eneko's vengeance. Before Iudila could question him, Eneko broke his embrace with Esti and stalked toward the man.

"On your knees, swine," he ordered. When the man hesitated, Eneko grabbed him by the hair to force him down. "Sweet Christ."

Rather than bringing the man to his knees, he succeeded only in tearing the scalp back.

The man cried out in pain, and Esti let out a gasp at the sight of raw, dirt-crusted flesh beneath the loose shock of hair.

Iudila was the first to find his breath. "What did they do to you?"

"What all good Christians do to those they enslave in faith."

Iudila and Eneko both looked to Esti.

"He's an apostate," she said. "He took of the sacraments then turned back to his heathen ways. The law says he must be punished."

"The children of Abraham are no heathens," the man spat. "Your own Apostle called Christians the spiritual heirs of Abraham. Does that not make us brothers, regardless of the day we keep holy?"

"A rapist and a Jew?" Eneko said. "Perhaps we should finish what the Goths started."

49

"No Goth did this to me. It was her people," he said, pointing at Esti with a sign of evil, the tips of his thumb and middle fingers touching.

"A Cantabrian would have finished the job," Eneko objected.

A grin spread across the Jew's lips. "Unless a band of Goths interrupted them. I ran from the Goths to be scalped by the Cantabrians to be saved by the Goths."

"To be killed by me," Eneko added, then yanked the man up by the arm and pushed him out the door.

The streets were eerily quiet, as the townsfolk had followed Eneko's instructions and holed themselves up in their homes. *Mari-Nadris's* crew—on finding the other fishing boats as bereft as the first—had been ready to murder the entire population and sack the town, but Eneko had led them to the house of Koldo, the richest man in town.

Koldo, who had sold Eneko into slavery. Koldo, who had tried to buy Esti for his son. Koldo, whom Eneko had slaughtered on the first boat, along with his brother and sons.

The man's riches—bought in part by Eneko's freedom and in greater part by his family's tragedy—now lay piled in front of Koldo's house. Smoke billowed from the shutters and roof thatch, while the surviving family members and servants huddled together and wept.

"Take any of them you want," Eneko told his crewmates, gesturing at Koldo's household.

The men hesitated, but Thanos broke the inertia and stepped forward. Mika and two others followed, and they dragged Koldo's wife and three daughters screaming into an alley.

"Not them," Eneko ordered as more of the crew started toward the group of shabbily dressed serving women. "They belong to me."

The men grumbled, then headed for the alley to take the leavings of their mates.

"What of him?" Milhma asked, gesturing to a boy of no more than six years, who sat crying in the dirt.

"By rights, I should sell him to you," Eneko said. He hoisted the boy up and dragged him, instead, toward the servants. "But, as they belong to me, so he belongs to them." He knelt before the oldest woman, smoothed her hair back, and spoke softly. "Ama?"

The woman looked at him, her eyes wild.

"Ama, Alaia, Nahia," he said, addressing each woman in turn. "It's Eneko. I've come home. You're free now." He jerked the boy to his side. "The last of Koldo's line. Do with him as you will."

The elder girl reached desperately for the boy, and Iudila feared she might tear him limb from limb. Instead, she pulled him to her breast and showered him with kisses and tears.

"Koldo's?" Eneko asked when he found his tongue.

"His son Odol's," his mother said. "They took him from Alaia when he was weaned, then forbade her ever speaking to the boy."

Eneko's face was a maelstrom of emotions, and Iudila knew his friend was torn between ending Koldo's bloodline and preserving his own. When Eneko stood, he laid a trembling hand on the boy's head.

"You will call him Arrano," he told his sister, "after our father. Now you."

He turned toward the Jew, whom Iudila held firmly by the arm. The blood rage had drained from the Cantabrian's face, but a look at Esti—still in her tattered gown—renewed his fury. He stormed forward, axe raised, and Iudila let go of the man's arm. The Jew fell to his knees, hands clasped together in prayer, rather than pleading. And then Iudila stepped in front of him just as Eneko swung back his axe.

"No."

Eneko froze, the axe high above his head.

"Stand aside," he said.

"You have shed blood enough today, Brother. Your blade won't miss this one."

"He dishonored my woman."

"Look at him," Iudila said. "He's been tortured. How does your honor tell you to treat the stranger under your roof?"

"Don't listen to him, Eneko," Esti cried. "Kill him. Kill them both if you have to. Just send the horned devil back to his master."

The axe shook in Eneko's hand. "Step aside, Iudila."

"You can redeem this day's shame by now showing mercy."

"Stand aside."

Iudila stared at his friend and shook his head. "You said you owed me a life. I claim that debt now." He pointed at the Jew. "I claim his life as my own."

Eneko's jaw tightened, his face crimson, but he lowered his axe, dropped the blood-stained blade to the ground.

"My debt is paid. There is nothing more between us."

The Cantabrian spun on his heel, took Esti around the waist, then led her and his family to the bakery.

Iudila helped the Jew to his feet, and his crewmates stood aside as he led the man to the well in the town's square.

"Why?" the Jew asked in a tremulous voice.

Iudila seated him on the well's edge and pulled a cloth from his pouch. He moistened it and daubed at the man's bloody scalp.

"Because, old man, you are Lemuel ben Iudah, brother to Tamara of Septimania. And I am your nephew."

9

THE *MARI-NADRIS* LAY AT ANCHOR that night under a pelting rain. The pirates had spread the sail across the split deck and now huddled beneath it while Iudila tended to their newest crewmate.

Lemuel had come aboard to fill Eneko's bench, but his body—soft from his years in Corduba's scriptorium—would likely prove better suited to the rowing drum or lookout post than to the oars. And with his uncle's perpetual squint, sharpened by tight-lettered parchments and poor light, Iudila was none too sure about the lookout post.

Eneko—his mood much improved after some time behind closed doors with Esti—had helped the pirates load Koldo's plundered fortune.

"You've kept your oath," he said to Iudila, hugging him fiercely. "When you are ready to reclaim your throne, call on me and I will answer." He then went ashore to lead his countrymen against the Goths' incursion, while *Mari-Nadris* returned to sea.

"You're supposed to be dead, you know," Lemuel told Iudila, his tongue made lazy with drink.

Iudila had liberated a wineskin from Koldo's plundered fortune, then soaked a fishhook and bit of thread in it. While Brehanu and Tesfa held Lemuel down, Iudila poured the strong Ceret wine onto the older man's separated scalp. After the screaming stopped and Lemuel had drunk himself into a stupor, Iudila began stitching his scalp back together.

"You know better than most that I've rarely done as I was supposed to," Iudila said in between tugs of thread.

Lemuel gave a crooked smile. "That is true. You were always—Not so deep! My brains are in no need of mending. Except, perhaps, from this." He took another pull of wine.

"Sorry." Iudila pulled a lamp closer. "But why am I supposed to be dead?"

"Because Lord Sisenanth said so. And when Sisenanth speaks, the very heavens must move to obey his command."

"Sisenanth?"

"Mm-hmm. Now, be a good lad and do finish that stitch. Ah, that's better." More wine. "Yes, our beloved Prince Sisenanth was pulled from the sea, the sole survivor of an attack by a most fearsome horde of pirates. Must have meant you fellows, hmm?" Lemuel raised the wineskin in salute to the other men, but Iudila stilled his uncle's hand before he could manage another sip.

"I saw him die. Well, I saw him thrown to the sharks."

"So that part's true, is it? With Sisenanth's tales, it's so hard to tell. But, no, he somehow evaded the beasts and was rescued by fishermen."

Iudila pulled the wineskin from Lemuel's hands and took a drink. His throat caught fire, while his eyes flooded.

"What did he say happened to me?" Iudila asked when he was able to form words again.

"He saw your throat cut and your body thrown to the sharks. Resilient stock, you Goths, eh?"

Iudila handed back the wineskin and silently finished tending Lemuel's scalp. He made his last stitch then tied and cut off the thread.

"Why?" he said finally. "Why would he lie? Why didn't anyone come after me?"

"Land, boy. Land and titles and power—which are all really the same thing. With you gone, the seat of Baetica was empty. The nobles slew King Witteric—small loss there. Sisenanth's father, Gundemar, became king, and he made Sisenanth Dux Baeticae."

"And he kept you as steward?"

"For Rosmunda's sake."

Iudila nodded, but Dingha asked, "Who is Rosmunda?"

"My aunt," Iudila said. "Sister to my mother and Lemuel, and Gundemar's queen."

"Sisenanth's mother?"

"Step-mother. But she would still have some influence over him."

"When Gundemar died last year," Lemuel continued, "the council elected Sisebut to the throne."

"Sisebut? The poet?"

"Poet, scribe, scholar—all-around pious fool. Clearly, the council wanted someone they could control, and the Church fared quite well in the bargain. Sisebut, of course, took Rosmunda as queen, to legitimize his crown."

"He took the king's widow to wife?" Tesfa asked.

"It's our old way," Iudila explained. "The king is selected from among the nobles, but to secure his claim he will take a queen of the Scarlet Thread, an ancient line that runs back through King David and the Pharaohs of Egypt."

"Whether she is willing or not," Lemuel added. "Poor Rosmunda. I suspect once Sisebut has gotten a son from her, he'll shut her away in a convent. If he feels merciful, that is."

"How is that merciful?"

"She is a Jewess. Sisebut has ordered the conversion of all Jews to the Roman faith. I refused. Rosmunda was powerless to protect me, so I ran. For all the good it did me."

"You're still alive," Iudila said, then took a hesitant breath. "What of Keinan?"

"She is safe in the care of Suinthila, Count of Eminio."

"In his care?"

Lemuel took a drink then handed the wineskin to Iudila.

"They are to be married."

"But she is betrothed to me."

"And you made her a widow before ever she was a bride."

Iudila tipped the wineskin to his lips but managed only a few drops before the slurry of dregs soured his tongue. He spat, cursed and threw the wineskin away. "I should have stayed ashore. I should have helped Eneko fight."

"Then you would have been slaughtered like a Pesach lamb. You and your men may fight well against ill-armed sailors, but you would have been no match for a trained army. Certainly not under Sisebut's best general."

Iudila caught the shift in Lemuel's eyes. "What general?"

The Jew looked about, as though searching for an answer on the air. He finally met Iudila's gaze.

"Sisenanth."

"He was there?" Iudila jumped to his feet. He would have leapt over the side to swim back to Cantabria, but Lemuel held him fast.

"Sit down, you fool. Sisenanth would kill you on sight, or as soon as he learned who you are. His rank, his wealth, his prospects all rest on the foundation of the lie of your death. He couldn't afford to have you tell the truth, and you are not strong enough to fight him."

"So you would have me run, as you did? Spend the rest of my days as a sea rat?"

"I didn't say that."

"What, then?"

Lemuel took a fresh flask from his pouch. He pulled the stopper, took a drink then handed it to Iudila.

"Get stronger."

10

RAIN LASHED AT THE WATER-LADEN SAIL that drooped more than billowed in the driving gale. Iudila and his mates dragged their oars through the choppy waters, but the oars slapped together and fell into wave troughs as curses and misstrokes rippled along *Mari-Nadris's* benches. Fortunately, the same troubles plagued their quarry, a Saxon trader by the look of her.

The pirates had taken to the waters off the northwest coast of Spania, growing rich from the plunder of Danes and Britons, Franks and Saxons en route to the Mediterranean. They ignored the fishing boats of the Cantabrians and, in return, found shelter in their coves and trade in their ports. The Goth navy was preoccupied with blockades of the Roman enclaves along the Mediterranean coast, giving *Mari-Nadris's* men a free hand in the northwest.

When the latest Saxon convoy had passed by, the pirates culled the trailing ship from her escort, driving her out to sea and away from protection. A storm had taken them by surprise, but with the wind to their stern, Milhma ordered the continued pursuit before disappearing into his cabin.

For half a day *Mari-Nadris* chased the Saxon, her crew taking turns at the oars to keep up their strength. The trader's crew was good, but *Mari-Nadris's* lateen sail had the advantage over the Saxon's square. That, combined with Dingha's skill at the steering oar, had slowly brought the pirates closer to their prey.

Lemuel beat his drum in the relative shelter of the bow deck, but each burst of wind snapped the sails and sent sheets of water cascading over him. His sputtering curses—an impressive mix of Hebrew, Latin and Greek—carried over the roar of wind and sea.

"Looks like he's a good Christian again," Dingha said.

"I think he joined us to get away from forced baptism," Iudila replied from his rowing bench.

"Jew, Christian, and now pirate," the helmsman said with a bellow of laughter as another wave cascaded over Lemuel's head. "He's been baptized by the sea now."

Dingha was in his element. This was his weather—a sailor's weather—where wind and wave fought each other, and the slightest misjudgment could founder a ship in the blink of an eye. But in the hands of a veteran, with all the finesse of a lover toward his fickle mistress, this was the sea at her finest.

"Now that's a big one," Dingha said, excitement in his voice. He smiled and set the steering oar for what Iudila knew was the heart of an approaching wave.

Iudila heaved on his oar, and his stomach plummeted as *Mari-Nadris* rose on the swell. The grey sky turned green. Iudila looked up to see the wave crest high above the mast. The oarsmen braced themselves as *Mari-Nadris* rode up the wave.

The climb became too steep and the dromon slid into the wet grasp, the sea's fist closing around her. Iudila opened his mouth to shout a curse at Dingha—who was now singing a raucous, unintelligible chantey—but the crashing water drowned his words and the *Mari-Nadris* somehow cleared the wave upright and afloat, though Iudila and the other aft oarsmen were buried beneath the sail, torn from its rigging. Lemuel left his drum and gathered the heavy canvas into a manageable bundle, then set to untangling the lines.

The Saxon ship had fared worse than *Mari-Nadris* and now lay athwart the seas, broken mast and rigging caught in an angry current that threatened to swamp the trader. Iudila leapt to the bow to judge the current, then guided Dingha on the best approach to avoid the floating debris.

"Ramming speed." Iudila gave the order with ever-increasing confidence, and the crew responded. The Saxons struggled to right themselves and resume their escape, but the pirates were quicker at their oars. Rather than the customary bow strike—which might overturn the wallowing Saxon vessel—Dingha brought *Mari-Nadris* in line with the stern of his target, then bore down on her.

"Unship larboard oars," Iudila ordered as the bow neared the other ship's stern, and half the crew slid their oars in through their holes. The other half feathered their blades and pulled the handles to their chests, making ready for the next command.

"Back paddle."

The steerboard crew dropped their blades into the foamy sea and pushed with all their might. A series of snaps echoed from the larboard side as Dingha brought *Mari-Nadris* crashing over the oars of the half-sunken Saxon. The clash of wooden hulls and the drag of the steerboard oars stopped the dromon midline-to-midline with her slightly longer prey. The larboard crew was ready with ropes and grapnels, which they tossed over the trader's gunnels, then lashed the boats together.

The Saxons—all long blond hair and scraggly beards—had abandoned buckets for blades and welcomed the pirates with a bristle of steel. Though out-manned by a brace of rowing benches, the pirates shouted their challenge and bore into the knot of the enemy. Tesfa led the way, struck down the largest man in the enemy line with a savage blow of his cudgel, then picked up the fallen man's sword.

The rest of the crew charged after him, driving a wedge into the line of defenders. The pirates formed a pair of shallow lines, back-to-back, that split the Saxons into two halves. Brehanu and Dingha joined Tesfa, their combined bulk holding back the aft part, while the rest of the crew swarmed the now-outnumbered forward half.

This was no mere trading ship, however. The Saxons—warriors all—wielded their swords and axes with practiced skill. From their rear ranks, targes were handed forward, and the front line of six men formed a shield wall.

Two pirates fell as they rushed the Saxons—one from an axe blow to the head, the other by the stab of a short-bladed seax to the groin. Other men filled their spots, but the Saxons gave a roar and a mighty heave with their shields, forcing the pirates a step aft and making room for one more shield as the beam broadened amidships.

The sea took no rest during the fight, and the belly of the Saxon vessel grew more swollen with each churn of the waves. Red-stained water swirled about the fallen men, their slackened limbs floating on the surface and threatening to trip the fighting men around them. Men spat curses and insults at one another in their different languages, but the song of their blades and the cries of the wounded shared a common tongue.

Iudila tried to force his way to the front of the fight, but the older men blocked his way on the narrow deck. A cry roared behind him, and he turned just as Tesfa fell to the water-logged deck, blood fountaining from a gash in his throat. Brehanu and Dingha fought on, but their line of attack—now reduced by a third—would be quickly overwhelmed. Tesfa clutched his sword even as Death called for him, and Iudila tugged the blade from his dying grip.

"*Gramawia*," Iudila shouted the battle cry that Tesfa had taught him. *Be Glorious.* He leapt to Dingha's side, swinging his sword. Brehanu roared with grief for his fallen brother and pressed the attack with a new fury. Dingha, too, redoubled his efforts, and the three men drove the Saxons back and back again until the rearmost man was forced up to the steering deck.

A shout rose above the fray, and Iudila looked up as the man leapt over the heads of his crewmates, sword held in both hands and pointed at Iudila's breast. Iudila knelt to the deck and raised his arms, blade up, to cover himself. The Saxon's feral scream ended when Iudila's blade pierced his throat.

The man's momentum carried him all the way to the sword's hilt, wrenched the weapon from Iudila's hand, and sent them both tumbling into the ever-reddening bilge. Iudila clambered to his feet, his head buzzing with fear and rage. Still clutching his short sword, he raced again to join Dingha and Brehanu, their original dozen Saxons down to seven.

Iudila ducked a sword swipe, snatched up a fallen axe from the water, and swung at the legs of his attacker. He caught the man behind the knee, watched him fall, then kicked him in the face.

Another man swung his axe at Iudila's skull.

The Goth crossed his sword and axe, caught the Saxon's shaft in the crook of his weapons, and snapped the head off. Iudila rushed the startled man, drove a shoulder into his belly and tossed him over the side.

He turned back to see that Dingha and Brehanu had dispatched four of the remaining men. The last Saxon in the rearward half scrambled over the side, to the relative safety of *Mari-Nadris's* deck. Iudila was about to give chase when a shout drew his attention forward.

The Saxon shield wall had stretched to eight men now and was slowly driving back the raiders. The pirates were pressed together, with no way for Iudila to join in and help. Instead, he leapt onto the rail. He had thought to run around the skirmishers and join the attack from the Saxon rear, but the view from above sent a chill down his spine and froze him in place.

It wasn't the tangle of bodies beneath the fighters' feet, not the spills of blood and gore, nor the bits of sailor meat that floated atop the calf-deep water like so much jetsam. Rather, the horror came from beyond the coupled ships, where winged, dragon-headed Death flew out of the storm.

Ruby eyes gleamed from a green- and gold-scaled muzzle, and a blood-red tongue lapped at the sea breeze. Twenty pairs of fins propelled the beast through the waves, its head bobbing and lunging with each stroke. The crack and rustle of its wings carried over the howl of the storm and the shouts of fighting men, but it was the cry of the beast—a mournful, soul-wrenching bellow—that turned Iudila's bowels to water.

At the beast's roar, the fighting paused for a moment as pirate and Saxon alike looked toward the sound. The Saxons recovered first and, with a cheer, renewed the fight, forcing the pirates to take another defensive step back.

"Lemuel, the sail," Iudila shouted above the fray.

"It's not ready yet."

"Get it ready. Now. Break off," Iudila shouted at his men. "Cross back."

He jumped over to *Mari-Nadris's* rail and hacked at the ropes that bound the two ships. The pirates shot confused glances at him. Confusion turned to fear when they saw the slackening lines and the growing rift between the vessels.

Without waiting for an explanation, Dingha roared at the remaining men. He grabbed one by the shoulder, spun him toward the rail and kicked him on his way. He shouted to Brehanu, and the two rushed to the advancing shield wall to cover their crewmates' retreat.

Iudila scrambled to the aft deck, gripped the steering oar in one hand and the mainsheet in the other. Lemuel perched atop the mast—having rethreaded the lines—ready to leap with the halyard to raise the sail on Iudila's command. Shouts rose from Milhma's cabin, but Iudila ignored them, instead focusing on the current to hold the ships as close as possible, and to give his crew time to escape.

Nine more men returned to *Mari-Nadris*, and Iudila shouted for Dingha and Brehanu to abandon the fight. Brehanu swung his sword like a fiend, giving pause to even the most fearless Saxon. Only when Dingha pushed him out of the way of an overhead axe blow did Brehanu's battle rage subside.

The axe glanced off Dingha's shoulder, peeling away a chunk of flesh. He screamed, stamped on the foot of the nearest Saxon, then ran his sword through the man's eyes.

Brehanu grabbed Dingha around the waist, hustled him to the rail and heaved him across the void. With a last glance, he hurled himself from the Saxon ship, leaving the corpses of his brother and six others in the company of the Saxon dead.

"Lemuel, go," Iudila ordered as Brehanu's feet left the Saxon rail.

The Jew leapt from the mast, trailing the halyard through its block, hoisting the canvas as he fell. The inflating sail slowed his descent, and he landed sprightly and looped the line about its cleat. Iudila tugged the mainsheet and pushed on the steering oar to turn *Mari-Nadris* away from the swamped Saxon ship. The gulf between the ships widened faster than Brehanu's leap could carry him, and he just managed to catch the rail.

The approaching beast bellowed again. Iudila looked back to see its wings flair, its fins rise in unison, and its flank turn to come in line with the crippled vessel. A dragon it was, but one wrought by human hands. The ship dwarfed *Mari-Nadris*, and if its forty oarsmen were half the fighters their countrymen were, the pirates were doomed.

Iudila turned the dromon fully with the wind as Dingha hauled Brehanu onto the deck. The sail spewed water in protest as the wind punched it in the belly and drove *Mari-Nadris* into the raging sea. Behind them, the dragon-ship paused to take on survivors from the swamped vessel, but her oars soon again beat the waves in pursuit of the pirates.

"To the oars!"

Even as Iudila shouted the order, the cries from Milhma's cabin turned into savage screams. The door burst open, and a Saxon—the one who had fled from Dingha and Brehanu—rushed onto the deck. His sword was smeared with red. His bare chest and back were streaked with bloody trails, his face white as canvas. He tossed his sword over the side, ran toward the nearest man, dropped to his knees, and clasped his hands together in supplication. Eyes wild, Milhma's twins shrieked in fury as they flew from the cabin and fell upon the man. His screams of horror were drowned out by the children's banshee cries. The crew looked on in morbid fascination as the pair dug claws and teeth into the hapless Saxon. His cries fell silent as the girl bit his throat, coming away with bloody shreds in her mouth.

"Oars," Iudila shouted again.

The men tore their eyes away from the grisly spectacle and dropped to the benches. The dragon-ship was gaining on them, and only eight of the pirates were fit to row. Exhausted though they were, they fell to the task with all the energy left to them. Their urgency, combined with Iudila's sense of the currents, gave *Mari-Nadris* the boost she needed to edge ahead of her pursuers.

The twins were now bathing in the Saxon's blood. A chill shot up Iudila's spine, but he shook it off. He checked on the progress of the dragon-ship, then settled in for the long escape.

11

THE STORM RAGED THROUGH another day and night, during which time Iudila drank little and ate even less. Sleep was but a distant memory to him, as none—not even Dingha—could tease the speed out of the wind and sea to match Iudila's skill. With the Saxons still perilously close, the pirates needed every advantage, and so—bone-weary, hands bleeding from the bite of rope and oar—Iudila stood his post through the deadly race.

The crew rowed in shifts, having bandaged the wounded and cleared the ship of every ounce of useless weight. The Saxon warrior—his body at last relinquished by the twins—had been the first to go, followed by empty water and food barrels, and even the plunder taken since the last port call. Anything that wasn't nailed down or needed for survival had been jettisoned.

Except for Milhma.

The captain lay in his cabin, covered by a wool blanket. As Iudila had pieced the story together, the Saxon had taken refuge in Milhma's cabin, holding a knife on the girl to force silence. When the pirates reboarded *Mari-Nadris*, Milhma rushed the man, expecting the crew to come to his aid. With their hurried retreat, however, no help had come. The Saxon spitted Milhma on his sword, only to meet his own bloody end at the hands of the children.

Iudila—indeed, most of the remaining crew—might have rejoiced at the captain's fate, had Death's scythe not stood so readily to hand. Whether joyous or mournful, remembrance of the fallen would have to wait until the Saxons gave up their chase—or until the crew joined their mates in the feasting hall of Hel, goddess of the dead.

"Still there?" Dingha asked as he climbed to the steering deck, having just been relieved at his oar. He spun his arms then winced as the motion brought a spate of fresh blood from his wounded shoulder.

Iudila shrugged, and that gesture alone sent spasms through his tortured muscles.

"Lemuel?" he called up to the lookout.

The Jew looked aft, shook his head and shrugged.

The crew had thought themselves safe on the previous morning, but the Saxons somehow tracked them through the sea's expanse and hounded them throughout that entire day and into the darkness. As night ebbed and the storm expended its last furies, Iudila adjusted his course for the changing seas and prayed dawn might find them alone on the waves.

With dawn's awakening—real daylight this time, not simply a fading of black to grey—Lemuel whistled down and pointed over Iudila's right shoulder. Iudila nodded, willed back his pain and fatigue, and nudged the ship a hair to larboard.

"Let me stand in for a bit," Dingha offered.

Iudila bit his lip and shook his head. "If they spot us, we'll need you rested for the oars."

Dingha grabbed the steering oar anyway and held out a cup of water. Iudila nodded his thanks and peeled his hand from the oar, leaving a stain of pus and blood on the handle. His hand trembled as he brought the cup to his lips. The salt-laced water scoured his parched tongue and throat. He rasped a thank you, handed the cup back and again took the oar.

The chase continued until the sun was halfway up its morning climb, its rays a gentle caress on Iudila's neck. He felt like an *nsambu*, one of the waking dead that Dingha had told him about—the lost ones whose souls had left their bodies, yet who still walked among the living. Instinct kept the sail trimmed and the steering oar in place, but Iudila's mind wandered in fitful waking dreams.

The endless beat of the drum seemed to him the heartbeat of some great beast. The grunts of the exhausted men at the oars played in his mind as the curses of the damned. The billowing white clouds on the horizon were plumes of smoke from Satan's furnace, and the smattering of green among the changeless blue of the sea.

From the depths of Iudila's not-quite-dream came a soul-rending shriek. A spatter of cold stickiness on his shoulder brought him back to his senses, and he cursed the gull that had shat on him. A few of the men laughed, but most were in the same catatonic state as Iudila had been.

Iudila stood straighter in his post, using the pain of cramped muscles to clear his fog-shrouded mind.

The gull and the clouds were signs of land. Land meant coves and the chance to hide from their pursuers. The patterned colors of the sea, though, puzzled him. He expected to see the waters fade to green as they drew nearer to shore, but not this far out, and not in random circles.

The mystery was solved sooner than Iudila could form the question.

At the center of a light-colored patch of water, the sea roiled to a seething cauldron. Green turned to white as a huge bubble erupted from the deep. The sea expelled its foul breath and the surrounding water rushed into the void. The surge sent a plume of water into the air, three times higher than *Mari-Nadris's* mast.

The noise and spray from the water spout jolted the crew from their stupors.

"Lemuel?" Iudila called up to the lookout.

"The water spots are everywhere." Lemuel gripped the masthead and looked in all directions. Even from the steering deck, Iudila saw his uncle's face turn pale. "We've already sailed past some. Any one of those could have swamped us."

"But they didn't," Iudila said. "I can see them from here, but I need you to tell me if I get too close. Dingha, secure the oars and bring the men on deck. If we hit one of these pockets, I want them to be able to get out fast."

Dingha glanced aft toward the pursuing dragon-ship. "If we stop rowing, they'll catch up with us in no time."

"I know," Iudila said. "That's what I'm counting on."

12

THE SUN WAS PAST ITS ZENITH by the time Iudila's plan came into play. He'd bled his sail and jinked the oar so that, slowly, almost imperceptibly, the Saxons closed the distance. Keeping well clear of the green patches, Iudila managed to place several of the pockets between *Mari-Nadris* and the dragon-ship. He wasn't sure what would happen when the Saxons fell into his trap, but he hoped the gamble would at least slow them enough to allow his rested oarsmen to reclaim the lead he had squandered.

The crew, for their part, showed little concern. At first, they were simply too exhausted to care. As they rested and recovered their strength, the Saxon advantage raised a few eyebrows, but Iudila's confidence seemed to satisfy them. Soon, the overflight of birds became more regular. The low clouds burned off to reveal a wooded, mountainous island. Its rocky shores promised refuge if the pirates could tuck the dromon into a hidden cove, resupply their water and food stores, and wait out the lurking Saxons.

Lemuel—who refused to leave his lookout post until Iudila surrendered the helm—called down, a feeble arm raised and pointing aft. Iudila looked back to find the Saxons closer than expected. He could hear the rapid beat of their rowing drum and the crack of the square sail filled with the northeasterly breeze.

His heart sank when he realized the hunters had passed several of the sea-pockets he had placed between *Mari-Nadris* and the dragon-ship. Whether they had gone around or simply passed through unharmed, he didn't know. He steered behind another pocket and called on Gabriel and Niord to shield him from his enemies.

The dragon's bellow—the blast of a hollowed-out ram's horn, he now realized—echoed across the waves.

"Ready to oars," Iudila called.

The order was met with a string of curses, but the men stretched their muscles and started toward their benches.

"They're coming in," Lemuel called down.

"I know," Iudila replied. "Ship oars."

"No—they're coming into a pocket."

Thirteen pairs of eyes looked back to see the dragon-headed prow cross the line from blue to green. The Saxons crested a wave and when the bow arced down—just across the pocket's threshold—the water seemed nothing more than foam. A clatter of oars and a string of curses and screams heralded the Saxons' fate as they plunged into the watery sinkhole.

The exhausted pirates cheered the two-score souls on their way to the depths, but Iudila gave only the grim smile of one who had temporarily cheated death.

He had, at least, guessed right about the pockets. This part of the sea must have lain over the backside of Oceanus. The Titan's sulfur-laden flatus rose to the surface in swarms of bubbles that lightened the water, both in shade and in density. The vitiated water could no more support a wooden ship than pond water could float a rock.

Iudila's second guess also proved correct. The falling dragon-ship crushed the bubbles in its path. As the sea rushed in to fill the void, it set off a cascade. Denser water filled the pocket until a plume vomited from the surface, bringing with it scraps of the doomed Saxon vessel.

Bits of wood, rope, and canvas fell like rain as the eruption settled. One oar survived intact, but all else was ruin. No bodies appeared amid the debris. It was as if the sea had consumed the entire ship then spat out the less edible parts like so much gristle.

As spectacular as the sight was, Iudila had seen too much destruction during the past few days and hadn't the stomach for more carnage. He tugged the mainsheet to capture the wind and aimed *Mari-Nadris* toward land.

13

IUDILA CLIMBED THE GRASSY SLOPE, his legs unsteady on solid ground. He had left Dingha and Brehanu to oversee the repair and provisioning of the ship, while he—for reasons he could not explain and did not himself fully understand—wandered alone to the island's interior. Part of the reason, he knew, was Milhma.

While few of the men had held any affection for the man, all were wary of his shade. None would risk offending the spirit of the slain captain, so his body would be consigned to a funeral pyre, appeasing the old gods with the sacrifice and releasing his spirit with fire and smoke and ash.

Iudila wanted none of it.

Milhma had been his captor, his tormentor. True, it had been years since Iudila last shared the captain's bed, and the boy was long since a man. But the scars on his soul were every bit as real as those on his cheeks. Milhma's shade would haunt Iudila for a long time to come, whether he took part in the funeral ritual or not. He needed to exorcise his demons in solitude and in his own time.

For now, he was glad to breathe in the earthy scents of laurel and leaf mould. A sailor he might be, but part of him longed for life ashore. A third of his life had been spent at sea, half of his remembrance. He dimly recalled the forests and fields of his childhood, the mountains and streams.

Spania was a rich land, and Baetica the fairest of all her provinces. Even without his titles, without Keinan, he might find contentment on a small patch of land beside a stream. Space enough to herd sheep, and water enough to keep them. Perhaps even a woman, one who neither knew nor cared about generals or princes or kings. A woman to shear his sheep, spin his wool, and hold him when the nights grew cold.

And when the nightmares came.

Iudila pushed through a stand of brush, and his breath caught. Before him lay a high meadow, as lush as the grazing lands of his imaginings. A brook giggled its way through the middle of the sward, its gentle cadence accompanied by mournful bird calls and the hum of dragonflies. Iudila looked around expectantly, as though a plump, fair-haired shepherdess might any moment emerge from the surrounding brambles.

Drained by the sea battle and the days at the steering oar, Iudila found a flat spot near the stream and stretched out on the ground. Warm sun and cool earth, gurgling stream and singing birds forged a somnolent conspiracy. Helpless to resist, he gave in to the call of sleep.

He awoke cold and stiff and confused.

Solid ground lay where a rolling deck should be. Instead of the rhythmic chant of the sea, the steady song of the brook tickled his ears. It was not the stench of brine and rotting fish and unwashed bodies, but the perfume of damp earth and sweet flowers. The sky was ominously dark, the stars surrounded by an unnaturally black horizon. It took a moment for Iudila to realize that all the spheres were in place, simply hidden by tree and hill and mountain.

The stream beckoned, and he heeded the call. The water ravaged the raw flesh of his hands as he ladled handfuls of the cool, sweet liquid into his parched mouth. His stomach rumbled, but Iudila had left the beach with no thought for food. A full meal would have to wait.

A shooting star blazed overhead, and he tracked its path until it disappeared behind the mountain at the island's center. As he turned away, a flash caught his attention from the corner of his eye—not the white trace of the fallen star, but a ruddy orange glow. He scanned the mountainside but could see nothing directly. Only when he looked to the side of the mountain could he make out the hint of light, almost at the summit.

Curious as to who or what could disturb the darkness in this deserted paradise at the edge of the world, he left the glade behind and started his climb.

Once among the trees, Iudila lost sight of the elusive glow, but the slope of the mountain guided the way. The air grew thin and chill as he climbed, his lungs burned for want of air, and his legs demanded rest, but Iudila ignored their protest and pressed on until he stood at the summit.

The island spread out beneath him, stretching east to west. The southern shore was blocked by another, lower range of mountains separated from his by a deep ravine. The moon, full and low in the eastern sky, revealed the crests of waves and the foamy line that tracked the tide's progress along the northern shore.

A red glow marked the spot where his crew camped, adjacent to an even brighter fire. Iudila knew the larger must be Milhma's pyre, which would burn through the night. He expected to feel something, but from this distance and with the benefit of his rest by the stream, there was only cool detachment.

A rustle in the brush made him spin around. Iudila's mouth fell open as an old man crested the peak from a hidden trail to the south. His head was shaved from forehead to crown, and his white beard stretched to his waist. He carried a lantern in one hand and a staff in the other.

"You're late," he said in terse Latin colored with a Hibernian brogue. "No matter. Come, come. The hour draws nigh."

As suddenly as he had appeared, the man turned and stepped back down the path. Iudila stared after him, dumbfounded, until the glow of the lantern disappeared. A gust of wind struck Iudila from behind, forcing him to take a step toward the path. He gave in to the momentum and stepped into the darkness.

The old man's stride went unchecked as Iudila caught up with him. The way was steep, narrower than any goat's track. A cold rock wall bounded one side. On the other, the mountainside plunged into a dark ravine.

The old man swept his staff in front of him, from the scrub at the trail's edge to the rock wall, and his *tap-clack* was the only accompaniment as he led the way to a rough opening in the rock face. He ducked low and stepped inside. Iudila followed.

The rasp of the old man's breath echoed off the stone walls, but his pace was smooth and even, suggesting he was accustomed to the thin air and to walking doubled over in this cramped tunnel. The way twisted and curved into the heart of the mountain, until the tunnel opened into a chamber.

The cavern was not only large enough for Iudila to stand upright, but its dimensions exceeded the humble lantern's ability to cast its light. At the top of the chamber, discernible only by the starlight that shone through it, was a small, round opening. Directly beneath it, where the old man now stood waiting, was a low altar covered with a white cloth.

A black cross stood at its center, equal-length arms sprouting from a circle decorated with serpentine figures. Carved marble pedestals stood near each corner of the altar. The two pedestals nearest the old man held candles, while the other two supported twin bronze spheres etched with strange shapes.

A small table stood nearby. On it rested a laver, a flask of oil, a dish of herbs, and a covered bronze pot suspended above a smoking brazier.

"Have you eaten?" the old man asked Iudila, his tone more perfunctory than cordial.

Iudila eyed the brazier, his stomach rumbling. "I've not. Only water since—" He paused. "I can't remember my last meal."

"Excellent." The old man rubbed his hands together, warming them at the brazier. "A hollow stomach focuses the mind. Come, wash."

Iudila dipped his hands in the laver, his bloody palms tinting the pure water the shade of summer wine. The old man offered him a cloth, and Iudila dried his hands. His mouth watered with anticipation as his host tipped back the lid of the brazing pot. It took Iudila a few moments to recognize the scent not as beef or fowl or even fish, but as rose-laden incense.

The old man set the lid aside, then sprinkled the oil and herbs over the incense. Smoke rose from the pot, and the man swept his hands through the plume, wafting the smoke over his face as though washing in it. He gestured for Iudila to do the same, and the Goth mimicked the motions, his eyes stinging from the aromatic smoke.

"Sit." The man gestured to a black cushion between the orbs, while he stood before a red one placed between the candles' stands.

Iudila did as instructed. The old man snuffed out the lantern, draping the chamber in darkness. Stars still shone through the oculus, but their light was too weak to illumine the space. Iudila could just make out the man's shape. He waited for him to speak or even to move, but the only sound was the quickening beat of his own pulse pounding in his ears.

After an age in the tomblike darkness, the old man clapped his hands together, the sound like thunder as it echoed from the cavern's walls. He hummed softly, beginning with a deep rumble then slowly raising the pitch until his voice resounded with power throughout the chamber. Using that same tone, he again spoke—in Hebrew, this time.

"*Yehi aur.*" Let there be light.

A faint blue glow shone between his gnarled fingers, growing brighter as he repeated the chant once, then again. He separated his hands, each palm supporting a small sphere of light, which he brought to the candles. He spoke the words again—an octave higher now—and the light changed to green, then yellow, then orange. With this last, he cupped his hands over the candles, raised his voice yet another octave and chanted, "Ahh—Ooh—Mmm."

The candles took flame, and the old man brought his hands together as in prayer. He whispered something Iudila couldn't make out, then spread his arms in a gesture of welcome. He settled onto his cushion and looked at Iudila expectantly.

"Who are you?" Iudila said. "What is this place?"

"I am but a humble brother of Christ who is honored to serve at *Heykhal v'Maharav*, the Temple of the West. For millennia it has stood as a signpost in the midst of the sea."

"A signpost to what?"

The monk sighed, shook his head and picked at invisible specks of lint on the altar cloth. "To what lies beyond."

"And what is that?"

The monk stopped his picking, looked up, and fixed his eyes on Iudila's.

"Why, your destiny."

Iudila stared blankly at the old man, whose eyes reflected humor and intelligence that belied his outward air of impatience.

"What do you know of my destiny?"

A smile tugged at the man's mouth.

"Much, Iudila of Corduba—son of Goiswinth, son of Athanagild, scion of the noble House of Balti. Your mother was of the Scarlet Thread, the Line of Zerah. Through her, you descend from Yahshua and Miriam, the Savior and his bride. Through them, your blood flows from David and the Pharaohs. You come from kings, king you will be, and from you will kings arise."

The old man cocked his head, as though listening to a whisper.

"But something stands in your way. The line whose blood you share has grown weak. Pretenders claim kinship even while denying its legitimacy. They bestow its birthrights on a corrupt Church, currying favor with those who would geld the lion and defang the serpent."

"How do you know all this?"

The monk arched a bushy eyebrow.

"How do you know the ways of the wind and waves? As surely as currents flow through the sky and the sea, so do they flow through mankind. As surely as you read changes in the wind, I can trace the patterns of your life."

"Patterns? Like the Fates?"

The man chuckled. "The three sisters do tend to meddle, but their influence has waned since mankind left Eden."

Iudila blinked at that. "The Garden?"

"What other? Eden represents humanity's early condition, when we communed with the gods, with nature, but without awareness—the same way a deer or a tree communes with the divine. For mankind to awaken, to reach its potential, it was necessary first to leave the Garden."

"You mean the Fall. Eve's original sin."

"Bah! You speak like a churchman. Eve should be praised for her actions, not vilified. Tell me, what was her sin?"

Iudila chafed at the scolding, but said, "She ate of the forbidden fruit."

"Yes, but what does that mean?"

Iudila looked away as his cheeks grew warm.

"Ah, of course. Your pious teachers would have you believe the sin was of a sexual nature. Eve was a temptress, and poor Adam—Adam, who walked in the Garden with the Almighty himself—was helpless to resist her. What chance, then, has an ordinary man against the wiles of the daughters of Eve? They must be shut away, stripped of any power, and made subject to man's authority."

Iudila made a gesture that was half shrug, half nod.

"Rubbish! It is that kind of thinking that saw Hypatia savaged at the burning of the Great Library. The same mindset that turned the Magdalene from the Bride of Christ to a lunatic and a whore. But tainted as the scriptures have become, they still hold some truth. Eve's fruit was not of temptation, but of—"

"Knowledge."

The monk nodded. "The knowledge of good and evil. The ability to consider different courses of action and to choose which to take."

"Free will."

"Precisely. But the Church has turned the act of awakening into woman's first sin. They have turned the serpent—the ancient symbol of wisdom—into a sign for evil. Their greatest sin, however, has been to take Lucifer—the Light-Bringer, the Christ-Spirit—and turn him into the chief of demons. 'And the woman and the man ate from the Tree, and their eyes were opened'—"

"And they became as the gods."

"Fellows of the Creator," the monk said with a nod. "Endowed with the power to create their own paths, their own destinies."

"Then what of fate?" Iudila said.

"All of Creation is under the agency of spiritual powers. The stars and planets, natural forces, the elements—each has a guardian that governs its place in the whole. It was the discovery—the memory, actually—of these guardians that gave rise to the first stories of titans and gods. Your Spinners were among the host of guardians assigned to govern mankind's affairs while still we lived in Eden. When we left the Garden, we gained the power to dictate our own fates."

"And the old gods lost their power?"

The monk shrugged. "Power is an intoxicating elixir. Once tasted, is not easily given up. This is as true for the spiritual beings as it is for men. The Garden was a place of beauty and peace and order, but freedom is a messy thing. A war began when humanity awoke to its true potential—a war between those who would again enslave us and restore order, and those who embraced the chaos as a means to the sublime peace that is freedom realized."

"Is it not better to have order?"

"Perhaps, but at what cost? Your ancestor was crucified by those who revered the law and wished to restore order. Can you imagine the chaos if people were free to choose their own destiny? To discover and serve the divine in whatever manner they chose? If—so long as they did no harm to others—they were left to determine right and wrong, good and evil for themselves? What kind of world would that be?"

"Paradise," Iudila said without thinking. "Mad and tangled and beautiful."

The monk smiled. "That is the New Eden. Restored communion with the divine, but with full awareness and purpose."

Iudila stared into a burning candle until a thought arose. "If mankind is free, then what need is there for the royal bloodline? What need for kings and priests and judges?"

"In the New Eden, little. But we have far to go before we achieve that blessed state. Until then, the ordained line is tasked to be not the masters, but the heart and head of the body of humanity."

"And we will lead them back to Eden?"

A nod. "Each generation has the opportunity to make a contribution, great or small. It is a long journey, measured in stars' ages, and the temptation is to leave the next incremental step to those who follow."

"If the steps are so small, what does it matter?"

"Little—for that generation. But then the next generation fails in its duty, and the next, and the next. Such complacency has led to the ruin of countless nations, and more than once has threatened mankind's very existence. Had your great ancestors not taken up the challenge, had they not embodied the spirit of the redeeming Christ, humanity would have plunged irrevocably into darkness, never to know our true nature, never to reach the heights to which we have been called."

"So Christianity is the true way?"

The monk raised his eyes to the cave's arch.

"Blessed Father Breandan, give me patience. No." He turned back to Iudila. "Christianity is an aberration, a perversion of the Truth of the Christ-spirit. It is a withered corpse animated by priests whose lust and greed would put Croesus to shame. They have done more to subvert the truth of man's divinity than a thousand-thousand Caesars or Alexanders could ever have done. They will reign throughout this age, and the earth will tremble like a frightened child under the lash of Holy Mother Church. Yet when the time is fulfilled, out of her will arise another savior who will usher in a new age of light."

"If another is to bring salvation, what is my part?"

The old man gave a wry smirk. "You are to plant the seed for the one who is to come. You have been chosen as the head of your line in this generation—you have only to find your heart."

It took a moment for the meaning to sink in. "A wife?"

"Indeed."

Iudila frowned and shook his head.

"The thought displeases you. Have you been so long among sailors that you would deny a woman's graces?"

"No, no." It was a feeble denial, and the fact that Iudila was still virgin—at least as far as a willing act—made him wonder just how deeply Milhma had scarred him after all. "I was betrothed to my cousin—the last of the Scarlet Thread—but she has married another."

The man gave no reaction, his expression neutral, as though waiting for Iudila to say something of worth.

"How can I marry, when the other half of my line belongs to another?"

"Just as Yahshua and Miriam reunited the splintered branches of David's line, so too was their line split. Your Heart lies not in Spania, but across the Sea of Atlas, where the holy seed was planted by Yahshua's son."

Iudila leaned back, stunned by the revelation. "But there is no land to the west. There is only the all-encircling Ocean Sea. The scholars have said—"

"The scholars who put the Sun in motion about the earth?" the monk taunted. "The scholars who would make a eunuch of your ancestor? Trust not the one who denies ancient wisdom to suit his own creed. The Phoenicians and Egyptians knew the shape and dimension of the earth long ago. Moses, son of Pharaoh, was initiated into the secrets of the mapmakers. He carried that knowledge into the Promised Land. The ships of Huram and Solomon sailed to the farthest reaches to bring back precious gems and metals, exotic woods and spices for the building and dedication of Jerusalem's temple.

"Why, my young friend," he continued, "do you suppose the Babylonians—and the Romans after them—were so eager to destroy the temple when they conquered Judea? Such a marvelous edifice, why not leave it standing and consecrate it to their own gods? Surely that would have been greater punishment to the rebel Jews than simply overturning every stone."

"They were looking for something. The Ark of the Covenant?"

"Perhaps, though it was removed long before. Solomon built his temple above a hollow in the earth, a natural crypt not unlike this one, or the one at the heart of the Pyramid at Memphis. Before Solomon—before even Melchizedek, the first priest-king of Jerusalem—seekers of Light would gather there to explore the secrets of the heavens and the earth. Solomon concealed the crypt within the foundations of his temple, ceiling it over with a grand arch. At its entrance were two pillars—"

"Yachin and Boaz," Iudila said as the faded memory of one of Lemuel's stories was restored to full light. "The names of the pillars: Foundation and Strength. And atop the pillars were—"

The old man smiled and raised his hands, indicating the orbs on either side of Iudila. "Two spheres of bronze, the terrestrial and the celestial. The secrets of heaven and earth." He creaked to his feet and gestured for Iudila to stand. "Behold, *Khug ha-Aretz*," he said, indicating the orb to his right, "and *Khug ha-Samayim*."

Iudila studied *Khug ha-Aretz*—the Sphere of the Earth. He touched it and found it spun freely on its pedestal. As it turned, its companion Sphere of the Heavens moved almost imperceptibly. "They're linked?"

"The movement of the earth and the stars are inextricably joined. The events of the one are recorded and foretold in the motions of the other. As above, so below. But, here, tell me what you see."

The man pointed to a spot on the terrestrial globe, and Iudila leaned in to study it in the frail candlelight. He tilted his head from side to side until a pattern emerged from what had before seemed meaningless shapes. Iudila had studied the *Geographia* during his early years at Ispali's cathedral school. The etches on the globe might have been taken straight from the pages of Ptolemy. Boot-shaped Italy jutted into the Mediterranean Sea. To its left, the bulb of Spania reached out to kiss Mauretania.

Iudila followed the coastlines around the basin of the Mediterranean, north along Spania's coast to Gaul, and across the channel to Britannia and Hibernia. The outline of Europe resembled well the familiar shape from so many maps and coastal charts, but Africa and Asia were far more expansive than any representation he had ever seen.

"The last navigational sighting I took was here." Iudila indicated a point near the northwestern corner of Spania.

The old man spun the globe under Iudila's finger, leaving the coast of Europe behind. Another brazen shoreline peeked over the globe's horizon, but the monk stopped the orb with Iudila's finger in the midst of the Sea of Atlas west of Mauretania, where the globe's smooth surface was marred with tiny dimples.

"The Isles of Atlas," the old man said, "where once flourished a great people. Alas, they too fell victim to complacency, and were scattered among the nations of the earth. Only whispers of their hallowed past survive them, and the secret of these islands and this temple has long been sheltered."

Iudila remembered something from Plato that told of a lost land beyond the Pillars of Hercules, a civilization forgotten in the mists of time. What intrigued him more was what lay beyond these hidden islands.

He turned the globe until the strange outline was fully revealed. Its shape called to mind a cornucopia, the horn of plenty, full at the top—where it nearly touched the extremities of Asia and Europe—and tapered at the bottom. The land in the middle narrowed like a hornet's waist, so that it seemed the flick of a giant's finger or the blast of an angry wave might forever sunder the two continents.

"There," said the old man, pointing to an area just above the isthmus. "There is where your heart lies."

"How will I find her in such a vast land? And how will I know her when I find her?"

"How did you find your way to these islands that do not exist? When the time comes, every necessity will be provided. Great guidance may come in the smallest of packages. But come. The hour has arrived."

The monk motioned Iudila back to his place and bade him kneel. He sprinkled more oil and herbs into the brazing pot, raising fresh plumes of aromatic smoke.

"In the name of the Serpent, the Light-Bringer." The old man stretched one hand over Iudila's head, the other pointed toward the aperture in the ceiling, now filled with the cross-shaped, starry head of Serpens. "A seeker stands between Heaven and Earth, ready for your inspiration. Fill him now with your light, with the wisdom of the ancients, that he may be emboldened for the trials ahead."

Iudila steadied himself as the old man laid a hand atop his head. A wave of heat rushed through his scalp, making him draw a sharp breath. Smoke filled Iudila's lungs, and he felt his soul twitch, as one who is halfway between sleep and waking. His vision blurred for moment. When it cleared, he found himself looking into the circle of the altar's cross, where a small spark glowed.

His sight narrowed until he saw nothing but the ebony ring, within which the spark grew in size and intensity until it filled his whole world with a burning sun. Slowly, a shadow crept across the face of the sun, blotting its light. In the full eclipse, he recognized the shape of the rabbit in the moon, while the corona of solar fire took the form of Ouroboros, the mystical serpent that consumes its own tail.

As the eclipse waned, the sun failed to reappear, leaving only a void where the moon had been, surrounded by the serpent that now faded from brilliant orange-red to muted blue and green. The snake released its tail and turned to face Iudila. Plumes rose to surround its head, more resembling a lion's mane than a cobra's hood.

The reptilian mouth opened, revealing white fangs set in a blood-red maw. From its throat, a fresh light grew, a new sun to replace the old. The serpent, the cross, the cavern—the whole world, it seemed, was consumed by the growing light.

When it could grow no more, it collapsed on itself, fading to nothing more than a shooting star, which flashed from the cross's circle, up to the heights of the cavern, then out the aperture to be lost in the night.

14

IUDILA'S EYES OPENED to a cloudless blue sky. Birds chattered, dragonflies hummed, and the stream gurgled nearby.

He sat up and looked around. Other than the angle of the sun—which suggested it was now mid-morning—the scene seemed little different than on the previous evening. The events of the night were already shrouded in fog, fading like the dream they must have been. Iudila looked toward the mountain. It was impossible that he could have managed the steep climb, exhausted and in the dark. It had seemed so real, but—no.

His stomach gave him little time for further reflection. He found some wild berries and washed them down with water from the stream. The not-quite-ripe fruit sat uneasily but it was better than nothing. He stuffed more berries into his pouch then followed the stream downhill. By noon, he had reached the coastal plain. After a last handful of fresh water, he struck out cross-country, taking as his guide the column of smoke from the funeral pyre.

He pushed through the brush at the shoreline to see *Mari-Nadris* drawn up on the shingle beach and leaning to one side, the low tide lapping at the tip of her steering oar. Six men scraped rocks against the exposed hull planks, stripping off half a year's growth of barnacles. The sail was spread across makeshift hurdles while Lemuel and another man mended the heavy cloth.

A cry rose from the direction of the pyre. Iudila turned to see Dingha rushing toward him. The helmsman's face was made even darker by soot and smoke, the grime cut through by snaky trails that ran from his eyes and nose to his heavy jaw. He wrapped his massive arms about Iudila and lifted him off the ground in a fierce hug, gabbling on and on in a tongueless rant that not even Iudila could understand.

Lemuel hurried over at Dingha's first cries, and the rest of the crew was fast to join them. Lemuel related the dry details of food and water collection, the condition of hull and sail. Then he cleared his throat and more haltingly told how the twins—disconsolate at Milhma's death—had walked hand-in-hand into the raging pyre. None of the crew was particularly grieved to be rid of the demon-spawned pair, but the manner in which they had returned to their birthplace was enough to unsettle even the coarsest among them.

When it was Iudila's turn to speak, he gave a poor telling of his wandering through the woods, the discovery of the glade, and his surrender to exhaustion.

"There's more," he later confided to Lemuel and Dingha and Brehanu.

The rest of the crew had returned to their tasks on the boat, while the four men sat by the campfire, a tree-bark bowl of boiled fish and clams in Iudila's hands.

"I don't know if it was a dream or a vision, or if it was real," he began, then told them of the monk, the globes and his promised destiny across the sea.

"I would follow you to the ends of the earth," Lemuel said, "but the others are sailors—simple, superstitious, and wary of the unknown."

"They followed me here."

"Their lives were in jeopardy. Even a sailor will plunge into the unknown if the alternative is certain, bloody death."

"What if it's not entirely unknown?"

Iudila reached into his pouch. Three pairs of eyes widened as he pulled out a cloth—the one given him by the crone in Tingis. He unfolded it and spread it on the sand before them. He had only discovered the change on his way to the beach, when he dipped the cloth in the stream to cool his brow.

What had been a plain weave was now embroidered with a partial pattern of the terrestrial sphere. The coasts of Spania and Mauretania gave way to the Sea of Atlas, dotted with its tiny islands. Beyond the strange lands in the west, the stitching left a broad gap before the mysterious coasts of India and Asia appeared along the top of the cloth, followed by the familiar outlines of Arabia and the Mediterranean.

Iudila supposed there could be a sane explanation for the map. Perhaps the stitching had always been there, unnoticed. Or maybe his sweat had simply stained the cloth with a pattern that just happened to approximate the Mediterranean.

Neither idea rang true. The more he tried to explain away the map's appearance, the less crazy it seemed that he had, indeed, received the revelation of an unknown continent from a monk in the core of a hollow mountain in the heart of an unmapped island in the midst of an uncharted sea.

"What is this symbol?" Brehanu asked, pointing to a pair of dots next to what looked like a four-leaf clover inside a circle.

Iudila looked sheepish. "My destiny."

The three other men looked at one another and nodded as they came to some silent accord.

"Then it is our destiny, as well," Lemuel said with a smile. "We'll just have to convince the others."

15

THE CREW AT LAST TOOK a well-earned rest. There remained water to gather and stores to fill, but with *Mari-Nadris* drowned, the bulk of the work was finished. The dromon lay in the tide channel of one of the island's rivers, her belly full of stones and the water flowing half a man's height above her gunnels. A few of the men wandered the shore, swords drawn, chasing down the rats that fled the sunken ship. From hiding places no man could hope to discover, the water drove out the rodents, along with the lice they harbored.

Everyone knew it wouldn't last. At the next port call—perhaps even while boarding their next raid—the pests would swarm back aboard to soil their decks and spoil their food.

For now, the crew were bathed and their hair—all their hair—had been combed or shorn clean of lice. Their clothes had been washed and smoked, the seams picked clean of vermin—both live and not-yet-hatched—then washed and smoked again. The patched, dripping, louse-free rags now hung over branches and rocks, while their naked owners stalked rats or lounged beside the river and traded lies.

Iudila listened to the banter but did not join in as he leaned against a rock and studied the river. The breeze was light but unnaturally cool against his skin, freshly shaved from cheek to toe. His thick mane of copper and gold remained, as he had chosen to suffer the ravages of Lemuel's makeshift comb rather than submit again to having his head shaved.

"What's that?" Brehanu called, and all heads turned toward the river.

"Grab it!" Lemuel shouted.

Thanos and Mika leapt into the river. A piece of wood had loosed itself from somewhere in the boat, and now floated in the lazy stream. The scrap would normally have gone unremarked, but the bored men raced toward it as though it were a precious relic.

The pair reached the wood in almost the same instant, but Thanos pushed Mika away and brought it ashore. The others crowded around the Greek, chatting loudly about what it might be.

"I know this design," Iudila said, and the others fell silent. "This mark," he continued, tapping a roughly scratched pattern in one corner of the plank. "It's from Milhma's cabin. See here, how the edge is beveled? As though it was meant to be lifted out." Iudila gave the men a stern look. "Did anyone go into the cabin after the body was removed?"

Every man made an emphatic denial.

"We would never violate his privacy," Mika insisted, and the rest nodded their agreement. "Certainly not so soon."

Iudila looked slowly from one man to the next.

"I believe you," he said at last. "If no living man disturbed his rest—"

"A ghost!" exclaimed Thanos. The Greek threw the wood to the ground, crossed himself, spat, and made a sign against evil.

"Lemuel, what do you make of it?" Iudila asked.

The older man stooped and picked up the piece without so much as a quiver—and why not? All the men knew that Jews regularly communed with spirits of the dead, demons, and the Devil himself.

Lemuel bowed his head over the board, muttered something in Hebrew, then went rigid. The muscles of his jaws stood out and spittle flecked on his lips. The men stepped back, but as quickly as the fit had come over him, it passed, and Lemuel fell to the ground.

"Bring him water," Iudila said, and no fewer than five men raced to find a water skin. Iudila knelt beside Lemuel, who gave him a surreptitious wink. "Nicely played, Uncle," he whispered, then more loudly, "Tell us what you saw."

"I saw the captain, standing on the mountain," Lemuel said, and nodded toward the looming peak. "He pointed toward the southwest and spoke in a voice that filled the heavens. 'You served me well, and gave due honor to my mortal remains. Alas, I stored up great treasure in life, only to neglect my fortunes in the next world.' Thank you."

Lemuel interrupted the tale to take a skin of water. He tipped it to his lips and took a long drink. He lowered the skin, loosed a sigh of satisfaction then took another pull. When he had slaked his thirst and stretched the men's patience to the limit, he spoke again.

"Now, where was I?"

"The next world," three men said together.

"Hmm? Ah, yes, the next world. 'To honor your service,' Milhma said, 'and in the hope that by giving my treasure to others I may yet find peace, I leave to you, my faithful crew, the secret of a land at the world's edge, a land of silver and gold.' Does anyone have a bit of fish?"

"Uncle!" Iudila chided him.

Lemuel shrugged then continued. "Where once this board rested lies a token of my sincerity and a sign of the way you must go. Find these, good crew, find my treasure, and let my spirit be at rest."

The men looked at him expectantly, but Lemuel said no more.

"That's all?" Mika asked.

"Every word."

"But how are we to divide the treasure?" Thanos demanded. "Who is to be captain in his stead?"

Lemuel shook his head. "He did not reveal these things to me, and a curse be on my beard should I put false words into the mouth of the dead."

The men nodded at his sincerity. They had heard the oath so often that none stopped to think that Lemuel's shaven beard—along with all the others'—was now nothing more than ashes.

The crew stood dumb, shifting from one foot to the other.

Brehanu, seeing that no one else would move, said, "'Where once this board rested.' Iudila, where did you say you had seen this?"

"In the cabin. It was long ago, but I think it was in the steerboard corner, behind his bunk."

Brehanu nodded and headed toward the river bank. The other men caught on to the meaning and rushed toward the sunken boat. Birds shrieked in alarm and leapt skyward as the raucous crew beat the water into a frenzy of foam. Men tugged at one another's arms and legs, striving to be the first to find the treasure.

Thanos outpaced them all and quickly reached the spot over the steering deck. He filled his lungs then dove under the water. Others followed his lead. In less than a minute, joyful heads breached the surface. The Greek's triumphant shout echoed through the glade, accompanied by half a dozen others. Thanos stroked awkwardly to the shallows then tramped across the tide-flooded marsh.

"Silver!" he cried. "A treasure in coin!" He tipped his hand over and let the glinting coins and bits tinkle to the ground. "And this," he added, handing an oilcloth packet to Lemuel.

Lemuel took the package, turned it over in his hands, then unwrapped the cloth. Some of the men raced back to the sunken boat for a second helping of coins, but the rest gathered round the Jew. The oilcloth had protected a folded parchment with two words scratched in charcoal, which Lemuel read aloud for the benefit of the mostly illiterate crew.

"Captain Iudila."

He gave the parchment to Iudila, who took the message, surveyed the men's eyes, and unfolded the sheet.

"It's a map," Iudila told the anxious men, their excitement rising. "Here is the coast of Spania, and here . . ." He gauged the sun's position, studied the angles of the shadows, then turned and oriented the map. "This must be the land of gold and silver," he finally said, indicating a scratch of land at the edge of the sheet opposite Spania.

"It is just as the shade of Milhma promised," Brehanu said, which judgment the others promptly accepted. "And he has passed the captaincy to Iudila, the ablest seaman among us. Does any man challenge this?"

Thanos opened his mouth, but snapped it shut at a growl from Dingha.

"What is your order, Captain?" Brehanu asked.

Iudila cleared his throat. "As your captain, half of all plunder falls to my share." The men bristled, nostrils flared. "As such, I claim for my share *Mari-Nadris* and the faithful service of her crew. The silver I leave to be divided equally among you, as a token of my gratitude and a promise of even greater treasure to come."

Another flock of birds hurled themselves into flight as the men's voices erupted in a cheer of acclamation, the loudest belonging to Thanos and Mika.

"Rest well this afternoon," Iudila told his men when their cheer ended. "We float *Mari-Nadris* on this evening's ebb. Tomorrow we will caulk her and provision her. And the day after that, we sail to our destiny."

PART II

KINGDOM OF SHUKPI, LAND OF SIBOLAT

610 C.E.

16

KAN-TUL SQUINTED AT THE BLAZING SUN. Her father had warned her otherwise, but curiosity got the better of her. Her eyes watered from the glare and she looked away. In the burning afterimage she saw the first bite taken by the sky serpent. She shuddered at the thought of the great beast devouring Kinich Ahaw, Lord Sun.

A scream filled the air.

Kan-Tul spun around and ran toward where she knew her mother writhed in agony. A strong hand grabbed her by one arm and lifted her off her feet. She kicked and cried out, but her captor pulled her to his chest and held her close.

"Hush, Little Bunny," her father whispered in her ear as he stroked her hair. Kan-Tul—her name meant "Precious Rabbit"—calmed as she heard her pet name. She wrapped her arms around her father's neck and clung to him. His thick hair smelled of smoke and incense, and she breathed deeply, drawing comfort from the familiar scent.

"The Snake is killing Mima," she said, envisioning the great fanged serpent that carried souls to the Underworld.

Uti-Chan, Lord of the city-state of Shukpi, clucked his tongue and rocked his daughter as he paced outside the birthing chamber. "Perhaps. He may be opening the Gateway to the North, but it is a journey that all must take. Some sooner than others."

Another scream sliced through the thickening noonday air. Kan-Tul cringed as a fist squeezed her heart, cold as river stone. She gripped her father's neck more tightly.

"Lord," the midwife said to Uti-Chan as she stepped from the chamber into the thinning sunlight. She glanced skyward and touched the tips of her thumb and middle finger together in a sign against evil.

"How is she, Siyah?"

The old woman grimaced and sucked air through her few remaining teeth. "The omens are not good. I will do all I can to save both mother and child, but the time may come ..." She shrugged her stooped shoulders.

"You are certain it is a boy?" the king asked.

"The signs are for a son. She carries the child low, and the maize kernel sprinkled with her urine sprouted sooner than the one with only water."

The king nodded and breathed a ragged sigh. He looked toward the darkened interior of the birthing chamber, then to his daughter and back to the old woman. "Save Lady Yashekh," he said. "Save my wife."

"My lord—"

Uti-Chan cut her off. "I may yet have a son, if Father-god wills it. I have many seeds but only one heart. You will do what you can to save her."

"Yes, Lord." The midwife bowed her head in submission.

Siyah's words cut to Kan-Tul's heart and the girl let out a whimper. After the midwife disappeared into the gloom of the birthing chamber, Uti-Chan turned away and started around the palace's courtyard, empty but for a few household servants who remained a discreet distance from their king. Uti-Chan walked to the center of the courtyard where a small pond lay, bordered by rocks and reeds. He pried Kan-Tul's arms from his neck and set her down.

"Come," he said. "Let us watch this dance in the heavens."

"But you said not to look," Kan-Tul protested.

Uti-Chan grinned. "And how well did you obey?"

Her cheeks grew warm. Her father took her by the hand and led her around the pool.

"Lord Sun is too resplendent for mortals to look upon," the king said. "In his mercy, however, he has given us ways to observe him, if we are clever. Is that not right, Tok-Ekh?"

Kan-Tul glanced over her shoulder as her uncle, shaman of the kingdom, approached from the shadows of the courtyard's arbor.

"Your pardon, Brother," Tok-Ekh said. "I wasn't listening."

"I was explaining to Kan-Tul the ways that Kinich Ahaw enables us to observe his actions."

Tok-Ekh looked up then clenched his eyes against the blinding light that raged against the shadow creeping across its face. Kan-Tul might have laughed but her awe of the man kept her in check. Tok-Ekh was tall—taller even than her father, who stood half a head higher than any other man in Shukpi. The shaman was made taller still by the wild shock of hair that fanned out from his head.

And he stank.

The blood and dung that stiffened his hair streaked all the way down to his feet, surrounding him with an aura of fear and death. His hemp sandals and shell anklets were stained with the crusted blood of countless sacrifices—some human, if the gossip of Kan-Tul's maids was true. The belt of Tok-Ekh's breechcloth was hung with the slender bones of his victims, and his bare chest bore numerous scars from self-inflicted bloodletting.

As fearsome as the rest of his appearance was, his face came straight from a nightmare. His sharpened teeth were black from rot and the blood of sacrifices, and inlaid with chips of jade and obsidian. His lips, cheeks and nose were riddled with puncture scars, his earlobes fat with stone flares.

Embedded in the middle of Tok-Ekh's forehead was a five-sided obsidian jewel. Even as her uncle shut his eyes against the sun's glare, Kan-Tul felt that third eye stare at her with cold, unblinking malevolence. Enthralled by the gem, she watched her own image look back at her from the shiny blackness. For a moment she was trapped behind the dark lens, imprisoned within the mind of the evil-smelling shaman.

"Only a reflection," she told herself, not meaning to speak the words aloud.

"Precisely." Uti-Chan beamed like a proud tutor. "And how might we observe the reflection?"

Kan-Tul struggled to free herself from the gem's hold. It took her a moment to remember her father's lecture on the eclipse. "A mirror?"

"Yes, but what kind?"

The smooth, shiny surface of obsidian was ideally suited to the purpose. Kan-Tul feared she might have to look into her uncle's jewel to observe the eclipse, so she gave the other possible answer. "The pond?"

"Excellent," Uti-Chan said with a smile.

He laid a gentle hand on his daughter's shoulder and led her to the pool. Small striped fish darted away, seeking cover among the rocks and water grasses as Kan-Tul's fading shadow crossed the pond's edge. The surface rippled with the sudden activity, and the sky was broken into hundreds of watery shards.

With the sun behind her, Kan-Tul glanced upward, staring in awe as pinpricks of light pierced the day sky. Chak-Ekh, the evening star, usually hid himself until just before Lord Sun retired to the Underworld each evening. Now he shone boldly even as his master grew darker and darker.

Though her father had told her what to expect this day, it seemed to Kan-Tul that the world had turned upside down, with the Underworld, Shibalba, now occupying the heavens. As the sun dimmed and the stars grew ever brighter, her heart quailed. She feared the world would not, could not right itself.

"Watch, Daughter," Uti-Chan told her. "Watch as Sak-Ishik dances before Lord Sun to tame his power."

Kan-Tul focused on the pool, its smooth surface now studded with reflected starlight. The divine drama played out in muted tones as silence settled over the courtyard and spilled into the streets of the city beyond. Little by little, the moon crept in front of the sun until there remained only a sliver of radiance that peeked out beneath Sak-Ishik's heavenly skirts.

A wail shredded the silence and filled the courtyard. Kan-Tul turned away from the pool as Siyah emerged from the birthing chamber. The midwife clawed at her own face with one bloody hand, while the other held an obsidian blade.

"I have failed you, Lord. Your son and wife are dead." The old woman plunged the blade into her belly, twisting it as she fell. Her eyes fixed on the waning sun as her final words rattled in her throat. "Darkness has won."

17

KINICH AHAW AGAIN RULED THE SKY as Kan-Tul trailed behind her father. She sucked in lungfuls of warm, thick air as she shifted the burden in her arms. Grief weighed on her as heavily as her dead brother, his body sticky and clotted with birth fluid. Her father's strong shoulders dropped as she followed him from the palace, along the river walk, and up the slope to the temple plaza. Mourners gathered with every step, a crowd large enough to fill the heavens with their cries. Kan-Tul tried not to look as she passed her uncle now in dressed in his full array of black feathers and Death's-head mask and holding a heavy staff topped with a peccary's skull.

Kan-Tul scaled the seven steps to the temple's apron, thinking the ordeal over, but her father led her across the threshold to another, longer flight of steps. On reaching the second level, she almost cried aloud when she saw still more stairs leading upward, until Uti-Chan turned down an echoing corridor. Kan-Tul followed him to a side door, a square of white light at the end of the hallway. Sadness filled her heart, but a flutter of excitement tickled her belly as she set foot on the temple's upper platform for the very first time.

All of Kan-Tul's eight years had been spent in this river valley, hemmed in by its hills and forests. As she stepped to the high platform's edge, she felt as though the goddess Sak-Ishik had given her the sky vision. She saw what a macaw might as it flew over Shukpi. Clusters of homes, storehouses, workshops and shrines centered around the royal palace. She looked down on the marketplace with its ballcourt and the broad ceremonial plaza dotted by massive stone markers.

Beyond the city, across the rolling hills, lay squares of fields planted with maize and squash. The valley was dotted by groves of fruit trees. Along its western border rose a great pine forest, to the east a thick jungle canopy. Grey smoke smudged the sky where farmers burned a patch of woodland to clear and fertilize the earth in preparation for the next planting season. The life-giving river, Hahkhan, flowed from its headwaters in the east, while the Sakbe—the broad ceremonial avenue—stretched away to the north.

Kan-Tul heard her name called, as from a great distance. She shuddered as her soaring spirit fell earthward. Her eyes opened to reveal her father looking intently at her. He offered an encouraging smile then laid his wife's body atop the large offering stone and pulled away the red shroud that covered her. He gestured to Kan-Tul and she placed her brother's body beside their mother.

Uti-Chan turned his face toward the heavens and raised his hands. The hundreds of mourners in the plaza fell quiet and the whole valley was filled with their silence.

"O great Father-god," Uti-Chan intoned, "whose glory is reflected in the splendor of Kinich Ahaw. O Lords of the Sky and of the Underworld. Accept these, our sacrifices. Look with favor upon your children. Open the thirteen gates before them and illumine the path, that the departed may safely travel to their eternal abode and rest forever in the shade of the great ceiba tree."

A calm washed over Kan-Tul as her father spoke. Grief loosed its hold on her heart and mourning turned to reverence. She felt herself change from motherless child to priestess and sensed a similar change in her father. From the plaza she had seen him perform many rituals upon this platform. As she watched him now, a different man stood before her. He was no longer simply her father, but the High Priest of Shukpi, the very voice and hand of the gods.

That hand now held an obsidian blade that hurled sunlight into Kan-Tul's eyes. The priest-king swept the knife at his wife's body. So keen was the blade that Kan-Tul first thought the stroke had missed. Uti-Chan thrust his hand into the wound and produced a bloody mass of meat, which he raised to the sky. The heart lay still in his hand, dangling strings of flesh. Thick crimson blood ran down his arm and dripped from the tendrils to make star-burst patterns upon the platform's stones.

"The radiant splendor of Na Yashekh, Lady of Shukpi, has embarked on the celestial canoe," Uti-Chan said. "What remains of her essence, we honor and take into ourselves."

Kan-Tul's mouth watered when her father sank his teeth into the heart. Tears cut ruddy trails through the stain around Uti-Chan's mouth as he slowly chewed and swallowed the meat. He turned to Kan-Tul and extended the offering to her. She reached out trembling hands, which were barely large enough to hold it.

Eyes locked on her father's, she lifted the heart to her lips and bit into it. Blood trickled down her chin, and she dug her fingers into the flesh to tear the bite away. She savored the rich tang before swallowing.

Uti-Chan took back the offering and placed the remains on a smoking brazier for the gods' portion. He handed the knife to Kan-Tul.

"Now you."

She blinked up at him, slow to understand. Her eyes widened as his meaning dawned on her, and she reached out a hesitant hand to take the knife. The leather-wrapped handle soaked up the dampness from her palm as she flexed her fingers about the hilt. She stepped toward the altar and studied the wound in her mother's abdomen, just below the rib cage. Part of her child-mind reeled in protest even as the priestess in her adjusted her brother's body for a better angle.

"Go on," her father said.

Kan-Tul struck out with the knife. She cringed as the blade caught on a rib, but wrenched it free and tried again. The second gash landed too low, nearer to the shriveled cord that hung from her brother's belly.

"Like this," Uti-Chan said.

He wrapped his hand about Kan-Tul's, guiding the blade along the downward slope of the last rib. The cut made, the king smiled in grim approval, took the knife from his daughter's hand and nodded.

Kan-Tul took a deep breath and plunged her hand into the opening. She forced her fingers past a thick wall of muscle then was surprised at how easily they glided over the organs. Her knuckles scraped under the soft ribs before turning beneath the sac of the lungs where she found the small, still lump in the center of the chest. She tugged at the heart, but it held firmly in place. She groped about, pinched through three blood vessels and tried again.

The heart tore loose but slipped from her fingers once before she managed to pull it from the body. She stole a glance at her brother's face, relieved that his eyes remained peacefully closed, his lips lightly pursed and undisturbed by the violation.

The heart barely filled Kan-Tul's fist as she mimicked the earlier ceremony, took a bite and offered the heart up to her father.

Uti-Chan shook his head. "All of it."

Kan-Tul nodded and obeyed. When she finished, her father took her bloody hands in his and led her to a stone canopy at the platform's edge.

"People of Shukpi," he said, his voice amplified by the carved stone enclosure, "the gods have moved among us this day. They have taken our beloved Lady Yashekh, along with the prince, her son."

A keen rose from the crowd. Uti-Chan allowed the mourning cry to peak before he gestured the people to silence.

"In his mercy, however, Kinich Ahaw has delivered a most wondrous sign. In the death of a queen, a princess is raised in her place. By the death of a prince, an heir is lifted up."

The king ushered Kan-Tul forward and stood behind her, his knife clenched in one fist as he raised his blood-stained hands to the sky.

"Kan-Tul has also died this day," he continued, and the girl's heart leapt to her throat. "But just as Lord Sun escaped the dark halls of Shibalba, so has Kan-Tul returned from the Underworld."

He opened his hand and dropped the blade. The obsidian shattered as it struck the limestone platform, and Uti-Chan placed his hands on his daughter's cheeks.

"Behold, my people, your new Lady of Shukpi, Na Chakin—Lady Two Sun."

18

"SO, WHOM SHALL SHE MARRY?"

Uti-Chan peered through the haze toward the speaker. Herbs smoldered on the brazier, and Popol Na, the Council House, was filled with smoke. The fire pit hissed and popped with new wood that added its heat to the already stifling air. Then there was the tobacco.

The weed's leaves had been dried and rolled, and the nobles set flame to the slender bundles and drew on them to punctuate their words with puffs and clouds and streams of heady smoke. A few of the men mixed other leaves and herbs into their cigars, the resultant smoke dragging them into blissful stupors.

The man who had spoken was not one of those men. Shan-Chitam might be the oldest man on the Council, but his scheming mind was always clear. He had recently seen his fourth *katun*, nearly eighty years—a rarity for a people whose men seldom saw two *katunob*. Grandson of a past king, cousin to Uti-Chan, he was the council's ranking member.

"Lady Chakin has expressed no preference for a consort yet," Uti-Chan said.

"Preference?" The old man spat out the word as he might an unripe berry. "You would allow a woman's—no, a girl's whims to dictate matters of state?"

"The women of Sibolat, more especially those of Shukpi, have long held the right to choose their husbands. Should it not be so for the very Lady of Shukpi?"

A few of the men mumbled agreement. Shan-Chitam would not be so easily put off.

"She is the last female of the line of Yash-Ahaw. Our great-father Khuk-Moh journeyed from Pah-Tullan in the land northward for the sole purpose of joining his blood with that of Yash-Ahaw, thus establishing this dynasty."

"I am well aware of our family's history," said Uti-Chan.

"Then you must be equally aware of the need to preserve its strength, its purity. Such a choice must be made rationally and deliberately, not left to a child's fancy. Remember, it was this council that recommended you to the Lady Yashekh as her consort, and to your father as his heir."

"As I recall," Uti-Chan said, "the council presented a number of candidates, including yourself. Lady Yashekh made her choice from among all those of the line of Khuk-Moh."

Shan-Chitam's cheek quivered at the reminder of his rejection in favor of Uti-Chan, but he proceeded calmly.

"An old man's memories are uncertain. It may be as you say. However, the council plays a key role in choosing the best candidates to present to the Lady of Shukpi."

Uti-Chan nodded. "It is yet some years before Chakin reaches marriageable age, but I naturally welcome the council's good judgment. Whom do you recommend?"

Shan-Chitam sat back and scratched his chin, as though he had not thought more on the subject.

"There are many options, of course. Khuk-Moh's line is a virile one, producing many strong men. Had you, Lord, produced a male heir, he would naturally be a leading candidate."

The dig cut to Uti-Chan's heart but he held his tongue.

"My grandson, Wuk-Oh, is of an age to marry," Shan-Chitam continued. The old man ignored the sputtered coughs of protest at the blatant attempt to raise his family's status. "He is a fine warrior, commander of a hundred."

"Would not Hul-Balam, then, make a better match?" suggested Nak-Makah, the royal scribe. "He is the finest warrior of Shukpi, commander of a thousand. And, with respect, he is closer to the reigning line, as half-brother to Lord Uti-Chan."

A chorus of approval met this suggestion.

"Hul-Balam is, indeed, an accomplished warrior and leader of men," Shan-Chitam said. "But if proximity to the ruling line is to be our chief concern, I submit that there is one nearer still to the god-seat. I speak of Tok-Ekh, full brother of our esteemed lord."

Silence greeted the old man's pronouncement. None could deny Tok-Ekh's royal lineage, but the looks on the assembled faces suggested that the other nobles shared Uti-Chan's opinion of the shaman's fitness as husband to Chakin.

"I thank the Council for its usual wisdom and sound advice," said the Lord of Shukpi. "There is yet much time before a consort must be chosen. I will consider the suggestions you have put forward. For now, the hour is late."

Uti-Chan dipped his fingers in a bowl of scented water and sprinkled it three times on the fire. He then lit a taper from the flames and drew a six-pointed star in the air. "Under the sign of Father-god, the Nameless One who is in all and through all, whose glory is reflected in the radiance of Kinich Ahaw, I bid you go in peace and serve our people in love."

19

"AND WHAT IS that one?" Chakin asked.

Tok-Ekh steadied himself with a deep breath. He squeezed his eyes shut and sank into the limestone embrace of the inclined viewing seat, slowly releasing his impatience with the air that hissed through his nostrils. The shaman needed to bring the child under his influence if he were to achieve his ambitions, so he rallied his forbearance and answered yet another question.

"Those are the Peccaries, my lady. One is here," he said, and held up a hand to match the shape of a line of stars, "and the other here." He cupped his other hand above and behind the first.

"But why are they standing like that?"

"They are mating."

"Mating?" The girl's eyes went wide in the starlight.

"Yes. Before the First Time, the Peccaries ruled the heavens. When they came together in their coupling, the boar's seed was so great that his mate could not contain it all. He spilled his seed across the sky to form the great cloud of stars that now guides our seasons."

"How go your lessons?" The voice came from behind them.

"Ahpa." Chakin squealed and leapt into her father's arms. "Tata Tok-Ekh has taught me all about the Shark and the Scorpion and the Peccaries. Did you know that the stars were made when the boy peccary planted seeds in the sky?"

"Is that so?" The Lord of Shukpi shot his brother a reproving look.

"I teach her the old stories," the shaman said as he stood, "so that she may learn to fathom in them the true ways of the gods."

"I see. That is probably enough study for this night. It is time for bed."

"Oh, Ahpa."

"My lady," Tok-Ekh said, "the Lord of Shukpi has spoken."

"When I am Lady of Shukpi in my own right, I shall stay up and look at the stars as late as I wish."

"I do not doubt it, Little Bunny," Uti-Chan said. "Until then . . ." He set her down and knelt before her. "A kiss for your father."

The princess obeyed with a perfunctory peck.

"There is a cup of spiced cacao waiting for you in your chambers."

The girl brightened, her smile shining in the moonlight.

"But do not forget to scrub your teeth afterward."

The smile faded.

"Say thank you to your uncle."

Chakin huffed and folded her arms across her chest, but said, "Thank you, Tata."

"You are welcome, my lady." Tok-Ekh touched his middle finger to the obsidian jewel in his forehead and gave a slight bow.

"Her lessons go well?" Uti-Chan asked after Chakin had gone.

"The child is bright, like her mother."

"Thank you for agreeing to tutor her. I know things between us have not always been easy."

"Do not think on it, Brother," Tok-Ekh said with a shrug. "Chakin is of my own blood, and that of Yashekh. I do an uncle's duty, for Shukpi and for its Lady."

Uti-Chan settled into one of the viewing seats and motioned for his brother to join him.

Tok-Ekh masked his surprise at the friendly gesture, and lay back in the seat next to Uti-Chan.

"Do you remember watching the stars when we were children?" the king asked.

Tok-Ekh's tone was matter-of-fact. "I remember squinting at them through swollen eyes after you had beaten me."

Uti-Chan turned to look at him. "Was I that bad a brother?"

"You were an older brother. That is simply the way of things."

"I am sorry," Uti-Chan said.

Sorry? Tok-Ekh wanted to scream. A king does not apologize. *Sorry?* Does an eagle apologize to the rabbit? Or the hurricane to the shore? The shaman kept a practiced, neutral expression as he asked, "How was the council?" He studied the king's face, which ever gave away his thoughts.

"It was—interesting." Uti-Chan's even voice did not match the irritated look on his face. "They are already discussing a consort for Chakin."

"Truly?" Tok-Ekh feigned surprise, for it was he who planted the seed in Shan-Chitam's withered mind. "She will not be a woman for several years yet."

"Which I reminded them. But, they were quite adamant that the process begin. Particularly Shan-Chitam."

"That old fool? And whom did our illustrious cousin recommend to the task?"

Uti-Chan swept his eyes from the night sky to his brother's face.

"You."

Tok-Ekh restrained a smile. "Me? You're joking. I should have thought someone like Hul-Balam to be a far better candidate."

"His name did come up, but Shan-Chitam made the case that you are closer to the throne, and therefore a more suitable choice."

Tok-Ekh pretended to weigh the words. "And what do you think?"

The king sighed. "You will forgive me if I speak plainly? You are, without doubt, knowledgeable in the ways of the ancient ones, as befits the kingdom's shaman. But to rule requires subtler skills: temperance, prudence, fortitude, justice. You are an adept of the old ways, but I believe it is the way of Yashwak that will lead our people to an age of goodness and prosperity."

What madness he spoke. The blood-path was the ancient way of the peoples of Sibolat, the means by which kings and priests maintained power over their people, standing between them and the gods. Yashwak—an ancient shaman and father of Shukpi's first Lord, Yash-Ahaw—had taught the end of blood sacrifice. He spoke of a single god, accessible to all the people without need of shamans or priests or kings.

Such nonsense. Tok-Ekh wanted to beat reason into his brother's head, or—better—to open his throat with the obsidian blade that burned impatiently in its sheath. Instead, he allowed a grin to crease his lips. "You persist in your belief in one god? It is a dangerous path you tread."

"Why should it be? I recognize the God above gods, but I acknowledge our ancient gods before the people. I permit them—I permit you to worship as you choose."

"Not quite as I choose."

"No," Uti-Chan agreed, "not quite. I will not permit the sacrifice of innocents, but there are criminals and enemies enough to satisfy your gods' hunger. Why, then, should it be of concern that I follow the path of the One?"

"That depends. If you are correct and your single god is one of love and mercy, then he will surely forgive the ignorance of those who have blindly served other gods. If, however, the old ways are correct and the many gods demand honor and sacrifice, they will feast on your soul when you pass the gates into Shibalba."

It was Uti-Chan's turn to grin. "That is a chance I have accepted, and that is why I will not force my beliefs upon the people. But neither will I deny them access to the means of finding the path to truth."

"I hope you are right, Brother," Tok-Ekh lied, "and I hope the gods do not hold the people accountable for the misjudgments of their lord."

"Yash-Ahaw's line ruled in peace for many generations," Uti-Chan said. "The line of our great-father Khuk-Moh has continued to do so. With only a few exceptions, the lords before me followed the path of the One."

"But those exceptions—including our own father—were whole-hearted in their return to the old ways, no?"

Uti-Chan did not reply, but Tok-Ekh savored the shudder that raced through his brother's body at the bloody memories. "Perhaps those few reinstatements of the old ways were potent enough to sustain the gods' favor."

"Or perhaps even they were not egregious enough to lose the blessings of the One," Uti-Chan countered.

Tok-Ekh laughed loudly at that. "You argue your point well, Brother. But how did we land on such a weighty subject? Ah, yes—Chakin. What will you decide?"

"The choice will be hers when she comes of age. Until then, if you wish, I will include you as a candidate as I think on the matter."

"I will, of course, serve Shukpi in whatever fashion I may."

Uti-Chan smiled and squeezed his brother's knee. Tok-Ekh tried not to shrink back from the touch. He returned the smile.

"I'd best look in on Chakin," the king said as he rose. "Good night."

Tok-Ekh leaned back against his seat as Uti-Chan's footsteps faded away. The stars were a glittering crown in the night sky, and the shaman smiled broadly at the prospect of the crown—and the other prize—that would soon be his.

20

THE BLACK APPEARED in the ether as a dark orb in the midst of infinite grey nothingness. Then another arrived, the Red, glowing like fresh blood. Each flashed a silent acknowledgement to the other and reached out smoky tendrils to form a psychic bond. In moments, three more spheres of light emerged: Yellow, Blue and Green. These, too, reached out to the others until the five were linked by a luminous pentacle bounded on all five sides.

In the name of the one we serve, the Green—Master of the Assembly—offered the invocation.

And of the secret light that illuminates him, the others responded.

So may it be.

No words were used. Rather, the ceremony was conducted in the pure language of thought forms and images that manifested in a white light at the heart of the pentacle. To speak would have been impossible in this realm of spirit. It would also have been fruitless, as there was no human tongue in common among any of the participants.

As below, the Green continued.

So above, the others replied.

To those in darkness has been shown a great Light,
But they understand it not.
The Light has blinded them,
For few may see the Light of Truth and live.

But for as many as look upon the Guardian of Light and see,
To them is given the power to be as the gods.
They shall be Watchers over the flocks,
And leaders to the blind.
Until the day of the Shadow Lord is attained,
And all the earth shall be called by his Name.

The five colored orbs grew brighter and larger, the rays between them pulsing in unison. The white light in the center shimmered and sparked, each spark forming a symbol that orbited the central light. When all the characters were formed, the light itself disappeared and the orbs with their connecting rays were all but extinguished, so that only the Name—timeless and ineffable—was visible.

The symbols made five revolutions then one by one, like the stars at sunrise, blinked into nothingness, their light replaced by the ever-stronger light of the orbs.

"Brother Exarp, your report," the Green said.

"Yes, Master Ahcoma."

Twice each year, at the extremities of the sun's path, the Order of the Pentad convened to discuss the progress of their work and to offer counsel to each other. In far more ancient times—beyond the reach of any written history—it had been possible for the Pentad to meet physically. As the races of humanity divided and filled the earth, however, the Brethren had accompanied them until great distances of land and sea separated them. Since that time, they had met in spirit on the Akashic Plane, the realm of thought, dream and prayer.

"The work goes well," the Blue said. "Certain among the people have become messengers of the Roman faith, and their word spreads like fire. The old ways will soon be forgotten, and the only light will be that of the Church."

"Excellent," the Master said.

The Roman Church was the Order's most productive, if unwitting, ally. The quest to shield humanity from the Light of Truth had nearly been undone six centuries earlier by the Nasoraean, a Jew from some backwater of the Roman Empire. His teachings of love and peace and the Kingdom Within might have spread throughout the Empire and exposed the whole world to the Light that reveals all. Fortunately, his political and religious rivals felt as threatened as the Order and they'd had the man crucified by their Roman masters.

That punishment failed to silence the Nasoraean, however, and the Way—as his movement was called—continued to spread until a member of the Order intervened. The esteemed brother first sought to crush the Way from the outside, murdering or discrediting its principal members. In a flash of inspiration that could only have come from the Shadow Lord himself, the brother had a miraculous conversion and became the movement's most energetic and outspoken apostle.

Within three centuries, the Way had been restyled into the cult of Christianity. The emphasis on personal access to the Light was subsumed into a bureaucratic hierarchy where the professed servants of the seekers became their masters. The teachings of the Nasoraean were cleansed of all that might lead the uninitiated directly to the Light. Those texts that could not be sanitized were destroyed or driven into obscurity. Even the very nature of the Nasoraean had been altered to the point that his own family might not recognize him, transforming the crucified man into a living god.

A handful of the original, dangerous teachings survived among the followers of Arius, Nestorius, Pelagius and others, but these had become so marginalized as to be rendered impotent.

Still, the farther one ventured from Rome or Constantinople, the greater was the risk that the Light might seep through the protective veil of the Church. It was in these remote places that the Pentad concentrated their efforts to keep the masses safely in ignorance, as they had done from time immemorial.

Though styled Brethren, the Order's members might be male or female. The Blue Exarp—named for the Angel of Air—was, in fact, a princess of the Saxons of Britannia. The Yellow Bitom, Angel of Fire, was a Silk Road trader among the Gokturks of Asia. The others—the Red Acnila, Angel of Blood; the Green Ahcoma, Angel of Water; and the Black Nanta, Angel of Earth—were holy men among their races.

"My people grow to great numbers," the Yellow said in turn. "They await only a strong leader to unify them, and they will move the very foundations of the earth."

"The time is not yet ripe," the Master said, "but keep them in readiness."

When it was the Red's turn to report, his orb flashed brilliantly. "The Light has been well and truly shielded in our realm. The line of the Nasoraean among the Franks has been subverted to the will of the Shadow Lord and has at last been ended among the Goths."

"As well with my flock," the Black added. "Only one remains, and that one shall soon be within our power. The people as a whole have forgotten whence they came, and the generations of the Light Bringer are at an end."

"And the relics?" the Master asked.

"Safely separated," the Black assured him, "until such time as they may be reunited under our control. For now, their secrets remain hidden, their meaning lost."

"It is well," acknowledged the Master. "Our mission among the Aksumites is also near completion. The Light has grown dim here and should be extinguished within a few years. Once my work is finished, a replacement shall be chosen, and I will join my essence with the Shadow Lord. One of you, then, will serve as Master in my stead."

"How will the new Master be chosen?" the Blue asked.

"That must be decided among the Brethren. Tradition places the succession with the next most senior, which would be Brother Acnila."

The Red flashed and the Black deepened its intensity, each for but a moment.

"However, if another is found more worthy, the mantle may fall to him. In this, as in all things, you must look to the shadowy one to guide your choice."

The pentacle quivered as the ray between Black and Red throbbed with energy. The assembly threatened to rupture with the psychic strain, but the Green sent a quieting pulse that eased the tension.

"If there is nothing further...?"

Silence.

As it was before the Beginning, the Master intoned the benediction.
Before the Word was spoken.
Let it be so again,
Now and forever.
So may it be.

21

TOK-EKH EMERGED FROM his trance and braced himself for the aftereffects. He abhorred these revolts by his body—the pounding in his head, the churning of his stomach, the fiery tingle in his extremities. But like the ache in his loins after a night of fierce rutting, the symptoms were a reminder of the exquisite power he enjoyed, so he accepted them without complaint.

In the early days of his work, Tok-Ekh had used the dream leaves, both to enter into a trance state and to ease the effects of leaving it. He found, however, that the drug caused him to drift while in trance and to lose focus. He had weaned himself from the leaves and seen his abilities grow until he was one of the most powerful members of the Order of the Pentad.

The shaman drew aside the heavy curtain at the doorway to his chambers and stepped into the courtyard of the royal compound. The afternoon sun reflected from flagstones and lime-washed walls, blinding Tok-Ekh after the darkness of his room. The pounding in his head redoubled its tirade. He staggered to a corner of his garden and vomited in the black dirt. He studied the pattern of blood and bile, then grinned with satisfaction.

"Are you ill, Uncle?"

Tok-Ekh turned at the sound of Chakin's voice, surprised that the omen should be so soon fulfilled. "No, my lady," he replied with a slight bow of his head. "Simply weary from my labors." He surprised himself by answering truthfully. Such was the power the princess held over him that she could command the truth from him in even the smallest of things. Even though Chakin had yet to receive her first moon-flow, and the celebration of her twelfth *tun*—the ceremony that would mark her transition to womanhood—was two *winals*, or forty days, away. Still a child by all counts, Chakin stood regally before the shaman, fully looking the part of Lady of Shukpi. The seven rows of shell anklets proclaimed her royal status, as did her breechcloth dyed in rich blues and greens, colors of the royal line.

She wore no covering over her chest where the first buds of womanhood had yet to appear. The ruddy glow of her skin was set off by strands of auburn that shone among the obsidian blackness of her hair.

The coloring was the gift of her mother. The Sibolan were people of the earth with black eyes, black hair and skin the color of dried cacao seeds. But those descended from Yash-Ahaw were a red people. Chakin carried some of the traits, but those in whom the god-line ran strong—her mother, for instance—looked as though they had stepped from the hearth of the creator god, Hurakan. Such ones had hair like flame, skin the color of fresh-cut mahogany, eyes of jade.

The thought of Lady Yashekh stirred emotions in Tok-Ekh he had long tried to bury. Killing her unborn son had been a simple expedient, both for his own desires and for the mission of the Order. He had intended to spare the queen, but that rancid bitch Siyah botched the abortion and took the mother with the child. She'd been wise to kill herself. Had the midwife died at Tok-Ekh's hand, her journey to Shibalba would have taken much, much longer.

"Uncle?"

Tok-Ekh blinked, late to realize Chakin had been speaking. "Forgive me, Lady. I was distracted by matters of state. You were saying?"

"I believe I know your remedy. Come to my garden and I will prepare the cure."

She turned to leave the courtyard, and Tok-Ekh followed. He studied her as she walked, her form still boyish but beginning to show a feminine grace. With each stride, the narrow breechcloth revealed long legs, slender and tanned, her calves and buttocks sculpted by daily climbs to the temple's summit.

He felt his passion rising, checked by the sharpened tip of a rib that he had positioned at the front of his grotesque belt. He winced in pain for a few steps until he managed to replace desire with resolve.

The girl would be a woman soon enough. He would be there for her first moon-flow, and he would drink of her divine essence. Then he would bleed her in a different way, and that taste would be sweeter still.

22

CHAKIN LED HER UNCLE through the gate into the private garden that had once belonged to her mother. She could never smell the tobacco flower, taste the vanilla bean, or hear the hum of the bees without her mother's shade running a chill finger down her spine. Chakin rubbed her arms to smooth the bumps that rose on her skin and directed Tok-Ekh to a deerskin cushion set beneath a linen awning. "Do the headaches come often?" she asked the shaman.

"A few times a year."

She placed her hand on the nape of her uncle's neck, then pulled back in alarm. "You are burning with fever."

"It—it sometimes comes with the headaches," he said, and it was the first time Chakin could ever recall his speech faltering.

She studied the man. His hair was lank, overdue for a treatment of blood and dung to stiffen it once more. His eyes were sunken but as bright as the obsidian that gleamed from his forehead. She took a moment to examine her reflection in the jewel and smoothed her hair back behind her ears.

"Besides the headache, fever, and nausea, any other complaints?"

"No," he stammered as she placed her hands beneath his jaw.

Finding no swelling there, she laid a hand on his scarred chest to gauge the meter of his heart, which seemed to quicken even as she touched him.

Tok-Ekh rose abruptly and paced to the center of the garden, where a papaya tree stood. Chakin's stomach tightened as he turned his back on her. She had once feared the man, but she now feared his rejection even more. She bit her lip to keep it from trembling, then set about the garden to gather the needed herbs. She tried not to look at Tok-Ekh but felt his eyes on her as she recited each ingredient's usage in a sing-song chant that Kehmut, her maid, had taught her.

"Cool water to cleanse the path, passionflower to ease the ache, primrose to rest the mind, and pepper seed to hasten the cure."

"You have it exactly, my lady," Tok-Ekh said, finally turning to face her as she sat at her grinding stone and began crushing the herbs.

Chakin's face grew warm at the small praise, and she could not hold back a smile. She swept the hand stone through its strokes with so great a vigor that she trapped a fingertip between it and the lower stone. She cried in pain and jammed the bleeding finger into her mouth to stanch the flow.

"Let me see," Tok-Ekh said.

He crouched before her, his longs legs folded so that his knees came next to his jaw and the bone fringe of his belt touched the ground.

"It's not so bad," he said as he examined the wound. He dug his hand into the pouch that hung from his waist. "But we mustn't take any chances. Chew this."

He gave Chakin a bit of hardened sap from the rubber tree. He pulled the stopper from a small clay flask, dipped in a finger and drew out a lump of grey paste.

"What is it?" Chakin said, wrinkling her nose as the ointment's stench invaded her nostrils.

"There are demons in the air who seek out fresh blood," the shaman explained as he spread the balm over her fingertip. "They enter a body through even the smallest wound, feed on the blood, and poison the body with their waste. If they are not properly exorcised, the wound will fester, their victim will take a fever and die within a few days."

Chakin gasped at his words.

"This, however, masks the scent of blood and forms a barrier the demons cannot penetrate." Tok-Ekh capped the flask and retrieved a small strip of linen from his pouch. "Spit," he ordered, and Chakin dropped the wad of softened gum into his outstretched hand. "There," he said as he stretched the sap over her fingertip then wrapped it with the small bandage. "No demons for you today."

Chakin grinned, examined her uncle's handiwork, then was crest-fallen as she saw her blood mingling with the herbs on the grinding stone. "It's ruined."

"Nonsense." Tok-Ekh pulled a wooden stirring stick from his pouch and mixed the blood and ground herbs into a thick red-brown paste. "Blood enriches the natural healing powers. The herbs alone do wonders but mixed with the blood of a great healer—a princess, at that—and my headaches are sure to cease." He scraped the paste from the stone, popped it into his mouth and swallowed noisily. "Delicious," he rasped, and Chakin giggled.

"Do the gods really need blood to survive?" she asked.

Tok-Ekh raised an eyebrow. "What does your father say?"

"Ahpa says my great-father Yashwak gave his heart-blood to Father-god, and the lesser gods will have to make do with that."

"Then why does the king still seal offerings with his own blood?"

Chakin thought for a moment. "It was taught by Yash-Ahaw, in remembrance of his father. By shedding his own blood before the gods, Ahpa follows Yashwak's example. Is it true?"

Tok-Ekh sat beside Chakin. "When your father hosts a great feast for the nobles and has eaten his fill, does that make you less hungry?"

Chakin made a face at the silly question.

"No. I am only full when I have eaten."

"Ah, of course. Then after you have had a large meal and your belly is out to here"—he puffed out his stomach, and Chakin laughed—"are you never hungry again?"

The girl shook her head. "I am hungry again the next day, or even that night."

"As am I. As is, I daresay, your father. Are we, then, to accept that the gods, having been fed once—even so great a meal as the very heart-blood of Yashwak—should never hunger again?"

Chakin rested her elbows on her knees and propped her chin in her hands as she tried to fathom her uncle's words.

"Long ago," Tok-Ekh continued, "before Yashwak and Yash-Ahaw came to Shukpi, rulers throughout Sibolat offered great sacrifices to the gods. At the beginning of each *winal*, every twenty days, a feast was laid on the tables of Shibalba, with flesh for bread and blood for beer. The routine sacrifices might be anyone—a criminal, a slave, a captive—but on the festival days of Kinich

Ahaw, six times each year, only the finest sacrifice was worthy of the gods. On these days, a member of the royal family was offered up."

Chakin's mouth went dry. "The royal family?"

"Yes. Of course, the kings took many wives then and had many children, so there were plenty to choose from. The strongest and most beautiful were given to the gods. You, my lady, would have made a most fitting sacrifice."

Tears moistened Chakin's eyes. She blinked them away and tried to calm her suddenly rapid breathing.

"But—but I don't think I would wish to die."

Tok-Ekh smiled. "I think I would not, either, but there are many ways to serve the gods. Sacrifice is simply the easiest."

"Easiest?"

"Certainly. You drink a potion to ease your fears, you climb the steps of the temple and lie down on the altar. The priest makes a cut here"—he ran a long fingernail high across Chakin's belly, and her stomach contracted with the touch—"then he reaches in and pulls out the heart."

"Does it hurt?" Chakin asked, remembering how she had performed the same act on her dead brother.

"Not if done properly. If the cut were clean and the motions swift and sure, you would feel no pain. You would simply see your heart raised before the gods, then fall asleep and wake beneath the Great Ceiba Tree in the heavens. Easy."

"But there is another way to serve?"

"Yes," Tok-Ekh said, and Chakin's stomach relaxed, "but the path is a hard one. It requires constant discipline and listening to the gods' voices, watching for their signs wherever they appear. It is a life of endless labor, of putting the will of the gods before your people, your family, even yourself."

"Ahpa says we serve the gods by serving one another."

Tok-Ekh laughed harshly. "That may be, but what the gods demand and what the people desire are not always the same. A wise ruler knows one from the other and gives his—or her—full devotion to the gods."

Chakin weighed the shaman's lesson, her brows pinched in thought. "Ahpa," she started, then bit off the word, now embarrassed at using the childish term. "My father often tells me to do things I don't want to do, though he says they are good for me. Might it not be the same with the gods and the people?"

"Even so, Lady."

She thought a few moments longer, then nodded and looked at her uncle. "I would learn to serve the gods, to hear their voices and read their signs."

Tok-Ekh's face spread into a smile. "That is excellent, Lady. Then let our lessons begin."

23

"YOUR BROTHER SEEMS quite taken with the Princess."

Nak-Makah sat with Uti-Chan beside the pond outside the king's residence. He was Shukpi's scribe, a member of the Noble Council, and Uti-Chan's oldest friend. He was also, it would seem, a master of the obvious.

"Your eyes do not miss much," the king said, "even through that mask of yours."

Nak-Makah rubbed his whiskered cheeks. The Sibolan were a smooth-faced people, but a few men in each generation developed facial hair, the legacy of distant ancestors from distant lands.

"One needn't have an eagle's vision to see it. Nor to read your opinion of the matter."

The king frowned. "She grows fonder of him each day, and the affection seems to be mutual."

"You don't think he would—"

"No, no. To violate a child is beyond even Tok-Ekh. But Chakin's moon-flower will soon blossom. Once she is a woman, I fear Tok-Ekh's restraint may vanish."

"The council will push for a decision soon," Nak-Makah reminded the king. "We are no longer young men, you and I."

"I have no intention of joining my fathers anytime soon."

"Nor I, but you have already seen ten years more than most men."

"Eight and a half."

Nak-Makah smiled. "Let us say nine. Who knows the will and the timing of the gods? Yes, you are in fine health. Yes, your father lived to be fifteen years older than you are now. But you are in the latter half of your years and the Lady of Shukpi has not yet come to maturity. Surely you understand the council's concern."

Uti-Chan grunted. "They would have me give my daughter to a man three or four times her age, that he might reign for only a few years after me? I would rather see Chakin choose someone like Hul-Balam over Tok-Ekh, but either way, she is sure to be a widow longer than she would be a bride."

"Then choose Wuk-Oh. He is nearer her age."

"That is so, and he has the makings of a fine warrior. He is, however, Shan-Chitam's grandson, and I am reluctant to dignify his house by giving Chakin into it." Uti-Chan paused and studied his friend. "Why have you not put forth Khu-Shul for consideration?"

Nak-Makah looked away. "My son will ever serve Shukpi, as I have done. Khu-Shul adores Chakin, and I would rejoice at the union of our two houses. But you know as well as I, the peculiar condition of the men of my line—Khu-Shul's in particular—make us better suited to record the history of Shukpi than to create it."

The gurgle of the pond and the calls of birds filled the void left by the men's words. A quetzal bird cried out, dipped low over the pair then flew westward. They followed its flight toward the distant mountains, and Nak-Makah clapped his hands together.

"Wakhem," he said, referring to the neighboring highland kingdom.

"What of it?"

"The new Lord, Oshlahun-Ak, is but a few years older than Chakin. He also has a sister, recently widowed. If you were to ally your house with his—"

"I will not make of Chakin a treaty-sow. She cannot be Lady of both Shukpi and Wakhem."

"But if you were to create an heir with ties to a neighboring royal house . . ."

"An heir? My friend, it is but three years since Yashekh went to her rest. I am not yet ready to love again."

"I said nothing of love, only of an heir. Were you to produce a son, the council would rest more easily. And, since Lord Oshlahun-Ak is some years away from his majority, should you hint at a possible union between him and Chakin, the council might be willing to allow more time before her betrothal."

"My lord?" A voice spoke from behind them.

The two looked up as Hul-Balam, captain of the royal guard, stepped into the courtyard.

"The people await you at the judgment seat."

"Of course." Uti-Chan rose. "Thank you, my friend," he said to Nak-Makah. "I will think on your words."

Hul-Balam fell in behind Uti-Chan as he followed the path from the courtyard, through the palace gate toward the river walk. Previous kings had built the great wall of stone to force back the waters of the Hahkhan and to form the foundations for the city's great plaza. Uti-Chan greeted fishermen and muckers who paused in their daily trade to bow and salute their king. Some dared to stretch out a hand toward him.

"More guards," Hul-Balam muttered.

The king smiled at his people and touched a few of the outstretched hands. "I am Lord of Shukpi by the will of Father-god," he reminded his captain when they had passed the group of well-wishers, "and lord I will remain as long as he desires. With or without more protection."

Within the boundaries of the city, the king took only Hul-Balam as an escort, while the rest of the guards—Shukpi's finest warriors—found useful work as potters, gardeners and weavers.

The men followed the river walk until they reached the broad ceremonial court where petitioners gathered before the temple. The king became judge as he climbed to the first level—the civic platform—and sat cross-legged atop the seat of justice, a slab of limestone an arms-breadth in length. It was an easy day with only eight cases to be heard. As usual, the most serious was saved for last, a merchant accused of cheating his customers.

"The gods detest dishonest scales," Uti-Chan said, rising from the judgment seat and stepping down from the platform, "but delight in true weights."

He reached into the man's pouch, pulled out a cacao bean and squeezed it between thumb and forefinger. The two halves of the pod slid apart and sand spilled on the ground. Cacao seeds were used both for their powder and as currency. By hollowing out the pod, filling it with sand and gluing the halves back together, the merchant had doubled his wealth, while halving that of his customers.

Uti-Chan signaled Hul-Balam, who drew an obsidian blade and placed it in the king's hand. The captain took hold of the merchant while Uti-Chan lifted the dagger toward the sun, touched it to the jade set in his turban, kissed the blade then touched it to his breast.

The merchant's screams shook the macaws from their trees as the king flayed his back—one strip of skin for each of the ten plaintiffs. Uti-Chan tied one of the bloody strands around the merchant's arm as a mark of his dishonor, then climbed back up to the platform and laid the other strips upon a smoking brazier. He raised his bloody hands to the noonday sun and spoke in a loud voice.

"Kinich Ahaw, Great Lord Sun, accept this offering as a sign of our obedience to your divine justice. May we follow in the example of your straight path that order and harmony may prevail, and your people flourish in the land you have given us."

Uti-Chan drew his blade across the heel of his thumb, adding his own blood to the sacrifice. The droplets sizzled on the hot coals, and he clapped his hands together to seal the covenant. He washed his hands in a copper bowl, then shook them off into the smoking brazier. As Hul-Balam dismissed the crowd, the king turned toward the temple's entrance.

Adorned with plaster renderings in brilliant greens and yellows and whites, the stucco walls of the temple were the fiery red of sunset. Twin images of Kukulkan—divine protector of the royal bloodline—flanked the doorway, the god resplendent in his serpentine plumage. Above the entrance, the likeness of Kinich Ahaw looked toward the west, where the great god died each evening. From high up on the façade, a snarling witz monster—guardian of the gateways to the Otherworld—glared down upon the plaza.

Uti-Chan left the sun-stoked platform for the dank shadows of the temple. He felt the familiar shiver caused not by the change in temperature but by the dread sanctity of the place, the shift from worldly to holy, from judge to priest. He paused inside the doorway, lifted a jeweled breastplate from its cushion and fastened it about his neck. The breastplate was made of copper and held twelve jewels that formed a six-pointed star, and as it rested against his chest, he began chanting in the priestly tongue, the language spoken by the distant ancestors of the Sibolan, now used only in the temples.

He continued the invocation as he climbed to the ceremonial level, matching his steps to the cadence of the blessing. At the landing, he dipped his middle finger in a bowl of pepper oil and sketched upon his face the symbol of the world tree, bridge between the Celestial, Earthly and Lower Worlds. His eyes watered as he traced the pungent oil down his forehead to the tip of his nose, then across his brow. Blinking away the tears, he climbed the steep, narrow stairs to the third level.

Holy became divine as Uti-Chan—king, judge and priest—entered the chamber of the god-seat. The small room at the top of the temple was lit only by a pair of beeswax candles and the small shaft of light that fell through a smoke hole high overhead. From the middle of the floor, a censer poured thick, aromatic smoke into the air.

On one side of the censer was a low wooden table bearing a leather-wrapped bundle. Uti-Chan folded back the oiled hide to reveal a stack of metal plates bound with a bark cover. The priest-king opened the book to its middle and stood it on end so the plates—brighter than his copper breastplate—reflected the dancing candlelight.

A thickly stuffed jaguar-skin cushion lay opposite the table, and Uti-Chan lowered himself onto it. He leaned over the censer and swept the smoke over his face, breathing in the purifying incense. His forehead burned from the pepper oil, and as he inhaled, the rush spread about his entire scalp.

From a small stand at his side, the Lord of Shukpi picked up a spindly *kish*, the stinger taken from one of the many sea bats that flew beneath the Sunrise Waters. Still intoning the ceremonial words, he stabbed the spine through his foreskin and set a small stone dish in place to catch the trickle of blood. He took a second *kish*, dipped its sharp end into a tincture of carefully selected mushrooms, leaves and oils, then forced the needle-like cartilage through his tongue.

The herbal tincture, the pain of the piercings, the smoke of the incense, and the burn of the pepper oil all worked to attune Uti-Chan's mind with the divine. Before his earthly senses abandoned him, he reached for a pair of large, translucent gems mounted in a copper frame. He fastened the gems over his eyes, and the candlelight split into dozens of flashing, ghostly patterns.

Uti-Chan gazed at the reflections in the metal plates, the images shattered by the jeweled lenses. He felt his spirit shift, twist, then float free of his body. He swirled about on the smoke of the incense, rushed up the column of heated air above the candles, raced through the smoke hole, and soared high above Shukpi.

A white rabbit darted from beneath the wall of the royal gardens, scrambled away from the palace, then raced down the Sakbe, the ceremonial highway that led to neighboring Ha-Naab. Behind the rabbit, a dark cloud followed, smelling of blood and rot. Trees and plants wilted as the noxious cloud passed by. Animals fell dead, their carcasses immediately blackened and bloated.

Uti-Chan followed the chase until the rabbit reached Ha-Naab and stopped at the banks of the river Hahshuk. The cloud caught up with the rabbit and enveloped it in foul blackness. Uti-Chan watched helplessly as the rabbit writhed and thrashed and screamed amid the choking mist.

The sound of a hundred conch shells split the air, and Uti-Chan looked east toward the noise. The Sunrise Waters seethed and boiled, whipped into a fury by a monstrous tail as a great serpent rose from the waves. Its glistening blue and green scales and the fiery plume of feathers could belong only to Kukulkan. The god breached the shoreline and raced up the watery trace of the Hahshuk toward Ha-Naab where the rabbit had all but ceased its vain struggles.

Kukulkan spread his wings and reared up in the water, his sinewy length rising high above the towering ceiba trees and seeming to scrape the halls of Kinich Ahaw himself. The feathered snake's belly rippled and undulated, the wave rising higher and higher until the divine beast opened his mouth and disgorged a flaming ball at the cloud. The ball shone like the sun, and the air whistled at its passing until the dark cloud opened and swallowed the flaming sphere. Uti-Chan grieved as the cloud grew blacker and thicker, engorged by Kukulkan's power.

Then a brilliant sliver pierced the cloud, followed by another and another until the blackness was riddled with light, like daylight through a poorly thatched roof. The cloud grew blacker still as it fought to overcome the light. The darkness was made nearly whole when the cloud shrank in on itself, then burst outward in an explosion of light and glory.

Kukulkan loosed a triumphant roar that seemed to shake the very foundations of Shibalba. He arched forward on his long neck, mouth opened wide as he plunged toward the rabbit and the ball of flame, devouring them both.

The god looked benignly at Uti-Chan, gave a beatific smile, then soared skyward with a great beat of his wings. The god flicked his tail to steer a course toward the setting sun. Without a backward glance, he disappeared behind the western mountains, bearing the king's precious rabbit out beyond the Sunset Waters.

24

THE DWARF GROPED his way through the clammy darkness. Somewhere in the distance water dripped, the sound echoing along the walls of the tunnel. The thought of the great volume of water held back by a thin slab of limestone made the young man stumble more quickly toward the circle of light ahead.

The air, while cooler than that outside, was heavy with stagnant water and bat droppings, and Khu-Shul thanked the gods that the bats that normally filled the tunnel had been evicted by the recent activity. He thought of how this place would soon be swept clean, then slogged through a mound of guano that rose to his thighs.

He dropped to filth-slimed hands and knees to crawl through a narrowing of the tunnel, then stood upright inside a small chamber. The dwarf breathed deeply of air sweetened by spices and oils and the light smoke of beeswax candles. In the pale, flickering light he inspected the workings of the chamber: paddles, spars, ropes, guides. He spun the massive wheel—four times his own height—against the direction of the tow to ensure it moved freely, then turned it back into place.

The machinery in this chamber had been unused since before Khu-Shul's birth, set in place by his grandfather for Lord Uti-Chan's accession more than thirty years earlier. Over the past few weeks—under the guidance of his father Nak-Makah and with the aid of trusted servants—the young man had lovingly restored it to proper order.

Khu-Shul had scoured guano and lime scale from the workings, plucked strands of rotted rope from the spool and guides, and installed the strong new hemp ropes woven by his own hands. The mahogany timbers of the great wheel had resisted the forces of time and decay, but he tested each linkage and greased the thick axle and rope guides with animal fat. By the time he'd finished, the machine fairly sparkled in reflection of his love and devotion.

The dwarf squeezed between a pair of paddles, then clambered up spokes and spars and braces until he reached the top of the great wheel. He heard the murmur of his servants' voices in the chamber above, connected to this lower one only by the holes through which the ropes passed. Khu-Shul forced a hand through one of those openings, stretching with all his might until the tips of his fingers brushed the carved stone of the object of his adoration.

He bathed in the thrill of that touch for as long as he dared, the hairs of his arms standing on end. With no more time to waste, he scrambled back down the workings, through the narrow entrance and into the shit-laden darkness.

Up the limestone path he hurried, one hand against the befouled wall, the other held in front of him. Even had the tunnel not been straight—had it the twists and turns and mazes and pitfalls of the other passageways his ancestors had cut into the bedrock beneath Shukpi—even then he would have needed no light. The pattern of the sacred labyrinth was as much a part of his heritage as the fuzz on his cheeks and the hump on his back.

The floor rose higher with each step, and Khu-Shul was breathing heavily by the time he reached the steep entry shaft where water trickled down the limestone face. Summoning all his strength, he groped for the water-slicked hand- and footholds and heaved himself toward the sunlit world beyond.

The dwarf emerged from the tunnel behind the crest of a hill that overlooked the royal city of Shukpi. He climbed the few paces to the summit under a sky laced with clouds that glowed pink in the sunset.

The eastern slopes of the neighboring mountains were already deep in shadow, while the waters of Hahkhan flowed blood-red under the evening sky. Behind Khu-Shul, a large pond, fed by the great river, rippled under a light breeze, thousands of tiny wave crests shimmering in the waning light. The dappled surface reminded him of skin gone duck-flesh under a loved one's touch, and a chill ran down his spine as bumps rose on his arms.

The sinking sun brushed the tops of the mountains, and Khu-Shul rubbed his skin smooth as he walked down the slope toward the pond. He climbed onto a small limestone platform positioned between the water's edge and the tunnel's mouth. A stout oak lever rose from a gap in the stone and lodged against the leaking block below. A rope circled the top of the beam and led through a pair of holes carved into the stone's face.

Khu-Shul gripped the rope's end and studied the sky, fearful that the thickening clouds might hide the signal for him to act. But as the sun dropped below the ragged horizon and the new day began with Kinich Ahaw's descent into the Underworld, the heavenly sign appeared.

Chak-Ekh, eldest brother of the night sky, shone through the hazy clouds. His light was a dim reflection of Lord Sun's glory, but among the gods of night he was the first and the brightest. Khu-Shul took a deep breath, coiled the rope about his hands and pulled. This was the most important of his duties this night, and the one that had been impossible to practice. He strained against the rope, his muscles bulging with the effort.

Hemp creaked and wood groaned, but nothing moved. Khu-Shul feared that years of disuse and contact with the pond's waters might have cemented the block in place. He crouched low, took a deeper grip on the rope and added the power of his legs to the effort.

The rope bit into Khu-Shul's hands, fire coursed through his legs and arms and back. He grunted against the strain, felt the veins stand out on his neck and forehead, and still he pulled. His body was small, but years of working with great blocks of limestone—first as quarrier, then as artist—had sculpted his muscles for this one purpose.

As his head buzzed and his vision turned red, he was dimly aware of a small shift, of the scrape of stone against stone. A great cracking sound thundered, and he tumbled over the platform's edge, the rope searing his flesh as it tore loose from his grip.

Khu-Shul pounded the earth, cursed the stubborn rock and the oak shaft that failed him. He shook his head to clear it of the echo of that failure, but the mocking thunder rumbled on, seeming to come from the earth itself. He opened his eyes, pushed himself up on burned, throbbing hands, then stood. His heart pounded, but a different rhythm flowed beneath his feet. He stepped toward the platform where the lever had not, in fact, failed him, but leaned sharply in its slot, shaking against the water that now rushed past it.

Mist rose from the opening of the platform, hissed from the mouth of the cavern, while the flood now raced down the narrow tunnel, cleansing it of the layers of mold and guano on its way to the paddlewheel chamber. Khu-Shul gave a triumphant shout, for even now the tide would be spinning that wheel, the ropes taking the force through the guide holes and into the upper chamber. His servants would be snapping into action to do their part, for on the floodwaters rose his labor of love, his gift to a princess.

25

THE PEOPLE OF SHUKPI milled about the great plaza. Their excited voices blended together into the sound of a giant beehive, accented by the calls of tree frogs and nightjars from the great forest around the city. Food and drink vendors roamed through the crowd, and the smells of dried fish and roasted meat filled the air. One clever merchant made a rapid trade by selling his cuts of duck, quail and monkey on skewers along with slices of tomato, squash, peppers and sweet potato. His trade was seconded by an older woman who sold a stew of beans and peccary meat, the portions wrapped neatly in maize flatbread.

More vigorous were the beverage sales. A young boy in a tattered loincloth did a token trade in water, his business generated more from pity than thirst. Chicha—the sweet beer made from maize—enjoyed a much greater popularity, along with balché made from fermented tree bark and honey.

Most favored of all, judging from the long lines in front of their booths, were the royal cacao vendors. The firstborn sons of all the noble families, Uti-Chan had chosen them to serve the people this night. The cacao bean was a currency of trade, and it was only on feast days—and with royal patronage—that the common folk could afford to drink money. The beverage of blended cacao and chili powder was the gift of Uti-Chan to his people. To ensure none came through the line more than once, each person had to present a tongue unstained by the dark beverage. Even more prized than the luxury of the royal drink, was the opportunity for the people to stick out their tongues at the nobility.

A subtler trade was conducted on the fringes of the crowd. The *tzanaob*—ladies of sacrifice—strutted about the plaza, seeking clients and arranging their assignations for the evening. No subtler—though less frowned-upon—were the young women of all but the highest classes, who worked to position themselves close to the handsomest soldiers or the wealthiest young nobles.

All had heard stories of riotous celebrations following such great ceremonies. Indeed, many had been conceived on similar occasions. Competition was fierce, and the objects of this hunt preened like cocks amid their bevies. The young men of humbler expectations skirted the flocks, hungry for whatever castoffs might fall their way.

Above it all—and eagerly absorbing each nuance—stood Chakin, who presided over the ceremony. The *katun*-ending celebration was rare, occurring only once every twenty years. A healthy woman could see two, maybe three *katun* celebrations in her lifetime.

From the priestly level of the temple, the Lady of Shukpi watched the celebrations of her people with a mixture of envy and pity. They would not see so lavish a display of food and drink until the girls that sidled up to the warriors saw their grandchildren weaned, whereas the delicacies they savored were common fare for the princess. The princess who so longed to be among the crowd, to breathe in the smell of roasted meat and fermented tree bark and sweaty flesh. The princess who dreamed of catching a young man's eye, of standing next to him as darkness filled the plaza.

Instead, the girl who was two moons shy of womanhood stood in the role of priestess, high above her people, arms outstretched and fingers tingling. At the sun's first caress of the mountain peaks, Uti-Chan had led Chakin to the second level of the temple. Her excitement at taking part in the ceremony quickly gave way to disappointment.

Her father instructed her simply to face Lord Sun and salute his journey to Shibalba by making the form of Wakah-Chan, the tree of life—feet together and arms spread at shoulder level. Disappointment soon became pain as her sinews turned to water and the bangles of seashell and jade at her wrists became like great blocks of limestone.

Chakin blinked back the tears brought on by the sun's radiance and her own frustration and agony. She mustn't appear weak in the eyes of her people or of her father. Least of all could she show weakness before Tok-Ekh. Using the techniques her uncle had taught her to detach mind from body, Chakin summoned deep reserves of strength. For a time this helped, but as the sun sank lower, as the crowd grew louder and the smells more enticing, Chakin's mind and body joined forces to rebel against the pointless ceremonial.

Just as she was about to flee in humiliation and anguish, she heard the familiar padding of her father's footsteps on the limestone platform behind her. Without a word, Uti-Chan draped a brightly colored shawl over her shoulders then fastened it in place with a string of seashells across her boyish chest. Coming around to face her, the king beamed with pride as he gently lowered her arms to her sides. Uti-Chan winked, then stood behind her and raised his arms high over his head.

"People of Shukpi," he called in a voice that might have stilled the waters of the Hahkhan. Immediately, the milling stopped, voices hushed and even the woodland creatures paused their noisemaking. "In the name of Kinich Ahaw, and under the patronage of Chak-Ekh."

As one, the people replied with the ancient blessing, "*Sak-lah*." May it pass in glory.

"Long ago the gods brought our fathers, Lords of the West, to Sibolat from across the Sunset Waters. Though we were few in number then, today we have become a great people, numerous as the stars in the sky. From glorious Shukpi to Pah-Tullan, the tribes and clans of the Sibolan fill the earth. Nine *katunob* ago, my great-father, Kinich Yash Khuk-Moh, arrived in Shukpi to add his seed to the branch planted by the First Lord, Yash-Ahaw."

Chakin—only half listening now—shifted her attention to the base of the temple's steps. The *khobah*, the great stone monument that bore testimony to her father's reign, had been removed during the previous night and a great bundle of reeds now stood in its place.

"Ten generations have passed from that time to this," Uti-Chan continued, "and the people and the land of Shukpi have flourished. Commerce thrives, hunger is no more, peace and justice hold sway throughout the land."

A murmur of approval rose from the crowd.

"This day marks the beginning of the third *katun* of our stewardship over the people of Shukpi. Before me and since the time of Khuk-Moh, only my grandfather Balam-Nan, blessed of memory, has served his people and the gods so long. It is right and proper that the gods should limit the time of lords and nobles, lest their pride grow too great. Already the gods have favored me with years beyond those of most men, years of peace and prosperity. The gods alone know what time is left before I go the way of all the earth and walk the dark road to the Otherworld."

Chakin stirred at those words. Though she was sometimes visited by memories of her mother, thoughts of death were strangers to her. Even Tok-Ekh's lessons about Shibalba brought with them only vague notions of the next world.

Now, a cold hand gripped her heart, and her breath turned shallow at the thought that her father might not walk with her in the land of the living forever. As though sensing her fears, Uti-Chan stepped closer to her, brought his arms around her and rested the backs of his hands lightly against her temples. Chakin's fears calmed at his touch, and she slowed her breathing as he continued.

"Na Chakin will soon reach the age of choice. That the god-seat might never be desolate, nor the people without a steward, I reaffirm her as Lady of Shukpi and mother to her people."

The king spoke the words as the last sliver of sun disappeared behind the western ridges and Chak-Ekh appeared high in the heavens. At the same moment, torches flared to life all about the plaza and the bundle of reeds at the temple's base burst into flames, sending the closest of the spectators scrambling. A rumble came from deep within the earth, accompanied by an otherworldly moan. Chakin tried to turn her head, to look up at her father, but he held his hands firmly against the sides of her head, keeping her still.

The reeds burned brightly and rapidly as the pyre consumed itself. The sounds from the earth grew louder and—just as the flames were about to die—the reeds erupted in spark and ash. The people shouted and Chakin took a sharp breath. As the air cleared and the fiery debris settled to the ground, a great cheer rose from the crowd.

Chakin was frozen in place by the acclamation and by the sight of the *khobah* that had appeared from the flames to replace her father's old marker. For there, carved in stone and staring back at her, were the images of Uti-Chan and herself.

26

SUCH A WASTE.

Tok-Ekh stood on the periphery of the great assembly, having just made his arrangements with a red-haired *tzana*. The hair coloring came from a solution of cinnabar, the shaman knew, and the girl would likely be dead or mad in a few years from the absorption of the dye into her scalp. For now, the madness had not yet set in, her body was trim and lithe, and she knew how to use her pleasure-slit to great effect. He had paid for her services before and knew that in the dim light of his chambers, he could almost convince himself that, instead of a whore, he rode the late queen, Yashekh.

It was not the girl, however, that made the shaman shake his head in dismay. Rather, it was Uti-Chan's squandering of this rare opportunity to strengthen his hold over the kingdom and his power throughout Sibolat. The *katun*-ending was the perfect time to begin a new building program, to initiate a war against his neighbors—or, at least, to squeeze his people for more tribute. Instead, Uti-Chan—just, merciful, insufferable Uti-Chan—used the occasion to patronize and coddle the peasants.

Tok-Ekh choked back his disgust as the Lord of Shukpi spoke of himself as steward to his people. What of King? Master? God-incarnate? How characteristic of this wastrel, who ruled with fleece and honey rather than flint and fire.

But he has style, the shaman grudgingly admitted to himself. Uti-Chan was dressed in a blue- and green-dyed kilt that exposed sculpted, muscular legs. Nearing his fiftieth year, still the king's belly was flat, his chest broad and adorned with pectorals of copper and strings of shells and gemstones. His outstretched hands were sheathed in jaguar skins embedded with the great cat's claws, while his ears were pierced with rich ornaments of jade.

Crowning it all—in place of his usual, simple linen turban—was a magnificent headdress that matched the image of Kukulkan on the temple's walls, with the face of a beaked serpent set about with smaller images of Kinich Ahaw and the twin maize gods. A great plumage of quetzal and macaw feathers sprouted from the headdress in such volume and splendor that it appeared the king might spread wing and take to the skies at any moment.

When the earth began to howl and the plaza blazed into light from the great pyre of reeds, Tok-Ekh inched his way closer to the temple steps until he had a clear view of the rising statue. He cocked his head and strained his ears to separate the noise of the crowd, the rush of the flames, the rumble of the mighty underground stream, and the creaking of machinery. The crowd roared as the *khobah* shuddered into place amid a cloud of smoke and embers, but the shaman focused his senses on the workings beneath the plaza.

Throughout the lands of Sibolat, the *katun*-ending would be celebrated with bloody games and spectacles leading up to offerings of scores of human sacrifices, or even hundreds. Alone among the seven great kingdoms, Shukpi's ruler forbade the ceremonial shedding of blood other than the auto-sacrifice of the presiding priest, which was usually Uti-Chan himself. But such an event as this—coupled with Chakin's confirmation—merited, demanded great sacrifice to imbue it with power and meaning. The *khobah* represented divine authority, and for the gods to bring life to the sculpture and legitimize the ruling family, life must be offered up in return.

As the underground paddlewheel lifted the stela—the troll Khu-Shul's gift to the princess—Tok-Ekh listened for the sounds of his own gift. The water sounds slackened, replaced by the barely audible clatter of wood and stone as Khu-Shul's slaves assembled supports beneath the *khobah's* stone slab. The subterranean noise changed character again and the shaman thought he heard shouts of confusion, then alarm from beneath the plaza's limestone flags. He closed his eyes and pressed his middle finger against the obsidian jewel embedded in his forehead.

In his mind's eye, the shaman watched as stones fell to plug the paddlewheel chamber's drain and the slaves' exit from the upper chamber. The troll would have shut off the flow from the holding pond by now, but the long tunnel held a great volume.

Tok-Ekh smiled as he envisioned the flood rising through the holes in the upper chamber's floor, swamping the ankles, knees, then the thighs of his sacrificial victims. The slaves shouted and pounded uselessly against the thick stone walls of the chamber, while the water rose high enough to snuff out the flames of the work lamps.

The shaman trembled as the scene fell into darkness, but still he watched the men's auras shift from orange to brown to sulfurous yellow, then finally a dull grey that faded slowly, inexorably to black. Tok-Ekh loosed a groan of pleasure and his back arched slightly as a chill ran down his spine. The thrill of sending more souls to Shibalba rivaled the one he would derive from rutting his whore while muttering Yashekh's name. Or, this time, perhaps Chakin's.

"Quite a spectacle, eh?" Nak-Makah jarred the shaman from his ecstatic reverie.

"It is that."

Tok-Ekh was repulsed by the other man. Scribe he might be, prince even, though the abominations of his line—stunted, monkey-faced and hunch-backed—would never claim the god-seat. Still, the vile creatures were not without use.

"Your son's talent rivals even your own."

The monkey-man beamed with pride, his eyes disappearing behind the whiskers. "Exceeds them, you mean. My best work is but a shadow of his skill. See how he has created almost a full profile in stone? Astounding."

Tok-Ekh studied the *khobah* and had to acknowledge the truth. Most sculptures or castings carried only a shallow relief, scarcely more depth than might be had from a drawing. Khu-Shul's work, on the other hand, had nearly a complete profile, the figures so lifelike it seemed the stone twins of Uti-Chan and Chakin might step from the rock at any moment.

"Tok-Ekh," Uti-Chan said in a booming voice from behind. "Nak-Makah. Incense and fragrance bring joy to a man's heart, but no more than the counsel of good friends, yes?"

His great headdress now replaced by his usual turban, Uti-Chan embraced each man in turn, then stood aside and gestured for Chakin to step forward.

The men bowed as the Lady of Shukpi approached.

"My lords," Chakin said in timid voice, and Tok-Ekh noted the delicious flush that rose in the girl's cheeks.

"Nak-Makah," Uti-Chan said, "you will excuse us while Lady Chakin and I discuss matters of import with my brother?"

"Of course, my lord," the scribe said. With a parting wink to the princess, he turned toward the cacao booths.

"Brother," the king said as he took the shaman by the elbow and led him to the side of the temple, away from the crowd. "You have been an able tutor to Lady Chakin these past years. As she is now affirmed as Lady of Shukpi, and is very nearly a woman, there is one more great favor I would ask of you."

Tok-Ekh's heart throbbed as he anticipated what the request might be.

"I am at your service, Brother."

"While she is not yet of marriageable age, a proper match involves many details and takes much time to arrange. Your cooperation in the matter, then, is of the utmost importance."

"Of course. I am your servant."

"Good," Uti-Chan said, clapping his hands together. "On the morrow, then, you will leave us and go to Wakhem."

Tok-Ekh's head jerked at the unexpected words, and his heart sank as he looked to Chakin to see her downcast eyes.

"There, you will serve as intermediary in my marriage to the king's sister, Sak-Chih."

The shaman managed to take a breath and to restart the beating of his heart.

"At your command, Lord," he stammered, and his hopes of taking Chakin for himself rekindled.

Until Uti-Chan's next words.

"And you will also commence negotiations for Chakin's betrothal to Oshlahun-Ak, Lord of Wakhem."

27

"YOU NEVER LET ME do anything," Chakin protested. "Why can't I go?"

"We have been over this time and time again. I do not want you to see such violence."

Uti-Chan's voice was calm as he repeated the tired excuses. Chakin's was not.

"If he asked, you'd probably let him." She gestured toward her half-brother, Khak-Imish, who grunted hungrily at his wet nurse's teat.

"If Imish asked me," the king said with a doting smile at the suckling whelp, "I should marvel at the gods' placing speech in the mouth of an infant."

Chakin clenched her jaw and fists, and glared at the foul thing, even as her father's face beamed with happiness. It had been bad enough when Tok-Ekh returned from his mission to Wakhem with the sister of that kingdom's lord.

Sak-Chih could not have been less aptly named, for she was neither fair nor deer-like. Her skin was oily and blemished, dark as maize dough left too long on the cooking stone. Her coarse hair, dried out by her years in the high mountain valley of her home, looked like frayed rope and stood out at all angles from her head, despite her maids' continual brushing. Her thighs were as thick as tree trunks, her hips as broad as a tapir's backside, and her laugh was like a howler monkey's.

And Uti-Chan doted on her.

He had been tentative at first, had even confided to Chakin his unease at being with a woman other than her late mother, Yashekh. But Sak-Chih had quickly charmed him with her foreign airs and bumptious ways. When she became pregnant, Uti-Chan's joy was greater than Chakin could ever remember seeing. And when Sak-Chih gave birth to that mewling, puking, stinking creature, it was as if the king's world was finally complete.

The sole bright spot in it all had been Tok-Ekh's return, but even that was sullied. Chakin's first moon-flow had come while he was gone, and she was eager to share the news with him. Rather than celebrate the arrival of her womanhood, the shaman had flown into a rage Chakin couldn't understand. He then disappeared into the jungle for nearly a year.

Following his return, it had taken months before Tok-Ekh again smiled at her, and Chakin still felt some invisible rift between them—a rift she hoped today's festival might heal. If her father would but show some reason.

"As Lady of Shukpi," she said calmly, trying a different approach, "I must share in the daily lives of the people, especially at such memorable times as this."

"She has a point, my lord," Sak-Chih told the king, speaking out of turn. "The union of the calendars happens only once in a generation. Most of the people—certainly the adults—will never see another. It is fitting that a member of the royal family preside over the festivities."

"Tok-Ekh represents the royal family," Uti-Chan said, "both as my brother and as shaman."

The queen smiled. "The shaman is a most important position, but not so important, I think, as Shukpi's Lord. Or Lady," she added with a wink at Chakin, who bristled but forced a smile.

Uti-Chan heaved a sigh. "I see the women of my household have conspired against me. If I am to have peace under my own roof, I suppose I must relent."

"Oh, thank you, Father," Chakin said with more enthusiasm than she intended.

"But," he added, "Kehmut will accompany you. You will watch from the royal viewing stand, and Tok-Ekh will perform the closing ceremony. Understood?"

"Yes, Father." Chakin kissed his cheek then raced back to her rooms.

"Kehmut," she called as she ducked beneath the stone lintel of her chambers. "Draw my bath and help me get ready. We're going to the games."

28

CONCH SHELL HORNS BLARED, and people shouted as banners snapped in the breeze. Smoke rose from giant censers placed around the ballcourt, both as fragrance-offerings to the gods and to keep swarming insects away on this steamy spring equinox. Tok-Ekh gestured to one of his slaves, and the woman—hair already plastered to her body with sweat—put more energy into her palm-frond fan to provide the shaman with a cooling breeze.

Tok-Ekh smiled as he sipped his balché. The people were thrilled to have their games back, and he was happy to receive their gratitude. Uti-Chan was, of course, the patron of the games, but it was his sow-queen who had convinced the king to restore them, and Tok-Ekh who had planted the seed of the idea.

How valuable Sak-Chih had proven. Uti-Chan was enamored of her, helpless to deny her wishes. If she wrote to her mother, the king dispatched a runner to Wakhem. If she wanted agave nectar to sweeten her bread, he sent a trade delegation to the embattled northern kingdoms to gather the desert flower. He had even begun referring to the gods in casual conversation, rather than his previous adherence to the One. Uti-Chan had yet to offer blood to those gods, but Tok-Ekh was more than willing to perform that duty in his stead.

The crowd cheered and gestured toward the royal viewing stand. Tok-Ekh rose and acknowledged them, then turned as Hul-Balam stalked up the steps ahead of Lady Chakin. The shaman had anticipated her arrival, having enlisted the queen's help in gaining Uti-Chan's permission. What he had not anticipated was the jolt her appearance sent through his heart—the heart inured to the pain and suffering of others, yet as susceptible to Chakin's influence as the tides are to the moon.

The girl had become a woman. True, her womanhood had bloomed years before. Tok-Ekh would never forgive his brother for sending him to back-water Wakhem just as the moon goddess Sak-Ishik first quickened Chakin's womb. After returning with Sak-Chih and learning of Chakin's news, the shaman had fled the city in rage.

For an entire *Chol-Kin*—the sacred 260-day calendar cycle—he stalked the daughters of the farmers and hunters and fishermen who lived in the great forests about Shukpi. With each full moon he found a girl ripe for her first flow and bought her for a few copper beads and cacao pods. Each month he drank of a young woman's virgin blood—that most potent elixir for opening the gates of the mind to the Otherworld—then offered her heart to the gods and her body to the river.

Eight times he fed the gods' hunger and slaked his own thirst. The paltry, fear-tainted offerings of peasant girls, however, could never match the willing gift of a princess and priestess of the lines of Yash-Ahaw and Khuk-Moh. The shaman had at last returned to Shukpi with a new resolve and with eight new ribs suspended from his belt.

Tok-Ekh absently stroked one of those ribs and was slow to realize that his jaw hung slack.

"I am pleased you chose to attend the games, Lady," he said when he found his tongue, then motioned for a slave to place a cushion next to his.

"More so than my father, I think. Thank you," Chakin added to the slave, then gracefully lowered herself onto the jaguar-skin cushion while her maid joined Tok-Ekh's slaves at the rear of the platform.

"Do you play today, Captain, or have you finally accepted that the games are for young men?" Tok-Ekh offered a smile to his half-brother, though both knew it to be a lie.

"Someone must keep the pups in line," Hul-Balam said. "Should you have any questions about the game, my lady, I'm sure one of the servants will know the rules."

"Thank you, Captain," Chakin said. "I wish you joy of the game."

"My lady." The warrior bowed, tossed a grunt in Tok-Ekh's direction, then left the stand.

"I will never understand why my brother persists in keeping that man as chief of his guard. He has seen nearly two *katunob*."

"He is one of Father's most trusted friends, and he is not so old as that," Chakin said, though the warrior was more than twice her age. "Is not our dear shaman older still?"

Tok-Ekh frowned at the words, despite the dazzling smile that accompanied them. "Only by two years. And shaman is an important role, demanding wisdom and experience."

"Is not wisdom a valuable trait in a warrior?"

"Give me twenty fools with spears, and they will crush one wise old man."

"Have I missed anything?"

The shaman turned at the sound of the voice, though he would know that grating timbre anywhere. Khu-Shul, the little troll of a scribe, clambered up the steps to the platform and waddled to where Chakin sat. Tok-Ekh dropped onto the stuffed pelt next to the princess, leaving no place for the foul creature to sit.

"Here," Chakin said, "share mine."

Tok-Ekh might have protested her offer to the dwarf, except for the fact that in making room for him on her cushion, the princess moved close enough for the hairs on the shaman's arm—standing on end—to touch her skin.

The scribe prattled on, explaining the forthcoming game to Chakin. Tok-Ekh pretended to examine the turf of the playing field, the crowd in the stands, the clouds overhead—anything but the princess—while from the corner of his eye he took in her every feature.

Her long, sleek hair was pulled over one shoulder, revealing an ear only just too large for her head. The jade ear-flare matched the flecks of green in her eyes, and a pang of longing shot through Tok-Ekh at the reminder of her mother. Chakin's head tilted toward the scribe on a slender neck from which hung strings of beads and feathers that could not fully hide the small mounds of womanhood newly risen upon her chest.

The roar of the crowd and the beat of the drums interrupted the shaman's discreet survey. Shukpi's players took the field, and the ballgame was set to begin.

29

"HERE," CHAKIN TOLD KHU-SHUL, "share mine."

She slid closer to her uncle to make room on her cushion, and a tingle ran up her arm as she brushed the shaman's skin. She felt Tok-Ekh's sidelong gaze, and she gathered her hair over one shoulder to give his eyes freer access.

"I'm surprised to see you here," Khu-Shul said as he dropped next to her.

"Why shouldn't I be?" Chakin said. "The alignment of the calendars happens only once in a lifetime. Someone should be here to represent the god-seat."

Two calendars governed daily life in Sibolat, each with a different number of days that realigned only once every forty-two years. This union of the calendars, commencement of the Great Year, was a time for renewal throughout all the kingdoms. Debts were forgiven, property redeemed, bond-servants freed. It was a time of celebration and rededication to the gods, solemnized by ritual games and sacrifice.

Across the land, fires were extinguished and hearths swept clean. At each major city, upon Kinich Ahaw's descent to Shibalba, a young woman from the royal house or the nearest noble clan lit a new fire using windfall, not chopped wood—virgin flame from virgin hands. Runners, often working in relays, then carried embers or torches lit from the new fire to each village and home. Within days of the celebration, every household through all the lands of Sibolat was purified and reborn.

"Will you be lighting the sacred flame?" Khu-Shul asked Chakin.

"Of course."

The scribe gave her a sly look. "Have you practiced?"

Chakin almost snapped at him. Though Khu-Shul was several years her elder, the fact that he stood only as high as her waist too often let her think she could treat him as a child. But it was in moments like this that she was reminded of his wisdom.

"No, I haven't practiced. What do I do?"

Khu-Shul smiled. "Not to worry. It is a simple thing to make a spark with flint and stone. And I have made certain the tinder will quickly take flame."

"That's cheating!"

A shrug. "Who's to say the wood wasn't coated with tallow when it was gathered?"

Chakin brightened and leaned against Khu-Shul. "You always take care of me."

"A scribe's work is never done. Nor that of a princess, I think." He nodded toward the playing field.

Chakin looked that way, and whatever words she was about to say died on her lips. Accompanied by the beat of drums and the cheers of the crowd, Hul-Balam led his men into the field's wide, open-ended northern zone. They paraded through the narrower central field, the east and west sides flanked by the public viewing stands. On they came to the southern zone, twin to the northern one but enclosed by the royal platform.

Across the captain's back was the pelt of a jaguar, the great jungle cat from which he took his name. The cat's stuffed head, with its garnet eyes, masked the warrior's face. His arms and legs were wrapped in fur so that he seemed the very creature made man.

His five men forming a line behind him, Hul-Balam led them to the royal stand. He crossed his arms, hands on opposite shoulders, and bowed to Chakin.

"My lady, your warriors await your command."

Chakin stood, stepped to the platform's edge and returned the salute. "In the name of Hun-Ahaw, Lord of the Games, play with honor and bring glory to the court of Shukpi."

Hul-Balam nodded, and Chakin's breath stuck in her throat as he stripped off the pelt.

An old man he might be, but his body was sleek and hard, his skin oiled so that his muscles—sculpted by years of training and battles and hunts—gleamed like polished stone. A dozen or more scars creased the skin of his arms and chest and legs. Not the ritual scars that decorated Tok-Ekh's body, but scars earned in pursuit of glory and service to Shukpi. These blemishes took nothing away from the captain's radiance. Rather, they added to his appeal as a brave and noble warrior.

Like Hul-Balam, the other players wore only loincloths. Flat stones were strapped to their right palms as protection against the hard rubber ball. Their hair was tied in top-knots so that every muscle from neck to calves was on full display. It took all of Chakin's self-control to keep her eyes fixed regally forward as the men moved to their side of the court and the opposing team entered the field.

To the accompaniment of mocking horn blasts and the jeers of the crowd, the six newcomers—taken from the savage Tolupan who lived south of Shukpi's lands—were herded down the length of the field. Hul-Balam had posted guards at the ballcourt's entrances, but two of the captives tried to escape through the stands.

One man was kicked back to the field by a spectator, then struck in the head with the butt of a spear. The other managed to scale the steep wall of the ballcourt, half again as high as a man. He made it to the fourth row of spectators before men, women and children descended on him in a crush of bloodlust and chaos.

The rest of the crowd cheered and stamped their feet on the stone risers as a scream rose from the midst of the press. The mob pulled back, laughing and blood-spattered. A pair of men tossed the player back onto the field. What had once been a human body squelched to the ground in a shapeless heap, like the bag of offal it had become.

"We should have rich sport today, indeed," Tok-Ekh said.

Chakin nodded, only half hearing her uncle's words. Her eyes were fixed on the trail of blood left behind as a pair of guards dragged the captive's body to the base of the royal viewing stand.

"You know the rules of the game, Princess?" Khu-Shul asked as he led her back to her seat.

Chakin shook her head. She knew the general premise but was thankful for the distraction.

"Wuk-Oh serves as judge," Khu-Shul explained as Hul-Balam's lieutenant entered the field carrying a ball made from the sap of the rubber tree and about a hand's-breadth in diameter. "He ensures the rules are followed and determines when a fair point is made."

Wuk-Oh spoke briefly to Hul-Balam, who indicated which of his men would sit out the game, evening up the number of players on each side. The teams faced each other in the southern zone. Wuk-Oh stood between them and tossed the ball into the air.

The men of Shukpi held back, allowing the captive team the first strike. One of the Tolupan gave a feeble hand shot toward the royal stand, but Hul-Balam jumped and blocked the ball with his chest, knocking it toward one of his men. Shukpi's players circled the men of Tolupan and passed the ball to one another using their heads, hips and knees.

"What are they doing?" Chakin asked.

"Showing off," said Khu-Shul. "This first part of the game represents the winter solstice, when Kinich Ahaw is the farthest south in his yearly journey. As we must offer prayers and sacrifice to encourage the great god to return northward, so must the players give honor. The first team to strike the platform marker with the ball earns the point."

Even as Khu-Shul spoke the words, Hul-Balam bumped the ball with his knee, knocking it against the platform's face. The crowd cheered as Wuk-Oh gave a shrill blast on a bone whistle. One of his men—stationed atop the western viewing stand—hung a blue banner from the neck of a macaw's-head marker carved in stone.

"That's it?" Chakin asked as the teams moved to the narrower central part of the field.

"Not yet. There are seven points in the game, representing the solar year. Our team just scored the winter solstice. Play moves to the central court for the spring equinox and zenith. The summer solstice plays in the northern zone. They return to the center for the summer zenith and autumn equinox, then back to the southern zone for the final winter solstice."

"And must we win every point?"

"The team that scores the most points wins." Khu-Shul had barely spoken the words when the whistle blew, the crowd cheered, and another blue banner was hung from the wall. "And it seems clear who that will be."

"I missed it," Chakin said. "Did we hit the side wall with the ball?"

"No. The marker disks are only in the north and south courts." He pointed across the field to the image of Kinich Ahaw that adorned the half-wall at the northern end. "In the central field, the play is divided into two sides, east and west. A team must keep the ball in the air while it's on their side. They may hit it off the wall, but it mustn't strike the ground. Once it passes to the other team's side, it may hit the ground once before they take control, but then they must keep it in the air until they return it."

Chakin watched as Hul-Balam and his men passed the ball from one to another. The crowd cheered each strike of the ball, especially the head and hip shots. When the ball bounced against the wall, laughing children reached down to catch it, only to be shooed back to their seats by the adults.

Hul-Balam set the ball in a high arc. One of his men slapped it down so it struck the ground just on the other side of the stone marker that divided the field. A pair of Tolupan players dove for the ball as it bounced off the hard turf. They collided, the ball bounced off the back of one of the men and rolled into the grass. Whistle, cheer, and banner marked yet another point for Shukpi.

"Do they stop when one of the teams reaches four points?" Chakin asked as the players moved into the northern zone.

"No. As with the sun's journey, each station must be passed before the game is complete."

"Why? If one team scores four points, the other side has already lost."

"Not necessarily. Points can be taken away for improper ball strikes. Yes!" Khu-Shul punched his fist in the air as one of the Tolupan intercepted a pass between a pair of Hul-Balam's men. Chakin gave him a curious look, and the scribe offered a grin. "I like to cheer the disadvantaged team."

"Given the stakes of the game, such generosity might be seen as treasonous," Tok-Ekh said, joining the conversation for the first time.

Khu-Shul bristled. "Considering that the poor devils have probably not slept or eaten since being taken from their families, I don't think a little encouragement is out of line."

The shaman shrugged. "The gods seek only nourishment and service. They care little how it is obtained."

"I should think they would want it honorably served," Chakin said. *"Sak-lah!"* She joined in the cheer as Hul-Balam headed the ball against Kinich Ahaw's effigy.

The teams separated to either side of the northern zone, and the crowd rose and milled about the stands.

"You said play continued even after the fourth point."

"It does," Khu-Shul assured her. "But just as we must take our midday rest during the heat of summer, so the teams are given respite following the solstice point."

Chakin accepted a gourd of watered balché from Kehmut, then leaned back and studied the clouds, while the players rested in the afternoon heat.

30

PLAY CONTINUED AS BEFORE, but with the outcome virtually assured, the crowd was less attentive.

Until one of Hul-Balam's men leapt after the ball, missed his hand-strike and kicked the ball across the dividing line.

Wuk-Oh blew his whistle, accompanied this time by the jeering of the crowd and the removal of the fourth banner from its marker.

"What happened?" Chakin asked as the players moved back to the northern zone.

"An illegal strike," Khu-Shul said. "The ball may only be struck by the head, chest and hips, or the right hand or knee. For any other strike the last point is taken away and must be replayed. That's why all seven points must be awarded. Until the cycle is complete, the other team still has a chance."

The Tolupan players recognized that chance and took it. Focusing their efforts against the player who had fouled the ball, they managed to keep control of play until one of their men kneed the ball against the northern marker.

Khu-Shul's cheer was drowned by the shouts of the crowd, but the players moved once more to the central field and—for the first time—a yellow banner hung from a marker stone.

The Shukpi player cursed and punched the air. He grew even more frustrated as the Tolupan continued to harry him. One of the captives struck the ball to the ground just across the line. Hul-Balam's man went to hit the ball with his knee and missed. He tried to turn for a hand strike, but one of his teammates pushed him out of the way. The man shoved back then looked up just as the ball struck his head and fell to the ground. A second yellow banner went up.

The crowd was on its feet now, shouting and stamping feet upon the stone risers. The two Shukpi players might have come to blows, but Hul-Balam sent them to opposite ends of the line. The rest of the men had caught their teammates' nervousness, however, and in three volleys the ball was again on the ground on Shukpi's side.

Chakin and Khu-Shul rushed to the edge of the royal platform as play moved again into the southern zone. Wuk-Oh's whistle was nearly inaudible as he put the ball in play for the last time.

There was no showing off among Shukpi's players now. Hul-Balam swung at the ball early, just as his opponent leaned forward to jump. The captain caught the man full in the jaw with his palm-stone, and the Tolupan's mouth erupted with blood and teeth.

The crowd roared its approval even as Chakin asked, "Can he do that?"

Khu-Shul gave a sour look. "The rules matter little in the final round, save the most important one: Win."

Hul-Balam's strategy for victory was clear. With his man down, the Shukpi players took each of their opponents in a fierce hold. Hul-Balam strutted unhindered around the players, bouncing the ball off his knee and urging on the cheering crowd.

"For Hun-Ahaw and Shukpi," he shouted, and lobbed the ball high in the air for the final shot.

As he leaned back for the strike, the downed Tolupan—blood streaming from his mouth—wrapped his hands around Hul-Balam's ankles and pulled.

The captain cursed as he fell, but managed to turn onto his back. The ball bounced off his stomach, and the Tolupan was there to hit it toward the end wall. Hul-Balam swiped at the ball as it flew toward the marker disk and hit home.

A few of the spectators applauded, but the majority refrained as Wuk-Oh blew his whistle and approached the players.

"A clean shot," Hul-Balam said. "I was the last to touch the ball."

The Tolupan shouted his objection and slapped his chest. His shattered jaw made the words unintelligible, but his meaning was clear enough.

"My lord, the point is disputed," Wuk-Oh said in a soft tone.

"Then make a ruling." Hul-Balam's growl resounded through the arena.

"I couldn't see it clearly. You'll have to replay the point."

"I already told you, Lieutenant. I hit the ball last. You men saw it?"

Every man of Shukpi shouted their agreement, but the Tolupan players all cried out in protest.

"The point is contested, Captain. We have to—"

Before Wuk-Oh could finish, one of the Tolupan players—the one who had earlier tried to escape—rushed Hul-Balam. The warrior dodged the attack, threw the man to the ground and stamped his heel into the man's throat. The crack of his larynx was even louder than the shouts of acclamation from the crowd.

The Tolupan clutched at his throat, his mouth opening and closing like a landed fish. His body twitched and his head jerked one way then another as he searched for the breath that would not come. The man with the shattered jaw crawled toward his dying comrade.

His brother? Chakin wondered. His son?

The man cradled the other's head in his lap and cried out to his gods, anointing the other with his blood and tears. Within a hundred of Chakin's rapid heartbeats, the Tolupan lay still, his eyes fixed heavenward and his kinsman shaking with sobs.

"I believe the dispute has been resolved." Hul-Balam bent to pick up the ball, raised it in both hands as an offering to Kinich Ahaw, and gave a victory shout.

His men joined him, and the crowd was not long in following as Wuk-Oh gave a final blast on his whistle and signaled the point for Shukpi.

31

THE GAME'S ENDING had been a foregone conclusion, and its timing was nearly perfect. The sun fell toward the western mountains, and the new Great Year would soon begin.

Tok-Ekh leaned toward Chakin to be heard over the crowd's noise.

"You have the option, Lady, of sparing them from the sacrifice. You may give them to the victors as slaves."

Chakin thought for a moment. "Such a worthy effort must be recognized. They deserve better than to be enslaved."

"We give them to the gods, then?"

Chakin hesitated and chewed on the inside of her cheek. She looked to Khu-Shul, but the dwarf just stared back at her. At last, she nodded.

"Let them go to the gods."

"It shall be as you say, my lady. Do you wish to pronounce the judgment?"

The girl lowered her eyes and shook her head, as Tok-Ekh expected. He had hoped she might surprise him, but he was pleased enough that she was willing to send the savages to Shibalba.

All in good time, he told himself, then rose to address the crowd.

"Seldom has this court seen so hard-fought a match as on this day." Tok-Ekh doubted the Tolupan savages understood the language of Shukpi, but his words were for the crowd, not the walking dead. "Lord Hul-Balam, I commend you and your men for such a spirited contest. And you, mighty warriors of

Tolupan, you could teach lessons on the ballcourts of Shibalba. And you shall soon have the opportunity to do so. Bring them."

These last words were swallowed by the roar of the crowd at the pronouncement of the sentence. Hul-Balam's men flanked the four surviving Tolupan who were too tired, too defeated to resist. The guards chivvied them through the ballcourt's southern gate where slaves waited to wash the filth from the savages in preparation for the holy rite.

Khu-Shul escorted the princess to one side as other slaves cleared the cushions and moved a large altar-stone to the front of the platform. Tok-Ekh's serving woman smeared a thin black paste on the lower half of the shaman's face, to give him the appearance of a missing lower jaw. She strapped a breastplate of ribs around his chest, and he was transformed into the image of Death. Around the arena, more of his men doused the censers, strangling the last remnants of the old fire.

A fresh brazier was set beside the altar. Khu-Shul personally laid the sticks that would give birth to the new flame. Kinich Ahaw was half-hidden by the mountains when all was ready, and the crowd settled into silence as Tok-Ekh stepped to the altar and lifted his hands.

"In the First Time, the gods instituted two marker stones to govern man. The *Haab* to track Lord Sun's journey through the heavens, and the *Chol-Kin* to measure man's journey from the Otherworld to this very land of the living. As the great period of these two calendars defines the span of a man's life, so their culmination marks a new beginning."

Tok-Ekh timed his words to match the sun's progress as he watched it from the corner of his eye. He gestured for Chakin to approach the brazier.

"Behold," she said, "the Old is passed away, even as it gives birth to the New."

Kinich Ahaw's crown dropped beneath the mountain, accompanied by the clack of flint on stone. It took only three strikes before a spark landed in the tinder, which instantly took flame.

Yes, Tok-Ekh thought, *the troll-scribe certainly has his uses.* The crowd had been holding their breath, and now exhaled as one. Chakin's face was luminous, both from the nascent flames and from relief at successfully striking the spark.

She stepped back as runners filed across the platform bearing torches to carry the light to the corners of the kingdom. Children followed, bringing candles to light at the sacred fire. Each bowed to the princess then carried the flame back to his family in the viewing stands. Soon, hundreds of lights flickered above Shukpi's playing field.

When the rabble had left the platform, Tok-Ekh again approached the altar.

"Kinich Ahaw is gone to the halls of Shibalba. As he has given of his essence to provide light and warmth to us, so ought we to give of our essence to sustain him in his night-walk."

The shaman gestured to the guards and they led one of the Tolupan forward. A second prisoner pushed past them and spread himself across the altar. Tok-Ekh grinned and waved off the guards who started to pull the man back. The order of sacrifice mattered little. If this fool wanted to show his bravery—or, more likely, to spare himself the horror of seeing his comrades butchered—it made no difference.

Tok-Ekh took the obsidian blade from a slave and lifted it to the sky.

"Gods of night, shine your dark light upon this implement of service, and with your rays purify it."

"*Sak-lah,*" the crowd said as one, adding their endorsement to the prayer

Without further ceremony, Tok-Ekh slashed the blade across the base of the Tolupan's ribs. He took a moment to savor the look of surprise and fear on the man's face, then thrust his hand into the wound. Up to his elbow in savage gore, the shaman found the pulsating lump of flesh and tore it from the man's chest.

"May the gods delight in this offering of meat and drink," Tok-Ekh shouted as he raised the heart toward the heavens.

The crowd cheered their assent. "*Sak-lah! Sak-lah!*"

Thick blood streamed down Tok-Ekh's arm while the heart continued its fear-hurried beat in a vain effort to carry life to its host. It was still pumping when the shaman threw the organ onto the brazier. The meat screamed in the heat as blood boiled and spat among the flames.

The guards tossed the man from the platform to join the broken bodies of his fellows, while the second sacrifice was placed on the altar. Tok-Ekh repeated the ceremony once more, then again. The third man reached out for his heart as the shaman offered it to the gods, and the crowd stamped approval of the effort as his body was added to the heap.

The guards laid the last sacrifice on the altar, and the crowd surprised Tok-Ekh by falling deathly silent. He turned to see Chakin again at his side. Khu-Shul followed at her heels, whispering loudly at the princess, but she paid him no heed.

"Let me," she said.

A bemused Tok-Ekh placed the bloody knife into her hand. Chakin raised the blade to the heavens, repeated the words of blessing—and hesitated.

She looked into the eyes of the sacrificial victim—the one with the broken jaw—and Tok-Ekh's heart sank at the look of pity and uncertainty that clouded Chakin's face.

"You must do as your gods require," the sacrifice said through shattered teeth, surprising Tok-Ekh with its knowledge of Sibolan.

Chakin's eyes softened and glistened with tears, but she nodded and swung the blade.

Tok-Ekh's heart filled with pride as Chakin stuck her hand into the wound. She had to lean close to the man to reach into his chest cavity, and her face came near to his.

"The peace of the gods be with you," she whispered. The man replied with gasps and grunts then convulsed as she jerked his heart free.

Chakin raised the beating heart with both hands and said, in a voice barely audible, "The meat and drink of Shibalba."

She squeezed, and the heart poured out its store of blood, showering her with crimson. She lowered the heart, tore a bite from the flesh, then threw it into the brazier.

The crowd was too stunned to react, but Tok-Ekh shouted, *"Sak-lah!"* as he stepped toward Chakin. The cry was picked up by the guards and servants, then by the whole assembly, until the ballcourt rang with the adulation.

Chakin wrung the blood from her hair, then ran her hands down her face, breasts and belly, painting herself with death.

Tok-Ekh resisted the urge to take her right there on the platform. There would be time later, and with the proper ceremony and herbs it would be all the more exquisite. For now, he satisfied himself with the knowledge that the old ways had a new priestess, and that the Light would not much longer shine in Sibolat.

32

"STUPID OLD MEN!" Chakin stormed into the observatory.

Tok-Ekh masked his amusement. "Troubled, my lady?"

"The council—our ever-so-wise elders—are trying to unseat me."

"How? You are the last remaining daughter of Yash-Ahaw."

"They, or I should say Shan-Chitam claims that the line of Yash-Ahaw is now fully imbued in that of Khuk-Moh. He says it is time the sons of Khuk-Moh claimed the god-seat in their own right, rather than leave it to a woman's choice. Oh, I may retain my position as Lady of Shukpi if I marry the next lord, but it must be one of their choosing rather than my own."

"Calm yourself, my lady. Such passions do not befit one of your stature."

Tok-Ekh lied. In truth, the fire that enlivened Chakin's features was quite suiting and most intoxicating. The shaman poured a cup of balché for the princess, motioned her to a cushion then sat opposite her. "The council will not press the matter with Lord Oshlahun-Ak?"

"That pimple-faced toad? No. The one good thing Sak-Chih has done is to convince the council that her brother is too young to marry."

"What do they propose?"

Chakin huffed. "They would have me marry Khak-Imish, my own brother."

Tok-Ekh shrugged. "This is not uncommon. The noble houses of Sibolat have long practiced familial marriages, the better to keep the royal blood untainted. Besides, he is only your half-brother."

"But he's an infant! Oshlahun-Ak can at least wipe his own backside. I'm already of marriageable age. I will not wait another ten or twelve years before I get—" She bit off the word Tok-Ekh was so anxious to hear drip from her lips. "Before I have a proper husband."

"Did they offer no alternatives?"

"I could marry Wuk-Oh, but I will never take one from the house of Shan-Chitam into my bed." She spat, wiped her chin on the back of her hand, then leaned on her elbows. "There was another suggestion."

"Yes?" Tok-Ekh tried and failed to keep his voice steady.

"Hul-Balam," Chakin said in a husky voice.

The shaman choked back the bile that rose in his throat.

"Oh, I know he's older," Chakin said, "but he's such a magnificent warrior. And he is my father's brother."

"Half-brother," Tok-Ekh snapped, then composed himself. "There is yet another option."

"Oh, Uncle," Chakin said with a pitiable expression that made him want to gouge out his eyes.

"No, no," he said with a forced laugh, and silently begged the gods to put him out of his misery. "I simply think there might be a way to claim the god-seat in your own right, rather than by marriage to a man of the council's choosing."

Chakin sat up. "How? Tell me."

"Chak-Ekh will soon appear from behind Kinich Ahaw's glory. This appearance, particularly just after the union of the calendars, has ever been the omen that the time for war is ripe. War for sacrificial victims, war for new territories—or war for the throne."

"I cannot go to war against my father."

"Of course not. But as you know, our little brothers in Ha-Naab have long provided us with captives—their criminals and imbeciles—to be taken in ceremonial battle, then offered to the gods."

"I thought they came from the Tolupan, like the one I—like the ones we sent to Shibalba."

"Some, yes, for the seasonal ceremonies. But these events in the heavens coincide with the calendar only a few times in a *baktun*. Such wonders require special sacrifice."

"Criminals and idiots?" Chakin said.

"Sibolan blood," Tok-Ekh corrected her. "For a normal sacrifice, any blood will do, even that of the creatures that live beyond our borders. For the rebirth of Chak-Ekh, only Sibolan blood will do."

Impatience grew on Chakin's face. "How does that help me?"

"Ha-Naab is a small town, but its ruler, Chan-Kawak, grows fat on the trade that passes up and down the Hahshuk, from Wakhem in the Highlands, all the way to the Sunrise Waters and the northern kingdoms. Chan-Kawak is weak, however, so Shukpi protects that trade. In return we get obsidian for our weapons, salt for our stores, and sacrifices for our gods."

Chakin nodded, but the look in her eyes made Tok-Ekh shorten the economics lesson. "Should the flow of trade goods cease," he explained, "Shukpi would be placed in a difficult position."

"But why would Chan-Kawak interrupt trade?" Chakin said.

"He would not, but if someone were to unseat him . . ."

Chakin waited for him to finish the thought, then her eyes locked onto his as she caught his meaning. "Me? Take the throne of Ha-Naab?"

"Were you to control the river trade, you would control Shukpi itself. Uti-Chan would never send troops against his daughter, and the council would be forced to treat with you as your position deserves."

The princess weighed his words as the tree frogs took up their night song and a jaguar screamed somewhere in the distant hills.

"It would break Father's heart if I rebelled against him."

"Do not think of it as rebellion. You are Lady of Shukpi. It is well within your rights to unseat your own vassal, to look after the trade interests of Shukpi, and to remind the council of its place."

"I would need an army."

"Hul-Balam commands all the warriors of Shukpi."

"But he would never act against my father or the council."

"You underestimate yourself, my lady. There is little he would not do to win your favor. He will help you claim your god-seat, and afterward—"

"He would expect to marry me."

Tok-Ekh cleared his throat. "Perhaps. But the choice would again be yours, not the council's."

"And if I chose another?"

The girl's fickleness amazed the shaman, but his cold heart fluttered with hope.

"Hul-Balam is a warrior. He serves the will of his sovereign. After defying your father, he will have no choice but to remain in your service at Ha-Naab. He needs only the hope, the expectation of your reward, and he will be yours to command."

Chakin leaned forward in anticipation, but her eyes dulled with the final objection.

"Father will never agree to send me into battle, not even a ceremonial one."

"Leave that to me," Tok-Ekh said. "Chak-Ekh appears in twenty days' time. Then it will be time to wage battle for the gods' glory, and you will claim your rightful place."

Chakin looked to the sky, as though to find some supporting sign there, then she slowly lowered her eyes to meet those of the shaman.

The princess nodded.

33

CHAKIN HELD SAK-CHIH'S HAND, the older woman's grip limp and clammy.

"Please, make it end," the queen begged Chakin, then pressed her free hand to her eyes as the very act of speaking—gasping, really—brought on a fresh wave of pain.

Chakin had tried all her remedies but none was any use in easing the queen's pain. The best Chakin had been able to manage was to put the woman into a stupor for the span of a bowl or two on the water clock. Each time, though, as soon as the effects of the herbs wore off, the pain reasserted itself with a vengeance, until Sak-Chih begged Chakin to let her suffer in full consciousness.

"My ladies."

Chakin turned as Tok-Ekh ducked through the heavy black curtain that spanned the doorway of the queen's chamber, a shield against any sunlight.

"Blessed shaman." Sak-Chih held out a trembling hand.

"How is she?" Tok-Ekh asked as he knelt by the queen's bed and eased her hand to her side.

"Her ailment is beyond my skills," Chakin admitted. "The symptoms are much the same as your headaches—"

"Which you have masterfully cured."

Chakin's cheeks grew warm as she dipped her chin at the compliment. "I fear I have failed to master this one."

"Let us see what we can find, then."

Tok-Ekh performed a cursory examination of the queen. He checked the pace of her heart, the warmth in the pit of her arm, the speed with which the blood returned after pressing her toenails. He asked about her most recent meal, her latest moon-flow, and the condition of her bowels and bladder, all of which Chakin had already noted.

"What do you think?" the princess asked, more out of concern for the state of her healing skills than for Sak-Chih's health.

Tok-Ekh shook his head. "I see no fault in your treatment. I would have tried the very same remedies myself."

Chakin gave a somber smile, her satisfaction tempered by the queen's groan.

"What else might it be?"

The shaman furrowed his brow and shook his head.

"There is naught else it could be. Unless . . . Bring a light, my lady." Tok-Ekh swept back Sak-Chih's hair, turned her head and peered into her ear as Chakin brought a lamp close.

"What is it?" Chakin asked.

"There is a certain parasite that inhabits the ear of its host. As it burrows, it causes great pain. There is no treatment but the removal of the pest."

"So we pluck it out, as a splinter?"

"No," Tok-Ekh said. "We would only separate its head from its body. The head would continue to cause pain, even madness. We must coax the thing out whole."

"How do you do that?" Chakin asked, pleased to be included in Tok-Ekh's plan.

"The parasite cannot tolerate seawater. We must bathe the queen's ears in it, and the creature will seek a more hospitable home."

Chakin blinked. "We must take her to the sea?"

"We will bring the sea to her. I need a gourd of warm water with this much salt." Tok-Ekh traced a circle on Chakin's palm.

"So much?" She was shocked at the amount of the precious mineral needed.

"Compared to the value of the queen's comfort, it is little," Tok-Ekh said. "Bring the water to a boil and add the salt a little at a time, so it may infuse the water with its potency. When you have added all of it, allow the water to cool until it is the temperature of your mouth. Then bring it to me and we shall rid the queen of her unwanted guest."

"And what will you do?"

"I will try to ease her pain until you return. Hurry now, my lady. She has suffered enough."

Chakin allowed Tok-Ekh to herd her from the room. She was unhappy to be given such a menial task, but did not wish to displease her uncle with complaints.

"Remember to let the water cool before you bring it," Tok-Ekh said, then drew the curtain shut behind her.

34

TOK-EKH LISTENED to Chakin's fading footsteps before turning back toward Sak-Chih. The queen's forehead glistened with sweat, while her broad, dark face was streaked with rivulets that shone in the dim lamplight. He moved to the bed, raised her to a seated position and whispered in her ear.

"In darkness, there is no pain."

As soon as he said the words, Sak-Chih's breathing eased. Her eyes fluttered open and fixed on the jewel in Tok-Ekh's forehead.

"Raise your arm," he ordered, and Sak-Chih obeyed. The shaman took a pair of tethered stones from his pouch and draped them over the queen's wrist as a test of his control over her. While under his thrall, she would keep her arm outstretched, regardless of the stones. Should her attention drift, her arm would bend under the weight and Tok-Ekh would know to reclaim her focus.

"Your husband opposes me," he said. "Lady Chakin must lead the raid on Ha-Naab. The gods demand it. The stars support it. Uti-Chan must permit it."

"How shall I convince him?"

"I care not. How you manage your husband is your concern. I require only that it be done."

The stones settled a bit and Tok-Ekh shifted the lamp to reflect its light from his jewel into the queen's eyes. "Heed my voice," he said, and Sak-Chih raised her arm once more. "Lady Chakin shall lead the warriors of Shukpi against Ha-Naab."

The Queen repeated the command.

"Good. Now, what must you ever do?"

"Heed the words of Lord Tok-Ekh."

"And how is the word given?"

"Mouth to ear, or spirit to spirit."

"How by spirit?"

"In sleep, I open my heart and my mind, that my lord's power might illumine my dreams."

Tok-Ekh had first brought Sak-Chih under his sway during their journey from Wakhem to Shukpi. Since then he had rehearsed the lessons many times, further strengthening his hold over her. The fact that the psychic connection brought the queen such pain mattered little.

"It is well," he said. "Our time is short. When we finish, your pain will return for the span of four hundred heartbeats, after which it will diminish, and you may sleep in peace through the night. Do you understand?"

"Yes."

Tok-Ekh removed the stones and placed them in his pouch, then unfolded a small cloth to reveal a fat, harmless grub. "Lower your arm and lie down."

The queen again obeyed, and Tok-Ekh inserted the grub in her ear. It would be flushed out with the saltwater rinse, Chakin would be convinced of the cure, and the queen would continue to be his most valuable servant.

35

"THERE ARE CRAFTSMEN to do that for you," Uti-Chan said from the gateway of Hul-Balam's quarters.

The warrior sat cross-legged on a reed mat, a rock in one hand and a lump of rough obsidian in the other. He started to rise, but the king waved him down and sat opposite him.

"Craftsmen are fine for sandals and ropes," Hul-Balam said. "When my life or the lives of those under my protection are at stake, I prefer to know firsthand the quality of my weapons."

He struck the obsidian with the rock and broke off a slab the size of his hand. The outer surface of the volcanic rock was covered in a lumpy, dull grey tuff, but the virgin surface of the sheared-off slab was glossy black and gleamed in the sunlight.

Uti-Chan picked up the slab and chipped at one edge with a smaller rock. He smiled at Hul-Balam's raised eyebrow.

"My life may depend on the sharpness of your blade," he said, and tested the edge with his thumb.

The pair worked in silence for some time, the void between them filled only by the strike of stone on stone and the growing pile of weapon edges. When they had formed blades for three spears, two daggers, a half-dozen javelins and enough shards to edge a wooden sword, only then did Uti-Chan speak.

"It will soon be time to pay a visit to Ha-Naab."

Hul-Balam nodded as he sorted through some of the smaller obsidian chips.

"I will, of course, call upon you to lead our men in the raid."

"I am yours to command, my lord."

Uti-Chan smiled. "You have ever been my most faithful servant. I would speak with you now as a brother."

Hul-Balam looked up at that and dragged a shard too quickly across his thumb. He cursed and pinched the wound against his index finger to stanch the flow of blood.

"Perhaps we should talk when there are fewer weapons about," Uti-Chan suggested with a smile.

Hul-Balam cracked a rare grin of his own.

"I've had worse. Now tell me—what troubles you?"

Uti-Chan's smile faded. "It is Chakin. I fear I am losing her, Brother. As a child, she was so close to me, would tell me anything. Now she is distant, irritable, secretive—"

"A woman," the warrior interrupted, and drew a rueful laugh from the king. "Surely, my lord, you knew this time would come. She is of the line of Yash-Ahaw, and will one day prove a wise and gracious queen. She is also of the line of Khuk-Moh, so is strong-willed and, at times, thick-headed."

"That is certain," Uti-Chan said. "I had hoped to be able to guide her through this, from the freedom of childhood to the demands of adulthood. As it is, she will hardly speak to me, let alone seek my advice."

"Is there none to whom she will listen?"

Distaste soured Uti-Chan's expression. "Tok-Ekh. She feared him as a child but now seems fascinated by him. It is my own fault, I suppose, for asking him to tutor her."

"The shaman is wise in many things," Hul-Balam said.

"He is a blood-thirsty wretch and he is shaping Chakin in his image. You yourself told me of her part in the ballcourt sacrifice."

"Is that what troubles you? My lord—Brother." Warrior and king locked eyes. "The blood path has formed the way of our people since before the First Time. It is natural—no, it is right that Lady Chakin lead the people in service to the gods."

"I am not speaking of religion," Uti-Chan said, his voice rising, "I am speaking of common decency. The offering to the gods should be sealed by one's own blood, not the blood of innocents. It is a sacred duty to be performed in reverence, not reveled in like a tzana at an orgy." The king was shouting now, and he took a deep breath. "Forgive me, Brother. You have done no wrong."

Hul-Balam shrugged it off.

"You have no need to apologize. I am but a warrior in my lord's service."

"But that is precisely my point," Uti-Chan said. "You are a warrior. You know the power and the value of blood, whether it be your own, that of your men, or even of your enemies. Tok-Ekh believes that taking the blood of others gives him power, and I fear that is the lesson he passes on to Chakin. I would have her learn that one must earn the power that gives blood its potency, then learn to use that power responsibly."

Hul-Balam weighed his king's words then slowly nodded.

"I am glad you agree," Uti-Chan said. "Because I would have you teach her."

"Me?"

"Chakin admires you. I suspect her feelings go beyond admiration." Uti-Chan paused, unsure how much more to say, but decided on candor. "The council has declared that Chakin must marry if she is to remain Lady of Shukpi, and she must marry one of their choosing. You, Brother, are one of those chosen."

"My lord, I—"

"I have delayed the matter as long as I could, but she is of marriageable age and the council will accept no more delays. I will not force the matter on you. Khak-Imish is the council's first choice, but I will not make Chakin wait for him to come of age. Tok-Ekh is also a candidate, and I cannot bear the thought of giving her completely into his hands."

There was also the golden-red orb borne by Kukulkan, but Uti-Chan's faith in his visions had long since begun to waver.

"That leaves you," he told Hul-Balam.

The warrior's mouth fell open, but no words came.

"Do not answer me yet," Uti-Chan said. "When Chak-Ekh makes his appearance, you will go to Ha-Naab to take captives. Chakin will go with you, to learn the warrior's way. If she proves herself—and then, only if it pleases you—I would have you become her husband and my heir as Lord of Shukpi."

PART III

THE LAND OF SIBOLAT

616 C.E.

36

DINGHA TUGGED ON the steering oar to position *Mari-Nadris* at full advantage of the wind and tides, her stern to the red morning sky. With the sail raised and the wind cooperating, the crew had stowed their oars and now lined the rails to take in the sight. For days, cloud banks and bird sightings had suggested the presence of land, but this was the first dry ground they had seen since leaving the Isles of Atlas more than a fortnight earlier. The crew had come close to mutiny at the first hint of land when Iudila refused to steer toward a promising cloud formation. Their course was set, he told them, and while he drew breath, he would not vary from it. Half the men had been willing to make that trade, but the other half included Dingha and Brehanu. The grumbling lessened even if it did not entirely stop.

Now, as a white-sand beach glided past them, its fringe a dense line of palm trees, all resentment seemed forgotten. Lemuel had called down his sighting of a natural harbor, and as Dingha navigated around the protective headland, thirteen mouths dropped open.

As beautiful as the sight of land had been, what met their eyes might have come straight from the shores of Paradise. A half-dozen women—dusky-skinned and bared to the waist—sauntered along the beach, the tide swirling about their ankles. Under their watchful eyes, a score of children played naked in the shallows. As they splashed and chased one another, their laughter carried over the sound of the waves.

The pirates cheered and shouted to the women. At the sound, every woman turned, scenting the air like deer sensing a predator. The children stopped their games and stared toward the approaching vessel, the playful scene now frozen somewhere between wonder and fright. The picture dissolved into chaos as the women screamed, herded the children out of the water then ran toward the shelter of the trees.

The men cried out after them, which only seemed to hasten their flight.

"Quiet," Iudila ordered, his voice overpowering even the combined shouts of his crew. "We need to talk to these people. We need food and fresh water. We need to find out exactly where we are, and whether the treasure is here or not." The lie of Milhma's hoard had become so natural that Iudila no longer tripped over the words. "If we go in there screaming like Saxons, we'll learn nothing from them."

The men looked balefully at him, not yet accustomed to taking orders from him instead of Milhma or Dingha—never mind that Iudila had been Dingha's voice for more than three years. They mumbled their acceptance and turned back to stare silently, if longingly, at the now empty shore.

"Man the oars," Iudila said. "Prepare to drop sail."

Brehanu dropped to the rowing deck, but the rest of the men remained focused on the beach. Only Thanos shot Iudila a curt glance, his eyes full of contempt.

"You know as well as I do that we need full speed to beach the ship properly," Iudila said.

The Greek spat over the side, left the rail and jumped down to join Brehanu at the oars. The other men slowly followed, none looking at their young captain as they took to their benches. With painful slowness, they shipped their oars.

"A captain shouldn't have to explain his orders." Lemuel spoke softly to Iudila after securing the sail and joining his nephew at the bow. "If that dirty Greek defies you again, you should take a few strips out of his back."

Iudila had been about to threaten just that, but the men were now at their oars. He feared continuing the battle of wills would only make matters worse.

"Make strokes for landing," he said, beckoning Lemuel to the drum.

The important thing was to get ashore, provision the ship, and determine their next step. Affirming his place as captain could wait. For now.

Lemuel settled behind his drum and the oarsmen fell into the practiced rhythm. Iudila looked back at Dingha, pointed out the piece of beach where he wanted to land, then braced himself against the bow post. The wait was short as the men's efficient strokes combined with the swelling tide to speed *Mari-Nadris* to shore.

The dromon hissed across the shallows then shuddered as she bore into the sand just above the high-tide line. Oars clattered as the men hurriedly secured them then poured over the sides. The pirates raced up the beach and toward the tree line, casting plumes of sand in their wake as they followed the women's footprints. Iudila dropped to the shore and shouted after his men, but his calls went unheeded.

"Mika, stop! Thanos, you half-blood bastard of a pagan whore!"

These words worked. The Greek had ever been proud of the purity of his blood, the orthodoxy of his faith, and the piety of his mother. The threefold insult was well calculated and perfectly aimed. He skidded to a stop, turned and raced toward Iudila. Bared teeth gleaming from his sun-darkened face, he roared a blood-thirsty challenge in his native tongue. His dagger glinted in the sunlight as he pulled it from its sheath, ready to bury it in Iudila's guts.

Brehanu and Dingha hurried to Iudila's side, but he ordered them back, dug his heels into the sand and braced himself to meet the mad Greek's charge. Thanos covered the distance with surprising speed. Iudila had no sooner positioned himself than he heard the blade's whistle. He leaned away from the dagger then hooked a forearm under his attacker's chin.

Thanos's momentum carried his feet out from under him. Iudila threw him to the ground, kicked the dagger away then drove a heel into his stomach. The wind bellowed from the Greek's lungs. His eyes bore a wild mix of fear and rage as he clutched at his throat and struggled to draw breath.

Mika rushed to his friend's aid but stopped short as Dingha and Brehanu stepped between him and Iudila.

Iudila knelt, his full weight on Thanos's chest, and spoke with steely softness. "I told you to wait. Never again make me repeat an order. Understood?"

The Greek's eyes flashed hatred. He looked ready to spew a fresh round of curses but the only thing to pass his lips was a feeble rasp. He averted his eyes and nodded.

Iudila stood and reached out a hand to Thanos. The pirate slapped the offer away, rolled onto his belly and struggled to his knees.

Women's screams erupted from beyond the trees, accompanied by the shrieks of children and the shouts of Iudila's men. The sound rolled out of the jungle for only a few rapid heartbeats before the cries of the women and children stopped. The men's shouts turned into unearthly wails of horror.

Iudila's blood turned to pitch and a cold hand of fear squeezed his bowels.

"Christ and Saint Frumentius, what was that?" Brehanu said.

The men looked at each other, fear in every eye. Even Thanos drew nearer to the men who had moments before been his enemies.

"Arm yourselves," Iudila said.

Dingha and Brehanu hauled themselves over the side of the beached *Mari-Nadris*, snatched an armful of weapons each and tossed them to the men below. Thanos retrieved his dagger and every man grabbed a sword.

"Stay close," Iudila said, surprising himself with the calmness of his voice.

He followed the crew's footprints toward the trees. The sand made child's play of the tracking. When the beach gave way to the ground cover of undergrowth and fallen palm fronds, broken branches and freshly scarred bark pointed the way. Despite the easy track, Iudila went slowly as the dense growth closed in around him.

The view ahead was limited to no more than five rows of trees, while the canopy of tatter-leafed palms turned the sky to a shadowy green field flecked with bits of blue and white. Iudila paused every few steps to scan the trees ahead, study the trail and check that the others were still behind him.

The trail led to a small clearing then disappeared. The pathway in was unmistakable. The dirt fringe was marked by numerous sets of footprints of women and children, overlaid with the larger prints of Iudila's men. When Dingha and the others caught up with him, Iudila bade them wait while he made a quick survey around the clearing. He found no tracks other than those at the clearing's entrance.

"Devils." Brehanu spat. "They must have snatched them into the air."

"Eight men and twenty women and children would have left some sign going through that canopy," Lemuel suggested.

"Quiet," Thanos hissed. "Listen."

Iudila strained his ears in the silence, then shook his head.

"No birds, no animals, not even a rustle of wind," Thanos said. "If they came in but didn't go out—"

"They're still here," Iudila finished the thought. A shimmer of light caught his eye from the center of the clearing. He recognized it as a small air current rising from the ground, a plume of heat. Scanning further, Iudila spied several more plumes scattered about the clearing.

"Stay here," he whispered to his men. "Keep an eye out and be ready to fall back to the beach."

He crept forward as silently as possible. If the raised hairs on his arms were any indication, he was already being watched and it made no difference how stealthy he tried to be. He crawled to the nearest plume and pulled back the ground cover of dried palm fronds.

A warm pool of fresh blood trickled from a headless trunk. By the tattoos on the stub of neck, Iudila recognized one of his men. He restored the makeshift grave then crawled to the next plume, where he found a similar scene. Iudila swallowed his disgust, turned back to his men then froze as the forest shifted.

Iudila rubbed his eyes, not trusting his vision. Then some of the trees sprouted arms. The whites of eyes appeared in the middle of the slender trunks. One of the living trees raised a branch to its newly formed mouth. Iudila heard a hollow rush of air, felt a prick in his neck and collapsed to the ground.

Unable to move, he could yet hear the shouts of his men, followed by more blowing sounds and the tumble of bodies. A cry rose from the trees that now stalked into the clearing, their treads surprisingly light on the brittle ground cover.

Someone rolled Iudila over. A shaft of sunlight stabbed through the canopy of leaves and into his eyes, which he could not close. A shadow intercepted the blinding light and slowly materialized into the face of a woman, brown-skinned and streaked with green. Her eyes narrowed and her mouth stretched into a feral, sharp-toothed grin just before Iudila's world went black.

37

THE HEAVINESS OF LATE AFTERNOON subdued the people of Shukpi as Kinich Ahaw sank toward his resting place in the western sky. The stones radiated the warmth Lord Sun had cast upon them during the day, and the usually festive atmosphere of the ballcourt was dampened by the hot, wet air.

Chakin waited before the royal viewing stand. Hul-Balam stood to one side of the princess, Khu-Shul on the other, with a hundred warriors arrayed behind.

Uti-Chan rose from his cushion and the elders of the council stood behind him. Sadness clouded the king's face.

Chakin raised her chin in defiance of the sympathy that tugged at her heart and urged her to rush into her father's embrace. No, she would not show such frailty. She was no longer a child, no longer her father's little bunny. However much the king might wish to deny it, Chakin was priestess and judge, hunter and healer. And soon she would be a warrior. From beneath the chin of her deer's-head mask, she peered at Uti-Chan as he spoke.

"Since the First Time, the stars have illumined mankind's path, denoting when to sow and when to harvest, when to tear down and when to build, when to make war and when to pursue peace."

The king pointed toward the western horizon where Kinich Ahaw's light dimmed and, out of his glory, Chak-Ekh—the Evening Star—made his first heavenly appearance of the season. Chakin's heart raced in anticipation of her father's next words.

"As Chak-Ekh arrives to watch over Kinich Ahaw's descent into Shibalba, now is the time for war."

Chakin noted the reluctance in her father's voice. The nobles and people, however, met the words with eagerness. They shook off the lethargy of the heavy air as the warriors rattled weapons against shields.

"Khu-Shul, scribe to the Court of Shukpi," Uti-Chan continued, "observe and record faithfully the forthcoming events, that they may be forever remembered before our ancestors and before the people. Hul-Balam, be glorious in pursuit of victory, and heed the words of your mistress."

Uti-Chan turned sad eyes to Chakin and addressed her directly.

"Na-Chakin, Lady of the Two Suns, I give into your hands the chosen men of Shukpi. May they bring honor to you and glory to the house of Kinich Yash Khuk-Moh."

"I accept their service." The great stones of the ballcourt seem to swallow Chakin's words, and she raised her voice. "I shall lead them back in victory, with tribute befitting the gods."

"*Sak-lah!*" old Shan-Chitam shouted.

The crowd and nobles picked up his acclamation. Uti-Chan kept silent but stretched his arms toward Chakin in a gesture of embrace.

The Lady of Shukpi gave her father a curt nod then turned to Hul-Balam.

"Lead us to glory, Captain."

Hul-Balam bowed to the princess, saluted his king then shouted an order to his men. The warriors split into two columns, clearing a path toward the open end of the ballcourt where a palanquin stood with eight litter-bearers. Chakin and Hul-Balam led the way through the lines of soldiers. The men nodded with respect and eagerness at their commander and their warrior-princess.

Drums pounded, horns blared, whistles shrilled, and the crowd cheered as Chakin stepped onto the palanquin and the bearers raised the platform onto their shoulders. Chakin barely heard the din over the thrum of her own heartbeat as the men stepped onto the Sakbe, the sacred white road that led toward glory and her destiny.

38

IUDILA TRIED TO BREATHE, to open his eyes. Every attempt to move—however slight—was greeted by stings all over his body. Even the beat of his heart set off a wave of pain that radiated through his limbs with each pulse.

With each pulse.

That, at least, meant he was alive. Iudila welcomed the pain, savored each prick and stab and ache. He drew a tentative breath and was rewarded by a burning in his lungs. He breathed deeper still. His head was swimming now, but the tide of pain ebbed with each breath.

His mouth tasted like a bilge, while his nose brought him the tangy smells of roasting meat. His eyes reported only a dull red field, darkened in intervals by fleeting shadows. A second beat pulsed in his breast. Out of time with his heart and twice as strong, this other rhythm was matched by the movement of the shadows and the ever-increasing thunder in his ears.

Iudila forced his eyes open and almost passed out from the pain of the light that stabbed through them. He willed his mind to focus and, surprisingly, it obeyed. His eyes adjusted and the blurs of light and shadow resolved into the figures of dancing women. All were naked save for anklets of shell and necklaces of bone that clattered with the women's steps as they danced around a high fire.

The second rhythm proved to come from a pair of drums, heads of tanned skin stretched across enormous frames, beaten in perfect, raucous time by wild-eyed youths. Children scampered around the legs of the women, whose dance was a wild display of complex, precise, erotic movements. Old men and women flanked the dance ring, all empty gums, pot bellies and scraggly hair.

While the dancing women beat the ground and made placating gestures toward the sky, Iudila chanced a look around. He was upright, bound hand and foot to a pair of spear shafts. One shaft was anchored to a tree while the other was counterbalanced by Lemuel. Brehanu, Dingha and Thanos were all similarly staked, with Thanos's spear tied off to another tree to complete the chain.

It took Iudila a moment to realize that Mika was missing, along with all their weapons and pouches. Iudila scanned the villagers but found no sign of the Egyptian. He also saw no men among them, other than the very young or the very old.

The drumming increased in volume and tempo. The women spun in mad circles, clawing at their breasts and flicking blood heavenward. A fat droplet struck Iudila on the cheek and was instantly pounced upon by a fly whose tickling trail Iudila was helpless to scratch. As one, the dancers stretched their hands toward the bound pirates, stalked in unison toward them, then strutted like hens in the opposite directions and cast their hands again toward the clouds.

For the first time since awakening, Iudila noticed the sky. The sun still shone, but threatening thunderheads chased after it. So heavy were the clouds, they seemed to absorb all the sun's light, casting the sky in a sickly green hue. The clearing—larger than the scene of his crew's attack and surrounded by thatch-roofed huts—was sheltered from the winds, but the treetops whipped back and forth in the gusts.

The drums fell silent and the dancers threw themselves to the ground. One woman, round with child, remained standing between Iudila's men and the fire. She cried out to the clouds and raised her hands to the lowering sky. One hand bore a black-bladed knife while the other was empty, fingers splayed. The other women, along with the children and the elders, mumbled and sobbed, lending their prayers to the pregnant woman's.

The pleas rose in pitch and intensity. Two other women stood and presented frond-covered wooden platters. The pregnant woman removed one of the covers to reveal Mika's head. She raised it by the scalp and shouted again to the sky. She passed her knife beneath the severed neck and threw the Egyptian's head into the flames.

Only then did Iudila recognize the shape of the roast over the fire, elbows and ankles tied to the heavy spit. Bile rose in his throat. The realization that Mika's head and body would be reunited in smoke and ash was small consolation—smaller still when the woman took the covering from the other platter. She lifted a bloody tangle of flesh and shook her hands at the clouds, dagger clutched in one, Mika's severed manhood in the other.

Whatever deity was the intended recipient of the offering, it seemed not to be placated. The wind screamed even louder, swept the phallus out of the woman's hand and knocked her off her feet. The sky tore open and loosed a downpour that extinguished the sacrificial fire.

The people shouted and ran. A few paused to help the pregnant woman and to usher the young and old, but most simply fled the village.

Rain lashed at Iudila's face and chest with needle-like drops. The wind sucked the air from his lungs.

"Can anyone get free?" he called to his men after snatching what breath he could from the marauding storm.

"The ropes are too tight," Brehanu called out.

The men all tugged at their bindings, grunting and cursing as they struggled against one another.

"Together," Lemuel suggested. "We should move together."

"He's right," Iudila shouted. "To Thanos. Now."

Each man pulled to the right, then toward Iudila and back again. The poles loosened in the sodden earth and the ropes slackened as they absorbed the rainwater. Iudila's spear sagged under his weight, and he slipped his bound wrist off the end of the shaft. Before he could untie his other hand, a clout of wind punched him in the chest. He whipped around, tugging at the stake he shared with Lemuel. The force overwhelmed the slender shaft, and it, too, broke free. The cascade continued until all five men were thrown to the ground.

Iudila lay in a tumble of palm fronds, dirt, and debris. The rain came in sheets now, turning the sand to mud and threatening to drown him each time he took a breath. He loosened the knot at his other hand, then his feet.

Iudila crawled to where the pregnant woman had fallen. The ground was a morass, but Iudila dredged the muck until his fingers brushed something solid. He closed his fist and pulled up the dagger.

As quickly as the wind and rain allowed, he cut the others loose.

"The boat?" Thanos said.

Iudila shook his head. "Trying to sail in this would be suicide. We should get to high ground."

"What if the women attack us again?"

As if in answer, an uprooted palm tree flew over their heads, struck another tree trunk and slid to the ground just feet from where the men huddled.

"I think they'll have other things to worry about," Iudila said. "Keep together, stay low and keep moving uphill."

The men locked arms and headed for what Iudila hoped was safety. Even with the wind to their backs, the going was slow. They slogged across the flooded ground and threaded around fallen trees and impassable piles of debris. The ground water had risen to their knees by the time the land started to rise. Free of the flood, they still had to contend with the mud, leaves, rocks and trees that rushed down the battered hillside.

A scream rose above the roar of the storm. Iudila turned to see a woman clutching a tree with one arm, the other vainly grasping against the wind. He followed the direction of her outstretched arm and saw the limp form of a child wedged against a fallen tree, face-down in the rushing flood.

"Keep moving," Iudila shouted to Dingha, and let go of the big man's arm. Dingha tried to stop him, but Iudila yelled, "Go!"

Iudila staggered through the wind and the flood. He fell, cursed as a rock sliced through his hand, then picked himself up and fought on. It took an eternity to reach the child, and Iudila's heart sank as he pulled the limp body into his arms.

His steps mired as in a nightmare, he lumbered back uphill. The woman staggered toward him, but the wind knocked her off her feet. Iudila half-crawled, half-ran to her, put the child in her arms and helped her up.

"Which way?" he shouted.

Iudila guessed she couldn't understand the words, but she pointed toward a stand of trees, their slender trunks bowed with the wind. Iudila wrapped his strong sailor's arms about the woman's waist. His long red hair tangling in the wind with her black, they climbed the hill together.

"Over there!" Iudila heard.

He looked up to see Brehanu and Dingha. They eased down the slope on their backsides until they reached Iudila and the woman.

"I told you to keep going."

"We did," Brehanu shouted against the wind, "and then we came back."

Iudila couldn't help a smile as the Africans anchored the group.

The woman pointed and shouted as they crested the hill.

"I see it," Iudila said when he spied the yawn of black against the brown of the muddy slope.

They staggered toward the opening, which proved to be the mouth of a shallow cave.

"Are you mad, turning back into that storm?"

Iudila ignored Lemuel's scolding, instead focusing on the woman. She held her son and whispered to him as she smoothed back his hair. His body was limp, his lips and fingertips a dull purple.

Iudila snatched the boy from her arms. He ignored her screams as she beat him and tried to reclaim the child's body.

"Keep them back," he shouted to his men as the other villagers rushed from the rear of the cave.

The pirates formed a ring around Iudila, the woman, and her child.

"I only want to help," Iudila said softly.

The woman seemed to understand. She crouched before him and hugged her knees to her chest.

Iudila bent the child over his knee. He pressed against the boy's belly and patted his back until water streamed from his mouth.

The woman screamed and reached for her son, but Iudila held on to him. He put his ear to the boy's mouth, but heard and felt no breath.

"No," he said, his voice but a whisper as he clutched the child to his chest. "No, no, no!" he screamed to the roof of the cave. "You don't get this one yet."

He laid the boy on the ground and bent over him. The woman's cries and beating began anew as Iudila placed his mouth over the boy's. The villagers shouted and fought against the pirates' ring. Iudila ignored them all. Twice more he bent over the boy and breathed into his mouth.

After the third breath, the boy coughed up more water. Iudila hurriedly picked him up and slapped his back until he stopped coughing and raised his head. The woman grabbed at the boy, and Iudila let her take him this time.

The pirates broke their protective ring. The villagers surrounded the woman and her son. The boy looked around to see what all the fuss was about.

"What did you do?" Lemuel said, as pirate and villager alike stared at Iudila with awe.

Iudila smiled. "You should know. After all, it was you who beat the Torah and the Prophets into me. Elijah and the widow's son? 'And he bent over the boy three times, and the soul of the boy returned with his breath, and he lived.'"

39

THE STORM RAGED through the rest of the grey day. With darkness came the calm and a damp, fitful night. Iudila's men slept in shifts, one of them keeping watch at all times.

The night passed without incident. In the new dawn the villagers took the pirates back to their clearing. The woman and the boy Iudila had saved led him by the hand, while the others danced and sang, picking at the pirates' clothing and whiskers as they went.

"How can you stand to have them touch you?" Thanos demanded of Iudila after shooing away one of the children. "They butchered more than half our men."

Iudila's stomach tightened but he kept his voice even.

"You should be grateful I called you back. Otherwise, you might be with them now. If they'd listened to me, none of it would have happened."

"The men meant no harm."

"Armed strangers arrive on your shore, shouting like devils, then chase after your women and children. You wouldn't feel the need to defend yourself?"

Thanos made no reply.

"Every one of their deaths is a knife in my gut," Iudila said, "but they brought it on themselves. Doing harm to these people won't bring them back. Anyway, I thought you'd be glad."

"Glad?"

"Your share of the treasure has more than doubled."

Iudila ignored the Greek's curses and tried to sing along with the villagers as they entered the clearing.

The storm had reduced the place to nothing more than a muddy swamp. The villagers seemed to care little as they set about collecting fallen trees and branches, cleaning up as best they could.

"Can you take us back to the beach?" Iudila asked the woman.

He used hand signs to try to get his point across. She eventually caught his meaning and called to one of the other women. The pair of them gestured for Iudila and his men to follow.

It was past midday when they reached the sheltered beach. Dirty runnels cut their way to the shore, scarring the land as the flood waters returned to the sea by whatever path they could. The front line of trees had been flattened by the wind, making passage from the jungle to the beach almost impossible. Iudila and his men squeezed, scraped and crawled their way through the debris, only to find a beach littered with death.

Shellfish, squid, and seaweed baked under the sun and filled the air with the stench of decay. The only sign of *Mari-Nadris* was the anchor, nearly buried in sand and closer to the tree line than it had been when they'd left the ship. Dingha tugged on the rope and raised it from its bed of sand as he followed it to the trees. When he reached the end of the line, he found it attached to its cleat, still fastened to its scrap of deck.

"Good knot," Iudila said.

He led his men into the trees, but it was no use. *Mari-Nadris* was dead, her body broken and strewn across the jungle floor, among the branches and—in one case—driven through the heart of a tree trunk.

"Gather what you can," Iudila said as he picked up a deck plank.

"You mean to put her together again?" Thanos asked.

"No. To cremate her."

40

"CAPTAIN," WUK-OH SAID, and Hul-Balam turned from his place at the fire. "The shaman has arrived."

Hul-Balam rose and followed his lieutenant to the camp's edge where Tok-Ekh waited impatiently.

"I am forbidden from entering my own camp?" the shaman snapped.

"The men were simply following my orders, Lord. No one—not even Lord Sun himself—is to enter camp without my direct permission. Well done, Wuk-Oh. You may keep your *tunob*."

The younger warrior smiled and patted his groin. "Thank you, Captain. I've grown fond of them. Eyes out, keep sharp," he told his men as Hul-Balam led Tok-Ekh away.

"You will want to speak with the princess?"

"In a moment." Tok-Ekh laid a cold hand on Hul-Balam's arm. "May we speak privately, Brother?"

Hul-Balam was too startled by the shaman's familiarity to recoil from the touch of his fingers. "Of course." He led Tok-Ekh toward the latrine pits and smiled as the shaman caught his breath. "We will not be disturbed here."

"With good reason," Tok-Ekh said, and wiped his watering eyes. "How well do you trust Khu-Shul?"

Hul-Balam instinctively looked around and spied the dwarf at Chakin's side by her fire.

"I would not want him by my side in battle, but I believe he is loyal to Uti-Chan and devoted to Lady Chakin."

"Are you certain?"

"What is your meaning, my lord?"

Tok-Ekh paused, took a breath then pressed on. "I fear that Khu-Shul may be conspiring against us with the Lord of Ha-Naab."

"Impossible. The scribe is like Chakin's puppy. He would never betray her."

"Unless he knew she would be lost to him anyway. You know of Chakin's troubles with the council?"

"I know they require her to marry in order to retain her title."

Tok-Ekh nodded. "Then you know that Uti-Chan has selected me to be her husband and to succeed him on the god-seat."

Hul-Balam's stomach turned to stone as the words burned into his ears. "That is not so. It cannot be so. He—"

Confusion clouded the shaman's face, then his eyes softened with understanding. "Oh, Brother, I am sorry. He made the same promise to you?"

The warrior managed a nod.

"It would seem that our lord the king has made many promises of late. Perhaps Khu-Shul is not entirely mistaken in his plot."

"What plot?"

"Uti-Chan sent me to Ha-Naab to negotiate the captives with Lord Chan-Kawak. While in his audience chamber, I saw a message listing the numbers of our men and our order of battle. Our scribe has a fine hand. I would know his writing anywhere. There is no mistake. He is providing information to the enemy."

"Chan-Kawak is not our enemy. He is a vassal to Uti-Chan. Perhaps the information was simply to apprise him of the timing of our arrival."

"Perhaps. But why would the Lord and the men of Ha-Naab be preparing weapons and armor for themselves? Every fit man was getting ready for war."

"That cannot be."

"I confess I am no warrior, but I know the difference between imbeciles and true fighting men. Chan-Kawak intends to challenge us on the field at Ha-Naab."

Hul-Balam struggled to find some other meaning.

"Perhaps Uti-Chan simply wishes Chakin to have a true victory, not merely a showpiece battle."

Tok-Ekh snorted. "Until Lady Sak-Chih persuaded him, our brother refused even to allow the princess to take part in the raid. You think he would allow her to see real combat?"

The warrior looked solemnly at the shaman. "What must we do?"

"How long until we reach Ha-Naab?"

A runner would have covered the distance in half a day, a trained army between dawn and evening of the same day. But this ceremonial escort, slowed by Chakin's litter, would take longer still.

"Two days," Hul-Balam said.

"More," Tok-Ekh said. "Slow down your men, create obstacles along the path. Do whatever you need to delay."

The captain narrowed his eyes. "Should we not go faster, to meet them before they are fully prepared?"

"No. They were very nearly ready for battle when I left them. To arrive early would give you no advantage. If you delay, however, Chan-Kawak may question the reliability of his information. His men will grow bored, tired. Arrive a few days later than they expect, and you will have the opportunity to surprise them."

Hul-Balam nodded. "What of Khu-Shul?"

"Give me two trusted men," Tok-Ekh said, "and I will take care of the matter."

41

"I DON'T UNDERSTAND," Chakin said.

Only moments before, Hul-Balam and two of his men had seized Khu-Shul and—ignoring her protests—dragged him away.

"Calm yourself, my lady," Tok-Ekh told her, and led her back to her place by the fire. "They are simply following my instructions."

"Your instructions?" Chakin's cheeks grew hot.

"Yes, Lady. Forgive me but there was no time to spare, and I did not feel it prudent to speak to you beforehand."

"Speak to me of what?"

Tok-Ekh sat beside the princess. "Khu-Shul discovered our plan, I fear. He was waiting only until you went to sleep, then he planned to return to Shukpi and tell your father everything."

Chakin's heart fluttered and her blood turned cold. "How did he find out?"

"I do not know, Lady. Perhaps he overheard something. Perhaps he sensed something—dwarves are blessed by the gods with many secret abilities. Regardless, I felt it necessary to stop him before he could undo our plans."

Chakin took a deep, calming breath and nodded. "Of course. I just can't believe he would betray me."

Tok-Ekh gave her a pitying look. "My lady, he loves you. One need only look at him to see that. Though he could never have you for himself, in Shukpi he could at least serve you as scribe and advisor. And should you be forced into a marriage not of your choosing? One can see how he might wish for your unhappiness in order to be of greater comfort to you."

"He would never be so selfish," Chakin said, unsure of the words even as they left her tongue.

Tok-Ekh shrugged. "Perhaps not. But the truth of the matter is that he was prepared to inform your father of your plans to take the god-seat of Ha-Naab. He was prepared to see you brought back to Shukpi to have your fate decided by Shan-Chitam and the elders."

Chakin's temper rose at the mention of the council. "They will never dictate to me."

"No, Lady."

Chakin stared into the fire, letting her thoughts dance with the flames as she tried to make sense of it all. "He was my closest friend."

"Friendship is a fickle thing."

Chakin looked up at that and blinked into the darkness until the remnants of the flames faded from her eyes. "He cannot return to Shukpi. But to keep him with us, he must be bound. I fear I could not stand to see him kept captive."

"If you wish, my lady, I will see to it that he does not return to your father."

Chakin met Tok-Ekh's gaze and was dazzled briefly by the fire's reflection in the obsidian in the shaman's forehead. Her eyes watered but she told herself it was simply from the light of the flames. She blinked away the tears, took another deep breath, and nodded.

Tok-Ekh gave a grim smile, rose, and turned away.

"Only—"

The shaman stopped and turned back to her. "Yes, my lady."

"Only, do not harm him. Please?"

Tok-Ekh started to speak, stopped himself, and thought for a moment.

"I give you my word, my lady. I will do him no harm."

42

THE SHIP BURNED through the night and into the next dawn. The men had gathered as much of *Mari-Nadris's* corpse as they could. They piled the scraps—along with their crewmen's remains—on the beach in a final, blazing farewell.

From buried stores, protected from the storm, the villagers had produced a number of clay pots that held a potent liquor. While the fire burned, villager and pirate alike drained pot after pot of the bitter brew. Morning found most of the revelers—including the children—sprawled on the sand.

"Do you know this sign?" Iudila asked a woman, the pregnant one who had led the ceremony in the village. They were among the few still conscious. In the sand, he drew the symbol from his map—two dots beside an encircled four-leaf clover. The woman looked at the sign and her face clouded over. She spat at the symbol, erased it with her foot, then rose and stormed back toward the village.

By the time Iudila's men awoke, the rest of the villagers had disappeared among the trees that lined the beach.

"What do we do now?" Lemuel asked, then raised a hand to his head and squeezed his temples.

Before Iudila could answer, a haunting song rose in the forest. The villagers reappeared, the pregnant woman in their lead. Behind her, the other women bore a log on their shoulders. These were followed by the children and old people, their voices raised in harmony.

When they reached the shore, the women lowered the log, which had been hollowed out and shaped into a narrow boat. In its belly were oars, the pirates' belongings and a few skins of water.

The pregnant woman stepped up to Iudila. She pointed at the smear in the sand where she had erased the map's symbol. She gestured three times northwest along the coastline, then three times more toward the southwest.

Without further ceremony, she led the villagers back toward the trees. Only the woman Iudila had saved paused. She turned with her son and waved before following the others into the forest.

"What was that about?" Thanos said.

"I'm not sure," Iudila said, "but I think she's pointed us toward our treasure."

43

IUDILA STEERED THE DUGOUT toward the mouth of the river. There was no breakwater, no natural harbor. The rising tide backed up the river, reversing its flow in the lower reaches. The men took advantage of this, riding the tide upstream for nearly a mile before the river's course reasserted itself.

For nearly a week the men fought currents and tides, following the instructions the villagers had given them. Three days of hard rowing northwest along the shoreline had brought them to a cape where the land doubled back on itself in a wide bay. Another three days of following the coast southwest had led them to the mouth of this broad river.

Unwilling to fight the river's current, Iudila steered toward a mud bank, beached the boat and waited for his men to fall over the low sides. He hauled the boat up the bank and tied it to a tree.

"Sweet Christ," Thanos said, not bothering to cross himself, "tell me we've made it."

"I hope so." Iudila dropped to the ground beside his men.

"Then where is it? Where's the treasure?"

"Milhma said to wait for a sign," Iudila said after a slight pause.

"What kind of sign?"

"He didn't say, only that we'd know it when we saw it."

Apparently too tired to argue, Thanos fell back onto the bank. Lemuel struggled to his feet, picked up the water skins and started upstream.

"You're tired, Uncle," Iudila protested. "Let me."

"Nonsense. You've been rowing for days."

"And you've been bailing."

"So let me bail a little more, only this time with fresh water. Rest. I'll be back soon."

"Don't wander far," Iudila started to say. He was asleep before the words passed his lips.

A sharp cry jolted him awake. He grabbed his sword and dashed upstream. The voice was Lemuel's. Iudila followed the sound of shouts until he saw the older man knee deep in the broad river, hopping and pointing toward the opposite bank. Iudila rushed to his uncle's side and pulled him toward the near shore.

"Look, look!"

Iudila followed Lemuel's pointing finger to the opposite bank. "I see nothing, Uncle."

"Beneath the tree, among the reeds. A basket—a basket of bulrushes, just as in the Torah!"

Iudila strained his eyes and could just make out the shape of something among the water grasses on the opposite bank.

"Wait here," he said, then gauged the strength of the river before wading farther in. Within a few feet of the bank, the water was above his waist. He swam into the current until he reached the shallows just upstream of the cluster of reeds.

The thing seemed, indeed, to be a basket—larger than an infant's cradle, but smaller than a practical boat. The basket was tangled among the reeds on the outside bend of the river. Iudila tugged on the basket, and a cry sounded from within the woven reeds—not a child's, but not quite a man's.

Another shout arose, this one from the opposite bank. Iudila turned to see Dingha pointing at him and plunging into the current. Iudila looked behind just in time to see a pair of bulging eyes and flaring nostrils moving toward him on the water's surface. The nostrils rose to reveal a pink maw bordered by twin rows of enormous white teeth. Iudila had time only to throw himself to one side before the teeth snapped together with a thunderclap. Stubby legs and a powerful reptilian tail beat at the water as the crocodile turned toward him, jaws opened for another snap.

Iudila tried to run but the water slowed his movements. He lost his hold on the river's bottom and floated—not quickly enough—on the current. The beast drew nearer to him. Iudila's leg was inside the sweep of the monstrous teeth that would crush his bones and carry him to the river's bottom, but the jaws sprang closed on empty water as the leviathan lurched backward.

Behind the beast, Dingha shouted in fury as he tugged the rough-scaled tail. The lance-shaped head twisted back and loosed a roar to match the helmsman's. It lunged at Dingha, who fell back into the water. Iudila remembered the blade in his hand and launched himself at the monster. He landed hard on the scaly back, his free arm wrapped about the slippery neck. The creature rolled and Iudila fought to hold on. So quick was the move that he had no time to draw breath.

Iudila tightened his legs around the crocodile's middle, straddling the thing as if it were some demonic charger. He plunged his sword into the soft underbelly. The beast writhed in anger, its blood clouding the already murky water. Again and again, Iudila stabbed the monster, but the blows did more to rouse its fury than anything else. Bubbles trickled from Iudila's mouth and streamed to the surface. His instinct screamed at him to follow but he dared not release his hold.

Stars flew across his vision even as black veils were drawn around the edges. He might drown or be eaten, though he had no doubt the crocodile could accommodate both fates for him. His vision was nearly eclipsed when, out of desperation, he loosed the grip of his arm, arced back and drove the blade toward the beast's head. With muscles starved for air and his motion dampened by the water, the blow should have been impotent, a last, futile act to crown a life of wasted chances.

The monster chose that moment to rear back its head, lending its power to Iudila's feebleness, and driving its skull onto the point of the sword. Steel pierced thick hide and brittle bone then slid into the jellied mass of brain. The beast gave a violent tremor that snapped the blade, then went still. Iudila kicked away and followed his last bubble to the surface.

His head ached, his lungs burned, his ears rang and he was fairly certain he'd pissed himself. But he was alive, and as he filled his lungs with the warm jungle air, he laughed for the joy of it. He laughed hard enough to draw in a mouthful of water, punctuating his laughter with spasms of coughing.

He swam to the nearest shore and found he'd been carried well downstream during the struggle. Dingha thrashed the water as he stroked furiously toward him. Iudila waved to signal that he was all right. He tried to stand but found his legs didn't work. The bladeless hilt dropped from his hand and he started shaking. By the time Dingha reached him, Iudila had curled into a tight, trembling ball. Dingha grabbed him by the shoulders and tried to still the tremors.

"I'm fine," Iudila managed to say.

"You don't look fine."

Dingha eased him to a sitting position and leaned him against a tree trunk. He bade him rest there while he plucked a giant leaf, filled it with brackish water, then gingerly held it to Iudila's lips.

"I'm all right, really," Iudila insisted. To prove it, he rose to his feet and took a few tentative steps. The terror had passed and his muscles seemed once again under his control. "Let's get the basket and find a way back across. Carefully."

Dingha nodded and picked up the stub of sword. He sharpened the end of a stout, slender reed then, holding the shaft like a spear, led the way upstream. Other than a few water snakes and some invisible skitterers that fled from their approach, no other creatures lay across their path. They reached the stand of reeds and found the basket where Iudila had left it. No sound came from within, but when Iudila nudged it, he thought he heard whimpering.

"It's all right. I'll get you out."

The basket was tightly woven of strong reeds, the top and bottom halves bound together by thick windings of palm leaves. Iudila took the sword from Dingha, slashed at the bindings with the broken blade then threw back the lid.

He had seen dwarves before—in the markets and fairs of Spania and Mauretania—but this one was different. The dwarf had skin the color of walnut, eyes more black than brown, earlobes punctured by thick wooden spools, and hair the color of night and cut short above his ears. His face was monkey-like—complete with tufts of hair growing from his cheeks—but radiated a keen intelligence and curiosity. And not a little fear.

"Don't be afraid," Iudila said, in as gentle a voice as his surprise allowed. "I only want to help."

The dwarf cocked his head dubiously, then clutched the sides of the basket as Iudila and Dingha pulled the woven vessel free of the reeds. He looked uneasily from one man to the other, but seemed to relax as they floated his basket-boat across the river. He sat up, jabbered at them in what might have been speech, then laughed and struck a noble pose as the pirates swam with ungainly sidestrokes across the deepest stretch of water.

Once on the other side, the dwarf shrank into the basket as the rest of the crew gathered around. Iudila told his men to stand back, and the dwarf stepped tentatively out of the basket. He tested the ground with each step, as though fearing the earth might vanish any moment. At last, he turned to Iudila, placed his fists together, and gave a small bow.

He said something in a nasally voice then stared at Iudila expectantly. Iudila looked to Lemuel, then to the rest of his men, but none could put meaning to the words. Iudila shrugged, and the little man repeated himself—this time more slowly and loudly, as though that would help—accompanied by meaningless gestures toward the river.

"I don't understand," Iudila said with another shrug and shake of his head.

The dwarf gave an exasperated sigh then looked around as if to find someone with any sense. Apparently finding none, he squatted and scratched a ragged line in the dirt. He pointed at the river then at the etched line.

"The river," Iudila said, repeating the gestures and kneeling opposite him.

The man smiled.

"Hahshuk," he said, and retraced the line in the dirt.

He then pointed at Iudila, gestured first one way then the other, up and down the ragged line, then held his hands up in question.

Iudila nodded, drew in the dirt to extend one end of the line into a small delta, and sketched the rough outline of a boat. "We came across the sea," he said, drawing waves beneath the boat, "and up the river Hahshuk." He poked dots along the river's course, then drew a line across the path and patted the ground. "And landed here."

"Ask him about the treasure," Thanos said eagerly. "*Thesauros?*"

"Let's work out the basics first," Iudila suggested. "You." He pointed at the little man. "You came from upstream?" He gestured along the dirt river's course.

The dwarf nodded, a pained expression on his face. He then launched into a description of what must have been an epic tale of tragedy and heartbreak. He replayed each detail of the story, animating the rapid-fire, indecipherable words with dramatic gestures. At length, he finished by sketching the figure of the sealed basket, then poked holes downstream until he reached Iudila's line in the sand. He sat down and dropped his chin onto his fists.

The other men looked at him with sympathy, though how he had ended up in a reed basket and abandoned on the river was still a mystery.

"Did he say anything about the treasure?"

Iudila ignored Thanos and crouched opposite the little man.

"My name," he said, and patted his chest, "is Iudila. Iudila."

The dwarf's eyes widened, and he looked from one man to another, as though to confirm the claim. He pointed at Iudila and said, "Uti-La?"

"Iudila, yes."

"Uti-La," he repeated in an awed voice, then patted his own chest. "Khu-Shul."

"Nice to meet you, Khu-Shul." Iudila then pointed at each of his men and spoke their names, which the man repeated—or tried to. Brehanu's gave him the most trouble, coming out as Blee-hanu.

"There," Thanos said. "We've made nice, we've introduced ourselves. Ask him about the treasure."

Unable to put him off any further, Iudila stooped to the sand and drew a jumble of dots surrounded by rays, as if to show a gleaming pile of coins. He then drew various geometric figures, representing cut gems. None of these made any impact on Khu-Shul, other than to raise expressions of pity for Iudila's obvious lack of artistic ability.

Iudila could think of no other way to communicate that they sought a treasure. The effort was doubly useless, as the treasure he sought was far different from what Thanos had in mind—and far more difficult to express in words, let alone stick figures.

He had one more idea—hopeless though it might be—and sketched the symbol from the monk's map.

Khu-Shul watched with patronizing interest as Iudila formed a rounded square. His interest became more genuine as the Goth filled in the curves. His eyes went wide when Iudila added the two dots. Khu-Shul looked from Iudila to Lemuel and the rest of the men, then scratched his own figure in the sand. His stubby fingers moved with surprising dexterity. In half the time it had taken Iudila to sketch his crude facsimile, Khu-Shul had crafted the symbol exactly.

"You know it?" Iudila said.

Khu-Shul pointed at the figure and nodded. "Chakin."

"Chakin,"Thanos repeated. "Chakin? Does *chakin* mean treasure? *Thesauros*?"

"Chakin," Khu-Shul repeated, nodding.

Thanos loosed a shout of triumph. The others—fully aware that Milhma had hidden no treasure—still could not help but share the Greek's excitement. None cheered more loudly than Iudila. After all the trials, all the doubt, his impossible journey had succeeded. The map had led them to a land that shouldn't exist. The strange symbol had been recognized. And guidance had, indeed, come from the smallest of packages.

Iudila looked at Khu-Shul, who smiled uncertainly at the crew's jubilation.

"Chakin—how do we get there?" He pointed to the symbol then to the crude map.

Khu-Shul extended the upstream line of the river. "Ha-Naab," he said with a sad expression, and drew a symbol on the river's northern bank. By the large square he drew around the symbol, Iudila took it to be the name of a city. The dwarf then drew the now familiar symbol across the river. "Chakin."

Iudila stared at the crude map, stunned to be so close to his goal, even in sketch form. "How far?" He pointed at the sun, rested an elbow in his opposite hand, and swept his arm in a vertical arc.

Khu-Shul nodded then took a moment to think. He paced deliberately beside the map, stopped beside the symbol called Ha-Naab and held up four fingers. He then made a rowing motion, followed by two fingers.

Only two days between Iudila and his destiny. "Brehanu, Thanos—bring up the boat," he said, and the two men hurried downstream to obey.

"We need food," Dingha said.

"I know." Iudila turned to Khu-Shul and gestured as though he were eating.

Khu-Shul nodded and smiled. He walked to the river's edge, and pointed across and slightly downstream—where the crocodile's carcass floated in the river, tangled among the reeds.

By the time Brehanu and Thanos returned with the boat, Dingha and Iudila had managed to haul the beast ashore. Lemuel went with Khu-Shul to find herbs or fruit or anything else edible that could easily be gathered. Through hand signs, Khu-Shul advised them it would be best to wait for morning before setting out. The exhausted men were only too willing to agree.

The storm that had devastated the village seemed hardly to have touched these northern shores. The jungle was thick with windfall and underbrush, damp but not soaked. Khu-Shul watched intently as Iudila struck his broken sword against a flint. After the tinder caught and a low, smoky fire took hold, Iudila handed the stub of steel to the dwarf.

Khu-Shul tested the blade with his thumb, tapped the metal, even tasted it before handing it back with his incomprehensible assessment.

"Do you recognize any of the words?" Iudila asked Lemuel.

"None. But perhaps we know something in common." Lemuel turned to Khu-Shul. "*Legum servi sumus ut liberi esse possimus*," he said, using his best Latin from Cicero.

The dwarf's blank expression was unchanged.

"*Ilthon balein eirinin alla machairan*," Thanos quoted from Greek scripture, but had no better result.

Brehanu tried his native Ge'ez, along with Sabaean and Coptic, while Iudila threw out some different Germanic tongues and even a few phrases in Persian. None had any result.

"*Shema Yisrael, Adonai eloheinu, Adonai echad.*"

Khu-Shul's eyes went wide as Lemuel spoke the words.

"That got through," Iudila said. "*Baruch sheim kvod malchuto lholam vayed.*"

The dwarf turned to Iudila, fear in his eyes. He clapped his hands over his ears and shook his head.

"All right," Iudila said. "No more." He placed his fingers over his mouth.

Khu-Shul gave him a wary look but took his hands from his ears and reached for a piece of crocodile meat.

The days-long row caught up with the crew, and they drifted to sleep. Iudila lay back but, despite his exhaustion, found no sleep as he awaited the dawn. A dawn that would bring him one step closer to his heart, to his destiny.

44

IUDILA SLAPPED AT A FLY the size of a small bird. Not for the first time, he cursed the man-eating creatures that infested the jungle. At the outset, the journey upstream had been full of novelty and excitement. Each new bird, fish, insect or beast was cause for wonder on the crew's part, while Khu-Shul chattered on in his strange tongue. The river's lazy current made the rowing no hard thing, and its many bends had provided surprises and new sights with each turn.

After four days of rowing, Iudila began to wonder whether it might have been faster to walk. The serpentine path of the river meant they had rowed several times the distance they had actually gained. For the past three nights, Khu-Shul had promised by hand signal that they would reach Ha-Naab the next day. Those promises were now wearing thin, as were the men's nerves.

The birds would not quit screeching. Fish kept fouling the oar strokes. Bugs drew blood and raised itching welts. And the animals—the wretched beasts seemed to have been created for no other reason than to try to feast on the men or to deny them peace with incessant cries and wails and calls. Every man was sleep-starved, his temper on fine edge. All but Khu-Shul.

The dwarf seemed inured to the sounds of the jungle. He slept peacefully at night, while the others tossed and fidgeted and slapped and cursed. During the day, as the crew rowed, he sat in the prow or walked the narrow length of the boat, threatening to capsize them with every step. Lemuel tried to engage him in conversation, using the Hebrew he had seemed to recognize, but Khu-Shul only pressed his fingers to his lips or clapped his hands over his ears.

Their guide seemed even more animated—and annoying—this morning. Iudila hoped the excitement meant they were nearing their goal. Khu-Shul had awakened before dawn, poked the fire to life, and had a breakfast of smoked fish and peppers ready by the time the men stirred from not-quite-sleeping to not-quite-awake.

The early start had given them a precious hour free from the swarming insects, but with the sun now climbing, that respite had long since passed. Iudila scratched his neck where his ill-timed slap had crushed the bug only after it had lanced him. He dragged his hand in the water to rinse off the blood and bug-gore, then adjusted his oar to steer around yet another god-damned bend.

45

CHAKIN PEERED ACROSS field and river to the city beyond. Ha-Naab glowed in the early morning light, its walls of red sandstone glistening like fresh blood. A mist hovered over the river banks, hiding the water lilies that gave the city its name, and screening the base of the walls so that Ha-Naab seemed to float in the air.

The jungle was silent, the creatures of the night having gone to rest and those of the day not yet awoken. Or perhaps the animals sensed what was to come and had quitted the area. Only the mosquitoes remained, as attested by an occasional slap by one of the men against some spot he had failed to smear with juniper oil.

Thin columns of smoke rose from the city as morning fires came to life. Women in groups of three and four went to the river's edge for their households' daily water.

"That does not look like a city ready for battle," Hul-Balam observed from beside Chakin.

"Perhaps Tok-Ekh was right. In delaying our arrival, we have lulled them into carelessness."

"We shall see in a few moments." The captain signaled his men on either side, and the commands were passed along the line. "Are you ready?" he asked Chakin.

The princess lied with a nod.

Hul-Balam rose with the fluid movement of the jaguar whose pelt he wore. Chakin felt none of the deer's grace as she lurched to her feet, steadied herself against her spear shaft and adjusted her armor. Greaves and gauntlets of thick deerskin protected her shins and forearms, while an apron of heavy peccary hide studded with stones and shells draped over her waist and thighs.

She struggled to breathe against her tight vest, the supple leather quilted with pockets of salt. Hul-Balam had been merciless when he cinched the bindings, squeezing the air from her lungs and further flattening her already small breasts.

"Short breath now is better than no breath later," he had replied to her protest.

Chakin adjusted her padded stone helmet, checked that her pelt and deer's-head mask were in place, and wiped damp palms on her apron. She bit her lip and nodded again, with only slightly more conviction.

Hul-Balam whistled his command and a hundred warriors and their princess stepped out from the cover of the trees.

At first, nothing happened. The fallow *milpah* was littered with last harvest's maize stalks and overlooked melons. Chakin's war party was halfway across the field before a woman looked up from the fog-shrouded riverbank, pointed through the haze and screamed. More women joined in the alarm and—amid the clatter of abandoned gourds and water jars—rushed back into the city.

Hul-Balam raised a fist and the line drew to a halt about a hundred paces from the river.

"Will they muster?" Chakin asked her captain.

"Most likely."

"Should we not advance to the bridge?" She gestured to the rope-and-log construction that spanned the broad river.

Hul-Balam shook his head. "We might prevent them from crossing, but we would become easy targets for hidden archers and huruk-throwers."

Chakin nodded nervously at that. She peered through the distance for any sign of men hidden among the thatched roofs of Ha-Naab. Archers worried her little. Only the best of bowmen could fire an arrow from the city's wall and reach Chakin's line, and the best archers of Ha-Naab had been conscripted into the army of Shukpi. But with a simple throwing stick, even a child could be trained to hurl a huruk—the slender flint-tipped javelin—from the walls to where Chakin now stood.

"Here they come," Hul-Balam said as forty warriors—fewer than half the number from Shukpi—emerged from Ha-Naab's river gate, raced across the rope bridge and formed their line along the Hahshuk's south bank.

Last across the bridge were Chan-Kawak and Tok-Ekh. The Lord of Ha-Naab wore his battle finery of leather armor, stone- and jewel-studded breastplate, and hammered copper helmet with a bright plumage of feathers—red and yellow and green—an arm's span across.

Tok-Ekh had ostensibly returned to the city for last-minute negotiations. He wore no armor, as befitted a servant of the gods. The only addition to his usual costume of breechcloth, shell, and bone was a mask made of bark that formed the image of a witz monster, guardian of the entryways to the Otherworld. Its jaw hung below Tok-Ekh's shoulders, its flame-red tongue lolling over sharpened teeth, ready to consume the hearts of the dead and dying.

Tok-Ekh's soot-blackened face was nearly invisible within the gaping maw, beneath the upturned snout and wrinkled jowls. Eyes of obsidian, enlivened by the sun's strengthening rays, surveyed the battlefield while the mane of black and dark blue plumage danced on the light breeze.

The shaman leaned toward Chan-Kawak and the pair stepped away from Ha-Naab's line, toward the middle of the field.

"Watch for my signal," Hul-Balam told Wuk-Oh. He gestured to Chakin, and princess and warrior went to meet the other pair.

"Greetings, Lady of Shukpi," said the Lord of Ha-Naab with an elaborate bow.

"You honor me with your presence on the field, Lord Chan-Kawak."

"My dear lady, where else would I be on such an auspicious day. The god-seat of Ha-Naab awaits your presence."

Chakin shot a confused glance at Tok-Ekh. The shaman remained silent, his dark eyes inscrutable.

"So you yield to me?"

"My lady, for one such as I, it is fruitless to resist such power as you bring to bear. I am entirely at your mercy." Chan-Kawak's smile and light-hearted tone were at odds with his words of defeat.

"I accept your surrender, then."

Chan-Kawak laughed. "Yes, yes—surrender, indeed. Now, it remains only to secure captives for the offering. How many men do you bring?"

"My men?" Hul-Balam said.

"Why, yes. It is customary for the bride's people to provide offerings for the wedding sacrifice."

"Bride?" Chakin looked to Tok-Ekh, whose expression was still blank.

"There shall be a wedding feast," Hul-Balam said, "but it is I who shall send your men to Shibalba, beginning with you."

The captain raised his war club—a heavy wooden sword inlaid with obsidian blades—but Chakin restrained him with a hand on his wrist.

"I shall marry whom I choose, at the time of my choosing," she said with a stern look at all three men. "Now, Lord Chan-Kawak, I have come to claim the god-seat of Ha-Naab. Do you willingly yield it or must we take it by force?"

The Lord of Ha-Naab made an expression of surprise. He opened his mouth to speak, but instead of words came a wheezing sound followed by a trickle of blood.

"That simplifies things," Tok-Ekh said as Chan-Kawak slid off the shaman's dagger and fell to the ground.

"Princess!" Chakin heard the cry from somewhere in the distance, but she had no time to look for its source.

Tok-Ekh grabbed her wrist. "They have slain Chan-Kawak," he shouted to the men of Ha-Naab as he pulled Chakin toward the northern line. "Kill them!"

Most of Ha-Naab's warriors were too stunned to react, but a few hurled javelins toward the opposing line.

"Lady Chakin," the distant voice again shouted.

Chakin lost her footing, unable to keep up with Tok-Ekh's flight. The shaman dragged her for a few paces, then lost his grip on her wrist. His mask fell off as he tumbled to the ground. He screamed in fury, a cry to match Hul-Balam's battle shout.

"Are you all right, Lady?" the warrior asked as he knelt beside the princess.

Only then did Chakin notice the blood on Hul-Balam's sword. Tok-Ekh looked at them both in pain and rage, one hand clamped over a bloody wrist. He cursed, rose and fled toward the bridge.

"Protect the princess," Hul-Balam shouted to his approaching men, then chased after the shaman.

Chakin looked down to see Tok-Ekh's severed hand still clamped about her wrist. She screamed, shook it off and scrambled away from the grisly thing.

Wuk-Oh and a few other men had reached Chakin by now. Most of the others had held back at their line, while a number of them had even run toward the trees. Shukpi's warriors carried mainly clubs, axes and spears—close-range weapons suited to taking captives, not defending at a distance. The few that carried arrows or huruks launched these at the men of Ha-Naab who now fled with Tok-Ekh across the bridge and through the corbelled vault of the gate.

Hul-Balam was halfway across the bridge when the last of Ha-Naab's men reached the city gate, leaving a dozen of their compatriots fallen on the field. Hul-Balam stopped, shouted a curse at the empty city walls then retreated to the south end of the bridge. He raised his mighty war club and chopped through the ropes of the bridge's mooring. The bridge bucked and swayed with each stroke until Hul-Balam cut the last line. The train of rope and timber slithered down the bank and into the waters of the Hahshuk.

"Princess!"

Chakin at last turned toward the persistent cry, then fell to her knees as tears flooded her eyes.

She opened her arms and Khu-Shul—somehow returned from Shibalba—rushed into her embrace.

46

"THEY TOLD ME you were dead," Chakin said through her tears.

"I was, Lady," Khu-Shul replied. "To be away from you is to be without breath, without life." The dwarf broke his embrace and turned on Hul-Balam. "And you! You and that—that fiend. Traitorous wretches! My lady, they sealed me in a basket and set me on the river to be a meal for crocodiles."

"Small meal, that," the captain muttered, then dropped his head at Chakin's stern look.

"Is it true, what he says?"

"Yes, Lady."

"Yet you helped me against Tok-Ekh."

The captain made no response.

"We will discuss this further, when we return to Shukpi."

"As you wish, my lady." Hul-Balam gave a small bow then shouted at his men. "Stand up, you laggards! Form your lines."

"Uti-La!" Khu-Shul called to a group of men on the shore as Hul-Balam cursed and harried his fighters. "These men saved me, my lady, at great risk to themselves. Be not afraid. They are frightful in appearance and their odor will stop the breath in your nostrils, but they are good men." He lowered his voice and beckoned Chakin to bend close. "And they speak the sacred tongue."

Chakin stared in disbelief at the dwarf, but he nodded insistently.

"Come," he said. "I will introduce you."

"You will not," Hul-Balam declared, placing himself between the princess and the strangers.

"You join forces with a traitor," Khu-Shul said, "but when friends come, you bar their way?"

Hul-Balam glared at the scribe and gave a menacing growl. "If they are friends, why do they come armed? They look like nothing more than thieves and barbarians."

Chakin looked past the captain. The men were indeed armed with blades of foreign material. They were a ragged band, grim looking, with complexions ranging from the shade of tanned leather to charcoal. Their chests were bared, but their lower bodies were covered by thin cotton leggings. All bore scars, the random patterns suggesting they were from battle or punishment rather than sacred ritual. Hair grew from their faces, shorter than Nak-Makah's or Khu-Shul's, but no less shocking. The hairs of their heads were just as short, though on the two darker-skinned men they twisted into tight curls.

All in all, they were a scruffy, dirty, sorry-looking lot.

Except for one.

The one called Uti-La had a thick mane of fiery hair that reminded Chakin of her mother's. Eyes the color of jade sat well spaced on either side of a broad, straight nose. His face bore stubble like the others, but the growth only accentuated the hard cut of his jaw. When the sun struck it, red and copper shone so brightly that it seemed Lord Sun had come to earth.

Indeed, his entire body glowed under Kinich Ahaw's warm gaze, from the broad shoulders and chest, to the sleek, muscled belly. His powerful arms ended in long, elegant fingers that seemed too refined for such a rugged frame. The leggings hung loosely from his slender waist, and Chakin's face grew warm under her deer's-head mask as she imagined what lay beneath the thin cotton.

"My lady?"

Chakin tore her eyes from the glowing stranger, thankful that the mask hid her blushing cheeks.

"Forgive me, Captain. You were saying?"

"Shall we slaughter them now, or bind them and carry them back to Shukpi?"

"I tell you they are friends," Khu-Shul insisted. "You need only speak to them and you will know. Uti-La! Uti-La, speak."

The sun-laced one looked puzzled and spoke to his companions in a strange, stilted language.

"You see? They speak with the tongues of demons," Hul-Balam said. "Let me send them back to Shibalba where they belong."

"Say something, Uti-La. Now!" Khu-Shul gestured strangely, as though at once forbidding and imploring the man to speak.

The copper stranger spoke briefly to one of his men—one with white among the black stubble on head and cheek—then handed him his weapon and stepped in front of the group, hands held to his sides. He opened his mouth hesitantly, then it was as though the breath of the gods flowed through him.

"Bereshith bara Elohim et hashamayim ve'et ha'aretz."

His accent weighed heavily on the words but Chakin could not mistake their meaning.

In the First Time, the gods molded the sky and the land.

47

"UTI-LA! UTI-LA!" Khu-Shul called, then added something Iudila couldn't understand. The dwarf stood next to a young warrior dressed in deerskin and with a deer's head over his face. A larger warrior—dressed as what appeared to be a panther—stood nearer to the pirates, his weapon held at the ready.

"What's he saying?" Iudila asked Lemuel.

"Whatever it is, the big one doesn't like it."

"Uti-La!" Khu-Shul shouted again. The little man covered his mouth and ears, then nodded emphatically and beckoned to Iudila.

"I think he wants you to speak," Lemuel said. "In Hebrew."

"What do I say?"

"The first thing that comes to mind. Just say it fast. The cat-fellow doesn't seem to be in a patient mood. Give me that first." Lemuel took the sword from Iudila and patted his shoulder.

Iudila held his hands to his sides, took a few steps forward and cleared his throat. He started to speak but his mind went blank. He struggled to think of something then took Lemuel's advice and said the first thing.

"In the Beginning, God created the heavens and the earth."

The deer gazed at Iudila from behind its mask. For a moment, no one moved except for a few of the fighters who flicked their weapons nervously. Then the young one gestured for the panther to lower his sword, and stepped forward. A slender hand rose to the mask and pulled away the deer's head.

Iudila's heart seized and his veins filled with honey as the deer transformed not into a boy warrior but into a young woman. A beautiful young woman at that, not much past her fifteenth year, he guessed.

Brown eyes, flecked with green, stared at him with intense curiosity and intelligence. Her nose was long and slender, and a dew of perspiration nestled in the cleft above her full lips. She pulled her hair free of her armor's padded collar to reveal flowing black tresses streaked with hints of auburn.

She stepped up to Iudila, her head cocked to one side as she examined him.

"You speak the priestly tongue," she said, clearly yet haltingly, as one who has not spoken a language for some time.

"The priestly tongue? You mean Hebrew?"

"Hiblu?" she repeated. "It is the tongue of the ancient ones, the first fathers who led our people to this land."

"What land is that?"

She looked at him as one might inspect an imbecile in the street.

"This land." She stamped her foot on the ground. "The land of Sibolat—the Bountiful Land."

"Sibolat?" It was Iudila's turn to repeat the strange word.

"Shiboleth?" Lemuel suggested. "It means 'bounty.' The ancient Gileadites used it as a password at the Jordan's crossing. Their enemies, the Ephraimites, could only pronounce it as Siboleth. Shiboleth—Siboleth—Sibolat."

The young woman looked from Iudila to Lemuel.

"Are you all priests?"

"We are but humble sailors," Iudila replied. "Only my uncle and I speak Hebrew—the tongue of your priests. It is also the language of our ancestors, our ancient ones."

"And where do you come from, humble sailor?"

Despite her unease with the language, there was no missing the irony in her tone. Iudila grinned. "We live upon the water but our homeland lies across a vast sea, many days to the east."

The young woman eyed him curiously. "And beyond this sea, is there another water, protected by two great pillars?"

"Yes." Iudila could not hide the surprise in his voice. "My own land contains one of those pillars, called Calpe."

The cat-warrior said something and pointed across the river, where men from the city were reeling in the fallen bridge. Spearmen lined the walls and jeered at the young woman's small band. The panther spoke insistently and the woman nodded.

"We must go," she told Iudila. "Khu-Shul says that you and your men are friends, so you may join us if you wish. My father will be eager to meet you and speak with you."

"Your father?"

"Uti-Chan, Lord of Shukpi. My name is Chakin, and you, Uti-La of the Sea, shall be my guest."

48

"WHEN DO WE SEARCH for the treasure?"

Thanos tugged at Iudila's elbow and whispered in his ear. It was a senseless precaution, as the man's Greek was as incomprehensible to the strangers as their native tongue was to the sailors.

"We should wait," Iudila suggested. "We'll never find the treasure on our own, so we'll need their help. And to gain their help, we have to earn their trust. We must prove ourselves good guests and worthy allies before we can impose on them."

The Greek muttered a curse but nodded his acceptance before falling back to join the rest of the crew.

They walked along a broad road cut through the jungle in a straight line as far as Iudila could see. The path reminded him of the Roman roads that yet survived in Spania. Instead of the cobbles of those highways, however, this road was paved with great slabs of stone so closely fitted that no gap was seen between them.

Also unlike the Roman roads, there were no chariots, nor even horses upon them. They walked in a wide column, a troop of spearmen in the lead, followed by an eight-man litter bearing Lady Chakin and Khu-Shul. Iudila and his men trailed behind, while a strong guard led by the surly warrior brought up the rear.

From time to time, Khu-Shul leaned out of the litter and beckoned for Iudila to walk alongside so the princess could question him about some aspect or another of his journey. Much as Iudila enjoyed the interviews, it was a relief that they were as brief and intermittent as they were.

Lady Chakin had removed her armor of quilted leather and now wore only a linen skirt that did little to hide the sculpture of her legs. While her long hair and strings of shells and beads offered some concealment of her breasts, her flat, supple belly was bare. When she tilted her head or gathered her hair over one shoulder, it was all Iudila could do to keep his eyes on hers, rather than on the small, firm breasts that peeked through the necklaces.

"Were you born upon the sea?" she asked him in one interview.

Iudila laughed. "No, Lady. The land of my birth is called Baetica, in a country called Spania."

She tried the words and gave a small grimace, as though they tickled her tongue.

"And your family? They are still in Baetica?"

"No, Lady. My mother died giving birth to me. My father died when I was a boy."

"My mother died in childbirth, also—with my brother. It is a hard thing to be without a mother. Doubly hard to be without a father too, I suspect. How did he die?"

Iudila looked away as he tried to think of something, anything other than the truth. Chakin's eyes bored into him, as to his very soul. He knew there could be no dissimulation where she was concerned. Strangely, that seemed as it should be.

"He rebelled against the king and his chief priest. He slew the king with his own hands but his fellow conspirators betrayed him. The king's son was set on the throne in his place, the priest was replaced by his brother, and I became an orphan."

A pained look veiled Chakin's face, and Iudila thought she might cry for sympathy.

"Your father dared shed the king's blood?" It was horror, not pity, that laced her words.

Iudila's shoulders drooped and his head bowed—in part from shame, but more from the sudden change in Chakin's voice. "He—well, yes, but—"

"You may go," the princess said.

He started to protest but Khu-Shul silenced him with a shake of his head. Iudila chanced a last look at Chakin—now cold and distant—then fell back with his men.

"No," he said, before Thanos could open his mouth to question him. "No treasure."

49

IUDILA CURSED YET AGAIN as his head bounced off a paving stone. He and his men were trussed up like wild boars taken in the hunt. Their wrists, knees and ankles had been bound together, a pole threaded through the lashings and supported by spearmen at each end. The difference in length between foreleg and arms put the pirates in a head-low position, and Iudila's head ached with the pressure of the pooling blood.

It was worse for Dingha and Brehanu, whose bulk made the poles sag, causing their shoulders and heads to scrape along the stone pavers. It might be worse, Iudila thought. At least they hadn't been field-dressed. Yet.

More painful than the physical stress was the sudden change in status. With one slip of the tongue, Iudila had fallen from revered guest to bound captive. Clearly, the honor accorded to those who spoke the priestly tongue did not extend to the sons of king-slayers.

"I have spoken with Lady Chakin."

Iudila turned his head to see Khu-Shul walking beside him. The dwarf's gait was made awkward as he stooped to speak into Iudila's ear while trying not to step on the Goth's long hair that dragged along the ground. It took a moment for Iudila to recognize the words.

"You speak Hebrew?" Iudila said.

Khu-Shul placed his fingers to his lips and shook his head. "It is forbidden to all but royalty and the priests." A shrug. "But one cannot help what one hears, no?"

Iudila managed a grin. "What did she say? Are we to be butchered?"

"If Hul-Balam has his way. He has to redeem himself after throwing in his lot with that traitor Tok-Ekh. The best way to do that is to fabricate an even greater treachery. Did your father really kill a king?"

"Yes, but I was only a boy. I hardly even remember him."

"That matters little. By tradition, the sins of the father accrue to his sons, even to the third and fourth generations. Hul-Balam would have been within his rights to cut you down on the spot. Only your knowledge of—Hiblu?"

"Hebrew."

"Yes. Only your knowledge of the priestly tongue has spared you and your men. The princess will present you to Lord Uti-Chan. Together they will decide your fate."

"What sort of man is this king of yours?"

"A noble man," Khu-Shul said without hesitation, "and a great lord. If you have any hope, it is in his justice and mercy. He is—"

A voice bellowed from the rear of the caravan. Iudila recognized the harsh tones of the warrior captain. Khu-Shul looked up. In that moment he stepped on Iudila's hair. Iudila shouted in pain, Khu-Shul stumbled, the rear porter tripped over him, and the foursome fell to the ground amid polyglot curses.

"Are you all right?" Khu-Shul asked.

"No worse than I've been," Iudila said.

"You're bleeding."

"It's nothing."

The spearmen got to their feet and hoisted Iudila's carrying pole roughly to their shoulders. Khu-Shul shouted at them in his native language then stooped to examine Iudila, turning the Goth's head from side to side. Iudila felt a chill when the dwarf touched the back of his neck.

"You bear a mark," Khu-Shul said, his voice hoarse.

"We all do. It is the way of seafaring men."

"Yours is different. I know this mark."

Hul-Balam shouted again.

"I must go," Khu-Shul said, excitement in his voice. "Be of good cheer, my friend. I will speak again with Lady Chakin, and this"—he tapped the tattoo on Iudila's nape—"this will speak for itself."

Iudila craned his neck to see the little man scamper ahead and pull himself up into the palanquin. Whatever the import of his tattoo, Iudila hoped it might serve to release him and his men, but the curtains closed behind the dwarf and stayed closed.

Iudila let his head fall back, and stifled a curse as he smacked against the pavement. His captors laughed and jostled the pole so that head met stone twice more. Iudila clenched his teeth and held his peace, then settled into his bonds as he swung and bounced toward his fate.

50

CROWDS LINED THE ROAD—Sakbe, Khu-Shul had called it—cheering and waving palm fronds and brightly colored cloths to welcome home their princess and her warriors.

Lady Chakin had donned her battle array and now stood in the palanquin, its curtains drawn back so she appeared in all her martial glory. The cheers grew louder at the sight of the pole-carriers bearing their captives. When Iudila and his men came clearly into view, those cheers quickly faded, and the rolling wave crest of jubilation fell into a trough of stunned silence.

Naked children gawped and pointed at Iudila and his men, the boldest among them trailing along with the procession. Lemuel and Thanos garnered some curiosity, but most of the stares were for Brehanu's and Dingha's dark skin and curly hair. Iudila's hair drew its own share of attention.

A young boy reached out a tentative hand, as though fearful the flame-red locks might burn him. When he came away unscathed, he signaled to his friends. The pack of brats yanked and tugged on Iudila's hair until the pole-bearers kicked them away.

Iudila lost count of the dozens, hundreds of people lining the road, their numbers rivaling the busiest of market days at Tingis or his own Corduba. When the parade turned a corner, the host of spectators who greeted them made any previous crowd he had seen seem like a small social gathering. His bearers carried him between a pair of massive stone slabs, set upright and carved with row upon row of indecipherable figures. The pillars were crowned with fearsome beasts that seemed as though they might at any moment shed their stone veneers, swoop down upon an unwanted visitor and make a short meal of him.

Past the foreboding marker posts, they entered what Iudila took to be the city of Shukpi itself. The people cheered even more loudly than those on the outskirts, offering flowers and incense rather than palm leaves. The dress of this crowd matched the increased richness of their tribute. Instead of naked children, these were dressed in brightly colored breechcloths. The plain costumes of the poorer men and women gave way to richly dyed skirts of fine linen, decorated with garish strings of feathers, shells and beads.

Around another bend, the procession entered an arena. Massive stone risers flanked the field, their rows crowded with celebrants. The warriors split into two columns and positioned themselves around the perimeter of the field.

Lady Chakin's litter-bearers carried her to the far end where a high platform stood. The pole-bearers arrayed Iudila and his men behind the princess, and Hul-Balam strutted from one captive to the next. Beneath the platform, musicians beat drums, blew on conch shell horns and plucked stringed instruments that sounded like cats being strangled.

The band went quiet as Hul-Balam stepped forward to salute those on the platform. The warrior then shouted in turns at the prisoners, to the crowd, and presumably to his gods. By the time he finished, the warrior had stirred up the crowd and the band to a clamor that pounded through Iudila's chest until he feared his heart would rupture.

Atop the platform, a majestic figure rose and strode toward the edge with slow, regal steps. He wore a white turban—not the rounded domes of the desert-dwellers Iudila had seen in Mauretania, but more resembling a stepped, inverted cone. A carved jade stone decorated the turban, and spools the size of Iudila's thumb pierced the man's earlobes. His muscled chest was bare, as were his feet. Bands of shell and stone wrapped his ankles and wrists, with a kilt of blue-green linen around his waist. From his dress and pride of place, Iudila knew this could only be Uti-Chan, Lord of Shukpi.

The king stood at the platform's edge and cast his gaze over the crowd, the prisoners, his warriors. Only when his eyes passed over Lady Chakin did Iudila notice a flicker of emotion.

After basking in the crowd's noise for a time, the king raised his arms. The audience and musicians instantly fell quiet, so that Iudila could hear the click of the shell bracelets that slid along the king's arms. As Iudila's heart had pounded with the din of the crowd, it seized with its silence. He held his breath as he waited for his fate to unfold.

51

CHAKIN BRACED HERSELF. Even with the litter-bearers' steps in unison, the palanquin swayed and dipped like a raft on a storm-swept lake. She could show no weakness or lack of composure, so she planted her feet, bent her knees, and did her best to appear motionless as the litter rocked and lurched beneath her.

Hul-Balam had sent runners ahead to Shukpi to announce their return. The messengers must have paused at every settlement along the way to spread the news. Chakin had seldom seen so many people, and their noise deafened her. Shukpi itself was home to more than two thousand people, and the outlying towns and villages hosted at least that many again. All of them, it seemed, had turned out for her triumphal return with the sacrificial prisoners. Instead, she feared, they would witness her defeat and shame as a warrior.

The crowd along the roadside was exultant, the spearmen proud, and Hul-Balam resplendent in his battle dress. Khu-Shul capered alongside the palanquin, and the crowd marveled at his return from the Underworld. Men, women, and children alike stared in awe at the strange-skinned captives, then redoubled their cheers at the martial skills of their princess, who had defeated the forces of Shibalba itself.

Only Chakin seemed to recognize this as the culmination of her failures. She had believed her uncle's lies, had agreed to his conspiracy against her own father, had even played a part in the attempted murder of her closest friend and advisor.

Had it not been for the arrival of Uti-La and his men, Tok-Ekh's plan might well have succeeded. Khu-Shul would be dead, and Chakin would now be a queen of rebels. The farmers who cheered her would instead be cursing her name as they prepared to go to war.

The real heroes, the men who had saved her father's kingdom—saved Chakin from herself—were now strung up like peccaries taken in the hunt, targets of the jeers and scorn of her people. Chakin breathed a prayer of thanks to Sak-Ishik for the mask that hid her emotions. She vowed that somehow, at any cost, she would make this right.

Where the Sakbe turned away from the river, the familiar jaguar guardians sat atop the stelae that guarded the city's entrance. Their stone eyes, carved by Khu-Shul's grandfather, seemed to narrow as they sensed Chakin's perfidy, and she squeezed her own eyes shut to avoid their accusing glares. Only when she felt the turn into the ballcourt did she again dare to open her eyes.

Her warriors lined the edges of the field. The crowds, who normally cheered their favorite players in the ball games, now acclaimed the princess who had almost torn the kingdom in two. The litter-bearers carried her to the south end of the court where her father waited in regal splendor. The crowd quietened enough for Chakin to hear the band that played beneath the viewing stand, while Hul-Balam raised his voice to the heavens.

"Revered Uti-Chan, Lord of Shukpi, heir to the House of Kinich Yash Khuk-Moh, Master of the Southward Land of Sibolat, he who breathes fire into the mouth of the sky. Your warriors have returned."

The crowd renewed their cheers as Hul-Balam strutted along the stands, jerking his arms skyward to encourage their shouting.

"In the ancient tradition and to the glory of the gods, your fighting men, led by Chakin, Lady of the Two Suns"—more cheering—"Daughter of Yash-Ahaw, Mother of Shukpi, and twelfth in the line of the great Khuk-Moh—"

The people shouted in a frenzy of religious and civic fervor. Hul-Balam soaked in the adulation before continuing, this time in a low voice that commanded attention.

"As did her ancestor Yashwak, father of Shukpi's First Lord, our lady led her forces to the very gates of Shibalba, there to reclaim one who had been untimely taken, the worthy scribe Khu-Shul of the House of Chuwen."

Again the crowd burst into cheers as Hul-Balam motioned toward Khu-Shul. The scribe glanced up at Chakin with a nervous expression, which he quickly changed to one of good humor. He bowed toward the royal viewing stand then raced around the palanquin while the crowd applauded him.

Hul-Balam strutted toward the prisoners.

"There in the heart of the Underworld, our lady entered battle with the dead legions. With her own sword she freed her friend and servant. One by one, she struck down the minions of Hun-Cameh, Dark Lord of Shibalba, and sent their souls back to our own Middle World, where they clothed themselves in these hideous forms."

A wave of jeers rolled over the crowd. Hul-Balam now turned on the prisoners.

"Foul beasts of the abyss! You pollute the very air with your breath. You corrupt the light of Kinich Ahaw merely by letting his rays fall upon you. The ground beneath you is soiled by your every step."

The band played more and more loudly as the captain stalked to the foot of the viewing stand and lifted his face and arms skyward.

"Great Lord Sun—you who grant light and life—I call upon you. I call upon the spirits of my father and mother, and upon the spirits of their fathers and mothers before them, back to the First Time. It is Hul-Balam who speaks—he who has slain the mighty jaguar, he who has climbed the great western mountain, he who has slaughtered a hundred-hundred enemies. Hear my words and bear witness that they are true. This very Chakin, Lady of Shukpi, has done all these things. Already she has shown her piety before the gods, her wisdom in the seat of justice. On her behalf, I now offer unto Uti-Chan—Lord of Shukpi, friend and brother to the gods—these captives of her sword, proof of her valor in battle."

The people raised their voices to the heavens, and Chakin thought the pressure of the noise would crush her. Hul-Balam's voice—trained on the field of battle—yet managed to rise even above this din.

"Long life to Uti-Chan and to Lady Chakin. May the gods favor the kingdom of Shukpi, and may the line of Khuk-Moh Ahaw reign forever!"

The roar of the crowd, the shrill of the horns, the beat of the drums, and the groan of the strings—all combined to shake the very stones of the ballcourt.

The palanquin trembled in resonance with the cheer and Chakin struggled to keep her balance.

Uti-Chan rose from his jaguar-skin cushion and stepped to the edge of the platform. He slowly surveyed the crowd, the warriors, and their captain. His eyes lingered on Chakin, and only the sanctuary of her mask kept her from turning and fleeing the look of pained accusation she read there. Her shoulders dipped when he released his gaze and swept his eyes across the prisoners. The king raised his arms toward the heavens, the noise instantly ceased, and Chakin nearly collapsed into the silence.

"Well spoken, Captain. Your achievements are well known to us. We accept your testimony on behalf of the princess. Lady Chakin, step forth."

The litter-bearers paced forward and lifted the palanquin off their shoulders, bringing Chakin level with the platform. She stepped toward her father, fighting the urge to fall to her knees, confess all and beg his forgiveness. She shuddered as he laid his hands on her shoulders and turned her toward the crowd.

"Na Chakin, Lady of the Two Suns, you have been acclaimed Mistress of the Land Southward. You have proven yourself Mother of the Poor and Tower of Justice. By the testimony of our trusted servant, Hul-Balam, we now declare you Champion of the Field and Sojourner of the Halls of Shibalba."

Chakin marveled that the people had any voice left, but they again roared their approval. Uti-Chan stepped back, raised his arms, turned his face skyward and joined his voice with the others', calling for the gods' attention.

"Lady Chakin," he at last continued, and her heart froze in her breast at what she knew was to come. "The gods have favored you, granting strength to your arm and swiftness to your sword. As proof of their blessing and affirmation of your place as champion, these prisoners are placed before us. Their souls are given into your care. What will you have done with them?"

The crowd went silent in anticipation of her verdict. Tradition dictated that the captives taken in battle be tested in the ballgame, and the losers' hearts given to the gods. The men she had previously delivered to the gods had been foreigners and innocent. These men, too, were foreigners, but heroes. Still, she had succumbed to Hul-Balam's fears and suspicions. The captain had taken the men unawares, beaten and clubbed them senseless, then bound them like animals for the journey back to Shukpi.

If what Khu-Shul told her of the mark on Uti-La's neck was true, his being here might be of greater importance than she could imagine. Yet she must give these captives—these men—over to the gods if she were to keep with tradition and satisfy her people.

Her father cleared his throat and Chakin felt the weight of thousands of eyes upon her.

She tried to swallow but her mouth was suddenly dry. She started to speak but the only sound to come out was that of a mewling jaguar kit. Playing for time, she shot her hands toward the ground then slowly raised her arms and her face skyward, bringing her fingers together to form the sign of the sun.

Sak-Ishik, give me voice, she silently prayed, then lowered her hands toward Iudila and his men, and said the words.

52

AS THE KING SPOKE, a surge of energy flowed through Iudila. It was as if the words entered his ears, coursed directly to his heart, and from there radiated to every part of his body. Other than Chakin's name, he understood none of the speech. The power in Uti-Chan's voice was equally foreign, while at the same time hauntingly familiar. Where the warrior captain had commanded attention, the king seemed to invite, coax, even seduce his audience to listen.

The people made not a sound, so enraptured were they by their king's words. Iudila was every bit as captivated.

When the king finished his speech—as brief as it was powerful—the movement of hundreds of eyes was almost audible as they shifted to Chakin. Though Iudila could not see the princess from his position, her features had been etched into his memory over the past few days. In his mind's eye, he saw the uncertainty in her brow, a nervous tic of her cheek, a lingering pout on her lips as she moistened them with her tongue.

"Gabriel, Guardian of the West, be our aid."

Even as Iudila whispered the words, Chakin jerked her arms downward, slowly raised them over her head then gestured toward Iudila and his men. After a slight hesitation, she spoke.

The words were in her native tongue, but they rang bright and clear across the arena. They were shortly followed by a great inrush of breath from the crowd.

The captain's body went rigid, his warriors looked dumbfounded, and Khu-Shul shifted from foot to foot. Uti-Chan took a small step forward, but Chakin gestured him back then spoke again. Her voice carried above the murmur that filled the arena and it soon stilled the crowd. She lacked the power of her father's voice, but the seed of it was there.

When she finished speaking, the crowd remained silent. Chakin turned to her father, who gave the slightest nod of his turbaned head. She stepped from the platform onto her palanquin, and her bearers gently lowered it so that, without missing a stride, she stepped off the far end directly in front of Iudila's pole-bearers. She spoke a word and the men eased him to the ground.

Iudila gave a groan of relief as the weight was taken off his bound wrists and legs. The tingle in his hands shot through his whole body when Chakin drew a dagger from its sheath behind her back and stepped toward him.

"Peace. Be still," she said in Hebrew, then slid the blade through the bindings.

Iudila's limbs fell heavily to the ground. Between the pain of the beatings and the stress of being bound to the pole for two days, Iudila's muscles refused to obey as he tried to rise. Chakin gave a command to her men. They picked up the Goth between them, draping a flaccid arm around each of their necks.

Khu-Shul rushed to Iudila while the princess freed the rest of the captives.

"It worked," he exclaimed. "She listened."

"What worked? Listened to what?"

"Your mark." Khu-Shul tapped the back of his neck. "The gods must favor you to give you such a sign. Expect to speak with the king soon."

Before Iudila could press for more information, Chakin gave a command to her captain. The warrior bristled but offered no protest. He made an elaborate bow toward the king, then growled an order to his men. He led them and the former captives past the viewing stand and out of the arena.

The hum of the crowd and the sound of the king's closing speech quickly faded behind the odd caravan of princess and dwarf, warriors and sailors.

A broad, stone-faced platform loomed ahead of them, three times the height of a man and at least a hundred paces across. Rather than climbing the wide steps to the summit, Chakin led the men around the broad base, where the path met a flagstone road that fronted the even longer side of the platform. They passed numerous buildings—some of dry-stacked stone with thatched roofs, others of dressed blocks with roofs of stone slabs.

At length, they came to a low, plaster-faced building, its walls dotted with openings from which drifted aromatic smoke. Chakin motioned for her men to assist the sailors inside. She stopped the pair who aided Iudila and gave a curt command to her captain.

Hul-Balam's jaws bulged and his nostrils flared with the ignominy of whatever the orders were. He snapped an order at his two remaining men and stalked toward Iudila. He stared down a broad, hooked nose at the Goth, his black eyes radiating contempt.

Iudila stared casually back at the warrior. The captain's lips peeled back in a silent snarl, exposing bright, sharpened teeth. He shoved one of his men away, hooked Iudila's arm across his broad shoulders then snapped at the other man, who fled after his companion. Chakin gave a slight nod, said something to Khu-Shul then disappeared into the building.

The dwarf came alongside Iudila, while the captain hauled him farther along the road.

"My men?" Iudila said.

"They will be cared for here. We are taking you to the royal palace."

"Why him?" Iudila jerked his head toward the captain.

"Hul-Balam is Lord Uti-Chan's most trusted warrior, for whatever that is worth."

The warrior glared at the little man at the sound of his name, but Khu-Shul ignored him.

"Only the greatest nobles or the king's most trusted advisors are permitted within the palace grounds."

Iudila was taken aback. "And I am to be allowed there?"

"Lady Chakin's orders. I must make preparations but I will see you soon." Khu-Shul ran ahead before Iudila could question him further.

"What do you make of all this?" Iudila asked the captain in his native Gothic.

The warrior just grunted, tightened his grip on the near-cripple, and hurried his pace along the roadway.

"That's what I thought."

53

IUDILA HADN'T BEEN SURE what to expect.

The palaces in Spania were generally artifacts from the great Roman builders, marble edifices that had been erected at least three centuries before. Where these had fallen into disrepair, wooden halls had been added on to the still serviceable portions of the original buildings, or built adjacent to those that were no longer good for anything but a quarry heap.

Iudila had heard of the grand palaces of Rome and Constantinople. These magnificent structures had vaulted domes that soared heavenward. They were paved with alabaster and adorned with the finest silk.

The palace of Uti-Chan matched none of these. Grand in its own scale, it was more of a compound, a cluster of interconnected stone buildings of varying sizes, grouped around several sun-drenched plazas. A high wall surrounded the royal residence, and Hul-Balam led Iudila through a narrow gate.

They passed a garden humming with bees and fragrant with fruit and herbs. Across a paved courtyard with a large pond in its center, they came at last to one of the smaller buildings on the periphery. Without ceremony, the warrior dropped Iudila onto a reed mat spread across a stone bench, then turned and ducked back out the low doorway.

No sooner had he left than a plump, middle-aged woman stepped through an interior doorway. Shock flashed across her face at the sight of the light-skinned, red-haired, swollen-limbed sailor.

Iudila imagined his expression matched hers as he stared at the tattooed, puncture-scarred, chisel-toothed woman. Used-up breasts rested atop her round belly. The only show of modesty was a narrow strip of blue, green and yellow cloth that escaped from between her thighs and was secured by a similar band wrapped around the approximation of her waist.

The woman's shock was quickly replaced by a look of matronly concern. Iudila distantly recalled a similar look on the face of Claudia, his childhood nurse—a look that had generally been reserved for when he came home covered with mud from the fields or forests or caves. The woman clucked her tongue in the manner of those accustomed to tending imbeciles and small children, and she promptly fell into her role.

She raked through Iudila's hair in search of vermin and, finding none, commenced a more thorough examination. Before Iudila could protest, she loosened the cinch of his trousers and stripped away the thin cloth. Her eyes went wide, and she raised her hands to her mouth to stifle a scream as she stared between his legs.

She pointed and gabbled something in her native language. Fearing some damage he wasn't aware of, Iudila looked toward the area in question but found nothing amiss. He smiled and shrugged, and curiosity replaced the woman's horror. She started to speak, then stopped and signed her question.

It took a few repetitions of the phallic gestures before Iudila understood that she had never before seen a man with a circumcision. "It's the way of my people." He knew she couldn't understand his words, and he wasn't about to try to explain the procedure with hand signals, so he again shrugged and smiled.

The woman looked at him dubiously but knelt and continued her examination. She took a moment to examine his unshrouded penis fore and aft, clucked in approbation, then proceeded to survey the rest of his nether regions, without regard to modesty or gentleness. Apparently satisfied that— missing foreskin aside—all was well, she hoisted him onto unsteady legs and helped him through the interior doorway.

Like the outer room, the inner chamber's walls were ringed with clear-burning candles and lined by a row of stone benches. But where the outer floor held a fire pit, this one was inset with a large, stone-lined basin of water. Steam rose from the surface, filling the air with an herbal fragrance.

Iudila winced as his toes met the hot water. The woman would brook no resistance, and dragged him into the cauldron. Helpless, Iudila knelt, yelped as buttocks and bollocks met the scalding water, then settled onto his backside.

The woman used a gourd to ladle water over Iudila's hair, then applied an ointment that made his skin first tingle, then burn as she rubbed it into his scalp. With a boar's-hair brush, she applied a similar treatment to the rest of his body from nape to sole, heedless of his rope burns or the strained joints and muscles.

By the time she finished her brutal ministrations, Iudila had acclimated to the water and longed to steep in its warm embrace. The woman had other plans, though, and she gestured for him to stand in the murky water.

She climbed to an edge of the basin where, from her elevated position, she was almost level with Iudila. She turned him by his shoulders to face away from her, draped a coarse linen towel over his head and scoured his already raw skin. She helped him out of the basin and led him to one of the benches. This one was covered with thick animal pelts, rather than the rough-woven mat of the bench in the outer room.

The woman gestured for Iudila to lie facedown. She lit a taper from one of the candles and carried the fire to a small brazier charged with rich aromatics. By the time the incense reached Iudila's nostrils, he had sunken deep into the soft furs. His eyes fell shut and he scarcely noticed as the woman murmured something and patted his head.

A sharp sting in the middle of Iudila's back roused him. He cursed as he jolted up and spun around to defend himself, then screamed as his back met the stone wall and a hundred more stabs registered along his spine.

"Be still."

The voice was soft but commanding, the words in Hebrew, though it took a moment for them to register.

"What have you done to me?" Iudila demanded. "Where did she go?"

Chakin reached out her hand, darted her eyes downward, then eased Iudila back into a prone position.

"Who? Kehmut?"

"The old woman. She was just here."

Chakin laughed, a charming, soothing sound that almost made Iudila forget the pain that coursed down his back.

"You've been asleep for two days. Much as Kehmut was taken with you, she does have other duties to attend."

"Two days?" Iudila winced at another sting. "What are you doing?"

The princess handed him a sharp lancet—its tip wet with blood—and continued her work.

"The spines of the stingray," she explained, and held a bowl of foul-smelling unguent under Iudila's nose. "We dip the ends in this and the needles carry healing power to the body."

"It's not my back that's injured," Iudila protested, then cried again in pain. "At least it wasn't before."

"Not all the barbs have been removed," Chakin said without apology. "They sometimes stick in the skin. And the needles do not need to penetrate the place of injury to bring healing. From along the spine, rivers of energy flow to the rest of the body. For example, a needle inserted here"—Iudila grunted through clenched teeth at a sting near his hip—"will bring relief to the lower leg. Do your people know nothing of medicine?"

"It would seem not," Iudila said. "Tell me of my men."

"They did not squirm as much as you." Another sting.

"You're doing that on purpose."

"Your men are resting now. The older one—Lemuel? He fared worse than the others, but he should be fine in a few more days. I noticed his—" She tapped her forehead just below the hairline.

"His scars? I'm afraid that was partly my doing." Iudila explained about the aborted scalping.

"Our legends say my *chak-chit*—my ancestor—had similar scars."

"Was he a Jew, too?" Iudila said with a rueful laugh.

"A what?"

Iudila shook his head. "No matter. It's a long story."

Chakin removed the last of the stingers and smeared some of the balm onto her hands. Iudila fought a shiver as she ran them down his spine and worked the ointment into his muscles. Iudila had given little thought to his nakedness while Kehmut bathed him. At Chakin's touch, though, he felt as Adam must have after his eyes were opened and he truly saw Eve for the first time. He wanted to slither away, to cover himself, but he also wanted to suffer her touch forever. Since there was nothing he could do to hide himself from her, he turned his face toward the wall and tried to relax under the pressure of her hands.

"What is to become of me and my men?" he asked.

"Whatever you wish," came the reply in a deep, sonorous voice that was decidedly not Chakin's.

Iudila turned toward the unexpected voice, but—given the effect of Chakin's touch—thought it best not to rise.

"How fares our guest, Little Bunny?" Uti-Chan said, standing behind his daughter.

Iudila's breath faltered as Chakin flushed at the nickname and her walnut skin turned an intoxicating bronze.

"He will survive, I think."

"Good. It would not do to lose so honored a guest." To Iudila the king said, "May I?" With strong but gentle hands, the king turned Iudila's head toward the wall, swept back his long hair, and thumbed the tattoo on the back of his neck. "It is even as Khu-Shul said. I offer you my sincere regret at the poor manner of your reception. If you will be so gracious as to bide a while with us, I shall amend each wrong with a thousand kindnesses."

"You are most generous, but no regret is needed. It is my men and I who are indebted as your guests."

Uti-Chan smiled and nodded. "See to him well, Daughter. When you are restored, Uti-La, it would be a kindness if you would permit me an audience."

"The pleasure would be mine."

The king smiled, nodded, and withdrew as silently as he had arrived.

"You will not tell him, will you?" Chakin rasped when her father had gone.

"Tell him what?" Iudila was struck by the fear in her voice, the glistening of her eyes.

"What I did. How I failed him. I will tell him myself, just not yet. You will not tell him?"

Iudila couldn't fathom what she was talking about, but he shook his head and smiled. "I won't say a word."

The princess instantly brightened and smeared more of the stinking ointment on his back.

"Good. Now stop squirming."

54

CHAKIN STEPPED INTO the observatory where her father reclined in one of the viewing seats. A cigar dangled from his fingers, its tip a bright red star fallen from the heavens.

"Father?"

Uti-Chan looked up and smiled, as though he had expected her.

"Father, I—" Chakin's throat clutched at the words and she fell to her knees. "Oh, Ahpa, forgive me." She bowed before the king, face to the ground, fingers tearing at the grass as her body shook with sobs.

Uti-Chan knelt, took Chakin by the hand and raised her chin.

"Hush, Little Bunny," he whispered, and pulled her to his breast.

"Ahpa, I'm so sorry."

"All is well, little one," he said, and stroked her hair, freshly anointed with his own tears.

When she could cry no more, Chakin sat back on her heels.

Uti-Chan smiled and dried her cheek with his thumb.

"You're so much like your mother."

"I'm nothing like her. She was strong and faithful and wise—"

"And impatient and hot-headed," Uti-Chan said. "And she, too, possessed my heart fully."

"How can you say that? I've acted horribly. I've been cruel to Sak-Chih and Imish. I—I even thought to rebel against you."

"Tell me," the king said softly. His face remained neutral as Chakin told of Tok-Ekh's plan to seat her at Ha-Naab. His eyes flashed with anger at the murder of Chan-Kawak, but the emotion passed with a blink. When Chakin had confessed all, Uti-Chan drew on his cigar. He held the smoke for a long moment before releasing the cloud into the night air.

"When I was a boy," he said, "I helped your grandfather inaugurate our temple."

"Yes, Father, I know the story." Chakin was puzzled at why he should bring up such a mundane subject.

"No, you do not. Have you never wondered at the temple's walls?"

"The walls?" Chakin shrugged. Where most of Shukpi's plaster buildings were naturally white, the temple was stained a deep red, like the mineral used to paint the bodies of the dead. "Are they not burnished with cinnabar?"

"My father captured hundreds of slaves for the building of the temple," Uti-Chan said, his voice flat. "For a year they labored to haul the great blocks of limestone to the temple mount and stack them into place. When it came time to dress the building, my father chose a slave each morning to provide the dye for the plaster."

Uti-Chan's hand trembled as he raised the cigar to his lips and drew on it, the red glow reflected in his glistening eyes.

"While guards held the slave down," he continued, smoke streaming between his lips, "I tugged on his hair to stretch his neck, and my father slit his throat over the tub of plaster. It took the span of a moon to make enough plaster to cover the temple. I was six."

Chakin laid a hand on her father's knee and looked into his moist eyes, but he would not meet hers. He looked only to the heavens, as though he might find peace there.

"On the day of dedication," he went on, his voice husky, "the remaining slaves were herded up to the second level and onto the upper platform. My father had a cauldron set there, with a conduit running to a cistern deep below the temple to serve the Earth Mother. The sacrifice went on for hours, my hands so thick with blood I could scarcely grip their hair by the end. Even Shmukaneh must have had her fill, for her cistern overflowed. Blood ran down the platform and onto the plaza. And the people . . ."

The king's voice faltered.

"It's all right, Ahpa." Chakin tried to console him, but he shook his head.

"It is not all right," he said. "When blood is taken without purpose, it changes people. While my father called on his gods, the crowd danced in blood. Children played in spilled life as they should only do in mud puddles. Our people—my people were reduced to nothing more than crazed savages that day, and it was my doing."

"You were only a boy."

"I was old enough to know it was wrong, yet I did nothing." Uti-Chan fixed his eyes on Chakin's. "I watched as Tok-Ekh increased his influence over you, and I did nothing. The council usurped my authority—not only as Lord but as a father—and I did nothing. I sought only to keep peace, to avoid conflict. I gave in to their demands rather than standing for the right and seeking your wishes. The wrong you have done is only what I caused to happen. Will you forgive me?"

Chakin's throat was tight, and she could only nod.

"Come, sit." Uti-Chan raised her by the hand and led her to the viewing benches. "We have much to restore, you and I. With our neighbors, with the council, with one another. Let us start here. If it is not too late, Lady of Shukpi, tell me what you wish."

Chakin leaned back on her bench, fixed her eyes on the sign of the Peccaries, and told him.

55

"YOU ARE RESTING WELL?"

Uti-Chan ducked below the tree's branches, and Iudila stood to greet him. The king was the tallest man among his people, but still half a head shorter than Iudila.

"Well enough, thank you. I would like to see my men, though."

The king smiled. "A true leader puts the welfare of his people before his own. I hope you will trust me when I tell you your men are being treated well. You will see them soon. Please, sit."

Uti-Chan gestured toward the reed mat beneath the tree, plucked a piece of pear-shaped fruit and sat opposite Iudila. He moved with fluid grace, his hair was thick, his skin taut. Only the webs of care at the corners of his eyes hinted at his age, which Iudila guessed to be nearer fifty than forty, a rare age indeed.

Uti-Chan cut the fruit with a knife, twisted the halves apart and handed one to Iudila.

Iudila took the fruit, sniffed at it and was rewarded with a delicate floral smell. He followed the king's lead and scraped out the cluster of black seeds. He bit into the soft flesh and wiped at the thick juice that ran down his chin.

"Delicious."

"It is called papaya. It settles the stomach, and the juice is excellent for cuts and burns."

Iudila fidgeted as an uneasy silence settled around them. Uti-Chan finished his papaya, tossed away the skin and picked some leaves to wipe the juice from his fingers.

"I am told your father murdered his king," he said in the same tone with which he might comment on the weather.

Iudila pitched the remainder of his fruit and met Uti-Chan's gaze.

"It is true," he said. "His brother."

"Was he a bad king?"

A shrug. "I don't know that I've ever seen a good king."

The Lord of Shukpi laughed and stood.

"Come, let us walk a bit."

Iudila followed him from the small courtyard.

"Tell me more of this king," Uti-Chan said. "Your father's brother?"

"His half-brother, by the name of Reccared. Three brothers were king before him, beginning with my grandfather Athanagild. My father was but a child when the king died, and the council bestowed the crown on Athanagild's brother."

"The council?"

"Our nobles—the leaders of our chief families—select the king from among their ranks. In older times, a queen was first chosen and her consort made king."

Uti-Chan shot him a quizzical look.

"The choice of king was left to a woman?"

"Yes. Not just any woman. She had to be a princess in her own right, descended from a royal line that stretches back hundreds of generations, before memory. Many dynasties have come and gone, but the Scarlet Thread of the female line has been unbroken for thousands of years."

"Yet your father tried to break that thread."

"He tried to restore it." Iudila's voice was louder than he intended. He took a calming breath. "His mother, Goiswintha, was of the Scarlet Thread. She chose Athanagild as her husband and king. When he died, Goiswintha was given to one brother then the next, until the youngest brother, Leovigild, managed to get a pair of sons from her. The elder son led a rebellion against Leovigild, which my father helped to put down. The younger son—this same Reccared—bribed the council with promises of new lands, and was elected king without consent of the queen, his mother."

"He broke your traditions?"

"He changed our religion."

Uti-Chan raised a curious brow.

"Mine is a fractured land," Iudila explained. "The native people follow their host of old gods or the god of their first conquerors, the Romans. My people have been in the land for fewer than a hundred years, but we have followed the path of the one god three times as long. To secure his election, Reccared converted to the creed of the Romans, seized the lands of our priests and those who refused the new faith, and gave those lands to his supporters."

The king gestured to a bench beside a small pond and the two sat.

"Tell me of this one god," he said.

"I am no scholar," Iudila said. "It's been years since I studied."

"Your god lives only in books?"

Iudila laughed. "No, though our priests would have us believe so, for they hold the keys to learning. In ancient times our book was nature. My people saw gods in thunder and lightning, the winds and the sun, even in war and birth and love. We named a god for each of these, gave them great powers and human frailties, built altars and shrines to them, and spent our crops and wealth and blood to please them.

"Then a man called Wulfila told us of the one god who is in all, and of whom the old gods are but different aspects. He told of the great teacher, Yahshua, who said that all are children of the One, that divinity is within each of us. Yahshua shed his blood as a final sacrifice to fulfill the requirements of the old ways and to begin a new one."

Uti-Chan's dark skin turned wan with Iudila's words.

"This—Yashwah, you said? He was hung on a tree?"

"Yes, and nearly killed. His family rescued him. He went into exile where he could be free to teach those who sought the path to the One. Many followed the way of Yahshua, but others taught that he had truly died and come back to life, that he was a god himself, to be worshipped and offered sacrifice."

"And did your Yashwah have children?"

"The Romans—those who made him a god—would deny it, but yes. Yahshua descended from a great line of priests and kings. His wife Miriam was of the Scarlet Thread. Together they were duty-bound to continue the line. One son, called Yusuf, traveled to the islands that lie north of my homeland, and established his line there. Another son, also called Yahshua, had no children and is lost to history. But a daughter, called Tamar, succeeded Miriam as Princess of the Scarlet Thread."

"And your mother was of her line?" Uti-Chan said.

"That's right. How—?"

"A guess. You have her hair, I suspect. And there is no record of the second son?"

Iudila shook his head. "Our family history says that his wife and child died in labor. Miriam, his mother, died about the same time, and father and son were both heartbroken. It is said that together they entered the mouth of the sea, never to be seen or heard from again."

Uti-Chan smiled. "What do you see?" He plucked a reed and played it across the surface of the pond.

Iudila rose and walked to the pool's edge. The broken surface reflected a hundred suns in as many cloudless skies, but a new image appeared as the waters stilled. The bottom of the pond was decorated with a mosaic of blue and green. Something in the pattern seemed familiar, and Iudila moved around the pond until the image became clear.

He shoved a hand into his pouch and pulled out the embroidered map. Some details varied but there was no mistaking the tiled pattern.

The bulges of Spania and Mauretania at the gates of the Mediterranean. The vast expanse of the Sea of Atlas. The undulating coast and islands of the western continent.

"I believe," the king said, "that your Yashwah—both of them—rose from the mouth of the sea here."

Fish scattered as Uti-Chan stabbed the reed into the pond and struck the map in the narrow neck of land between the two great masses of the continent.

"Nearly six hundred years ago," Uti-Chan went on, "a pair of holy men arrived on the shores of Sibolat from the Sunrise Waters. The elder bore scars relating to North, East, West and South." He indicated his forehead, each hand and his feet as they corresponded to the directions. "Another scar related to the fifth direction, the Center." He placed a hand on his side. "The other man, his son, bore a sign similar to yours. His hair was like fire, also similar to yours.

Both of these are marks of the gods' favor. He established his dynasty here, and it is from his line that the Ladies of Shukpi descend."

"Chakin?"

"And her mother, her mother's mother, and so on, back thirty generations. As with your people, stewardship of the throne—the god-seat—belongs to the Lady of Shukpi. Her consort becomes next in line of succession. Or, if her choice of heir is too young to be her husband, she sustains the throne until he comes of age."

"Chakin will choose the next Lord of Shukpi?"

"Yes. But I fear I have placed her in a difficult position. As did your King Reccared, our Council of Elders would dispense with the old ways and remove the selection of Lord from the hands of a woman. In trying to secure Chakin's position, I placed her between two powerful men."

Iudila remembered the fight by the river before he first met Chakin. "The man at Ha-Naab, the Death's-mask?"

"Tok-Ekh, my brother."

"Brother?"

"He is the shaman—or was. Our priests and kings are not so separate as yours seem to be. Here, the lord stands as chief mediator between the people and the gods. For the shaman to become king is not unheard of. Sadly, Tok-Ekh lacks certain qualities I should like to see in my successor."

"And in your daughter's husband?"

"Even so. He seeks power as a macaw seeks baubles. It matters not whether the power can be of benefit to him, let alone to the people. It matters only that he have the power and that others do not."

Iudila thought of Milhma, now a smear of ash on some sandy shore. "I've know such men. And the other?"

Uti-Chan smiled. "The other you know fairly well, though I would not yet call you friends."

"Hul-Balam?"

A nod.

Iudila thought a moment. "He certainly looks the part of a king. He is a warrior, he knows how to lead. And I daresay he's devoted to you and your household."

"He is all of that and more, particularly where Chakin is concerned. He would be a just and brave ruler. I fear only for his lack of forbearance. A king must be judge, as well as warrior and priest. Hul-Balam is less likely to hear argument in a dispute than to cut the throats of both parties to stop their prattling. And they do prattle on."

Iudila grinned. "That would hurry along the process, though justice might not be best served that way. Are there no other candidates?"

"There is one, of as noble birth as Chakin and much nearer in age than either of the others." Uti-Chan looked intently at Iudila.

"Me?"

"I have seen more strength in Chakin in just these past few days than ever before. She has told me of the events that preceded your arrival. While I am saddened she felt the need to deceive me, she has proven that she is no longer a child. The time is right for her to have a husband, and it will be one of her choosing, council or no."

"She would choose me?" The words snagged on Iudila's throat.

"She has said as much. From what I have seen of you, I can think of none better suited."

"There is much you do not yet know."

"I know enough. Think on it. The council requires her marriage soon, but I will not force the matter."

"Yes," Iudila rasped.

The king blinked. "Yes, you will think on it?"

"No," Iudila said, and fixed his eyes on the king's. "I accept."

56

"WE WORRIED ABOUT YOU, BROTHER."

The Green glowed warmly as the Black appeared in the ether. The latecomer flashed an acknowledgement then stretched his dark, luminous tendrils toward the others to complete the pentagram.

"We have a problem," he reported after the opening ritual was complete. "The sea barrier between our lands has again been breached."

A charge flashed among the members of the Pentad at the news.

"From which direction?" demanded the Yellow, the Gokturk trader. "My people's knowledge of Fu-Sang has long been suppressed. None has left our shores for a thousand years."

"Your efforts have succeeded, so far as I can tell," the Black said. "No, this latest incursion came from our east, as before."

"The monk Breandan was silenced," said the Blue Saxon princess. "His story has been so confounded with dream and fantasy that none will take it seriously."

"I speak not of your monk, but of the one he served, the Light-Bringer who reached our shores half a millennium ago."

The ether crackled and four pulses of energy surged toward the Red.

"That is not possible," the Red insisted. "The Nasoraean's line in Spania has been cut off. All that remain are in the Frankish lands. These are so mired in politics and warfare that they are more ally than enemy to our cause."

"Yet one is here who claims descent from the Light-Bringer. He speaks the language of your Church and he bears this sign."

A line appeared in the void between the five, as though drawn by a smoky black finger. The line stretched into five more to form a six-pointed star. At its center, the Black sketched an eye with a long, sweeping tail.

"Iudila."

The other four again focused on the Red.

"You know this sign?" asked the Green, Master of the Pentad.

"Yes, but he died years ago."

"Resurrection must run in his family," the Black said. "You killed him yourself?"

The Red hesitated and took on a deeper hue. "No. I assigned the task to others, but they assured me it was done. I later searched the ether for Iudila's presence, and it was not there. He was gone."

"Yet here he is. How do you explain that?"

"Peace, Brothers," the Green said. "How no longer matters. The important thing is what to do about it. You have him in your power?"

It was the Black's turn to hesitate. "Not yet. His arrival fouled my plans and forced me to retire while I prepare a new strategy."

"But the other," the Yellow chimed in, "the Nasoraean's daughter? She is still in your control?"

Another pause. "I had no choice but to abandon her for the time—"

"You left them together?" the Red demanded. "You fool! Do you realize the consequences if they join their lines?"

"I had no way of knowing who he was," the Black exclaimed. "If you had done your job properly, none of this would have happened. Thanks to your incompetence, we have lost time and I have lost a hand."

"Brethren, be at peace." The Green's command was accompanied by a paralyzing jolt, and all the others fell silent. "I am sorry for your loss, Brother Nanta," he said to the Black. "Your sacrifice is noted and your service will be rewarded when you have completed your mission.

"As for you, Brother Acnila," he continued, addressing the Red, "I trust you will be more thorough in your future assignments. We must all be diligent in our efforts to shield humanity from the Light. The Nasoraean loosed his seed and his spirit into the world, and both have been far more persistent than our forebears in the Order could have anticipated. Fortunately, the potency of his seed diminishes with each generation as the bloodline becomes diluted. When two distant lines are reunited, however, that coupling may make up for centuries of decline."

Silence reigned in the ether for a time as the others considered the Master's words.

"Brother Nanta, you will do all in your power to prevent the union of these two lines. While I previously endorsed your plan to subvert the daughter of the Light-Bringer to our cause, the risk to our mission is too great. Both lines must be cut off."

Tension throbbed in the Black's links with his brethren as he first resisted the command, then finally relented.

"I understand, Master Ahcoma."

"The Light is seductive," the Green reminded the others. "It warms and guides, but it can also burn and blind. In darkness is peace. We who stand in the Light must maintain the peace of the world, whatever the cost. Now, Brethren, as it was before the Beginning. . ."

The Black joined in the closing ceremony, even as the rest of his mind planned how he would bring that peace with a sword.

57

IUDILA WONDERED if he had been forgotten.

Three days had passed since Uti-Chan's brief visit. Iudila's injuries were nearly healed, but he had no word of his men. For that matter, he'd had no communication with anyone, save for the serving girls who brought his food and drew his daily bath.

Whether reality or fantasy, Iudila had the distinct impression that—should he wish it—the young women would also provide for his more carnal needs. Beauties all, and dressed only in simple breechcloths, they offered strong temptation, but Iudila's concerns were for his men, his own desires notwithstanding. And, he admitted to himself in the long, dark hours of night, their combined beauty was but a flickering candle next to the blazing sun of Chakin's splendor.

Iudila was well treated. He had plenty of food, ample rest, and had been given a blue- and green-dyed kilt of fine linen to replace his tattered trousers. But he felt more prisoner than guest. Any attempt to pass through the gate of the small garden outside his house was politely, if firmly, turned back by the gardeners during the day, and less cordially by Hul-Balam during the night.

The surly captain's was the only familiar face Iudila had seen in days, but it bore a perpetual scowl. When Iudila tried to speak with Hul-Balam, to ask after Chakin or his men, each question was greeted with a baleful glare and stony silence. Iudila resigned himself to the solitary confinement. He spent his days studying the plants in his courtyard and the cracks in the plastered walls, and his evenings studying the new stars visible along the southern horizon.

"That is the Great Turtle," he heard on yet another night of stargazing.

Chakin's bare footfalls had been swallowed by the cool, damp night, masking her approach from Iudila. He slowly turned to face her.

Chakin pointed toward the stars near Orion.

"Long ago, the First Father descended to the Underworld to face the gods of death. He was killed and his bones buried beneath the ballcourt of Shibalba."

She spoke slowly and distinctly, her voice as clear as the moonlit sky. Her large, almond eyes gleamed with starlight as she swept them across the heavens, the garden, even the paving stones of the little plaza—anywhere but at Iudila, who stood intently watching her.

"One day," she continued, "his sons journeyed to the Underworld. After many trials, they defeated the Death Lords and watered the ballcourt with their blood. First Father was reborn as the Maize God, who sprouted from a crack in the earth, the Great Turtle's shell. His annual sacrifice and resurrection sustains our people, our daily bread made from his flesh."

"That's a nice story," Iudila said, his voice flat. "Now tell me of my men."

Chakin chanced a look at him, the barest hint of a smile on her lips. "They are well. Even Lemuel is quite recovered. They keep their servants busy with requests for food and drink—and other things."

"When may I see them?"

"Tomorrow, after the ceremony."

"Ceremony?"

Chakin's eyes finally settled on Iudila and ensnared him in their depths. Her hair was pulled back, exposing her broad forehead and high cheeks limned by the pale moonlight. Her lips were like ripe fruit, and it was all Iudila could do to restrain his appetite.

"Tomorrow is the culmination of the sun's northward journey, one of the holiest days of the year. Father thinks it is no coincidence that you arrived in time for the festival, and he wishes you to take part."

"Me? I'm honored, but why?"

"Because of the sign you bear." Chakin tapped the back of her neck. "It is the mark of Shemesh Baal—Lord Sun, whom we call Kinich Ahaw. Surely, you are favored by the great god, so it is only fitting that you take part in his celebration."

Every prince of the royal Balthi clan received a unique identifying sigil, tattooed on the boy's nape before his hair grew long enough to cover it. Lemuel had chosen Iudila's sign, a representation of the Eye of Horus, the ancient Egyptian sky-god. So how had a millennia-old Egyptian symbol come to represent the chief god of a foreign people half a world away? The same way Hebrew had become the priestly tongue, he reasoned.

"You are displeased?" Chakin said when Iudila made no reply.

"No, just confused."

Chakin blanched, and uncertainty clouded her eyes.

"Father said he had spoken with you, that you had agreed—"

"Yes," Iudila said, more eagerly than he intended. "Since I've heard nothing these last few days, I feared you'd changed your mind."

Chakin gave him a condescending look with which he was already becoming familiar.

"All great undertakings require a period of preparation and reflection," she said. "Come. Lord Sun is even now approaching his farthest descent into the Underworld. The time to aid in his ascension draws near."

"I may bear his mark," Iudila said, "but I have much to learn of the ways of Kinich Ahaw. I am your student."

"Come then, pupil," Chakin said with a broad grin. "Your lesson awaits."

She led Iudila in silence from the royal compound, along a broad stone jetty beside the river, and up a sweeping ramp to the wide platform in the center of the city. Their short walk was followed by the curious stares of the handful of fishermen, watchmen and others still about at this late hour. Ever vigilant, Hul-Balam stalked a not-so-discreet distance behind the pair.

On reaching the summit, Iudila nearly tripped over his own feet.

The platform was larger than the parade grounds or equestrian rings the Romans had left behind for their Goth inheritors, far larger than any marketplace or plaza in Spania. The moon cast an ethereal glow upon the limestone pavers, so the very ground seemed to radiate its own heavenly light.

A scattering of buildings sat about the perimeter. Iudila's eyes were drawn to the largest, a magnificent structure that anchored the eastern side of the platform, looming over the river. Unlike the other buildings, this one cast a reddish glow, like the moon in eclipse. Elaborate carvings decorated its face, though Iudila could make out few details. Light flickered from openings on three levels, and smoke rose from the lofty pinnacle.

Iudila turned instinctively toward the great temple, but Chakin caught his hand and led him toward one of the smaller buildings. Though her fingers were cool, they sent a surge of warmth up Iudila's arm, to his heart, and through the rest of his body. Hul-Balam loosed a low, menacing growl, but Iudila made no effort to free his hand.

When they reached the doorway of one of the buildings, Chakin turned and said a few words to the captain. Hul-Balam glowered briefly at Iudila before turning away. As the slap of his bare feet against limestone faded, Chakin squeezed Iudila's hand and ushered him into the building.

The single room was a small cube, barely large enough for Iudila to stand upright. Three stone benches lined the walls, centered on an empty fire pit. The interior was dark, and became darker still when the princess pulled a linen curtain across the doorway.

Iudila's sight quickly adjusted as Chakin guided him to a far corner of the room. She let go of his hand and pressed against a portion of the wall, releasing a hidden latch. Chakin tugged on one corner of the far bench, and it slid away from the wall to reveal a stairway.

Iudila balked at climbing down into the darkness, but he reminded himself he'd already gone to the end of the earth to find Chakin. According to Hul-Balam's version of events at Ha-Naab, he had been to the Underworld and back, as well. A short detour into this manmade cavern was nothing compared to the ordeals he'd already passed. Iudila took a calming breath and followed Chakin down the steps.

At the bottom of the stairs, Chakin pulled on a toggle, which drew the bench back into place. Iudila had the feeling of a tomb being sealed from the wrong side. Chakin's fresh grip on his clammy hand kept his dread at bay, even as she led him farther into the blackness.

Just enough light diffused into the tunnel for Iudila to see side passages out of the corners of his eyes, but the openings disappeared when he looked directly at them. Chakin counted out her steps in a sing-song cadence, her low voice nearly drowned out by the sounds of their footsteps and of running water somewhere in the distance. She paused occasionally, made a deliberate turn left or right, then restarted her rhythmic counting.

As they passed through more and more side tunnels, Iudila realized this was a labyrinth to rival that of King Minos. He hoped the thread of Chakin's memory was as sound as Ariadne's ball of twine, and that no Minotaur lay in wait at this maze's end.

At last, a soft glow appeared around a bend. The light grew stronger with the next turn and the next, then bloomed into brilliance as the pair entered a small candlelit chamber. Iudila's relief was short-lived as the light, made red by the deeply colored walls, revealed the narrow ledge he shared with Chakin. The rest of the chamber was filled by a murky pool of water.

Without a word, Chakin released Iudila's hand, stripped off her skirt, and motioned for Iudila to do the same. He hesitated, but when she stepped closer to assist him, his inhibitions evaporated.

As his wrap fell to the stone floor, he pulled Chakin to him, his arms crushing her body against him, his mouth covering hers. She returned his kiss, her tongue at first tentative, then hungrily engaging in the duel with his. Iudila's need rose between her thighs, and the pressure of it made Chakin gasp and break away.

Iudila opened his mouth to plead for her forgiveness, or to beg for another taste—he wasn't sure which—but she silenced him with a touch of her fingers to his lips.

"Not yet," she said in a husky voice, "but soon. Now come."

Before Iudila could reply, she turned and dove into the pool, disappearing beneath its dark surface. Iudila plunged in after her. The water was warm and closed around Iudila in a gentle embrace. He swam underwater to where Chakin waited beside a narrow hole in the rock wall. She flashed him a smile—bubbles forming like pearls against her teeth—then disappeared into the opening.

Iudila's shoulders barely fit inside the tunnel. There was little room to kick and even less to use his arms. Fear edged his consciousness as his lungs started to burn and the rock seemed to squeeze around him. He tried to wriggle out of the tunnel but couldn't move forward or back. Just as panic threatened to overwhelm him, strong hands gripped him by the wrists and pulled him through the tunnel.

Chakin guided him to the surface, and they stroked to the edge of a second pool. Iudila wiped the water from his eyes to see a chamber larger and brighter than the first. The plastered walls were painted a soft blue that suffused the space with a peaceful, calming influence.

"Do all of your suitors face this ordeal?" Iudila asked when he'd caught his breath.

"Only the ones favored by the gods. Come, we have farther to go."

Iudila turned to look at Chakin. "How much farther?"

"I do not know. I have never been here before."

"Then how do you know where to go?"

"Because that is where the path leads."

She pointed to a low doorway at the far end of the chamber. Chakin rose from the pool—water flowing like lovers' caresses down her slender form—and walked fearlessly toward the opening.

Iudila marveled at her boldness and her beauty, then rose and followed. He stooped through the doorway where Chakin waited at the junction of six new tunnels cut into the earth, each one stretching into the darkness. Chakin turned to him, her confidence replaced by uncertainty.

"What is it?" Iudila asked.

Chakin shook her head. "I do not know which path to take."

"But you found your way through the first maze."

"That was different," Chakin said. "I knew the way."

"You said you'd never been here."

"I have not. The path was told to me in a song my mother sang when I was a child."

"A song?"

Chakin nodded. "About a young maiden who travels to Shibalba to find her love. On reaching the Underworld, she walks ten days toward the Sunrise Waters, five days chasing the summer sun, and so on, until she reaches a sacred pool where her love awaits."

"Then what?"

Chakin grinned and lowered her eyes.

"I see." Iudila stepped toward her, cupped his hand under her chin and kissed her gently. "And what after that?"

"Together they return to Kab, the Middle World."

"Back the way they had come?"

Chakin shook her head. "They first go to the place of the Sun. After they are purified and receive the blessing of the gods, only then do they return to Kab."

Iudila studied the openings. "You say they returned together?"

A nod. "Hand in hand, side by side, they climbed the path to the mount of the Sun."

Iudila took her hand and led her to one of the passages. "We go this way."

"How do you know?"

"'Hand in hand, side by side.' It's the only one wide enough for us to walk together."

Chakin looked at the other doorways, smiled and nodded. Together they struck out on the upward path.

58

TOK-EKH CREPT through the darkness, fifty men from Ha-Naab behind him. The men had wrapped their weapons in leather or cloth to silence their rattles, and caked their bodies in mud against both the biting insects of the night and the moon's reflection.

The war band had left Ha-Naab two days earlier, picking their way through the trackless forest to avoid the small habitations and the guards who would surely be posted along the Sakbe.

Now only the flat expanse of Shukpi's marketplace and ballcourt lay between the shaman and his goal. The temple mount loomed vast and dark in the thin moonlight. Tomorrow the platform would be packed for the celebration of Kinich Ahaw's mounting, when the sun began its annual journey toward the south. The people of Shukpi and all the villages along the Hahkhan river valley would unite to mark the solar festival.

In the dark of the night, however, the upper and lower plazas were empty. Tok-Ekh led his men toward the ballcourt.

Shukpi had no walls. Marker stones proclaimed the city's boundaries, invoking the gods' blessings on those who came in peace and their wrath on those who did not. The shaman made a show of appeasing the gods and concealing from them the intent of his mission before crossing the protected border. The men of Ha-Naab were tentative as they followed him, but gained courage when none was struck by lightning or consumed by demons.

"You four, come with me." Tok-Ekh pointed to the best warriors. "The rest of you, stay in the ballcourt. Once we have secured the upper plaza, we will signal for you to join us. Shukpi has governed Ha-Naab long enough. Tomorrow the roles reverse."

The men did not cheer, but their smiles shone in the moonlight as raised fists silently punched the air.

Tok-Ekh nodded his approval. He led his chosen men first to the ritual bath to wash off the hardened mud, then through the warriors' gate of the ballcourt, beneath the royal viewing stand.

A broad, stepped terrace led to the temple mount, but the shaman passed this, moving to a narrow stairway cut into the face of the upper plaza's wall. The lower landing was guarded by a pair of sharp-fanged, snake-tongued witz monsters that peered out from the limestone. Tok-Ekh stretched his left hand—his only hand now—into the mouth of one of the beasts while one of his men reached into the other.

At a nod from Tok-Ekh, the two pressed hidden trip-stones, and a click echoed in the night. The other men pushed on a stone at the base of the stairs. The slab slid away to reveal a second set of steps leading beneath the foundations of the temple mount.

"We have no torches," one of the men said.

Tok-Ekh cautiously descended into the opening, groping blindly ahead of him. A smile flitted across his face as his fingers closed around a string played out on the floor.

"We won't need any."

59

IUDILA GUIDED CHAKIN up the sloping path, her arms tight about his waist.

"How can you see anything?" she asked as he led her around a pile of rubble.

"As long as I can remember, I've been able to find my way in the dark," Iudila said. "When I was young, a friend and I explored a cave with some older boys. They took the torches and left us, but I was able to see well enough to find the way out."

"Why would they leave you like that?"

"The Goths have an ancient warrior tradition. Our young men constantly challenge each other—younger or older, it doesn't matter. The struggle is even greater among the nobles. If a man cannot survive a challenge, he isn't a fit leader for his people."

"But you were only a boy."

"I was ten," Iudila protested. "He is no warrior who hasn't passed an ordeal or bloodied his spear by that age."

"No son of mine will be put through such a thing when he is little more than a baby."

Iudila grinned in the darkness. "Your sons will be great warriors and wise leaders of men."

"Is that so?" He heard the smile in her voice as she cinched her arms more tightly about him.

"Oh, it's so." He squeezed her in return, savoring her scent, her warmth against his skin, the slickness of their mingled perspiration. "Is it getting warmer?"

Chakin first giggled, then said, "It is. There may be a steam chamber ahead."

"Steam?"

"For spirit quests. The heat, with certain herbs in the air, can induce visions."

"Whatever it is, we must be getting close. Can you see that?" As they turned a corner, a faint glow appeared in the distance.

"Yes," she said. In the dim light—bright as day, after the utter blackness that had engulfed them—Chakin loosed her grip on Iudila.

Two side tunnels met theirs. Air whistled from the inky depths into the main passage, which narrowed as it approached the glowing wall. The air moved faster, cooling the pair with the blessed breeze. The relief vanished as they rounded a bend and the glow turned into a raging fire set in the middle of the narrow path. The air drove them forward as it rushed in to feed the hungry flames.

Iudila felt the snick of the cord against his ankle, knew in that instant what had happened, and knew that he was helpless to stop it. He stepped through a trip wire strung across the path, and before he could shout a warning or spin around, a great slab of stone crashed to the ground behind them, sealing off the tunnel and trapping them between rock and flames.

The inferno guttered, its air supply cut off. As the blaze lessened, Iudila saw past the scorched walls surrounding the fire, to where the smoke rose through a narrow shaft, a chimney cut from the rock. And hanging from the shaft . . .

"A rope!"

"I see it, but how do we get there?" Chakin's voice was weak, her words slurred as the fire greedily consumed the last rations of air.

Iudila answered by slinging her onto his back, her slender arms about his neck.

"Deep breath."

Chakin tensed and buried her face in his long hair as he started toward the flames.

Iudila recalled the Eastern mystics from the festivals at Tingis, how they trod their paths of hot coals at an easy pace, and how their drunken imitators howled in pain when they tried to run the same path. Flames on one side and scorching rock on the other, Iudila threaded the middle path where the fire had burned down to embers. He resisted the urge to run. Instead, he clenched his teeth against the heat and the need to breathe as he stepped onto the glowing trail.

The smell of scorched flesh and singed hairs filled Iudila's nostrils, but he took the five searing paces across the firebed, then three more to where the rope dangled in the smoky murk. He paused only long enough to slap the dull embers from between his toes, then grabbed the rope and hauled himself up.

Iudila would normally have pitted the strength of his arms against any man's, but his muscles were taxed by the days of inactivity. Chakin's added weight, the oppressive heat of the tunnel and the lack of air didn't help. He grunted against the strain, loosing some of his precious breath, but he forced himself to reach up for one more handhold, then another and yet another.

Iudila's arms ached and his lungs raged. His eyes watered from the smoke. His fingers cramped and burned as they alternately squeezed then slipped on the greasy, soot-stained rope. Chakin's breath was faint in his ears as she breathed through the filter of his hair, her heartbeat soft against his back. That low, slow pulse metered his progress as he drew them higher.

Just as Iudila thought his arms must fail or his lungs burst, his upraised hand closed on empty air. He felt about and found a deep ledge. Using handholds gouged into the rock, he clawed his way onto the flat surface. Chakin rolled away from him. The pair coughed and sucked down lungfuls of fresh air that rushed up another tunnel to dilute the fast-rising column of smoke in the chimney.

"Next time you feel like taking a walk," Iudila said, the words grating against his smoke-roughened throat, "let me pick the trail."

Chakin smacked his chest, and the tunnel rang with the echoes of their laughter and coughs. When they could again breathe easily, Chakin led the way down the slight grade of the tunnel that was only high enough for them to crawl.

A pale light glowed soft and green and round at tunnel's end, and they emerged into yet another chamber furnished only with a stone wash basin and a pair of sponges. They rinsed the worst of the soot and sweat from themselves and each other—too drained to take any greater pleasure than soft caresses.

Beside a square-cut doorway lay a pair of folded linens dyed the familiar blue and green, along with twin necklaces of bone and jade and obsidian. They wrapped the linens around their waists then placed the necklaces about one another's necks.

Iudila smoothed Chakin's hair over the loop of her necklace, took a moment to appreciate the way the beads nestled against her breasts, then kissed her gently. Her return kiss was one of passionate strength, if not the hunger of before—a sharing of their breath, their souls, rather than a devouring of one another. When Chakin broke the embrace and stepped back, she laid a hand on Iudila's grizzled cheek.

"There is one more test before us," she said. "It is, perhaps, more dangerous than what we have already passed. If you—" She lowered her eyes and turned away. "If you do not wish to go farther, we may leave the temple without shame."

Iudila stepped close behind her and placed his hands on her shoulders.

"Do you wish to go on?"

She gave the slightest of nods.

"Then our path lies together. Where you go, I will follow."

Iudila took her hand, her slender fingers intertwining with his calloused ones. On tired legs they passed through the doorway and climbed a steep, winding stairway lit by candles at each landing. Iudila wondered if they had, indeed, descended all the way to the Underworld, so long was the upward climb.

After they had passed a dozen candles, a curtained doorway appeared. Through this doorway, Chakin led with a confident stride down a narrow corridor to another set of stairs.

"You know this place?" Iudila asked.

"We have reached the temple," she said, and pointed through a window slit to indicate the plaza and the tiny building where the night's ordeal had begun.

Chakin led Iudila up the stairs, then up yet another flight to a small chamber in the summit of the temple, lit only by the coals of a smoking brazier.

The smoldering light revealed Uti-Chan, Lord of Shukpi, seated cross-legged upon a cushion. His head was covered by the strange, conical turban, his broad chest decorated with pectorals of finely carved jade. His hands rested on his knees, a serene look upon his face. He opened his eyes as Chakin and Iudila approached, and he gestured for them to sit opposite him.

"In the First Time," he said, "a divine mist enveloped the earth. Gods and nature-spirits moved in the mist, and man had but to breathe to be as one with them and with each other. It was not good, however, for man's mind to remain clouded. Father-god—he whose reflection is the glory of Kinich Ahaw—poured forth his light and dispelled the fog. No longer was man shrouded in mist. In the clear light of day, however, he lost his intimate knowledge of the gods and became separated from his brothers and sisters."

The priest-king sprinkled a handful of herbs on the brazier, filling the room with an aromatic cloud that made Iudila's eyes water.

"Lord Sun delivered his children into light, but he saw how they longed for the union they once knew. In his divine mercy, he gave to us fire and smoke, that in the embrace of those most sublime elements we might again be as one with our neighbor and with the gods. Breathe now, my children, and find the oneness that was our first state, and is our ultimate calling."

Iudila and Chakin leaned toward the brazier and inhaled. A tingle traced down Iudila's throat, and he tried not to cough as the sweet smoke filled his lungs.

"Chakin," the king continued, "Lady of Shukpi, daughter of the great Yashwak. And Iudila, favored one of Kinich Ahaw, you who crossed the Sunrise Waters. Together, you have traversed the fields of Shibalba and ascended to the Temple of the Sun. You have passed the ordeals of earth and water, fire and air. Only the test of blood and spirit yet awaits you before you cross the threshold of Sak-Ishik to that divine union of heart and body. The way of the goddess is one of the utmost joy and pleasure, but it also holds much heartache and danger. In the arms of one another, you will find all to gain and all to lose. Is it your will to embark on this greatest of trials?"

Iudila glanced at Chakin through the smoke. The low light of the brazier cast shadows upon her face, sharpening and accentuating her features. Iudila thought his heart must break with the beauty of her. Her eyes met his, and he saw in them the girl's playfulness, the woman's resolve and the warrior's strength. There was also something of the child's uncertainty, which he hoped to allay.

"It is my will," he said, not taking his eyes from her.

Chakin smiled, her eyes shining through the smoke.

"And mine."

"So be it," Uti-Chan said.

He drew back the cloth from a low table to reveal a pair of quills joined by a cotton thread with knots along its length. Beside these was a small bowl containing a thin brown liquid.

"As you share communion with the gods through the divine breath, so may you commune with one another through the joining of blood and spirit. Take the kish—the needle that sharpens the mind—and with it join your souls."

Iudila and Chakin each took one of the stingray spines.

Uti-Chan turned to Iudila and said, "The heart is the seat of bravery and strength. Its pulse enlivens the body, and its rhythm orders the life of a man. Pierce, now, the heart-center, and draw from it your courage."

Iudila wasn't sure he understood correctly, but the king pointed to a pair of round scars above his own left breast. Iudila nodded then clenched his teeth as he threaded the quill through his skin, the knots tugging at the wound.

The priest-king looked at Chakin.

"A woman's tongue is the instrument of wisdom. By it, she may embolden or humble a man, call forth praise or curse. I charge you now to consecrate your tongue that, by it, you may temper the heart of the one you have chosen."

Chakin's eyes watered, but she made no sound as she forced the needle through her tongue and pulled with it the knotted thread that bound her to Iudila's heart.

Uti-Chan motioned for them to trade spines, then directed Chakin to pierce her navel, center of the will. He at last turned back to Iudila.

"A man must subsume his passions to the will of his beloved, ever placing her needs above his own desires."

Iudila nodded solemnly, then froze as the king pointed between the Goth's legs. He looked to Chakin, and she smiled, blood staining the thread in her tongue. Iudila spread the skirts of his kilt, and forced the needle through the skin of his penis, pulling the thread tight.

Uti-Chan clapped his hands three times, then cut the quills off and tied the ends of the thread. He lifted the bowl from the table and carefully poured the liquid, first along the thread between Chakin's tongue and Iudila's heart, then the crossed strands. He set the bowl between the pair and put the ends of the thread into it. The cotton acted as a wick, drawing the liquid along the string's length. Iudila's blood burned as the potion seeped from the thread into his veins. His eyes grew heavy even as his head became lighter. His chin drooped and his eyes settled on the line strung between Chakin's belly and his breast.

A glow emanated from the thread, a blue-green radiance that grew and coalesced, then surged up the string and pierced his chest. He drew a sharp breath, and the light's heat surged through his body. His flesh was consumed, organs burst, bones melted, until only his soul remained. He merged with the light, his spirit becoming one with the sinewy radiance.

When his vision returned, he found himself on a broad plain—a patchwork of barley and wheat and rye—ringed by high, snow-capped mountains. A pond lay amid the fields. Iudila stooped to drink, but stopped when he saw his reflection.

A serpent's face gazed back at him through green eyes he recognized as his own. His great mane of hair was replaced by a feathery hood of golden red that shone in the sunlight. Nostrils twitched in a pointed snout, and when he opened his mouth in surprise, sharp fangs unfurled, dripping with venom. He craned his long neck to examine the rest of his body, finding short, taloned legs that supported a long body covered in iridescent blue and green scales.

A cry sounded from across the pond.

Iudila looked up and saw, caught in a bramble, a white rabbit he somehow knew was Chakin. He leapt over the pond, and wings unfurled from his back to carry him across the water. He tore away the encumbering brush, and Chakin's spirit form came to him and nuzzled her velvet nose against his scaly one.

A sound came from behind them. They turned to face a great white cloud, lit from within as by the sun. The cloud rumbled like summer thunder, then shot a tongue of flame over their heads toward a black cloud that descended from the distant mountains and stretched across the horizon.

The dark menace brought with it a driving rain that flattened the crops and drowned the fields. From the floodwaters there arose a giant shark whose thrashings destroyed whatever survived the black cloud's onslaught.

Iudila launched himself after the shark that despoiled the land—Iudila's land—but at Chakin's cry he looked back to see the black cloud engulfing her. He turned and flew to her rescue.

The wind abandoned Iudila's wings the moment he entered the cloud, and he tumbled to the sodden ground. The cloud drained his lungs. Iudila snapped his teeth and lashed his tail against the life-stealing force, but the evil wisps evaded his attacks.

In a final effort, Iudila flared his hood. With his last breath, he loosed a roar that shook the muddy fields. The roar turned into a gout of flame that spewed from his mouth to evaporate the dark mists. He paced in a circle about Chakin's inert spirit-body, burning away the cloud until sunlight again shone. Its rays quickly dried the earth and scattered the last of the black storm.

Iudila leapt skyward to return to the shark but the beast had returned to the abyss whence it came, leaving only ruin in its wake. Iudila winged once around the plain. It lay empty save for Chakin and the fire-cloud that hovered benevolently over her. He swept down in his plumed-serpent form. The cloud flashed once and disappeared, leaving the pair alone.

Iudila nudged Chakin's still form. He teased the air around her with his forked tongue, bent a scaly ear to sound out her heartbeat, but there was no sign of life. Tears flowed from his reptilian eyes, and he threw back his head in a roar. He unleashed a fiery torrent that turned the pond into steam, while his tail reduced to stubble the few grain stalks that still stood.

Through his rage, a memory surfaced, a long-forgotten legend from childhood. The Balthi, royal clan of the Goths, claimed their descent from a beast not unlike his present form, a serpent whose venom held the power to destroy or to save.

With nothing to lose, he stooped next to Chakin, nudged her once more, then plunged a fang into her breast. Venom pulsed from its sac, and the rabbit went stiff with the influx. Iudila retracted the fang, and Chakin's pink nose twitched, a brown eye flicked open, and her furry chest rose with new breath.

Iudila's heart soared as Chakin pushed herself onto her feet and took a pair of tentative steps as the steam cloud from the vaporized pond drifted toward them. Iudila spread a wing to shelter Chakin, but the gesture was in vain. The mist saturated the air around them, a moist veil that hid Chakin from view.

Dew settled on Iudila's scales, first in drops, then streams, then sheets that flowed and spread across his body like quicksilver. The watery sheath hardened and contracted, squeezing his body, crushing him with its weight. The world about him grew larger as his perspective diminished to that of a dog, a worm, a gnat—nothing.

Consciousness barged in on his senses as he opened his eyes to see Uti-Chan looking at him expectantly.

Iudila glanced to where Chakin sat, now stirring from her own trance. The look on her face matched what he felt, and he knew that—while the events of the vision may not have been real—their sharing of it had been very real indeed. A bond was forged between them that would not be sundered.

"Ponder what you have seen," Uti-Chan directed them as he cut and removed the threads, "for it portends the nature of things to come. Your path is not fixed. You may choose another way, if you wish."

Iudila looked from father to daughter, from priest-king to—what?

A princess? A bride? A treasure whose loss—even if only in a vision—still gnawed at his belly, but whose restoration even now lifted his heart.

"I will face whatever that path may bring," he said, then turned to Chakin, "so long as you are by my side."

Chakin smiled, her eyes bright in the brazier's glow.

"If the gods will it, then our path lies together. And I pray it is their will, for it is the fervent desire of my heart."

Uti-Chan clapped his hands together and rose.

"So be it. Rise, children, and come. Lord Sun is at dawn's threshold. Let us greet his awakening and seek his blessing for your new journey."

60

THROUGH A NARROW WINDOW in the temple's wall, Iudila saw the plaza teeming with people. Some milled about while others clustered together against the cool dampness of the predawn. Their noise filtered through the stones of the great temple, where Khu-Shul fumed at his staff and fussed over the wedding party.

The temple servants had already dressed Uti-Chan in his ceremonial finery. Strands of shells reached from his ankles to his knees. He wore thick leather bracers on his wrists, while bands of copper strained against his biceps.

A jaguar pelt hung from the king's shoulders, its forelegs stretched across his chest, the great paws fastened together with a brooch of jade. From his neck hung a copper plate studded with twelve gemstones in the pattern of a six-pointed star. He wore his usual turban with its jade headpiece, and carried a wooden baton, its surface intricately carved, worn and oiled by the hands of those kings who had gone before him.

Khu-Shul directed his attentions to Chakin, doting on the princess and making certain that every adornment was perfect.

A hide of white deerskin hung from her shoulders to her knees, setting off the dusky glow of her skin. Her hair was coiled atop her head, held in place by a headdress of heron feathers that formed a halo about Chakin's face, as radiant as the moon she represented. She wore no jewels or shells or beads, nor needed any. The simplicity of her costume made her natural beauty all the more evident.

Iudila was the last to fall under the dwarf's scrutiny, though his dress was the most elaborate. Khu-Shul appraised his design as one of the servants applied the last bit of makeup around the Goth's eyes.

"Are you ready?" Khu-Shul said.

Iudila nodded tentatively.

"I will tell you when to go out," Khu-Shul assured him. "You will not need to speak. Just follow the king's directions and Lady Chakin's lead." A look of doubt flashed through the scribe's eyes. "You—you are what you say you are?"

Iudila knelt before Khu-Shul—not a simple act, given the restraints of his costume—and spoke in a soft voice.

"All I have told you is true. I know you've loved her far longer than I. But I swear on the blood of my ancestors, I will do all in my power to prove worthy of her, to use my every breath to bring her happiness."

Khu-Shul nodded gravely at Iudila, then clapped his hands and drove the servants from the room. Iudila rose as Uti-Chan approached him.

The king examined Iudila's costume.

"You are truly favored by Father-god. May you walk in his path, in wisdom and fortitude."

"Thank you, my lord."

Uti-Chan turned to Chakin, kissed her on each cheek and pulled her into a gentle embrace. He said something Iudila didn't understand, then father and daughter smoothed tears from each other's eyes.

The Lord of Shukpi cleared his throat, stepped through the doorway and onto the temple's terrace. The people greeted him with a roar that shook the foundations of the temple mount itself.

61

THE VERY ROCK seemed to quake with the shouts of the crowd, and Tok-Ekh feared his eager troops had acted too soon. It was not long, though, before the raucous cheers turned into a chant of his brother's name, that pulse-pound of adulation that had sickened Tok-Ekh for years.

A king's name was to be spoken in whispers, in tones hushed with awe and dread. The people should fear the king—the lord of their destinies—not love him. Yes, a healthy degree of gratitude should be expected, for it was the king who stood between the people and the gods, shielding them from the devastating power of the divine. But that gratitude ought ever to be tempered by the knowledge that he could at any time withdraw his benevolence.

All would soon be as it should, the shaman promised himself. By day's end the gods' order would be reestablished. The people of Shukpi would be restored to their rightful place, protected from the divine light that burns the unworthy.

The cheers at last subsided, and Tok-Ekh continued through the tunnel. His one hand held fast to the guiding thread while a square wooden shield covered the stump of the other. His men stumbled behind him, and he smiled at their heavy breathing and stifled curses as they jostled one another in the darkness.

They were warriors, yes—tested in the ballcourts and proven in battle—but warriors of Lord Sun, whose battles were fought by daylight. It was he—the dreaded, reviled, oft-mocked shaman—who would lead them through the bowels of Shibalba to the field of glory where they would become true warriors of the night.

Tok-Ekh felt the knot in the string a moment before he jammed his toe against the stone step.

"Quiet, fools," he snarled at his men as they clattered to a stop behind him. "Watch carefully."

He released the string and fumbled in his pouch for a flint, which he struck against the stone wall. The brief flash of light nearly blinded him after more than an hour in utter darkness, but it revealed what he needed to see before the blackness again swallowed them.

"You two, up the stairs," he ordered the warriors immediately behind him.

While they crawled up the stone steps, Tok-Ekh groped for the toggle he had seen in the flash of light. He found the wooden handle, tugged on the line and felt the release of a latch.

"Now, heave."

He heard the men on the stairs brace themselves and plant their hands against the stone slab. Without demanding so much as a grunt between them, the concealed paver slid noiselessly on its pivot. Predawn gloom trickled into the tunnel and the men visibly relaxed. Even Tok-Ekh breathed more easily as the crushing weight of the darkness lifted.

"Not a sound until my signal. You know your positions and your duty. By the shades of your ancestors, do not fail me."

The men uttered not a sound, simply nodding their heads. Fear, Tok-Ekh decided, was a great motivator indeed.

The shaman and his warriors filed up the steps and into the small room, then—one by one, so as not to draw attention—out onto the plaza.

The crowd filled the temple mount, a greater number than Tok-Ekh could remember having seen for many years, perhaps since the dedication of his father's temple. The people stood in rapt silence as Uti-Chan, the pretender and impotent Lord of Shukpi, invoked the gods, imploring them to bear witness on this holy day.

Tok-Ekh suppressed a grin. The gods would certainly see quite a spectacle— if they deigned to answer his brother's summons—though it would not be the one the king had planned.

Keeping to the shadows, Tok-Ekh crept to the rear of the low building and found a ladder and spear set in place. He climbed to the roof, out of sight of the crowd but with a clear view of the temple platform. He settled in just as Uti-Chan summoned Chakin, and the shaman's heart fluttered.

He had last seen the princess only days earlier, yet she had gained years in beauty and poise. Her youthful charm was still evident, even from this distance. A new aura of strength and confidence shone about her, however, adding a womanly grace he had seen in no one else since her mother. The white headdress captured the remnants of moonlight, illuminating her graceful features, while the simple deerskin frock outlined her lissome form.

Tok-Ekh breathed deeply to still his desire. He surprised himself by blessing the gods for Iudila's untimely arrival. Had the sailors not arrived, the shaman would have taken Chakin at Ha-Naab. He would have missed her transformation into the earthly goddess who stood now between the Middle and Upper Worlds. The pleasure of their union would now be all the greater.

As Tok-Ekh's heart settled back into rhythm, Uti-Chan raised his arms and voice to the heavens in the age-old ritual of dawn and called upon Kinich Ahaw to rise from his slumber.

A gasp rose from the crowd, and even Tok-Ekh's breath caught. The demon-spawn Khu-Shul might be a foul little creature, but the monkey's bastard knew his stagecraft and used it to full effect.

From beneath the temple's apron, the embodiment of Kinich Ahaw rose to meet the day. His hair glowed with flame, his face radiated in splendor, and his sculpted body shone with magnificent light. As the great god stepped forward to join the king and princess, the sky came awake with the first glimmer of day.

For once, Tok-Ekh could forgive the mob their superstitions, for Khu-Shul's art had been perfectly executed. The shaman knew the vision before him was largely a trick of bright metal and reflective paints, but even he could feel a tickle of the divine.

The foreign prince shone with the brightness of Lord Sun himself, and Tok-Ekh despised him. He loathed Iudila for his physical perfection, for his nearness to Chakin. Mostly, he hated him for his pretensions. About each of the foreigner's eyes was painted the symbol of the great god, as though this resplendent worm could claim kinship with the divine.

Tok-Ekh suppressed a groan of agony as he tore his eyes from the brilliant spectacle and looked to Chakin. The princess stared enraptured at her bridegroom. The fascination was similar to that she had shown when the shaman had shared with her the great mysteries of the gods and of the spiritual powers. But there was more.

Even from across the plaza, Tok-Ekh saw in Chakin's eyes the look he knew he gave her in his unguarded moments. Only her gaze of adoration was for the sun-washed sailor.

Iudila would die first, Tok-Ekh vowed. Chakin he would take for himself, and he would spare Khu-Shul if he could. Such talents as the dwarf possessed would be useful, indeed, in harnessing the gullibility of the people. Not only was Khu-Shul's dramatic flair unparalleled, but his timing was perfect. The entire event had been managed so that Iudila stepped toward the audience just as the sun burst above the horizon behind him.

While Uti-Chan spoke his blasphemous litany, the solar disk climbed higher, its light shining through the openings in the temple walls aligned specifically for this day of the year. The sun cast a gentle aura about Iudila's body, then flared into a corona around his head as Chakin stepped to his side.

Rage filled Tok-Ekh's body. His breath quickened as his pounding pulse filled his ears. He could not hear the words Uti-Chan spoke to the couple, nor did he need to. He rose from his hiding place—heedless of the fact that his men were likely not yet in place—and shouted his defiance.

62

CHAKIN STOOD BY HER FATHER, only half hearing the words he spoke. She was dimly aware of the crowd and their breathless anticipation, of Iudila's men near the foot of the temple, of Hul-Balam's careful watch over them.

How strange, Chakin thought, the course her life had taken in just the last few days. One moment she had been willing to sacrifice everything—her home, her position, her father's trust—for what she now knew to be Tok-Ekh's false promises. Had the handsome stranger not arrived when he did, the gods only knew what pain and bloodshed would have been wrought.

And what of Iudila? Could he truly be the answer to her heart's cry? There had been an immediate attraction—at least on her part—and their shared ordeal of the night just past had drawn them even closer. But they had known each other only a few days. Was it possible to know love in such a short time?

Yes, she admitted, it was. In his arms, she knew at once the thrill of desire and the peace of a soul come home. How had her mother once put it? Love is finding in another the harmony to your heart's song. In Iudila, she found just that. They had much to learn together, of life and of each other. Chakin craved the learning of it as a racing deer craves the stream.

And then he arose.

Chakin missed her father's words but there was no missing the rumble of the rising platform or the awed gasp from the crowd. Chakin turned to see a god rise from the earth. Though the sun had yet to awaken, Iudila glowed with the full light of day.

His hair had been teased and stiffened into twelve rays about his head like the crown of Kinich Ahaw. Bands of copper adorned his legs and spanned his arms. His linen kilt was embroidered with strips of copper and gold, and lozenges of the same metals spanned his chest on a copper wire. His skin, kissed by the sun god himself, was smooth and oiled, and glistened in the light to reveal the contour of each sculpted muscle.

Iudila stepped toward Chakin at the very moment the true sun peeked above the horizon. The temple walls were built with openings aligned to the various solar festivals. The rays of Kinich Ahaw now shone through the set designed for the summer solstice, bursting about Iudila's head in dazzling splendor. Chakin moved to meet him, not because the ceremony dictated it, not even because she desired it. She went to him for the same reason the moon seeks the sun in eclipse—it is simply the natural way of things, the fulfillment of their wanderings.

"Even as Sak-Ishik tames the fire of Kinich Ahaw," she scarcely heard her father say, "so must you temper and balance one another. Together will you bind night and day, capturing the positive aspects of each, while dispelling the negative. If it is your will to be united, stand before one another and join hands."

His words were needless, for Chakin had already locked hands with Iudila, her eyes fixed on his. She forced herself to breathe, and the scent of him, earthy and raw, filled her nostrils.

"Tell him the words," Uti-Chan said as he approached the couple and wrapped their hands with the tail of his jaguar pelt.

"Now there is no rain," Chakin translated her father's words, her voice little more than a whisper, "for you are shelter to each other. There is no cold, for each is warmth to the other. No longer is there darkness or pain, for you are light and comfort to one another. Two bodies, but your hearts are joined and the two are now made one."

Uti Chan stood behind and between the couple then raised his hands toward the sky to invoke the gods' blessing.

"No!"

Chakin cringed at the shout. She knew of Hul-Balam's objection to the marriage, knew that he had wanted her for himself. But as she looked toward the captain, she saw a mask of confusion that must have mirrored her own. She looked past him, past the crowd to the edge of the temple platform.

The sun illuminated a tall, lean figure atop the very building where the previous night's ordeal had begun.

Tok-Ekh shouted again in rage. He stamped his feet against the roofing stones then hurled his spear toward the temple. Chakin watched its flight through tear-blurred eyes. She cried not for fear, not for sorrow, nor even for pain as Iudila's body fell against her and swept her to the ground. In that moment she wept with anger, for on this most sacred of days, hate had stalked love to the gates of Shukpi.

63

IUDILA TURNED TOWARD the shout. He caught the glint of sunlight on the spear's blade, heard the faint whistle as the weapon took flight. He reached for Chakin, their hands still fastened by the jaguar's tail. He swung her around, battering the king with her body and bringing the three of them to the ground in a tangle.

The spear grazed his shoulder before it skidded across the platform, its shaft clattering against the stone. So fine was the blade that Iudila only noticed the cut when blood spilled down his arm. He ignored the wound, freed his hands and helped Chakin and the king to their feet. Shielding them with his body, he hurried them through the temple's doorway where Hul-Balam came racing up the steps to meet them.

"Take care of them," Iudila ordered the captain, not caring that the man couldn't understand him. Iudila raced back out the doorway, snatched up the spear and shouted to his men. "*Mari-Nadris!* On me!" He leapt from the temple platform.

"We've no weapons," Brehanu told him as Iudila landed among his men.

"Then we'll have to take them," Iudila said.

Brehanu and Dingha smiled savagely.

Iudila looked over the heads of the fleeing crowd and spotted the tallest figure hurrying in the other direction.

"This way."

He led his men against the tide of bodies, in pursuit of the man he remembered from his first meeting with Chakin. The crowd thinned as the sailors neared the north end of the temple mount. A little girl wailed in fear and pain, clutching an arm that jutted out at an obscene angle, broken in the stampede from the plaza. Iudila snatched her up and put her in Lemuel's arms.

"See to her. Find her mother," he said, then led the others down the platform's steps before the older man could protest.

Tok-Ekh was already running across the lower plaza. A guard stood at the foot of the steps.

"After him," Iudila shouted.

The guard turned and raised his weapon against Iudila rather than Tok-Ekh. The man's bellicose grin turned to a grimace of fear as his eyes focused on Iudila in his god-like array.

Iudila had no time for superstitions or treason. He lifted his spear, feeling its weight and judging its balance, then hurled it down the steps ahead of him.

He reached the ground at the same time as the guard's body. Iudila wrenched the spear free of the sucking wound in the man's chest, then continued the chase. Thanos snatched up the fallen man's sword while Dingha finished him with a heel to the throat.

Iudila rounded a corner where the shaman had disappeared. He nearly tripped over a pile of bodies that littered the alley. Some of the men had their throats cut in ragged, yawning gashes. Others had gaping wounds in their backs, testament to their cowardly murders. The pirates searched the bodies with practiced hands but found no weapons on the fallen men.

"Steady on."

Iudila led his men past the bodies to the alley's end. He paused there, listening for a hint of what lay beyond the alley walls. He heard nothing over the continued cries of the crowd at the temple. On instinct, he stuck the butt of his spear past the entrance to the alley. A club immediately crashed down on the slender pole.

Dingha was ready for this. He leapt upon the club, crushing its owner's fingers between wooden handle and stone pavement. Iudila cut off the man's howl of pain with a blow of the spear's shaft to the side of his head, then silenced him forever with a quick slash of the blade across his throat.

The fallen man's cry had been enough to draw his comrades. Half a dozen warriors charged the sailors. Dingha tossed his club to Brehanu then loosed a feral howl of glee.

Two of the attackers hurled spears, which Dingha dodged with an ease that belied his size. The others charged him and, before the rest of the crew could join him, Dingha had batted aside one attacker and crippled another with a kick to the knee. A third he grabbed by the wrist and rent shoulder from socket with a pop that was nearly as loud as the man's shriek. Dingha gripped the wailing man about the waist, wrapped his meaty paw about the man's useless weapon hand, and lashed out at the remaining assailants.

Iudila, Thanos, and Brehanu came to his side, each of them now armed. Their faces, hands, and weapons dripped with the blood of those foolish enough to attack them.

On seeing their compatriots' fate, the remaining three attackers turned and fled the way they had come. The pirates charged after them with a battle keen that matched the continued cries of Dingha's wracked victim.

Down the street, around a bend then through a gateway that Iudila remembered from their arrival in Shukpi, and they were in the arena.

Where an army waited.

64

TOK-EKH CURSED THE FOOLS who had surrendered their lives and their weapons to the foreign dogs. He cursed himself for his own outburst and the premature release of his plan. But he blessed the gods now as they delivered his quarry into his hands.

Blessing turned again to curse as his men fell back a step at Iudila's approach. Even without the dwarf's clever lighting, Tok-Ekh had to admit the foreign prince was striking. Costume and makeup aside, his stature and frame—seemingly thrown on the pottery wheel of the gods—were sure to strike awe in the hearts of his friends, and fear in his enemies'. His hair, bright as flame, marked him as favored by the gods, perhaps even brother to them. Except for one thing.

"He bleeds, idiots," Tok-Ekh shouted. "He bleeds from the cut of my own spear. He is no god, but a man, an imposter who must pay for his blasphemy. Shall he live, this man who would put on airs of a god? He who would supplant the gods of your ancestors with his foreign demons?"

"No," a few of his men answered, daring a step toward the sailors.

"Shall he live, he who led his minions of Shibalba up from the watery abyss?"

"No." More men joined the chorus.

"Shall he live, he who would take your wives, your children, your fields, and lay them waste before your eyes?"

"No!"

"Then take them. Send them back to Shibalba, whence they came."

His army rushed Iudila's men. It was all the shaman could do to keep from cackling with glee. His ought to be the blade to silence Iudila's heart, his the ear to capture the death rattle, his the lips to take in the exhalation of Iudila's spirit.

"Save the red one for me," he called to his men, not really caring if they heard him.

So long as Iudila died, that was the important thing. After that, Tok-Ekh would see to his brother.

And then to Chakin.

65

"BACK!" IUDILA SHOUTED to his men. The army that faced them could not have been more than fifty men, but with a ten-to-one advantage, even this small army could spell disaster. Iudila led his men to the gateway at the arena's entrance, where the close stone walls would protect their flanks and squeeze the raiders into a narrow column.

"This isn't our fight," Thanos said. His was the only remaining clean blade.

"That bastard tried to kill me," Iudila said. "He brought the fight to us, and I'll by-God finish it."

"Shit." Thanos spat but stood his ground between Dingha and the right wall. "Some shields would be nice."

"We'll just have to make our own," Brehanu said.

"That's right," Iudila said. "Beginning with these."

The attackers reached the portal's entry and jostled one another for the honor of being first in, first to bring down the enemy. Five men squeezed through the narrow archway, their ululating war cry ringing from the stone walls. They charged Iudila and his men. They then became the first course in the defenders' wall.

Another four rushed the sailors, faces contorted with rage, weapons raised in two-handed hate.

Iudila took one man with a spear stroke to the groin. Thanos parried a second man's sword, spun away to let him pass, then slashed his blade through the man's kidney. Brehanu shattered his assailant's skull, while Dingha—hefting a sword in each hand—countered the attack by hacking through his man's upraised arms, nearly severing the warrior's head before his blades came to a stop.

Blood washed the plastered walls of the gateway. The sailors yanked the blades from their victims' bodies and gathered the fallen men's weapons. They took two steps back so the next wave would come at them off-balance after passing the hurdles of the fallen.

"Behind us!" Thanos shouted.

Iudila turned to see a fresh band of warriors racing toward the arena, spears bristling from beneath lowered shields.

"Dingha, with me," he yelled, and the man came to his side while Thanos and Brehanu held the inside line.

The new men charged into the gateway, but their leader lowered his weapon as he approached Iudila.

Hul-Balam removed his jaguar-head helm. He looked Iudila up and down and took in the bodies and the blood-spattered walls. For the first time since they had met, the captain cracked a smile. He said something in his native tongue, then laughed and slapped Iudila on the back.

Iudila grimaced as the captain struck his wounded shoulder, but he forced a smile and gestured toward the interior of the arena.

"Shall we finish this?"

Hul-Balam caught Iudila's meaning. He nodded and, side by side, prince and warrior advanced ahead of their men toward the enemy.

Dingha growled a deep, chest-rattling rumble. He beat his weapons together as he followed Iudila over the morbid barrier. The other men took up the cadence, beating spears on shields and filling the stone-walled gateway with the sound of their fury.

Tok-Ekh's men in the front ranks backed against their companions, fear growing on their faces. Their war cries turned to shouts of panic. As the clash of Shukpi weapons grew ever louder, the rear ranks seemed to understand the threat.

The invaders turned and ran.

Hul-Balam raised a triumphant shout, accompanied by the voices of his and Iudila's men. They chased after the fleeing rabble, slashing with their spears at the ankles of the stragglers. Iudila scanned over the heads of the fleeing warriors to see Tok-Ekh far in the lead. The shaman's long legs carried him quickly past the city's marker stones and onto the wide road toward Ha-Naab.

They chased the men along the Sakbe, the would-be raiders dropping swords and spears and shields as they ran. Tok-Ekh dashed into the trees but the others raced along the thoroughfare.

Iudila whistled at Hul-Balam, who had continued forward with his men.

"Tok-Ekh!" He pointed into the woods when the warrior looked back. "Tok-Ekh," Iudila repeated, then picked up an abandoned shield and led his men off the road in pursuit of the shaman.

"What are we doing?" Thanos demanded, his voice ragged with the chase.

"Defending the kingdom." Iudila drew his men to a stop and scanned the trees.

"It's not our fight," Thanos repeated his objection.

"It's mine now. There!" Iudila pointed to a broken branch, its exposed flesh moist and green. "Stay if you want. If you're with me, spread out and keep up."

Iudila ran deeper into the forest, following the loose trail of broken twigs and disturbed piles of humus. The dense growth blocked his men from view, but heavy footfalls told him that at least Dingha and Brehanu were with him.

The sun climbed. The air grew thick with moisture and with the sounds of the jungle. The land rose in a gentle slope, and Iudila paused at the crest to catch his breath. A rustle in the leaves made him look up, but he saw only shadows among the thick foliage. He flexed his fingers on the grip of the strange sword, its wooden blade inlaid with obsidian shards. He whistled to his men and a trio of replies echoed back to him.

Iudila studied the trees, picked up the trail again and continued down the slope. The rush of a river sounded from somewhere ahead of him and grew louder as he raced along the track. Another broken twig pointed the way, and Iudila burst past a tangle of branches.

His feet sank into a cushion of decaying leaves but he slogged ahead through the ankle-deep mould. Iudila stopped when he saw the tracks he left behind, realizing there was none before him. He turned around, caught a movement from the corner of his eye, and looked up just in time to see Tok-Ekh falling toward him.

Iudila dropped to a crouch and raised his shield. The hard wood absorbed the spear thrust, but the shaman's momentum tore the shield from its grips, leaving Iudila exposed. He rolled away from another stroke, this one slowed by the weight of the impaled shield. Iudila remembered his sword, which he brought to bear as he struggled to get his feet under him. The slope behind him pitched ever more sharply downward until it plunged toward the river below.

Iudila found his footing and advanced a few steps toward Tok-Ekh. The shaman had already managed to clear his spear tip. He swept the weapon in a wicked stroke, which Iudila parried with his sword. The blade's jagged pieces of obsidian caught on the spear's shaft. Tok-Ekh deftly flicked the sword away, leaving Iudila defenseless.

The shaman pointed the spear at Iudila's belly and backed him toward the bluff's edge.

"Your master may have failed to deal with you properly, but I shall finish his work." Tok-Ekh's Hebrew was perfect, if laced with hatred.

"I have no master," Iudila said, "but do what you will."

Tok-Ekh sneered and drew back the spear to strike.

Iudila braced himself, ready to bat aside the spear thrust, trusting in his oarsman's strength against the shaman's speed. Neither came into play, as another shape fell from the trees.

Tok-Ekh jerked his spear toward the falling creature to give it a swipe. It loosed a haunting snarl, struck out and knocked the weapon from the shaman's hands. Tok-Ekh fell on his backside and scuttled away from the beast.

Iudila might have thought the thing a huge, living shadow, but for the slender trail of red where the spear had opened its skin. The great cat's coat was black as night and patterned with rosettes that appeared only in the shifting sunlight. Its amber eyes leered at Iudila as it sniffed the air and lashed its tail. A rumble that might have been a growl, might have been a purr, radiated from its deep chest.

The panther turned on Tok-Ekh. The shaman had edged farther away but stopped as footsteps crashed through the brush.

Hul-Balam emerged from the trees, closely followed by his and Iudila's men. The cat snapped at the newcomers, who slid to a stop.

Taking advantage of the distraction, Tok-Ekh drew his dagger and leapt.

Iudila had no time even to raise an arm in defense. The blade should have pierced his heart, but the jaguar pounced and caught Tok-Ekh in midair. The tangled pair tumbled over the bluff's edge. The screams of wild cat and feral shaman echoed up the steep sides of the river gorge.

Hul-Balam rushed toward Iudila. He helped him up and the two peered into the water-cut valley. The sun had yet to reach the depths of the gorge, leaving the river shrouded in a thick mist that hid from them Tok-Ekh's fate.

The warrior spat over the edge, looked Iudila in the eyes and said something in his native tongue. Iudila followed him as he stalked back to the waiting men and led the way to the road.

"What did he say?" Iudila asked Chakin later, repeating the Sibolan words.

Iudila smiled when she translated them.

"A waste of a good pelt."

66

THE BRIDGE AT HA-NAAB had been repaired. The gates of the city stood open and unguarded. Chakin, Iudila and Hul-Balam studied the open field between the tree line and the river but saw nothing out of the ordinary.

The march from Shukpi had been just as unremarkable. Hul-Balam's one hundred warriors were augmented by a shoddy collection of farmers and fishermen who had stoically endured the forced march, resting only during the few hours it was too dark to have detected any potential traps.

No snares had lain in wait. The only signs of passage left by the men of Ha-Naab were the abandoned spears and swords and shields along the way.

"He says it is still too dangerous," Chakin interpreted Hul-Balam's objection to Iudila's plan, hatched during the march.

"There can't have been more than thirty men who left Shukpi on their own feet," Iudila explained again, as Chakin relayed the words to her captain. "By my count, every one of them left his weapons somewhere by the road. There are how many people in the city?"

"Five hundred?" Chakin said after a moment's thought.

"Which means that nearly every fighting man was in Shukpi yesterday. Even if they left some defenders behind, the men who returned were frightened. Fear is as good a weapon as a spear. Certainly better than fishing gaffs," he added with a wave toward the array of makeshift weapons carried by their conscripts. "How far will a spear fly?"

Hul-Balam scratched his cheek then pointed from the city wall to a point about midway across the field.

"That is the throw of a great warrior. How about a frightened farmer?"

The captain grunted and smiled. He indicated the area adjacent to the river.

Iudila nodded. "Bring your men to the midpoint of the field. Chakin and I will go to the bridge. Your long arm can still protect us there, and it's unlikely their feeble weapons will touch us."

Chakin relayed the words. The warrior's face made it plain he saw through Iudila's flattery. Nevertheless, he nodded and snapped an order to his men. A few of the conscripts muttered at the too-short rest they had enjoyed, but they followed the lead of the trained warriors and soon fell into line.

"What of us?" Dingha asked.

"Stay with him." Iudila nodded toward Hul-Balam. "Keep in sight and keep your weapons ready. And try to look mean."

"Try?"

Iudila laughed and clapped Dingha's shoulder.

"Ready?" he said to Chakin. With her answering nod he took her hand and led her onto the field. "Are you all right?" he asked as he felt the tension of her body through her hand.

"The last time I was here . . ."

"I know. That's behind you. Now these people need to see a princess, a warrior, the very representative of the gods."

She squeezed his hand and nodded. As she squared her shoulders, the anxious girl again gave way to the regal woman. "I have much yet to learn," she admitted.

"And much to teach. And we will take our lessons together," Iudila promised, "after we have reclaimed this city."

Chakin flashed him a smile and the pair went ahead of their army toward the bridge. Before they reached the abutment, a keen rose from behind the walls. The gates filled with a screaming mob that raced across the bridge. Iudila tensed and was about to signal his men, until he saw the mob consisted solely of women and children. Their cries were not of war, but of its daughter, mourning.

The women lined the southern bank of the river, their children arrayed in front of them. A few men followed them out the gates and stood in two columns on the bridge, eyes fixed on the wooden runners.

The presumed matriarch of the city—a woman Iudila judged to be in her late twenties, with four children clinging to her legs, and a fifth clamped on a swollen breast—stepped tentatively forward. She looked from Chakin to Iudila, then shielded her eyes, as against the sun itself.

"Our men have shamed us." Chakin whispered the translation to Iudila, though he found he could already understand some of the words.

"The shaman Tok-Ekh led them astray with flowered words and false promises," the woman continued, "but our hearts are with Uti-Chan Ahaw. Take these men if you must. Only leave us our children and our fields that we may live, and we will serve Shukpi faithfully." She raised her eyes to Chakin and arched a brow. "Or leave the men to us, and we will surely put them in their place."

Iudila's plan had been to play on the people's superstitions, to capitalize on his new-found association with their Lord Sun, and to demand the surrender of the rebels. Feminine good sense, however, seemed to be the victor this day, so he stilled his bravado in deference to Chakin.

"You speak wisely," the princess said. "My heart cries at the betrayal of Tok-Ekh and the men of Ha-Naab, but your words give comfort. Much blood has been spilled, and I have no desire to draw more. Many of your men have paid the full price for their foolishness. I trust that the justice due those who remain will be more aptly given by your hand than mine."

The woman nodded.

"How many men have you lost?" Chakin asked.

"Between those who found justice yesterday and those whose women will no longer have them, thirty-one hearths are in need of tending."

"Yours included?"

The woman smiled. "My own hearth went cold before this one drew breath." She patted the back of her suckling babe. "With the right spark?" A shrug.

Chakin turned and signaled to Hul-Balam, who came running to meet his princess.

"Lady?" he said.

"Who is your best warrior?"

"Wuk-Oh," he said without hesitation.

"Call him."

The captain signaled his lieutenant, who sprinted across the field.

"I greet you, Wuk-Oh," Chakin said, "and name you as captain of my guard."

"My lady?" both warriors said at once.

"I do not understand, Princess," Hul-Balam continued, pain shot through his face. "I know I failed you before, but—"

"Ha-Naab is without a father. You will choose thirty—" Chakin glanced at the woman with her children. "Make that thirty-one men, to serve you here and to ensure that such as yesterday's foolishness is never repeated." She turned toward the people lining the river and spoke in a strong, clear voice.

"This is Hul-Balam, who has slain the jaguar, who has climbed the western mountain, who has defended Shukpi and slaughtered her enemies. In the name of Uti-Chan and with the blessing of Kinich Ahaw, I now declare that he is Lord of Ha-Naab. You will serve him well, that peace may again reign between us, and that the ancient kinship between Shukpi and Ha-Naab may ever be remembered."

Children cowered as the women burst into cheers. The men on the bridge looked uneasy, but a few nodded in approval.

"My lady, I—" The warrior, now made lord, struggled for words.

"You are a good man, my lord. You have been a good friend. Now be a good ruler."

"What of your father?"

"Let him be your example. I am confident he will approve of my decision. He will rely on your friendship in healing the rift between our cities. Now go, choose those who will join you in this great task."

Hul-Balam nodded and went to select his men.

"And you, Captain," Chakin said to Wuk-Oh, "assure those who wish to remain here that they will always have a place among us. Families may quarrel, but Shukpi is elder brother to Ha-Naab. That bond must be maintained."

"It shall be as you say, Lady. And thank you." The warrior bowed then followed his former captain across the field.

"You have both the beauty and the wisdom of Sak-Ishik," said the woman of Ha-Naab. "May the goddess bless you, and may your hearth be always warm." With this last, she gave a sly look to Iudila.

Chakin smiled, took Iudila by the hand and led him back to their waiting men.

"That's it?" he asked.

"What more is there?"

"How do we know they won't attack again?"

Chakin stopped and looked into Iudila's eyes.

"You do not know the women of Sibolat. Once we have resolved something, it is as good as done."

"Is that so?"

"It is so. And now, Husband, our marriage is more than a day old. I resolve that not another noon shall pass before we have made our marriage bed."

Iudila glanced heavenward, to the sun just past its zenith.

"Then we must hurry. Far be it from me to stand between a woman and her resolve."

67

THE SUN'S LOW RAYS bounced off the waters of the river Hahkhan, bursting into shards of light as fish broke the surface to make a breakfast of the insects that swarmed in hazy clouds. Iudila and Chakin led their small band—Wuk-Oh, the three pirates and as many chosen warriors—through the gates of Shukpi to the stunned looks of the posted guards.

"Captain, you will report to the king," Chakin said, "and tell him of our success. You other men have earned your rest. Be certain, my father will hear of your service."

Wuk-Oh bowed and headed toward the palace. The warriors turned back to the gate—not too tired, it would seem, to trade lies with their compatriots.

Though they had marched through a day and a night, though they had taken only a few hours' rest in the past four days, Chakin kept her shoulders straight and moved with a fluid grace Iudila couldn't help but admire. His own men, tireless sailors and fighters in their own rights, dragged their feet and muttered at the madness of these people who used their roads for walking rather than riding. They cheered somewhat as Khu-Shul and Lemuel came down the steps from the temple mount to greet them.

"Princess!" Khu-Shul rushed to Chakin, wringing his hands, his eyes red and bleary. "How are you back so soon? Where are the rest of your men? What's happened?"

"Give her time to breathe, Scribe," Iudila said in clumsy Sibolan.

The dwarf blinked up at him. "How did you learn our tongue?"

Iudila smiled. "One cannot help what one hears, yes?"

"Everything is fine, Khu-Shul," Chakin said. "I will explain later, but now our guests need food and rest."

"Yes, Lady, I will see to it."

"Bring them to the palace this evening," she added. "We have yet to share our wedding feast."

"Of course. Will there be anything else?"

"Nothing. Absolutely nothing." Chakin took Iudila's hand and led him to the palace. If they passed anyone in the streets, they did not see them. If anyone greeted them, they heard them not. Their world was condensed to the warmth of flesh on flesh, the rush of blood in their veins, and the fragrant air of love that surrounded them.

A warm bath waited in Iudila's chambers, where they undressed each other and slid into the water's embrace. They were exhausted and sore, but the fatigue drained away with the road grime as they bathed one another. They soon abandoned their wash cloths, rose from the basin and explored each other's body with hands and lips and tongues.

Chakin's mouth was hot and moist on Iudila's, her skin taut and smooth, save for the gooseflesh that rose under his caresses. She moaned as her flower opened first to his gentle touch, then further to his kiss and the deeper probing of his tongue. He drank from her nectar, consuming and consumed. Her cries filled the room as her passion bathed his tongue. He rose along her body to kiss her navel, her breasts and again her lips, sharing the taste of that sweet ambrosia, that elixir of life.

Iudila's racing heart beat in time with Chakin's as their bodies pressed together, the rhythm echoed by the thrum in his ears and by pulsing shadows on the fringe of his vision. He felt transported, taken out of his body. And then pleasure turned to fear, then to rage as Iudila fought against a rising tide of lost memories. He flinched as he imagined Milhma's rough hands crawling on his young flesh. His ears rang with Milhma's mocking taunts and whispered endearments. His eyes clouded as visions of Milhma's funeral pyre faded into scenes from back alleys in coastal cities where the muffled screams of women echoed from behind dilapidated whorehouse doors. Iudila drew back from

Chakin and the nightmarish sounds were replaced by a low growl as he grabbed her by the shoulders, spun her around and tried to force himself into her from behind. She gasped in pain as he wrapped his hand in her hair and yanked her head back.

"No!" she cried out as she twisted and kicked her way out of his grasp, then scuttled across the room, out of his reach. Breathing heavily, her eyes were wide with surprise and fear.

The pounding in Iudila's ears subsided. The voices faded, and the visions of the pirates' raping their victims, taking whores in the alleys of Tingis, and the years of torture under Milhma's hands—all these vanished. He was left in the quiet half-light of the wedding chamber, his bride huddled in the far corner, knees drawn tight to her chest.

"Chakin—"

"Don't!" Her voice was red with hurt and anger.

His own voice was ragged, barely a whisper as he pushed himself onto his knees and crawled toward her. "I didn't mean … forgive me, please."

"Don't come any closer."

Iudila stopped beside the bath, the stones still wet with the prints of their bodies.

"I am so sorry and … ashamed." His tears added to the damp patterns on the stone. "I … I have known only the ways of violence and lust. Never giving and receiving. Never tenderness. Never this." He choked back a sob. "Never love."

Chakin's face softened. She came to her husband as he curled onto his side. She sat beside him and cradled his head to her breast. "Never force me like that again," she said, and his silent weeping became racking sobs as he wrapped his arms tightly about her waist. "Shh," she whispered, and stroked his damp hair.

Chakin rocked him for a long time, until Iudila's shaking stopped and his tears no longer fell.

"I am so sorry," he whispered finally. "I was just a boy when I was captured and the captain … he … he …"

"Shh. It is over. That man is dead, and I am not hurt," she assured him. "You forget, I am warrior as well as princess. And I am also a bride. Come."

She led him to one of the stone benches, cushioned with thick pelts. She bade him sit, then pushed him into a supine position. It was his turn to moan as she teased his skin with fingers, lips and long hair. Guilt and pain turned again to passion, and she lay beside him, drew him atop her, and guided him into her.

Chakin gave a soft cry. Iudila started to pull back, but she gripped him firmly, and pulled him deeper. She held him there and fixed her tear-moistened eyes on his.

"I am the Surface of the Deep," she said in breathless tones, "the sacred font from whence springs all life."

The words startled Iudila, but from somewhere in the depths of his soul, he found the reply. "I am the Spirit of God, the will of the One whose seed brought forth Creation."

And the Spirit of God moved upon the Surface of the Deep.

68

A HAND ON IUDILA'S SHOULDER shook him awake.

"Again, my love?" he mumbled. "Even the Almighty took a day of rest."

Iudila opened his eyes to see the wrinkled skin, pierced nostrils and chiseled teeth of Kehmut. He yelped as the old woman stripped away the covering linen and inspected his manhood.

"Seems to have worked well enough," she judged, "even being half cut off."

She herded the newlyweds into a fresh bath then gathered up the pelt stained with their lovemaking and Chakin's virgin blood.

"The feast begins soon," she told them. "Do not be late."

Kehmut took the pelt, and a cheer rose from outside as she left the pair to their bath.

"It seems your people approve," Iudila said, and kissed Chakin.

"Their princess approves," she said. "That is all that matters."

She returned his kiss and ran a hand down his chest and beneath the water's surface. The day of rest could wait.

69

CHAKIN AND IUDILA ARRIVED LATE. From the royal courtyard came the sounds of laughter, clattering cups and the squeals of serving girls.

"Greetings, my lady," Wuk-Oh said. "Your father would have a word."

Rather than ushering them into the feast, the newly-raised captain of the guard led them to a tall, plaster-faced building. Stucco reliefs adorned walls brightly painted with murals depicting battles, sacrifices and celebrations. From the decorations and trappings of jaguar pelts, colorful feathers and richly-dyed linens, Iudila took this to be Uti-Chan's audience chamber.

The king sat cross-legged on a cushioned platform. Behind him and to one side stood a squat, round woman with a squirming toddler in her arms. An older man stood to the other side, thin and with a face like an axe blade. Wuk-Oh took his place against the side wall, while an older, bearded man lay prostrate before the king. Chakin took Iudila's hand and stepped toward the royal dais.

"I'm sorry, Father," she said. "We didn't mean to be late."

"It is not that," Uti-Chan said. "I fear unhappy news must sully this joyous day. Captain?"

"My lady, it is my sad duty to inform you that the scribe Khu-Shul has been arrested for treason."

Chakin's face went pale. "That's not possible. He is my most trusted friend."

"I took it upon myself to determine how the rebels gained access to the plaza," Wuk-Oh continued. "I enlisted Khu-Shul's assistance in examining the tunnels beneath the temple mount, where I found this." The captain produced a spool of twine.

Chakin shook her head. "I don't understand."

"This thread was strung between the upper entrance and the river gate. I believe the scribe was in league with Tok-Ekh, that he provided the means for the traitor to gain access to the temple mount."

"What does Khu-Shul say?" Iudila demanded.

"He denies it, of course," the captain replied. "He even seemed surprised when I discovered the string. He doubtless assumed his fellow conspirators would gather it up behind them."

"Or perhaps he knew nothing about it," Iudila said.

"The tunnels are part of the sacred temple space," Uti-Chan said. "Only the royal family and the scribes have access to them, and none knows them as well as the scribes."

"Why is that?"

"Khu-Shul's grandfather laid out the tunnels," Chakin said, having found her voice. "He and his family know every path, every chamber."

"He knows the tunnels," Iudila acknowledged. "That does not explain why he would help your uncle. Tok-Ekh tried to kill him."

"But who else could have done it?" Chakin said, then lowered her eyes. "Khu-Shul has long been fond of me. Perhaps he acted from jealously."

"I want to talk to him," Iudila said.

"That will not be possible," the king replied. "Judgment has already been passed."

"What sort of judgment?"

"The penalty for treason is death."

Chakin leaned against Iudila, and the man before the dais choked out a sob.

"However," Uti-Chan continued, "the law requires two reliable witnesses for a sentence of death to be carried out. Given the absence of positive proof, and in light of his family's long record of faithful service, Khu-Shul has simply been banished."

The bearded man clasped his hands together.

"May all the gods above and below bless Uti-Chan Ahaw for his mercy."

"Khu-Shul's father," Chakin whispered.

"Where has he been sent?" Iudila asked the king. "May we see him?"

The woman stepped forward. "I have arranged with my brother Oshlahun-Ak, Lord of Wakhem, to host our deluded little Khu-Shul. Be assured, he will be well cared for."

Chakin brightened and gave a sad smile. "Thank you, my lady. You are most gracious."

"Rise, Nak-Makah," the king ordered, and the bearded man obeyed. "As the son is liable for the sins of his father, so is the father responsible for his son's. The most aggrieved party has the right to speak your punishment." Uti-Chan gestured toward Iudila.

"Me?"

"Your blood was shed by treachery," the king said, "your wedding bed kept from you."

"I believe the families of the murdered guards have a greater claim than I, but I will presume to speak for them."

Iudila felt the stares of all present, their eyes boring into him.

"Nak-Makah," he continued in halting Sibolan, "you will kneel—"

The man started to his knees, but Iudila caught him by the elbow and raised him.

"You will kneel three times daily to beg your gods for the well-being of the people of Shukpi, the health of their lord, and the restoration of your son's good name."

Tears dampened the man's whiskers.

"I shall pray five times daily, Lord." He took Iudila's and Chakin's hands in his. "And I shall also pray for the joy and prosperity of Shukpi's Lady and her love."

"About that," said the narrow-faced man beside the king. "I believe we have one more order of business before this court."

Chakin nodded, released Iudila's hand and stepped toward the dais. Iudila started to follow, but Nak-Makah took his arm and shook his head.

Chakin stood to one side of the dais, and the other woman—"The queen, Lady Sak-Chih," the bearded scribe whispered in Iudila's ear—stepped to the other side with her child. Chakin reached for the boy, but he shrank back from her. The queen cajoled him, and he loosened his grip and allowed Chakin to take him. She shifted him to one arm, then laid a hand on his head.

"I am Na Chakin, Lady of the Two Suns, Mother of Shukpi, Daughter of Yash-Ahaw and of Kinich Yash Khuk-Moh."

The narrow-faced one held out a bowl of oil. Chakin dipped in her middle finger then drew a cross on the boy's forehead.

"As Lady of Shukpi, I anoint Khak-Imish, son of Uti-Chan Ahaw and Na Sak-Chih, as heir to the god-seat of Shukpi, under the patronage of the god Khawil." Chakin handed the boy back to Sak-Chih, dipped both thumbs in the oil and traced a pair of crosses over the queen's eyebrows. "I further relinquish my title as Lady of Shukpi and bestow upon Na Sak-Chih the authority of the same. This I do in the name of Sak-Ishik, she who reflects the glory of Kinich Ahaw."

"Shan-Chitam," the king said to the old man who wore a crooked smile of victory, "as chief elder, you stand witness to the transfer of titles. Nak-Makah—scribe and elder—you will faithfully record the same and will prepare a khobah as a permanent remembrance before the people, before the venerated ancestors and before the gods."

Uti-Chan stood, embraced Chakin and led her back to Iudila. Shan-Chitam bowed and started to leave, but the king was not yet finished.

"Let it also be witnessed and recorded that on this day I claim Uti-La of the Sea as my son, and name him protector of the sacred treasures of Khuk-Moh."

"My lord—"Shan-Chitam started to protest.

"It shall be duly recorded," Nak-Makah cut him off.

"And witnessed," said Wuk-Oh, a look of defiance in his eyes.

"So it is done," the king said. "If there is no further business before the god-seat?"

Shan-Chitam was plum-faced but he held his tongue.

"Then let us attend to the wedding celebration. Captain?"

Wuk-Oh nodded, struck the butt of his spear three times on the stone floor, and led the assembly through the doorway.

"What was that?" Iudila asked Chakin as they joined the procession behind Uti-Chan and Sak-Chih.

"The council would never abide Shukpi's Lady being wed to a foreigner, not even so distant a cousin." Chakin's eyes were moist, but she wore a smile of contentment. "That, Husband, was my bride price."

70

"REMIND ME WHY we're doing this," Thanos said.

Iudila looked up at him. "You want to eat, don't you?"

"I want to be able to pay for my food and have it served to me, not to catch and cook it myself."

The pirates were now fishermen. Uti-Chan had offered his patronage to keep them as guests of the royal household, but Iudila knew his men—knew himself—too well. He judged that with ease would come restlessness. With restlessness was sure to come trouble. So he had asked only for a canoe, a dugout similar to the one the Tolupan had provided them. Instead of sailing the coasts for plunder, they now plied inland waters, the web of rivers that fed the Hahkhan from its headwaters in the east to where it spilled into the Hahshuk.

After stepping aside as Lady of Shukpi, Chakin had taken on the duties of shaman. She spent her days gathering herbs and listening to the stories of the old ones, filling in Tok-Ekh's half-formed history lessons with the folk memory of her people. By night, she tracked the stars' wanderings. It was a rarity for her and Iudila to be abed at the same time, but they made the most of what stolen moments they could.

"Come with me," Uti-Chan said from the dock as Iudila and his men brought their canoe in with a good morning's catch.

"Mustn't keep Papa waiting," Thanos said under his breath.

Iudila ignored him, tied the boat to the dock, and walked with the king along the wharf.

The two men walked up a ramp and into the southern entrance of the temple. Iudila followed the king's example, washing his hands and wafting incense smoke over his face. Uti-Chan then led the way up the steps to the third floor.

It had been dark the first time Iudila entered the temple's uppermost level. Now the anteroom was brilliantly lit through clerestory openings that admitted the sun's rays but held out its heat. Iudila followed the king into the inner sanctum where the only direct light came through a soot-stained smoke hole in the high roof. Mirrors of obsidian reflected light from the anteroom onto the whitewashed walls to illuminate the inner chamber.

Uti-Chan sat beside a low wooden table and motioned Iudila to the opposite cushion. The king raised the lid on a woven box to reveal a pair of linen-wrapped bundles.

"Open them," he said.

Iudila pulled away the wrappings to reveal a pair of large, cut gemstones set in a frame of copper wire. The second packet held a stack of metal plates bound with a tree-bark cover.

"The treasures of my great-father Khuk-Moh," Uti-Chan said.

Iudila opened the cover to reveal a series of hammered copper plates covered on each side with uneven rows of rough-handed inscriptions. The characters were not the glyphs Iudila had begun to recognize on the buildings and monuments of Shukpi. Nor were they any alphabet he knew, though they bore some resemblance to the runes used by Celts and Northmen.

"What do they say?" Iudila asked the king.

Uti-Chan's frowned. "I had hoped you might tell me. You cannot read them?"

"It's no script I've ever seen." Iudila picked at a scale of green patina that marred the plates along their edges and on the exposed surfaces. Even if he could read the words, he feared much of the message would prove lost to corrosion.

"What about this?" Uti-Chan said.

The king turned past the copper plates until he came to a series made of bronze. The writing was neater than on the copper and became neater still as Iudila turned more and more plates.

"I can't make sense of any of it," Iudila said.

"And the gemstones?"

Iudila lifted them from the table. The jewels were each about half the size of his palm, as thick as his thumb, and cut with neat facets. One of the gems appeared to be of ruby, the other of sapphire. They were connected along their edges by a copper wire about a finger joint in length, with a hand's-breadth of wire trailing from the opposite sides.

Patterns of colored light danced on the walls as Iudila studied the gems. Red and blue moved independently, even with the same motion of the lenses. Iudila placed the jewels over his eyes, and the room split into dozens of distorted images.

"Would you raise your hand, my lord?"

Uti-Chan did so and a host of red- and blue-tinted images mimicked him. Some were sideways, others upside-down or even in mirror image. The effect made Iudila dizzy, and he placed the gems back on the table.

"We call them seer-stones," Uti-Chan said. "They help in seeing past the veil between this and the Otherworld."

"Where did they come from?"

"Khuk-Moh brought them from Pah-Tullan when he left there to join his seed with the line of Yash-Ahaw. His was the last hand to inscribe the plates. It would seem he was the last to be able to read them, as well."

"But there were others before?"

"Oh, yes," Uti-Chan said, and stroked the plates reverently. "Many years ago the Lords of the West—the distant ancestors of the Sibolan people—left their homeland across the Sunset Waters. They brought with them these and the other treasures of Khuk-Moh."

"Others?"

The king nodded. "When Khuk-Moh left Pah-Tullan, he brought only the plates and the seer-stones. The rest he left behind."

"What are they?"

Uti-Chan tapped the metal book. "What he left behind, and where, are written here. The plates also contain the record of our people—here in Sibolat and in the land across the water—back to the First Time."

"And none can read them?"

Uti-Chan shook his head.

"Do your legends not record the stories? Surely your elders know them."

The king laughed. "Legend has a way of changing over time. Wars are won or lost, families feud or make peace, and memories change to suit one party or another. Had we no writing at all, we might be more diligent in preserving the past. As it is, we record our deeds, but succeeding generations may change or destroy the past as they see fit."

"So even these plates may not be a true reckoning of events."

"Perhaps. I suppose we will never know."

Iudila scratched his chin. "There may be a way. My uncle is well learned in many languages, some that are no longer spoken or written. He may recognize in these plates what we do not."

Uti-Chan brightened. "He would consent to become a scribe rather than a fisherman?"

"I don't think he would mind the hardship."

71

IUDILA TRACED HIS FINGER along Chakin's spine. Perhaps even more than their lovemaking, he treasured these times of blissful communion as they both lay spent, their heartbeats slowing from the frantic pace of only moments before. He'd once heard a mystic speak of that moment of ecstasy when a man's mind is drained of conscious thought, freeing him to glimpse the divine. In climax he caught a flash of that vision but it was here, in the afterglow, that the veils between Heaven and earth were drawn apart enough for the holy light of Paradise to shine through.

"Iudila, come quickly!"

The voice called from outside his chambers, and the heavenly veils dropped in place once more. Iudila sprang to his feet, grabbed his sword and raced through the doorway to find Lemuel clutching a sheaf of tree-bark paper.

"I didn't mean that quickly," Lemuel said. "Put away your sword and come to the temple. Bring Chakin. But do get dressed first, hmm?"

72

"WHAT'S SO IMPORTANT, old man?"

Iudila and Chakin joined Lemuel in the small scriptorium on the temple's second level. The plates and seer-stones had been moved here both for the better light and for the fact that Lemuel—though honored as a scribe—was not permitted within the sacred space of the highest chamber.

"Oh, it's not so important, really," the Jew said, "unless you want to know what the plates say."

Chakin and Iudila both stopped midstride.

"You can read them?" Chakin said.

"Partly. I've identified the base script, but it changes as the text progresses. Given time, I should be able to work out the later portions."

"How did you do it?" Iudila asked as he sat next to Chakin, across the table from Lemuel.

"With these." Lemuel held up the wire-bound gems.

"I tried them," Iudila said, "but I couldn't read anything."

"Nor could I at first." Lemuel stood and bowed as Uti-Chan joined them.

"Sit, my friend, please," the king said. "I understand you have made progress."

"I have," Lemuel said as he sat and smoothed his kilt. "I reasoned the copper plates must be the oldest, given their state of corrosion. I also assumed the gems must be some sort of lenses through which the text might be made plain. No matter which way I viewed the text, its secrets remained closed to me."

Iudila had long been accustomed to his uncle's round-about manner of storytelling, but Chakin had yet to learn his patience.

"What next?" she asked.

Lemuel's eyes lit up and he leaned close to the princess. "The idea came to me that the copper plates might not be the first part of the book. My people, the Jews—and the Egyptians before them—have long known the secrets of combining metals. Copper by itself will eventually turn to ruin, particularly in a damp environment. However, when cast with just a small amount of other minerals, it forms another metal, bronze, which is relatively impervious to corrosion.

"If the plates originated across the seas, it stands to reason they might have been made of bronze. On reaching these shores—where copper can be had, but the other minerals seem nowhere to be found—the manufacture of bronze became impossible. Eventually, the skill was forgotten."

"It may be as you say," the king said, though he sounded dubious. "Go on."

"I then began viewing the bronze plates through the lenses, trying different combinations until . . ."

Lemuel picked up the gems and made a show of twisting them around the connecting wire before he handed them to Iudila. "What do you see?"

Iudila gave his uncle a skeptical look but fastened the jewels over his eyes, the end wires wrapped behind his ears. The result was much the same as the first time he had looked through them—vertigo and confused images.

"I see nothing of any sense."

"Ah, my fault. Turn them over so the red is over your right eye. Red is the color of the earth."

"What does that matter?" Chakin asked as Iudila flipped the lenses.

"The earth is the Great Foundation," Iudila explained, "the base upon which all else is built. In the great temple of our ancestors, there were two pillars before the altar. The one on the right was called Yachin, which means—"

"Foundation," Chakin said.

"As brilliant as she is beautiful," Lemuel said. "Now, what do you see?"

Iudila looked once more at the open leaves of the book, this time with a much different result.

"I can see regular figures, but I don't recognize them."

Lemuel slapped his forehead. "Forgive an old man. I've left it upside-down." He turned the book so the first plate of bronze lay to Iudila's right. Immediately, the lenses bent the images of the plates so that partial characters from the opposite pages were overlaid, and Iudila could make out the first lines of text.

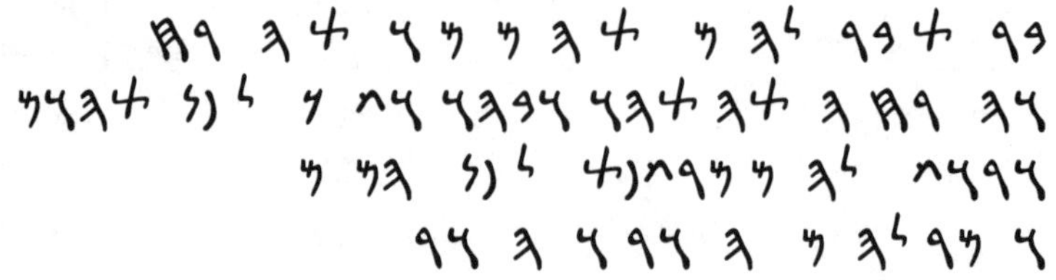

"It's Punic," Iudila said, then explained to Chakin. "The Punics were early settlers of what is now my land of Spania. They left inscriptions on rocks and in caves all along the sea coasts. Unfortunately, no one knows how to read them."

"You are partly correct," Lemuel said.

Iudila removed the lenses to see a rather satisfied look on his uncle's face.

"What have you done?"

"It was only a guess, really," he said with uncharacteristic modesty, then placed on the table a piece of bark on which he had written two rows of characters.

"What is it?" Uti-Chan asked.

"My lord," Lemuel explained, "the top line is the script of my people, in which our holy book is written."

"A short book," the king judged, "if you have not even thirty words."

Iudila smiled. "There are more words than thirty, my lord. Many more. Each of these characters represents but a sound. The sounds are then put together to form words."

Uti-Chan nodded slowly, but still looked skeptical. Lemuel pointed to each of the Hebrew characters in turn, giving their sound. The king seemed more convinced. "And the second line?"

"I believe they represent the same sounds, written in a different way."

"How did you work that out?" Iudila asked.

"As I said, it was a guess. Here." Lemuel set another sheet on the table, this one containing the first few lines of text from the plates. "My dear," he said to Chakin, "would you be so kind as to draw the twins to the characters?"

Chakin picked up a wooden stylus and scratched the matching Hebrew figures beneath those from the plates. It took some time for her to form the foreign shapes, and Iudila's eyes grew wider with each stroke.

"You wish to speak the words?" Lemuel asked him when Chakin had finished.

Iudila's throat was dry, but he somehow found his voice. "In the Beginning, the gods brought about the skies and the land. The land was all chaos and desolation, and darkness rested on the surface of the abyss. The breath of the gods stirred the seas—"

"And they said, 'Bring forth light,'" Uti-Chan said, and all eyes turned toward him. "It is part of our sacred ritual, the words that revive Kinich Ahaw and bring him back from his winter sojourn in the south. These are the writings of our ancient priests."

"And of ours," Lemuel said.

Chakin shook her head. "But how?"

"The Punic kingdoms were established by Phoenicians, a sea-faring people," Lemuel said. "They originated on the eastern end of our great inland sea. When my distant ancestors formed their kingdom, they took the lands of the sea-people, seized their cities—"

"And adopted their alphabet," Iudila finished for him.

Lemuel nodded. "Our Hebrew script was not formed until after the return from captivity in Babylon, a thousand years after Yahshua led the Israelites into Canaan."

"Your Yahshua?" Uti-Chan asked Iudila.

"A different one. He was a great military and religious leader, three or four baktuns before Yashwak."

The king nodded. "A distinguished name. Friend Lemuel, you have done well. You believe these plates hold the key to the rest?"

"The script changes as the text progresses," Lemuel said. "Once I am familiar with the base script, however, I should be able to trace it through the later plates, to follow it through time, if you will."

"Make every effort," Uti-Chan said. "You shall have all you require to that end. In the mean time, my children, I believe it is time for you to make a journey."

73

"UP, YOU RASCALS!" Iudila pulled aside the curtain at his men's doorway. Sunlight flooded the room and sailors cursed the brightness.

"It's midday," Thanos protested. "We've been out since before dawn. Now is our time to rest."

"You're right," Iudila said. "Go back to sleep. I'll just go after the treasure on my own."

The Greek dropped back down on his mat and draped his arm over his eyes. It took a few moments before he slowly lowered his arm, sat up and looked at Iudila. "What did you say?"

"Pah-Tullan," Iudila said later, after his men had joined him in the audience chamber.

One wall of the room was painted with a map of the Sibolan kingdoms. Shukpi lay in the south, and Iudila pointed to a symbol in the far north.

"The king's ancestors came from there two hundred years ago. He has asked us to lead a trade mission."

"Why us?" Brehanu asked. "We are not merchants. We know nothing of these lands." He swept his hand across the broad expanse between the two cities.

"Mutul and Lakam-Ha"—Iudila pointed to the cities north and northwest of Shukpi—"have long been at war. The whole central region of the land is in upheaval. Runners rarely make it through the lines, and even diplomatic embassies have been captured and killed."

"Wonderful," Thanos said. "Your new king sends us to commit suicide. Wouldn't it be simpler just to kill us here?"

"Wakhem is the queen's home city," Iudila said, ignoring the objection. "They control trading ports on the western coast. We will follow the river to Wakhem, then sail up the coast to Pah-Tullan."

"We'll be at sea again?" Dingha said, his broad, dark face lighting up at the prospect.

Iudila smiled. "We'll be at sea. If all goes well, the king envisions several trading trips each year, carrying fruit and herbs and pelts. In return, he expects—"

"Gold?" Thanos's eyes were wide.

Iudila looked at him sternly, then slowly softened his expression and let a grin twist his lips. "And silver and gems the likes of which this city has never seen."

Thanos loosed a triumphant shout, and Wuk-Oh rushed into the chamber, spear at the ready. Iudila waved the weapon aside. "It's all right, Captain. You may tell the king he has his crew."

74

"NO WORD YET?" Chakin asked Nak-Makah.

The scribe shook his head. "Nothing."

It had been weeks since Khu-Shul's exile to Wakhem, but news of his arrival there had yet to come.

"I will ask after him," Chakin said, and kissed the old man's whiskered cheek. She forced another kiss on Khak-Imish, and the boy squirmed away, wiping his cheek. "I will deliver your letters to your brother, my lady."

Sak-Chih took Chakin's hand.

"May the gods smile on your travels."

Chakin finally turned to Uti-Chan.

"My heart will mourn each day you are gone," he told her.

Chakin pressed his cheeks and kissed him. "Then pray that Father-god makes our journey quick and successful."

Iudila embraced Lemuel in parting. "You will send word?"

"As soon as the plates open their full meaning to me," the older man promised.

"The king awaits your success."

Lemuel smiled and winked. "Both my kings, I think." He placed his hands on Iudila's and Chakin's foreheads, his middle fingers forming vees. He raised his face to the heavens and said, "Yahweh bless and protect you. Yahweh shine his face upon you in mercy. Yahweh watch over you in peace."

Iudila helped Chakin into the canoe then stepped down from the pier. Other families hurried their good-byes as Iudila and his men pushed the boat into the Hahkhan's current to lead the convoy of dugouts to Wakhem. Traveling with the flow of the Hahkhan, they reached the junction of the Hahshuk by the end of the first day. There, a pair of boats from Ha-Naab joined them for the nine-day journey upriver to Wakhem.

"Do you think Lemuel will find the hiding place?" Chakin asked Iudila one night as they lay in their riverside camp beneath a tent of heavy linen.

"If anyone can, he will."

While the outward goal of their journey was to reopen the coastal trade route with Pah-Tullan, Uti-Chan had charged the pair with the separate task of recovering the rest of Khuk-Moh's treasure. Lemuel had deciphered the alphabet used to inscribe the plates. The first set of bronze plates proved to be a copy of the Torah—the Hebrew book of law written by Moses. It also included a genealogy that traced a line of descent from the patriarch Joseph through the tribe of Ephraim, down twenty generations to a pair of brothers called Laban and Malachi.

Only that first set—the Torah and genealogy—had been inscribed in the separated script, requiring the seer-stones to read the characters. A second set of bronze plates and the copper plates were covered with undisguised script. As near as Lemuel could determine, the plates had been engraved over a period of a thousand years. The changes in the script and language structure during that time were gradual, but significant enough that he had to read from the beginning in order to interpret the later plates.

By the time Chakin and Iudila left on the trade mission, Lemuel had determined Khuk-Moh's treasure to consist of a sword of steel—a material unknown in Sibolat—and a bronze orb, an astrolabe or star-finder. He had yet to learn where Khuk-Moh had secreted them, or why. Uti-Chan promised to send a messenger to Pah-Tullan as soon as the hiding place was discovered.

For now, Iudila was again charged to go into the unknown. Only this time, he had Chakin by his side. He pulled her close as a falling star streaked across the sky, lighting their path to the west.

75

THE GREAT PLAZA at Pah-Tullan left Iudila dumbfounded. Man-made mountains—only slightly smaller, it seemed, than the natural ones surrounding the valley—anchored a broad avenue that ran more than a Roman mile along the central axis of the city. A third mountain towered over the middle of the avenue, larger than the other two combined.

Staggering as the proportions of the giant pyramids were, their decorations were even more so. The massive steps and ramps were sheathed in plaster, covered with brightly-painted murals and inlaid with gems and gold and silver that dazzled the eye and bathed the plaza in colored light.

Chakin and Iudila led their party from the canal at the south end of the plaza to the looming temple in the north. They carried the royal boon—that part of their tribute set aside for Pah-Tullan's king—while receiving agents had already begun ransacking the canoes for trade goods.

Of the twenty dugouts that left Wakhem's port, four had been lost with their cargo and passengers during the three-week voyage along the coast, tribute to the angry gods of wind and sea. All the remaining boats had survived the twenty-day journey upriver to Pah-Tullan, though three men had been claimed by Kinich Ahaw as they paddled through the breezeless canyons of sun-scorched rock.

It was, then, an exhausted, parched, sunburned delegation that traversed the long avenue.

The day was not a solar festival, not an alignment of the calendars, nor a feast day of the gods. Even so, the plaza was filled with thousands, tens of thousands of people. Royal guards cleared a path for Chakin, Iudila, and the handful of servants bearing the royal gifts. When they reached the base of the northern temple, the escort formed into lines on either side of the stairway and bowed as Chakin and Iudila continued upward with their train.

The face of the temple was steep, but Iudila blessed whatever architect had sunk the steps into the sides so the angle wasn't quite so punishing. Still, he lost count of the steps somewhere after eighty, and by the time they reached the summit, Chakin and Iudila dripped sweat, while their porters were drenched.

As they passed the final step, a band of flutes and bells greeted them, along with a company of dancing girls dressed in brightly colored skirts. The temple's plateau was nearly the size of Shukpi's sacred plaza, with a half-dozen buildings around its perimeter. The band and dancers led them to a pavilion at the center of the platform.

Beneath the shade of a heavy linen canopy, a group of people rose as Chakin and Iudila approached. At their center stood a boy whom—by his pride of place, the size of his feathered headdress and the wealth of gemstones, silver and gold ornaments—Iudila assumed to be the king.

The boy stared open-mouthed at Iudila until an older woman leaned forward to whisper in his ear. The king closed his mouth, nodded, and gestured to a serving woman, who poured a gourd of water for the guests. His voice cracked as he said. "As water enlivens the desert, so may it revive your spirits after so long a journey."

Iudila had to guess at some of the words, as the language of Pah-Tullan differed from Shukpi's as much as Saxon differed from Gothic. Chakin caught the meaning faster, and she accepted the bowl, drank, and handed it to Iudila. He also drank, then returned the gourd to the servant.

Chakin bowed to the king. "Lord Khal-Ayin, I bring you greetings from Khak Uti-Chan, son of Kinich Yash Khuk-Moh who was brother to your great-father, Yatah-Itzat."

The king returned the bow. "In the name of the great god Gukumatz, I accept the greetings of my brother, and bid welcome to you, my sister. All that Pah-Tullan has to offer, I lay at your feet."

"My lord is most gracious," Chakin said, "but your good will is gift enough. If it please you, I offer a humble token of esteem from the lords of the lands southward."

She gestured the porters forward, and they set down their bundles of jaguar pelts, peccary hides and tobacco leaves. Others presented baskets of feathers from quetzal and mot-mot birds, spines from stingrays, and pieces of jade. The king and his court nodded politely at all these, but eyes went wide and hands covered whispering mouths as the final gift was presented.

"A calendar wheel," Chakin said, "commissioned by Uti-Chan and crafted by the great scribe Nak-Makah."

The wheel—a large disk of obsidian—had somehow survived the journey. It had taken four men to carry it up the pyramid. A porter placed a mahogany stand beside the king's cushion, and the men heaved the wheel into place.

The king examined the brightly polished stone, his face reflected in the central image of Kinich Ahaw. Around the circumference were emblem glyphs for each day of the Haab—the solar year—while an inner ring represented the Chol-Kin, the human year. A third ring held representations of the thirteen constellations that governed the night sky throughout the year.

"It's beautiful," Khal-Ayin said as he traced the image of the Great Turtle.

The older woman—the queen-mother, Iudila guessed—cleared her throat, and the king squared his shoulders and resumed his air of indifference.

"The workmen of Shukpi are talented, indeed. My thanks to Brother Uti-Chan, and my compliments to your scribe." The king clapped his hands and a half-dozen attendants stepped forward. "You must be weary from so great a journey. My servants will guide you to your rest. I will call on you soon."

Attendants led Chakin and Iudila back down the temple steps. As he descended, Iudila surveyed the great city, and his heart sank. Besides the three giant pyramids, hundreds of smaller buildings flanked the great avenue. Thousands more lined the lesser streets and plazas and canals that radiated from the central artery.

Iudila quailed at the thousands of acres covered by the city's buildings. Even if he confined himself to the pyramids alone, it might take months, years to search the tunnels that must cut through the artificial mountains.

As if sensing his dread, Chakin took Iudila's hand.

"Among all the lands of Sibolat, and all the lands northward and southward, all the great islands of the sea, you found your way to me. How difficult can this search be?"

76

"MOTHER SAYS I SHOULD STAY in the temple and palace, but what good is being king if I can't do what I want?"

During the past several weeks, Khal-Ayin had taken to visiting with Iudila and Chakin after the noon meal, while the queen-mother slept through the heat of the day.

"A king must place the needs of his people ahead of his own desires," Iudila said sternly, then laughed at the boy-king's downcast look. "I do not see that your visits cause any harm to your people, however. In this case, you may do as you please."

Khal-Ayin brightened and reached for a piece of flatbread, which he dipped in a bowl of agave nectar. "Tell me again how you crossed the waters." He popped the bread into his mouth and a drop of syrup trickled down his chin.

The boy was fascinated by Iudila and his men, so different were they from the people of Sibolat. He seemed never to tire of their stories of the sea and the lands on the far side of it. Iudila told him again of the great storm, of the sea of foam, and of the temple on the island.

"And how did you find your way over so long a journey?" the king asked.

"I followed my heart." Iudila said, and Chakin took his hand and placed it on her belly, recently swollen with child. "But the sun and stars also helped."

"They told you where to go?" Khal-Ayin asked, his mouth filled with flatbread.

"In a sense," Iudila said. "Certain stars hold their place in the sky, always in the same direction. If you know where you want to go and you know where your star is, you can always find your way."

"Like the Lakhin-Na," Khal-Ayin said.

Iudila shot a glance at Chakin. "Lakhin-Na?"

"A copper orb," Khal-Ayin explained. "A star finder. My ancestors crossed the waters like you, only they came from the other direction. They used the Lakhin-Na to help them find their way."

Iudila's heart beat faster at the prospect—slim though it might be—that Khal-Ayin spoke of the orb of Khuk-Moh.

"I should like to see this Lakhin-Na."

"I can show it to you," the boy said eagerly. "Our priests and shamans use it only a few times a year, to mark the seasons for sowing and harvesting. But I'm the king, so I can use it any time I wish." Khal-Ayin's expression turned guarded. "That won't harm my people will it?"

"No, my lord. It won't harm them at all."

The king's face brightened. "Good. Then I will show you tonight."

77

IT WASN'T SUPPOSED TO BE this easy. Uti-Chan had charged Iudila to seek out the lost treasure of Khuk-Moh, to reclaim it at any cost, and so restore the legacy of his ancestors. Now, instead of the grueling search and life-threatening recovery he'd feared, Iudila had only to follow a boy into the heart of a mountain.

Kehmut had forbidden the pregnant Chakin to join them, so it was only Khal-Ayin and Iudila who approached the central pyramid.

"My lord." A pair of spearmen snapped to attention and dipped their heads in salute as the king led Iudila up the western stairway.

The king waved the men aside.

"Don't worry," he said to Iudila as they started up the steps. "We don't have to go all the way."

Iudila craned his neck to look toward the temple's summit. The pyramid was a gaping black wound against the moonless sky. A chill gripped his spine, and he felt as though he were falling into the great primordial void. He thrust a hand against the stairway's wall to steady himself.

"Don't look up," Khal-Ayin said. "Or down, either. It's best just to look a few steps ahead."

They continued up the slope, Iudila counting the steps as they went. When he reached ninety-one, he found himself on the first of four terraces that spanned the pyramid's circumference.

"This way," Khal-Ayin said.

The terrace was wide enough for eight men to walk side by side, but Iudila ran a hand along the facing stones to make certain he didn't wander too close to the edge. He followed the king along the west side of the temple, then around to the north face until the way was blocked by a high stone wall.

Iudila scanned up and down the wall, finally recognizing it as the edge of the broad ramp that ran up the north side of the pyramid. His survey took only a moment, but when he looked back down, the king was gone.

"My lord?"

The echo of laughter suggested the boy hadn't vanished, so Iudila ran his hand along the wall until he found a gap in the stones. Feeling around the edges, he realized that where the giant limestone blocks met the ramp's wall, some of the stones had been left out to form an entrance to the pyramid. He crawled into the gap, groping his way through the darkness and around a corner where the tunnel emerged into a larger chamber.

Khal-Ayin stood there grinning, holding a pair of torches.

"Did I surprise you?" He handed Iudila one of the torches.

"You did indeed, my lord."

"Only the priests, shamans, and scribes know about the doorway. And me."

"The very wisest minds of Pah-Tullan."

"It's this way."

The boy led Iudila down a long, sloping corridor until they reached another chamber beneath a corbelled vault. The air was heavy, as though weighted down by the incalculable mass of stone above their heads. Iudila held his breath and studied the arched ceiling to be sure it wasn't closing in.

No stones moved, but some seemed to sparkle. Iudila looked more closely and discovered several shafts running straight through the pyramid's walls.

"They were built to align with certain stars on specific dates," Khal-Ayin explained, "like a great calendar stone. The priests haven't said anything, but I think it's broken."

"Broken?"

The boy's face grew serious.

"I've watched for the stars' appearances and compared them with Kinich Ahaw's annual journey. The alignments are at least five days early, sometimes six."

"That doesn't seem so bad. Perhaps they were misaligned from the start."

The king gave Iudila a reproachful look.

"The temple—indeed, the entire great plaza—is aligned to the divine pattern. The gods themselves ordained and blessed the plans. Either they were wrong then, or we have somehow displeased them so that they no longer order our seasons."

Iudila nodded solemnly, though he failed to share the young king's concern. Throughout the lands formerly and currently governed by the Roman Empire, if the calendar was found to be in error, the emperor simply added or removed the requisite number of days—or changed the calendar altogether.

"What will you do?" Iudila asked.

"For now, watch and pray. The priests say that only a great blood sacrifice will restore the gods' favor. But we have lost only five or six days in the five hundred years since the temple was built. Perhaps we can reclaim the gods' favor and win those days back through devotion and service alone. If it gets worse—" Khal-Ayin shrugged.

Iudila patted the boy on the shoulder. "I'm sure the gods will recognize your wisdom and sincerity. The people are in good hands."

The young king smiled at that, and his excitement revived. "Let me show you how the temple was laid out."

He led Iudila to the center of the chamber and looked at him expectantly.

Iudila glanced around the empty space. The far walls were barely visible in the thin torchlight, and he saw nothing that might have been a help to the ancient architects.

"Not out there," the king said. "Here." He stamped his foot, and Iudila looked down.

In the plaster-coated floor—worn with time, but still legible—were five large circles. East, south, west and north were arranged about the central one.

"This is Pah-Tullan," Khal-Ayin said, pointing to his toes as he stood in the middle of the central circle.

An inlay of gold spanned the diameters of the south, central and north circles. Iudila studied the patterns and called to mind the image of the terrestrial sphere from the Temple of Atlas. He realized the middle figure must be that of a globe centered on Pah-Tullan, with north and south depicting the views with the globe rotated toward those directions. Similarly, the eastern circle described the lands of Sibolat on its left, with the familiar shapes of Europe and Africa to the right.

Khal-Ayin stepped to the inner edge of the western circle, then paced across a sea of stone, skirting the long northern coastline until he reached the shores of what Iudila knew to be Arabia. The king walked north through the Red Sea until he came to Jerusalem, the Omphalos, the navel of the world.

"This is where my ancestors came from," the boy said.

"Amazing," Iudila said, his voice little more than a whisper. "They came all this way, then fashioned these maps. How?"

"'The sword divides the earth under the guidance of the stars.' That's what the old priests say. Come, I'll show you."

Khal-Ayin started toward one side of the chamber. Iudila's heart fluttered as he followed. He was only steps away from completing his task.

But how was he to remove the treasures from the temple? He couldn't harm Khal-Ayin, a boy of sacred blood whose only fault was being too trusting. Perhaps Iudila could take the torches and leave the lad in the darkness. There was only one path in and out, and Khal-Ayin would find his way before long. Were the king to be discovered missing, however, there was no chance that Chakin and Iudila would be permitted to leave the city.

No, he decided. The best course was to learn the location of the treasures, then recover them just before returning to Shukpi.

Iudila almost bumped into the boy when he stopped before a pair of wooden doors. Khal-Ayin handed Iudila his torch, raised the latch and pulled the doors open.

A pair of jaguar-skin cushions sat on shelves inside the cabinet. One pillow was long and narrow, the pelt marred by a stain of rust in the shape of a sword blade. The other was square, its center molded with a circular impression.

The gutter of the torches was the only sound as Iudila and Khal-Ayin stared at the empty cushions.

The treasure of Khuk-Moh was gone.

78

KHAL-AYIN COLLAPSED INTO SOBS at the realization of the lost treasures.

"You don't understand," he said when Iudila tried to comfort him. "It is my duty to preserve the calendar. The sole purpose of the royal family—of the very city itself—is to interpret the will of the gods, to govern the lives of the people by means of the calendar. My only job, and I've failed."

Iudila half-carried the boy up the tunnel from the map chamber and along the temple's terrace.

"You are still Lord of Pah-Tullan," he said when they reached the western stairway. "You must act like it before your people."

Khal-Ayin managed to descend the stairs under his own power, nodding as he passed the guards. Iudila led the king to the guesthouse in the emissaries' quarter, a group of small pyramids near the northern temple and palace.

Iudila needed only to look in Chakin's eyes to tell her something was wrong. She poured a cup of *octli*—the fermented sap of the agave plant—and placed it in the king's trembling hands. The boy drained the cup but coughed up half the contents as his throat rebelled against the liquor. He wiped his face and held out the cup for more.

"Have any other visitors been here recently?" Chakin asked after Iudila told her about the theft of the relics. "Another member of the noble families? A priest or shaman?"

"No one." Khal-Ayin's speech was slurred after his third cup of *octli*, and he rubbed his eyes as he tried to think. "No, only the dwarf."

Chakin and Iudila traded looks.

"A dwarf?" Iudila asked.

Khal-Ayin waved off the question. "A traveling performer—juggling, acrobatics, fortune-telling. He arrived during the equinox festival and left soon after. I wouldn't even remember him, but for the fortune-telling."

"What did he say?" Chakin asked.

The king shrugged. "He told me darkness is greatest in the belly of the earth, but the light that shines there is greater still."

"That's all?"

Khal-Ayin nodded and yawned as the *octli* seemed to dampen his dread over the lost treasures. When the boy could no longer sit upright, Iudila draped the king's arm over his shoulder, helped him to his feet and took him back to the palace.

"It's time to go," Iudila told Chakin when he returned and they lay on their mat together.

She turned onto her side, pulled his arm about her and pressed his hand over where their child grew.

"It can only have been Khu-Shul. But why would he want the relics?"

"The same reason as your father. To have them all together."

"But the plates and seer-stones are still at Shukpi."

"For now. Your father charged me with recovering the orb and the sword. I failed. He also charged me with protecting the other treasures. I can't do that from here."

"Do you feel that?" A ripple moved beneath the taut skin of Chakin's belly. "Your son quickens."

Iudila's breath came short as he felt the movement, proof of the miracle that lived inside Chakin. "He begins his journey," he said. "Let us resume ours."

79

A SULLEN KHAL-AYIN STOOD at the canal with Chakin and Iudila. His desperation had waned in the days since discovering the theft, his time filled with final trade negotiations and plans for a royal visit to Shukpi. His shoulders drooped, though, and he walked as if burdened by an enormous weight.

"You will return soon?" he asked Iudila.

"It will take some months to gather the next trade shipment and to build proper ships." Iudila had been impressed with the boats of Pah-Tullan, made from bundles of dried reeds. With a broad hull, they were much more stable than canoes, could carry more cargo and—Khal-Ayin had assured him—were well suited to the open sea. "But, yes," he added on seeing the king's downcast expression, "I will return as soon as I am able."

Iudila crossed his arms, hands on either shoulder, and bowed to the boy-king of Pah-Tullan. He climbed into the canoe where Chakin, Kehmut, and the crew waited.

Onlookers waved from the banks of the grand canal as Iudila led the little merchant fleet toward Naab-Malah, the salt lake on Pah-Tullan's western boundary. From there, they would follow the series of rivers back to the coast.

"Paddle faster," Thanos said under his breath, "before they change their minds."

The others laughed and maintained the slow, steady strokes that would see them through ten hours of rowing each day for the next several weeks.

Iudila understood the Greek's concern, though. The trade seemed a generous one. For sixteen boatloads of pelts, rocks and feathers, they were returning with a fortune in gold, silver and gems.

"It isn't that impressive," Chakin said. "We return with far less than we brought. They might at least have offered something useful, like copper."

Takin—the word meant "sun dung"—represented the Sibolan attitude toward gold, at least among those who had little of it. While the metal might please the eye, it was too soft to be useful like copper or flint or obsidian. Nevertheless, Khal-Ayin had been generous with the baskets of gems and pelt-shaped ingots of gold and silver. These had been distributed among the canoes, which all sat low in the water.

"Consider it ballast, my Heart," Iudila said. "It will keep our boats steady and bring us a safer journey."

"And faster, I hope. I want my son to be born in Shukpi." Chakin leaned against Iudila's knees as he steered the canoe around a bend.

She began singing, a song about the wooden men that were the gods' first attempt at populating the earth. Kehmut picked up the tune, which carried to the other boats until the water's surface echoed with the harmony of their voices. The paddles stroked in rhythm with the music as they made their way toward the sea and home.

80

"YOU DO WOMAN'S WORK."

Iudila looked up from the grinding stone as Uti-Chan stepped into the courtyard. "Chakin does enough work just in carrying our son around. Grinding a little maize seems a small thing in return."

Chakin and Iudila had been back in Shukpi for a month, Iudila's men having remained at Wakhem to oversee the building of the new trade fleet.

"She fares well?" the king asked.

"She's fine," Iudila assured him. "Kehmut tends to her constantly. I fear the boy will emerge with his hands clamped to his ears, so great is her chatter."

Uti-Chan laughed. "That is well."

"And the queen?"

"Sak-Chih's headaches have returned. She rests little and wakes more exhausted than before she slept. Chakin tries to ease her pain but with little success."

Iudila brushed maize dust from his hands and motioned Uti-Chan to a cushion.

"And how is the Lord of Shukpi?"

The king sat.

"My children have returned home, we have renewed relations with our ancient brethren in the land northward, and my people are secure and well fed."

"And yet?"

Uti-Chan looked deeply into Iudila's eyes. "And yet an uneasiness overshadows the land. What do you know of the Prince of the West?"

"I hear whispers of him among the servants, but nothing more."

"The West is the abode of darkness," Uti-Chan explained, "the place where Kinich Ahaw dies each night, where his fire is consumed. The Prince of the West is the one who nightly overcomes Lord Sun, and it is only by the power of the gods of the Upperworld that Kinich Ahaw escapes to be reborn in the morning."

Iudila nodded slowly, unsure of Uti-Chan's meaning.

"You," the king added, "are the Prince of the West."

"Me?"

"You and your men have been among us more than two years."

"And your people have continued to thrive in that time."

"That is true," Uti-Chan agreed. "By day they see you as my son, husband to Chakin and defender of Shukpi. But superstitions run deep. By night, you are Prince of the West, the demon of Shibalba. Children are made to behave with threats of giving them into your hands, to feed your craving for blood and fire. The old ways persist among the people. Any misfortune, great or small, is laid at your feet. If a man stubs his toe in the dark, it is because you have placed the rock in his path. Ancient relics disappeared, you have hidden them."

"A queen suffers headaches . . ."

Uti-Chan nodded. "She had none during your absence."

"Surely you don't believe—"

"Of course not," the king assured him. "She suffered such maladies long before you came to our shores. I know not whether they are natural or due to some evil influence, but I know they are not your doing."

"And the relics?"

"It seems clear that Khu-Shul stole them from Pah-Tullan, but I cannot believe he did so for himself."

"Tok-Ekh," Iudila suggested.

Uti-Chan nodded. "We never found his body."

"Even if he survived, why would he want the relics?" Iudila said.

"My brother has ever hungered for dominion. He lusted after my first wife, both for her beauty and for the power her bloodline would give him. He desired

Chakin for the same reasons. Her marriage to you and her stepping aside as Lady of Shukpi have taken the ancient authority from her hands, but not from her blood.

"Were Tok-Ekh to possess the ancient relics of Khuk-Moh," the king went on, "were he somehow to claim the power of Yash-Ahaw's bloodline, he could position himself to rule not only Shukpi, but all of Sibolat. He would plunge the people into the old ways of human sacrifice and blind obedience to the king as interpreter of the gods' will. He would undo all the progress we have made in the six hundred years since Yashwak and Yash-Ahaw arrived on our shores."

Iudila shuddered at the prospect, but he kept his tone light.

"That is something to be avoided then."

Uti-Chan nodded solemnly. "What do you recall of your vision?"

"From our wedding day? I remember everything. The fire, the flood, the black cloud—" Iudila locked his eyes on Uti-Chan's. "Tok-Ekh."

"Black-Cloud. His name as well as his spirit form," Uti-Chan said. "He has appeared so in many of my spirit walks."

"You've had visions of him before?"

The king nodded. "And of you."

"Me?"

"Years before you came to our land, I foresaw your arrival, heralded by Kukulkan, divine guardian of the sacred bloodline."

"Did you see all that was to happen?" Iudila asked.

"Uti-La! Ahpa!" The words rang through the courtyard before Uti-Chan could answer.

Khak-Imish dashed through the gate. "Chakin," he said, breathlessly. "It is her time."

"Go to her," Uti-Chan told Iudila. "We will talk more on this later."

Iudila needed no further encouragement. He raced across the royal compound. Sak-Chih—her face drawn and wan—greeted Iudila at the doorway to the birthing chamber and ushered him to the inner room.

Chakin sat upon what resembled a throne of stone. Kehmut had just finished emptying a basin and placed the vessel back on its stand beneath the princess. Chakin's dark hair lay damp with sweat and clung to her face and neck. Iudila knelt before her, stroked her cheek and smoothed a lock behind her ear.

"How does my son treat his mother?"

Chakin managed a smile. "He is eager to greet you, it would seem."

"And you?"

"She will not greet you for some time," Kehmut warned him.

"But all is well?" Iudila pressed.

The old woman nodded. "My lady is strong, and the child is surprisingly well-behaved, given his father's nature."

Iudila took the gibe in stride. "Good." He took Chakin's hand and was rewarded with a grip that might have crushed a melon. Chakin's scream filled the stone room.

Kehmut stroked Chakin's arms and hummed a tune as the wave of pain—judging from the strength of her grip—crested then ebbed.

"That wasn't so bad," the old woman judged as Chakin released Iudila's hand and fell back against the stone seat. "Your son knocks at the gate, Lady. You." Kehmut turned on Iudila. "Out."

"But—"

"You did your part in the sowing. The harvest belongs to the women. Out."

Iudila knew arguing was useless. He kissed Chakin, received a swat to the back of his head from Kehmut, then let himself be herded from the room.

"What are they doing to her?" Khak-Imish asked, wide-eyed, as Iudila joined him in the courtyard."

Iudila shook his head. "It is a mystery only women can know. Come, let us walk while we await your nephew."

The boy looked with horror toward the shadowed doorway where a fresh scream emerged, but he took Iudila's hand.

"How is she?" the king asked as he joined the pair. He took Khak-Imish into his arms and offered Iudila a cigar.

"She seemed well enough before they banished me. Kehmut says she is fine."

Uti-Chan nodded. "She loves Chakin as a daughter. She will do all in her power to conduct her through this ordeal."

"And after?" Iudila asked. "What becomes of Chakin after giving birth to the son of the Prince of the West?"

Uti-Chan glanced down at Khak-Imish, who was already snoring against his neck.

"How do your people view marriage to outsiders?"

Iudila shrugged and took a long pull on the cigar. "So long as there is political or mercantile advantage, there is no objection. The priests might say otherwise, but their concerns matter little in that regard."

"If a prince of the royal line took a wife of foreign blood, it would not compromise his claim to the throne?"

Iudila grinned as he caught up with the king's reasoning. "If she were also of noble birth, it might strengthen his claim."

"More so, I should think, if she brought a dowry of gold and silver and the promise of continued trade," the king suggested. "I told you of my earlier visions, before ever you arrived in these lands. In them, Kukulkan carried you and Chakin across the sea to the west."

"But my land is in the east."

Uti-Chan shrugged. "Visions may be certain or they may only hint at what is to come. I know only that I saw your arrival from the east, your defeat of Tok-Ekh, and the great god taking you and Chakin to the west."

"That may be, but I can't ask Chakin to leave her home, to leave you."

Uti-Chan smiled. "For a bright young man, your eyes can be slow to open. You are Chakin's family now. You are her home. She made that decision when she chose you over her titles. The council will limit any influence she or you might have in Shukpi. Already they amend the official records to remove any mention of her or her deeds." He took a slow draw on his cigar. "Chakin's ability to guide and serve our people diminishes with each passing day. In a less rigid kingdom, who can say?"

"Have you spoken with her about this?"

The king shook his head. "I do not need to. She is my daughter. I know her heart and mind as my own. It will yet be some time before she is able to travel. Until then, there is a task you have yet to complete."

"The relics."

"I believe Tok-Ekh yet lives, and that he is behind the theft of the treasures from Pah-Tullan."

"He has been invisible for years," Iudila said. "How do I find him?"

"If it is known that you travel with the remaining treasures of Khuk-Moh, I suspect he will find you. What I ask of you is dangerous."

Iudila looked into the king's eyes. "I am Guardian of the Treasures of Khuk-Moh. Far be it from me to shirk my duty. What am I to do once I have retrieved the relics?"

"That, I do not know," the king admitted. "I know only that they rightfully belong with the line of Yash-Ahaw, the line of Chakin."

A scream tore through the air.

The men spun toward the birthing chamber. Iudila's heart stopped when the cry was cut short, but his pulse began anew at the sounds of a wailing child.

Uti-Chan clapped a hand on Iudila's shoulder.

"And the line of your son, it would seem."

81

IUDILA FOLLOWED UTI-CHAN up the temple's steps, the burden in his arms doing little to keep his feet from floating off the paving stones. The crowd was not so large as he had seen on previous occasions—and as nothing compared with the multitudes of Pah-Tullan—but all eyes followed the Lord of Shukpi and the Prince of the West as they stepped to the apron's edge.

Uti-Chan abandoned his usual eloquence, instead stepping aside and gesturing to Iudila.

"My son!" Iudila shouted without preamble. He raised the squirming, mewling child into the air. A chorus of cheers swelled across the temple mount. "See, Lord Sun," Iudila called to the heavens. "Hear me, you gods of my fathers. Bear witness, Yash-Ahaw and Yashwak, my great-father. I am Uti-La of the Sea, he who crossed the Sunrise Waters. Today I am given a son. He shall be called Two-Water, for in him are the lines of Yashwak reunited, and through him shall the light be continually kindled for the guidance of his people and for the sake of the One."

The people shouted the name—Cha-Naab—and Iudila lowered the screaming infant. He stroked his son's cheek—purple with rage—then pacified him with the tip of a finger between hungry lips.

A tear rolled down Iudila's face. He had been duke and slave, pirate and prince, warrior and husband. He was now guardian and father, and the joyous fear of those honors swelled his heart to bursting.

Kinich Ahaw kissed the edge of the distant mountains as Iudila followed Uti-Chan back down the temple steps while the people returned to their homes. Lemuel and Nak-Makah joined them at the royal compound where waited tables of food and pots of balché.

While a shaman plotted and a queen in her chambers dreamed dark dreams.

82

"IT IS STILL TOO DANGEROUS. Cha-Naab is too young to travel." Iudila gave the argument for the tenth time, hoping against hope that the reason of the simple words would this time sink in.

Chakin rolled her eyes as she had nine times before. "You have run the roads for six months and have had no sign of Tok-Ekh."

It was true. Iudila had traveled the roads and rivers from Shukpi to Wakhem and down to the western coast where the new merchant fleet—according to the report Thanos had recently brought—was nearly ready to sail. Three times Iudila had made the journey, each trip preceded by rumors that he carried the plates and seer-stones of Khuk-Moh. Each time he had returned to Shukpi unmolested.

"You go to carry more trade to Pah-Tullan," Chakin continued, "to bind my father's covenant with him."

"Yes."

"And I go as the representative of the House of Khuk-Moh. Khal-Ayin is my kinsman. If trade is to persist between our peoples, it is right that an heir of Yash Khuk-Moh carry the treaty."

"Well—"

"And where I go, my son goes. No." Chakin held up a hand to silence Iudila's repeated objection. "Cha-Naab is strong but he cannot yet be without his mother. I will no longer be without my husband. Perhaps your women of

Spania bear fragile whelps, but the children of Sibolat—more especially those of Shukpi—are of hardy stock. We will go with you."

Iudila opened his mouth to object, then thought better of it. "It shall be as you say."

Chakin wrapped her arms around Iudila's waist and rested her chin against his chest. "That wasn't so hard, was it?"

"No," he said in a pained voice, then bent to kiss her.

"But this is," she said as she pressed her hips against his.

"What about Cha-Naab?"

"He's fine with Kehmut," Chakin said as she led him to their bed.

"I thought he was too young to be without his mother."

"Do you want to be right, or do you want this?" she asked, and dropped her linen wrap to the floor.

Being right, Iudila decided, was not everything.

83

THIS JOURNEY TO WAKHEM proceeded much faster than before. With the onset of the dry season the Hahshuk ran with less force but was not so low as to be blocked by rocks or sandbars.

Hunters foraged each evening for rabbits or deer to supplement the more readily available fish. Most of the trade party camped beside the river. Kehmut insisted that Cha-Naab needed the pure air carried by steadier breezes, so Chakin and Iudila pitched their linen tent atop the riverbank.

By the fifth night, Wakhem remained only a half-day's row away. Hunters and fishers went out as usual, but all returned empty-handed. No game—not a fish, not a bird, not even a tree frog—was to be found. The travelers made a paltry dinner of leaves and berries and flatbread, then went to their mats in the unnatural silence of the evening.

Hours later, Iudila lurched upright, his breath coming in gasps as he shook off the remnants of a dream. The visions quickly faded, leaving him with only the memory of being violently shaken. As he came to his senses, his heartbeat and breathing eased, but the shaking did not.

Chakin sat up beside him and touched his arm.

"It is only the *Pawahtuns* shifting their grip as they support the earth."

Iudila lay back down and pulled her close.

"How long does it last?"

"It will stop soon," Chakin mumbled, and buried her face in Iudila's neck.

Within the space of two deep breaths—warm and moist on Iudila's skin—Chakin's words were fulfilled. The ground again slept and the night fell once more to silence, save only the creak of leather as Cha-Naab's cradle swung from its hanging place.

Then came the horror.

The ground lurched. The night's stillness was ruptured by the sharp crack of a giant's whip. Cha-Naab came awake with a wail, and cries arose from the other shelters. With no time to dress, Iudila snatched the boy from his cradle, thrust him into Chakin's arms, then carried them both from the tent.

"High ground! Run!" he called to Thanos and the others who spilled from their tents by the water.

They had made only a few steps up the bank when a howl rose from the west. A wall of water swept down the course of the Hahshuk, its foaming crest edged by the pale moonlight.

Screams erupted from the lower camp. Men and women stared at the wave, their feet unmoving. A few gathered their senses and tried to run, but watery death overtook them, sweeping people, boats and supplies into the swollen current.

Only Thanos had reached the lip of the bluff. Iudila pulled him onto high ground then looked back toward the bank, now a muddy mess that showed no signs of life. Chakin let out a cry that Iudila first took to be grief, until he turned to see the Greek's arm about her and Cha-Naab, an obsidian blade held to Chakin's throat.

Iudila started toward them, but Thanos pressed the blade to Chakin's skin and shouted, "Stop where you are."

Iudila stopped and held his hand to his sides. "What are you doing?"

"Securing my treasure," Thanos said. "You lied to us. There was never any here. It was always in the north. I saw how their king lives, how their nobles live. Gold and silver and jewels at every turn. I intend to live like that, as soon as you're out of my way."

"That's fine." Iudila tried to keep his voice even. "I'll get out of your way. Just let Chakin go."

"You think I'm a fool? She's the key to my treasure. Without her, I'm nothing but a foreigner, a nobody. With her, I'm a prince—maybe even a king, hmm?"

"If that's so, you'd best keep her safe. Put your blade down."

Thanos glared at Iudila but eased his blade away from Chakin's throat. He tightened his grip about her and took a step backward.

A branch snapped overhead and Thanos looked toward the sound. He cursed as Chakin raked her anklets along his leg, the shells biting into his flesh. She spun out of his grip and raced toward Iudila, Cha-Naab still in her arms.

Thanos lurched after Chakin then fell to the ground beneath a mass of black. The living shadow loosed a roar, eyes gleaming yellow in the moonlight. The Greek tried to crawl away, then screamed as a great black cat dug its claws into his back and closed its maw about his head.

The scream died the same instant Thanos did, as the jaguar crushed the man's skull. The cat shook its head, and the sound of the snapped neck echoed in the night. The beast dropped its prey and stalked toward Chakin and Iudila.

Iudila stepped in front of Chakin and Cha-Naab. The jaguar continued forward, a deep rumble in its throat. The moonlight revealed a streak of white along the black flank, and Iudila realized he had last seen that mark as a bloody cut made by Tok-Ekh's spear. As the cat came closer, Iudila held out his hand. The jaguar pressed its robust head against Iudila's palm and redoubled its purring.

"I gather you're friends," Chakin said as she stepped to Iudila's side.

Before Iudila could answer, the jaguar staggered to one side and the purr turned to a snarl. The cat gnashed its teeth at the air from where two spears had flown to pierce its side.

A cry erupted from the trees as a score of warriors rushed forward, weapons lowered. Iudila placed himself between the warriors and Chakin, even as the jaguar leapt.

Four men joined their spears to meet the great cat's attack, and the beast fell heavily to the ground. The forest rang with feral shrieks long after the jaguar went silent, as the men took turns thrusting their spears into the inert form.

"Enough!"

The shout came cold from the darkness. The warriors ended the blood-orgy, circled around Chakin and Iudila, and held their spears at the ready.

"I see you're none the worse for the earthquake."

Iudila looked toward the voice. His blood ran cold as a ghost stepped from the darkness into the ring of spears.

84

TOK-EKH HAD CHANGED LITTLE since his failed rebellion. He might be thinner, but with his skeletal frame it was hard to tell. He smiled his black, gruesome smile as he stalked toward Chakin.

She felt Iudila tense, heard the beginnings of a rumble in his chest. Whatever protest he was about to make was cut off as the shaman lashed out at him. A sickening clash of metal on bone dropped Iudila to the ground.

"Quite the improvement, wouldn't you say?"

The shaman's eyes gleamed with madness as he stepped over Iudila's body and raised his hand for Chakin's inspection. The stump created by Hul-Balam's sword was now capped by a hand of molded copper, an obsidian blade imbedded along its outer edge. "What, no word of greeting for your dear Tata Tok-Ekh?"

He reached out his natural hand to brush Chakin's cheek. She clutched Cha-Naab to her breast and tried to shrink back. Two of his men grabbed her and held her fast.

"No!" she screamed as Tok-Ekh wrenched Cha-Naab from her arms.

The boy cried out but Tok-Ekh paid no heed to mother or son. He lifted Cha-Naab by the ankle and held him high.

"May this tainted blood be purified in the holy waters of Shibalba," he said, then drew the sharpened edge of his hand across the squirming child's throat.

Chakin's heart collapsed. She opened her mouth to scream, but only a pinched hiss of air escaped her throat. Tok-Ekh dropped the boy's body atop

Iudila's. Chakin's vision narrowed as her world, her life drained away with Cha-Naab's blood. Her knees buckled, but Tok-Ekh's men kept her upright.

The shaman stooped to look her in the eye, his nose almost touching hers.

"You will have other sons," he said, the words all but lost in the dark cloud that enveloped Chakin. "Sons of pure blood, unspoiled by this corruption." He kicked Iudila. "Together, we will restore the glorious rule of Yash Khuk-Moh. As he and his brothers established their dynasties in this land, so shall your sons—our sons—carry the line once more into the land northward, to reestablish the glories of the First Time."

"You're insane," Chakin wanted to say, but had no strength to form the words.

Iudila's slowly moving chest gave her some hope, but it was small comfort against the still form of Cha-Naab.

Tok-Ekh stripped the bloody cloak from Thanos's mauled body and wrapped it around Chakin's bare shoulders.

"You mustn't catch a chill," he whispered in her ear, his mouth wet on her skin. "And you will never again expose yourself before any but me." The saliva that dripped onto her neck seemed to burn her as it ran down her shoulder. "Bind her," Tok-Ekh told his men. "She's meek enough now, but she'll fight like a jaguar bitch before long. Treat her with respect, though. She is a princess and will be queen over all Sibolat."

The men hurried to obey.

"What of these?" one asked, indicating Iudila and Cha-Naab.

"Give the child to the river. Perhaps a crocodile will find it and carry the abomination back to Shibalba. As for him"—he again kicked Iudila—"his heart will still be beating by the time we reach Wakhem, or each of yours will serve as substitutes."

"Yes, Lord," the man said, and hurried to carry out his orders.

Chakin nearly collapsed at the sound of the splash that was her son's farewell, but she lacked any strength to respond, even with tears.

"Place her in my litter," Tok-Ekh ordered.

Strong hands lifted Chakin and carried her into the woods. A curtained litter waited beside a trail, and the guard set her gently inside. He stood, turned, then crumpled to the ground as Tok-Ekh rammed a spear into his chest. "So shall be the fate of any who dares to lay a hand upon Chakin, Lady of the Two Suns. She is my wife, and none but I shall ever touch her again."

The men all nodded their submission then took their positions at the litter's poles or in the vanguard.

Tok-Ekh climbed in beside Chakin. Her stomach reeled as the litter rose onto the men's shoulders, then it twisted as Tok-Ekh ran a hand beneath her cloak.

"I've waited a long time for this."

85

CHAKIN SHIVERED IN THE DARKNESS. She wanted to scream her fury. She longed to cuddle Cha-Naab to her breast, to have Iudila fold her in his arms. Her heart demanded she cry out to the gods of vengeance against the murderer Tok-Ekh, or that she herself take arms against him. Her body, however, would not obey her. She could only lie on the stone floor and tremble in her rage and grief.

Her head throbbed and her ribs ached. Tok-Ekh had tried to take her in the litter on the way from the river to Wakhem, but he could not muster his resolve. His arms had not shared the impotence of his manhood, however, and he had savagely beaten her. Chakin endured the abuse in silence, praying to Sak-Ishik to guide the shaman's obsidian-edged hand across her throat to end her torment. But the goddess withheld her mercy, as all the gods seemed to have done.

A sound echoed in the corridor outside her chamber and a faint glow spilled across the threshold. Her cell had no door, nor needed any. Even if she'd had the strength to move, she still could not have found her way through the maze of tunnels beneath Wakhem's mountain.

Tiny feet stepped into the room. Chakin's misery was made whole as Khu-Shul entered, a leather-wrapped bundle in his arms.

"My lady!" The dwarf rushed to her side, dropping his burden.

"Get away from me," Chakin managed to say, though she still lacked the strength to enforce her will.

"Princess, please. Let me help you."

"No," she feebly insisted. "I trusted you. I mourned for you, and you betrayed me. You serve him."

Khu-Shul gripped her by the shoulders and raised her to a seated position. His very touch sent a wave of revulsion through Chakin.

"No!" she cried, and summoned the strength to push him away.

That power just as quickly abandoned her, and she fell again to the floor in the grip of violent tremors.

"See to her injuries." Khu-Shul spoke to a pair of serving women who had followed him into the cell. He gathered the fallen bundle and opened it. "Put the balm on her injuries and be certain she drinks the tonic. Dress her and make her ready for Lord Tok-Ekh. The ceremony must begin soon."

The women nodded. Chakin had no strength to resist as they daubed her wounds and brushed her hair. She could only hurl hatred with her eyes at the retreating form of Khu-Shul. One of the servants tipped a small clay flask to Chakin's lips. A sour taste flooded her tongue and crept down her throat.

Chakin thought to spit, but the servant cupped a hand over her mouth and nose, and she could only swallow. The potion acted quickly, stilling her tremors and quieting her raging thoughts. Her eyes became heavy, and she fell into a deep, black silence.

86

"UNACCEPTABLE! She must be awake for the ceremony."

"Not to worry, my lord. I followed your instructions exactly. The effects of the tonic will ease soon."

Chakin sensed herself awaken, but she could not move or open her eyes. She was seated, her body cushioned by pillows, but she knew nothing more of her surroundings. A pair of shadows—one tall, the other short—moved across the red field beyond her eyelids.

"It had better," she heard Tok-Ekh say, "or your heart will also feed the gods."

"Even as you say, my lord. Shall I make preparations for Lord Oshlahun-Ak to attend the ceremony?"

Tok-Ekh scoffed at that. "Why should I honor that little toad?"

"He has been of great service to you, has he not?"

"He performed adequately," the shaman allowed. "He followed his sister's instructions, that is all. It has cost me much to keep Sak-Chih under my command from this distance, but my brother's wife will no longer be needed." A cold hand brushed Chakin's cheek, but she was unable to recoil. "Once I have taken my bride, we shall together claim our rightful thrones."

"And the relics," Khu-Shul prompted him.

"And the relics," Tok-Ekh said.

"Will not Khal-Ayin wish to reclaim them for Pah-Tullan?" Khu-Shul drew near to Chakin and placed his fingers on the inside of her wrist.

"Let the pup come," Tok-Ekh sneered. "Let him throw his weapons against Wakhem. Let Shukpi and Ha-Naab sully their blades and let the Hahshuk's waters run with blood." His voice rose in pitch as he spoke. "Let the land be desolate from Pah-Tullan to the land Southward, from the Sunrise to the Sunset Waters, and let the people be bereft of hope." The shaman fell silent and the only sound in the space was the echo of his breathing.

"And then," he continued in a voice scarcely above a whisper, "when the earth is saturated, when the gods of have had their fill of blood and flesh, then will I lead the people back to their first estate, to the unerring service of the gods."

Chakin tried to cry out against Tok-Ekh's madness, but it came out only as a whimper.

"As I promised, my lord," Khu-Shul said, "she stirs."

The numbness slithered from Chakin's body. She blinked her eyes open to see the scribe's and shaman's faces only inches from hers. Khu-Shul wore an expression of sympathy and concern, but Tok-Ekh was painted with the visage of death. Chakin was about to scream, to leap out of her chair and claw at those masks, but something in Khu-Shul's eyes made her stop.

"See to the sacrifice," Tok-Ekh ordered the scribe, his voice deep and low.

"Yes, Lord." Khu-Shul gave a last look to Chakin then turned and left the chamber.

"You seem in better spirits than the last time we spoke," Tok-Ekh said with a smile.

Chakin held her tongue.

"Your silence betokens your wisdom."

He stepped back from her and Chakin saw that he wore only his bangles of shells and belt of bones. His virility had failed him earlier, but Tok-Ekh laughed as her eyes were drawn to his manhood, now proud and tumescent.

"The gods give us powerful elixirs," he said, "and you shall soon see just how powerful. But first. . ."

He took a pair of tethered stones from a peg on the wall and moved to Chakin. "Raise your arm," he commanded.

Chakin had thought herself unable to move but, as of its own accord, her right arm stretched out in front of her.

Tok-Ekh draped the stones over her wrist and knelt before her. He adjusted a candle stand to cast reflected light from the obsidian in his forehead into Chakin's eyes.

Chakin gave a start as the jewel reflected her face, painted with a Death's mask that matched Tok-Ekh's. The shaman held her in place, though, and her eyes lost focus as he spoke.

"In darkness there is no pain . . ."

87

IUDILA OPENED HIS EYES, but the pain that shot through his head forced them shut again. The world spun about him and his stomach revolted. He tried to roll over, to turn his head, but he could not move.

"Help him," a voice commanded as he started to choke.

One wrist was cut free, strong hands turned him onto his side, and the bitter flood drained from his mouth. He coughed to clear his throat then retched again. Every spasm threatened to burst his skull. When he rolled again onto his back, the pain ebbed enough for the rest of his body to register.

His ankles and one wrist were tightly bound, while the other hand burned with restored blood flow. His side ached, his ribs protesting each movement, every breath.

"Drink this," the voice said, and Iudila's head was lifted and a bowl set to his lips.

The brew was warm and thick and tasted of the earth. His stomach quivered at the influx, but he managed to keep the drink down.

"How long will it take?" another voice asked.

"Even now."

Iudila could make no sense of the words until a ball of coldness formed in the pit of his stomach, grew, and shot tendrils throughout his body. With his free hand he pressed against his chest, trying in vain to stem the creeping tide. The coldness flowed past his shoulder and reached to his fingertips, then his arm went limp. A hand gripped his wrist, raised and released it, and his arm fell heavily to his side.

"It is done," the first voice said.

Fingers stretched his eyelids open. The orbs refused to work together, but as they came into separate focus, his double vision filled with the gnomish face of Khu-Shul.

88

"YOU SERVE TOK-EKH NOW?"

The guards had carried Iudila to a new room and laid him upon a stone slab. Khu-Shul drew decorations upon Iudila's face and body.

"I serve my lady Chakin," he replied in Hebrew, "as I ever have."

The drug had taken complete hold over Iudila, paralyzing him and causing his bladder to empty. The effects were waning now, enough for him to focus his eyes, form a few words at a time, even twitch a finger.

"You will want to keep still," Khu-Shul said in a sing-song voice that must have sounded like senseless chanting to the half-dozen guards that ringed the chamber. "I gave you only a small dose and the effects will soon wear off. You must not move until theirs take full hold."

"Theirs?"

Before Khu-Shul could answer, a horn sounded outside the room. The plaintive tone echoed through the darkened tunnel and off the chiseled stone walls of the chamber. Iudila's heart quickened, but whether due to the effects of Khu-Shul's potion or the haunting sound he wasn't sure.

The guards came to attention, drawing their spears to their shoulders. A torch-bearer strutted into the chamber followed by a pair of trumpeters, their conch-shell horns strung with feathers of red and black. These were followed by a sword-bearer, his steel blade cleared of most of its rust and flashing in the torchlight.

Behind him strutted Tok-Ekh, clad only in his strings of shells, beads and bones. His hair shone with a fresh coat of blood and dung. His face was painted in a hideous Death's-mask, jaw and eyes blackened, lips and cheeks painted with a white skeletal grin.

Next came a pair of litter-bearers. Iudila's breath caught at the sight of Chakin. Her costume called to mind the bridal array from years earlier. While she had then represented the full moon, the dark of the moon now had its expression in the black gown and headdress. Her face paint matched Tok-Ekh's, and her eyes were vacant and glassy in the dim light.

"Wait," Khu-Shul whispered beneath the din of the trumpets. He leapt down from the stone slab and went to help Chakin from her litter. The horns fell silent and the sword-bearer handed the blade to Tok-Ekh.

The shaman pointed the sword toward the ground. "Lords of Shibalba," he intoned in a sonorous voice, "you who bring darkness upon the Middle World, who shield men's eyes from the unbearable light of Kinich Ahaw. Heed now the words of Tok-Ekh, servitor of the Dark One."

As if in response, the earth trembled. The guards shifted nervously. Even Tok-Ekh seemed unsettled by the gods' response to his summons, but he went on when the tremor ceased.

"See here, O Guardians of the Black Road. I bring before you Na Chakin, she of the line of Kinich Yash Khuk-Moh, who bore the words of the ancients, and of Yash-Ahaw and Yashwak, who dared to bring the light of Kinich Ahaw to this Middle World. Imbue me with your power, that I might overcome light with darkness. In return for which—"

A conch shell clattered against the stone wall as one of the trumpeters stumbled back on his heels. The torch flared as its bearer dropped his arm then quickly raised it again.

"In return for which," Tok-Ekh growled, glowering at his men, "I give to you the heart of one also of the line of Yashwak. Slake your thirst with his blood, fill your bellies with his flesh, as recompense for the one who stole Death's feast from your table." Tok-Ekh brought the tip of the sword to Iudila's left breast and pricked the skin. The shaman's eyes filled with hunger at the small pool of blood that welled up. He drew the blade down Iudila's chest, leaving a red trail that ended just below his rib cage.

"Feast on the spawn of the Light-Bringer." Tok-Ekh brought both hands—the one of copper, the other of flesh—to the hilt and drew the sword back above his head, holding it like a great dagger. He would surely have plunged the blade into Iudila's belly, but the earth heaved again, knocking the shaman off balance.

Iudila seized the moment. He rose and leapt from the altar stone.

"Take him!" Tok-Ekh cried.

A pair of spearmen lowered their weapons and charged. They took no more than three steps before their legs buckled beneath them. The rest of the men managed not even that much, collapsing where they stood.

"Vile wretch," Tok-Ekh said, his sword pointed at Khu-Shul, his words dripping with venom. "I should have known better."

"You should have," the dwarf agreed, then smiled as Iudila crashed into the shaman, driving him into the wall.

Iudila had not fully recovered from the drug given by Khu-Shul or the blow to his head given earlier by Tok-Ekh. The chamber spun sideways and the floor rose to greet him.

Khu-Shul rushed the shaman, but Tok-Ekh easily batted aside the dwarf's attack. The shaman retrieved his sword and stalked toward Iudila.

"Death's table awaits." Tok-Ekh again drew back the sword but stopped as Chakin stepped unsteadily toward him and laid a hand on the blade.

"He is mine, Husband," she said, her voice flat, her eyes still vacant. "My hand shall deliver him to Shibalba."

Joy flooded Tok-Ekh's face. "The earth trembles in anticipation of our union, Lady." He gave her the sword, took her hand and led her to where Iudila lay. "Now, my dear. The dark lords await their feast."

Iudila searched Chakin's eyes but saw no sign of recognition there. "Chakin, don't do this."

She ignored his plea and raised the sword. "So shall be the fate of any who dares lay a hand upon Na Chakin, Lady of the Two Suns."

Iudila's eyes went wide as she drove the blade home.

Tok-Ekh's eyes widened, too, as the blade slid into his belly. Chakin put her weight behind the hilt and drove the sword deeper. The shaman's legs faltered, but she kept him upright as he dropped to his knees. She stooped to look into his dark eyes, their noses almost touching.

"I am the wife of Iudila of the Sea, Prince of the West. None but he shall ever touch me again."

She drove her fingernails into the shaman's flesh. Tok-Ekh screamed as she tore the obsidian jewel from his forehead. His scream redoubled as she twisted the blade and wrenched it from his body. The cries ended only when she plunged her hand into the wound.

Understanding dawned in the shaman's eyes as he felt what his countless victims had. His eyes darted from Chakin to Iudila to Khu-Shul but found nothing but coldness in any face. Tok-Ekh's mouth gaped in a final, silent cry as Chakin pulled her hand from his chest, bringing with it the beating heart.

Struggling to his feet, Iudila half-expected the thing to be made of pitch or stone, but the flesh was little different than any he had taken from a deer or peccary. Chakin studied the pulsing meat, as though she might find the cause of the evil that coursed through the man it had served, but it held no answers. She set the heart on the altar, picked up the fallen torch, and plunged flame into flesh.

The meat sizzled and popped in its own death throes, then fell silent and still even as Tok-Ekh went limp. Chakin threw the torch away then collapsed into Iudila's arms. "I couldn't save him," she sobbed. "He took our son and I did nothing."

"There was nothing you could do," Iudila said, knowing the words brought no comfort.

The earth heaved again.

"We must go," Khu-Shul said.

"What about them?" Chakin indicated the fallen men. Their bodies were still but their eyes darted in unfocused fear.

"They chose their master," Iudila said. "Let them serve him in Shibalba." He took up the sword then pulled a torch from its wall bracket and gave it to Chakin. "Stay close," he said, and led the way out of the chamber.

"Wait!" Khu-Shul scrambled to the litter that had borne Chakin. He tossed its cushions aside, pulled out a leather-wrapped bundle, looped its string across his chest, then rejoined the pair.

The scribe led them through the smooth-walled tunnels with familiar ease.

"Did your grandfather design these tunnels, too?" Iudila asked him.

"Don't be foolish. It was his cousin, but the sacred patterns are everywhere the same."

The tunnel rose and fell and wound its way through the earth, but Khu-Shul guided them unerringly.

Chakin stumbled, and Iudila caught her about the waist and helped her on.

"Where exactly are we?" he asked.

"Witz Wayah, the sleeping mountain," Khu-Shul said. "Its brothers occasionally belch fire and smoke, but this mountain has slept for generations."

"It's awake now," Iudila said as another tremor shook the tunnel. Cracks opened in the rock walls and the air filled with dust.

"This way. Hurry!" Khu-Shul turned down a side tunnel.

"We're going deeper," Iudila objected.

"It's the shorter way out. Come!"

"Trust him," Chakin said, and they followed the dwarf deeper into the earth's rumbling belly.

As they rounded a bend, Iudila smelled a hint of rotten eggs. The odor soon passed, and he forgot it as he caught a glimpse of moonlight through the veil of dust.

"Almost there," Khu-Shul said. He raced along the tunnel then suddenly collapsed where the path bottomed out.

"Khu-Shul!" Chakin cried, and rushed toward him.

Iudila tried to stop her but he was too slow. No sooner had she reached Khu-Shul than she, too, fell to the ground.

The earth heaved again, and the rain of dust and rocks intensified. Iudila tossed his torch to the opposite slope. The flame guttered as it passed over Chakin and Khu-Shul, but burned brighter once it passed the dip in the path. Iudila took a deep breath then ran down the slope. He dropped the sword, took Chakin in one arm and Khu-Shul in the other, and carried them up the far side and out the mouth of the cave. The ground still shook, but rocks no longer fell on them. Iudila set the pair down.

"Chakin?" He patted her cheek until she coughed and opened her eyes.

"The sword," Khu-Shul said when he, too, had found his breath. "Where—?"

"I had to leave it," Iudila said. "And we have to move."

"No. We must save the sword." Khu-Shul loosed the bundle from about his chest and thrust it into Chakin's hands. Before Iudila could stop him, the dwarf staggered back into the cave through a hail of ever larger rocks.

Chakin started after him, but Iudila caught her wrist.

"Let me go. I can save him."

"It isn't safe."

As soon as Iudila spoke the words, a cloud of dust spewed from the cave's mouth. Rocks filled the void where Khu-Shul had disappeared, sealing him in the earth.

"No!" Chakin broke free of Iudila's grip, threw herself at the rocks and tore at them.

Iudila tried to pull her away, but she shook him off.

"Help me or leave me."

The look in her eyes proclaimed she would not be dissuaded, so Iudila joined her in digging. A gap opened near the top of the cave's mouth, and Chakin grasped the little hand that emerged, scratched and bleeding. Khu-Shul drew his hand back and the sword's hilt appeared in the opening.

"Take it and go," he shouted.

"We won't leave you," Chakin yelled. "Just a bit longer and we'll have you out."

"There's no more time," Khu-Shul insisted. "Iudila, you must go. You are the protector of the relics. Take them. Take Chakin and go."

"Relics?" Iudila asked.

"You must go to the sea," Khu-Shul said. "Get to the boats. Go!"

Iudila wasted no more time. He grabbed the hilt and pulled the sword from the tomb of stone. Taking up the bundle Khu-Shul had left, he tied it around his waist, surprised by its weight. He slung the sword through the makeshift belt, then wrapped both arms around Chakin.

She kicked and screamed, but Iudila kept his hold on her. He cradled her to his chest and ran, slid down the mountain's side toward the moon-studded surface of a lake below.

Chakin's struggles slowly turned to sobs. Where she had fought and pounded against Iudila, she now clutched at him as her body shook in his arms. By the time they reached the lakeshore her fury had passed, even as the earth again fell silent.

"It's over," she said when Iudila set her feet upon the steady ground. "We can go back for him."

The hairs rose on Iudila's arms and neck as he remembered the calm following the first tremor at their river camp.

"It's not over."

He clamped his hand around Chakin's wrist and pulled her into the water. They waded until the water reached Iudila's waist. He wrapped an arm across Chakin's chest and stroked farther out.

"What are you doing?" she demanded.

Iudila said nothing, but continued swimming until he felt the lake's flat surface heave. "Deep breath."

He gave Chakin just enough time to obey, then dragged her beneath the surface. Her eyes were wide in the murkiness, but Iudila held her steady, counting the heartbeats that pulsed in his ears.

It didn't take many—perhaps only ten—before the lake seethed. The water crushed them as in a giant's fist, threatening to squeeze the air from their lungs. Iudila closed his eyes against the pressure, but even through the lids he could see the night sky flare red above the water's surface.

The glow subsided but the lake wasn't yet finished with them. The water seemed to fall away beneath them, and they breached the surface gasping.

"Breathe!" Iudila pulled Chakin close and shielded her as best he could as an enormous wave rolled over them.

The water dashed them against each other and against the rocky lakebed until—its anger spent—the lake once more slept. Chakin and Iudila stroked to the surface. They were bruised and scraped by the rocks, but otherwise unharmed. They swam toward the spot where a river led from the lake to the sea, then crawled onto the beach.

Iudila took in the devastation around them. "By Sak-Ishik's crown," he swore.

A column of smoke rose from the mountain's flattened peak, while glowing tendrils of liquid fire spilled down its sides. Brush and grass burst into flame at the approach of the burning streams, while trees smoldered, their leaves and needles scorched black and filling the air with ash.

"Here."

Chakin tore strips from her would-be bridal dress. They wrapped the wet cloths over their mouths and noses to filter out the worst of the smoke.

The river seemed the safest path to the coast. The water now ran low, but there was no missing the signs of the flood that had gone before them. Trees were bent or broken, some of them with large rocks tangled in their branches.

The ground continued its unrest as they traveled downstream. Iudila kept an ear tuned for the sounds of yet another killer flood, but none came.

The eastern sky had turned from black to grey by the time Chakin and Iudila—dry-mouthed, ash-caked, exhausted, and heart-broken—reached the narrow delta at the sea's edge.

"Which way to the harbor?" Chakin asked.

Iudila searched the horizon. "South."

"Are you sure?"

"I'm sure," he said, and pointed toward a sky bright with flames.

89

IUDILA LED CHAKIN along the beach, their way lit by the flames of a half-dozen ships. The bundles of dry reeds with their pitch-lined seams burned like giant torches. Several of the great wooden pilings—driven deep into the sand to keep the ships upright on their narrow keels—had burned through, allowing the ships to spill over in heaps of glowing embers.

"This is the work of man, not of the gods," Chakin said.

Iudila grunted his agreement, for the beach was littered with spear shafts. Bodies lay in the sand amid pools of blood that glistened black in the firelight. He picked up one of the abandoned spears and leaned heavily upon it as he searched among the dead for his friends, but all were Sibolan.

Chakin laid a hand on Iudila's arm and indicated the burning ships.

"They may yet be there."

Iudila examined three more corpses—a pointless gesture, as Dingha's and Brehanu's bulk would have made them obvious. He looked toward the burning hulks.

As the tide came in, the waves lapped at the smoking sterns. The sea would soon claim what little the flames left behind, and the beach would be swept clean of the blackened scraps. What remained of Iudila's friends would be food for the fish and crabs of this foreign shore, so far from the lands of their fathers.

"What have I done?" he cried.

In answer, a shout rose from the direction of the shore.

The voice was Dingha's, and Iudila feared the big man still lived among the cruel flames. Then Brehanu's voice joined in, and Iudila realized their calls came from beyond the ships, from the sea itself.

He dashed to the shore to see another reed boat atop the waves with Dingha and Brehanu at the oars. Iudila plunged into the foamy sea and swam toward them.

Dingha dropped his oar and leaned out from the bow to grasp Iudila's wrist. He hauled the Goth over the side and wrapped him in a crushing embrace, nearly capsizing them in the process.

"Your boat is foundering, Dingha," Iudila chided him.

The helmsman reclaimed his oar and matched Brehanu in the four strokes it took to reach the shore. They landed well clear of the burning wrecks and dragged their boat above the high-tide line.

"My lady," Brehanu greeted Chakin as she came to join them. She welcomed each man with a warm embrace.

"What happened here?" Iudila asked.

"We were nearly finished with the ships," Brehanu explained, "when a war-band came over the dunes. A few of our men fought, but most turned against us. Had the mountain not erupted, we would not have lasted. The blast distracted them long enough for us to fall back to the boat and escape to sea."

"And you're all right?"

Brehanu nodded. "But what happened to you?"

"Tok-Ekh," Iudila said.

Chakin burst into tears at the mention of the name. Iudila pulled her close and stroked her hair but could do little else to ease her suffering.

Brehanu's eyes burned. "I thought that bat's-turd was dead."

"He is now," Iudila assured him. "As is Thanos. As is our son."

Brehanu and Dingha had never even seen the boy, but each man laid a hand on Iudila's shoulders. They whispered prayers to their gods to welcome the child to whatever reward awaited the innocent in the afterlife.

Iudila nodded his thanks to the men. "We need to leave," he said. "The mountain may already be sleeping. As soon as the way is clear, your friends will likely come back to be sure their job is finished."

"May we not find shelter at Wakhem?" Brehanu asked.

"No," Chakin answered. "They were Oshlahun-Ak's men in the cave, and likely here as well. He was in league with Tok-Ekh. We will find no shelter with him."

"Perhaps we can go around his forces and return to Shukpi," Iudila said.

Chakin shook her head.

"He will have men posted at every pass coming up from the coast. Pah-Tullan is also closed to us. Khal-Ayin believes we stole the sword and orb of Khuk-Moh."

"Why would he think that?"

Chakin briefly explained what she'd overheard from Khu-Shul and Tok-Ekh.

"We must return to Shukpi," Iudila said. "If Sak-Chih is conspiring against your father, we have to warn him."

"No," Chakin said. "With Tok-Ekh gone, Sak-Chih should have no memory of what she has done. It would needlessly break my father's heart to learn his own wife had betrayed him, even unknowingly."

"Then what do we do?"

Chakin looked toward the mountains, then to the sea. "We go west."

Dingha grunted something that Iudila didn't catch, but Brehanu spoke over him.

"Lady, there is nothing but water to the west."

"Then it is good we have a boat," Iudila said. "We have crossed one great sea, we can cross another. Chakin's ancestors sailed these waters a thousand years ago. We will trace back their steps."

The men stared blankly at Iudila, but Chakin wiped her cheeks with the back of her hand and took his arm.

"It shall be even as you say."

Dingha grunted again, insistently, and all eyes turned to him.

"What is it?" Iudila said.

Dingha pointed toward the bluff above the beach.

Where an army stood in battle array.

91

THE BEACH WAS A MESS of bloody, fiery and ashen ruin, save the small cluster of life that stirred on its fringe. Khu-Shul breathed a sigh of relief then launched himself over the lip of the dune and slid down the bluff.

"Princess! Uti-La!"

Chakin dropped to her knees as the dwarf ran to her.

"How?" she said, her voice choked with tears. "You were trapped."

"That was the fastest way out, not the only one. I went another way to find help." In a loud voice he added, "Unfortunately, all I could find was this rabble."

The war chief had left his men atop the dune and now walked up behind Khu-Shul.

"You wouldn't know a good warrior if he slit that round belly of yours," he said, then lifted the jaguar-head mask.

"Hul-Balam." Chakin stood and embraced him.

"Lady. My lord," Hul-Balam added to Iudila with a bow of his head. "I see your men yet live."

Iudila stepped toward him and gestured along the beach. "Is this your work?"

The Lord of Ha-Naab reared back his head and roared with laughter.

"If this had been my work, they would not be standing here. No, my men did not do this." He drew his sword, its massive wooden blade and obsidian shards red with fresh employment. "But we found the ones who did," he added, then licked the blade and gave a cat-like grin.

"How did you know to come?" Chakin asked.

"When the first bodies washed past Ha-Naab, I sent messengers to Shukpi and led my men upriver." The warrior bowed his head. "I brought your son from the river with my own hands. He will be in Shukpi now, to rest with his fathers."

Chakin had no words as fresh tears drowned her eyes. She could only nod as she squeezed Hul-Balam's hand. "Thank you, my lord," Iudila said.

Hul-Balam bowed then turned and waved to his men, who started down the bluff.

"Your father sent runners as soon as he received my message. He gives you his blessing and prayers for a safe journey."

"Journey?" Chakin said.

"To your husband's kingdom. To return to Shukpi with the treasure of Khuk-Moh could well start a war between your father and Khal-Ayin. He begs you take the treasure to its rightful home."

"Put me down, you ruffian!"

Hul-Balam smiled at the outburst behind them.

"All the treasure."

One of the men from Shukpi carried on his back a wood-framed litter with a narrow seat.

"I'm not an invalid," came another shout as the man reached level ground.

The porter knelt, untied the straps about his chest, and released his burden.

"Barbarians," Lemuel spat as he rose on shaky legs. "I might have settled for a wheelbarrow, but no. They truss me to a chair and run me across the mountains like a bundle of laundry. Hello, my boy." His tone softened as he hugged Iudila then wrapped his arms about Chakin.

Hul-Balam took a leather-wrapped bundle from another porter and gave it to Iudila. "The plates and seer-stones of Khuk-Moh. You have the other relics?"

Iudila pointed to the boat where he had left the sword and orb. "They are safe."

"Good," the warrior said. "You were a *winal* in crossing the Sunrise Waters?"

"Yes," Iudila said, "twenty days."

"You have food and water for twice that time," Hul-Balam assured him as more men set their packs beside the boat. "I trust that is enough?"

"It will do." Iudila directed Dingha and Brehanu to load the provisions, then took the bundle from Hul-Balam.

The Lord of Ha-Naab nodded.

"We have little time. Oshlahun-Ak will send more warriors once the earth settles. For the sake of peace, my men and I must be well away from here by then. Turn your face just north of west. Our merchants claim that after a few days you will find the seas run fast toward Kinich Ahaw's evening rest."

"How can we thank you?" Chakin said.

Hul-Balam's chin quivered. "Live, Lady. Thrive, and bring the best of Sibolat to the heathen dogs across the sea."

Iudila laughed at that, clasped Hul-Balam's wrist in parting, then turned to help his men secure the provisions.

"The people of Ha-Naab are fortunate, indeed, to have you as their lord," Chakin said. "You have been a good friend to my father. I pray you continue to be so, and to my brother when his time comes."

"I will serve him as I would have served you, Lady—with all the strength of my sword and of my heart."

Chakin reached up, pressed her forehead to his and kissed him. "Tell my father that Khu-Shul is my most trustworthy friend, to be reinstated to his service." She knelt before the dwarf. "I don't have the words. All you have taught me. All you have done for me."

"Be happy and well, Princess," Khu-Shul said. "The land of your birth has been unfair to you. Perhaps your new land will be kinder."

"I will think of you often." Chakin wrapped Khu-Shul in a tight embrace.

"The tide beckons, my Heart," Iudila said softly.

Chakin rose, laid on hand on Khu-Shul's cheek, then Hul-Balam's. Iudila lifted her over the side of the boat where Lemuel was already settling in. The tide had reached the high-water line and lapped at the bow. Iudila, Dingha and Brehanu tugged on the boat's lines. With the help of Hul-Balam and his men, they slid the craft into the water. The warrior continued pushing until the water reached his chest. Iudila and his men pulled themselves over the sides and shipped their oars.

"Are those tears I see?" Khu-Shul said as Hul-Balam came dripping out of the waves.

"Bah! It is only sea spray." Hul-Balam stood by the dwarf, looked out to sea and wiped saltwater from his face.

"You did a good thing this day, my lord," Khu-Shul said.

"It is a pity that no temple will ever bear their dedication, that no khobah shall stand for them before the people."

"A pity indeed, but the council would never have it. Though perhaps . . ."

The two men shared a smile. "Write them well, scribe," Hul-Balam said, a hand on Khu-Shul's shoulder. "Write them well."

~ fin ~

Historical Notes

IN 1929, A MAP WAS DISCOVERED in the Topkapi Palace in Istanbul, Turkey. Dated to 1513 CE and ascribed to the great Ottoman admiral Ahmed Muhiddin Piri (more commonly known as Piri Re'is), the map shows the west coasts of Europe and Africa, along with the east coasts of North and South America, including Cuba and other Caribbean islands. While Piri never sailed west of Spain, he noted that his map was compiled from a score of maps from other sources, as recent as Christopher Columbus (d. 1506 CE) and as early as Alexander the Great (d. 323 BCE).

While the map repeats errors known to exist in identifiable source maps, it demonstrates a number of striking accuracies. First, the longitudinal (east-west) distance between Africa and South America, a feat that bested other cartographers until the advent of the marine chronometer some 260 years later. Second, the extreme southern end of the map appears to show known features of Antarctica, not officially discovered until around 1820. Finally, the map appears to indicate features of the Pacific coasts of Colombia and Panama, first discovered by Europeans in 1513 (the same year as the map was created), and not officially mapped for some years afterward.

When I first learned of this curious map, I wondered how the original materials might have been developed, who could have explored these far reaches prior to their revelation to orthodox history, and what other secrets might accompany them. Thus began the story you now hold in your hands.

The choice of a Visigoth as protagonist was a matter of some iterative thinking. Initially, I'd placed my hero in 9th-Century Byzantium (present-day Istanbul). As I began exploring the logistics, both of making such a voyage and of its being lost to history, the story began to slide westward and backward in time, until I arrived on the shores of Spania around 130 years after the collapse of the Western Roman Empire.

As it turns out, while Europe was sinking into what came to be known as the Dark Ages, across the western sea the Maya civilization was nearing its zenith. Borders were expanding, new cities were being founded, and great monuments raised. As the greatest city along the southern frontier, Xukpi (present-day Copán, Honduras) seemed a most likely spot for the central action of the story. And what a happy circumstance that turned out to be.

Copán is one of the most studied sites of the ancient Maya world, having been investigated, explored, and excavated for nearly 200 years. Lost to history soon after the collapse of the Maya civilization, and far from the cultural centers of the Yucatan, the site remained undisturbed for nine centuries. Its great treasure of buildings and monuments survived relatively intact, save for some erosion by the Copán River. Given the remarkable state of preservation of the site, with its numerous engraved marker stones and a monumental stairway inscribed with more than 2200 hieroglyphs, much of what we know about Quiché Mayan (the dialect of the southern reaches of the Maya civilization) comes from Copán.

Specific to our time period (roughly 610-620 CE), Copán was under the rule of its second-longest reigning Lord (Ajaw), K'ak' Chan Yopaat, also known as Butz' Chan (here, rendered Uti-Chan). In the 400-year recorded history of Copán, his 49-year reign was exceeded only by his son, Chan Imix K'awiil (Khak-Imish), who reigned 67 years.

A number of monuments either date to or refer to Uti-Chan's rule. These include Stela 7, Stela P (which inspired Chakin's coming-of-age ceremony), and Altars Y & X. Though dated to well after Uti-Chan's reign, Altar Q (8th century) provides detailed relief carvings of the first sixteen rulers of dynastic Copán, of which Uti-Chan is the eleventh.

The most extraordinary find, in my opinion, came in 1989. While excavating beneath the central pyramid-temple at Copán, archaeologist Ricardo Agurcia discovered a second temple, of a very different design and entombed intact within the structure of the familiar stepped pyramid. While tradition dictated demolition of earlier temples to become part of the replacement's foundation, this temple (called Rosalila by her discoverer) had been carefully preserved by Khak-Imish when he built his great monument around it.

The visual remains left to us by the Maya, especially those at Copán, provide fascinating (if mute) hints at the ceremonial lives of the rulers. Altar Q, along with statuettes of the rulers found in Khak-Imish's tomb, depict the strange goggles and breastplate here used by Uti-Chan. Other engravings and codices depict otherworldly creatures, elaborate costumes, heart sacrifices, self-mutilation, and myriad other glimpses into this distant culture, to which I have attempted to provide context in this story.

In doing so, it was necessary to make a number of leaps in logic and imagination. First was related to the calendar. I'm generally a stickler for historical authenticity and using time reckonings as my characters would. In this case, however—short of including a doctoral thesis and thoroughly alienating my readers—it wasn't possible to pick one. In Europe, the BC/AD system was in its infancy and wouldn't become widespread for another two centuries. With the collapse of the Western Roman Empire, dating based on the year of an emperor's reign became moot. A dating system based on the reigns of Visigothic kings would have been even more problematic, as several never reached their first anniversary. (Three backsides warmed the throne of Toledo during the span of this tale alone.) The most common dating system at the time in the Visigothic realms was the æra hispanica, or the Spanish era, dating from 38 BCE and the establishment of Roman governance over the Iberian peninsula.

In the case of the Maya, things become even more complicated. The primary calendar was the Long Count system, of 21 December 2012 fame. This system is simply a counting of days in a base-18 and base-20 system beginning with the foundation of this world (era or epoch), believed to correspond with 11 August 3114 BCE. The units of this system were the kin (1 day), winal (20 kins/days), tun (18 winals, 360 days), katun (20 tuns, 7200 days), and the baktun (20 katuns, 144,000 days). Dates in this system are commonly written as a decimal series with the first number relating to the baktun, the second to the katun, and so on.

Katun-endings were rare in a given lifetime, occurring about every 20 years, and were cause for celebration and great ceremony. The katun-ending of 9.9.0.0.0 (7 May 613) here coincides with Chakin's coming-of-age ceremony.

Based on two inscriptions (out of thousands among the known Mayan corpus), it is speculated that 13 baktuns complete the cycle. This really messes with my OCD, but gave rise to the 2012 shenanigans, 21 December of that year equating to the completion of the 13th baktun (1,872,000 days from the beginning of the present long-count cycle).

The Maya also had more pragmatic calendars. The haab' consisted of 18 months of 20 days each, plus five inter-calendrical days, for a 365-day year. This calendar would have been used for events relating to the natural solar year. Since the actual solar year is slightly longer (by not quite a quarter of a day), and since there was no provision for leap year, the alignment of the calendar with solar events such as the solstice or equinox would eventually become noticeably out of sync, thus giving rise to Khal-Ayin's concerns about the broken calendar.

The tzolk'in calendar consisted of 260 days, 20 months of 13 days each, and was used more for religious and ceremonial events. This calendar would have been used for naming of children (based on the date of birth), beginning monumental construction, and so on. It has been speculated that this 260-day calendar corresponds to the human gestation period (approximately 38 weeks, or 266 days), which would make this a more feminine, lunar calendar as opposed to the masculine, solar nature of the haab'. The alignment of these two calendars (the union of the divine feminine and masculine) occurs mathematically every 52 years, and this would also be cause for great celebration.

Language was, of course, the other obvious challenge. My general principle is that I serve as a translator and, so long as I don't have any gross anachronisms (e.g., mentioning steel in a society that has no iron-working), use of contemporary American English will be most effective in telling a story and entertaining a broad audience. I don't doubt that there will be purists who object to my using captain and lieutenant instead of contriving more authentic Mayan titles, but I imagine I caused enough cerebral damage with people and place names as it was.

Which leads to the central conceit (and likely most controversial idea) of the story: the collision of Mayan and Hebrew languages and the commingling of Visigothic, Hebrew, and Mayan bloodlines. Let me explain—no, there is too much. Let me sum up.

The Book of Mormon provides as its unique origin story the tale of a 6th-century BCE Hebrew family of the tribe of Manassesh (son of the patriarch Joseph). Having been warned of the coming destruction of Jerusalem by the Babylonians, the family packs up their fortune (including a steel sword and a set of engraved brass plates), and sets out on a great voyage. The family receives a divine gift called Liahona (here, Lakhin-Na, or Place of the East), a brass orb that guides them across the Indian and Pacific Oceans to a new promised land. There they settle and raise great temples, all the while continuing to record their history on plates of brass and copper, even gold.

After many generations, the people had filled the land, intermixed with other tribes, and developed their own unique (and often warring) societies. One bright and shiny day, a divine messenger appeared in the heavens, claiming to be a distant cousin. Having founded a new religion back in their ancient homeland (and having been killed for his troubles), he came back to life and crossed the ocean to see if this branch of his family might be more receptive.

Now, I don't personally put much stock in this tale, as far as an account of divine revelation. However, from personal experience I know that stories don't come from nowhere. So what if a branch of Hebrew people migrated to the New World two millennia before Columbus? What if, having survived crucifixion, a heretical Jewish prophet passed the Strait of Gibraltar and crossed the western sea? What if...?

The idea of Jesus having fathered children is nothing new. But what good is a royal/semi-divine dynasty without offspring with stories of their own? The European branch has been explored, but what of those "... other sheep, which are not of this fold ..."? Now that makes for some fun storytelling.

Iudila is a historical figure, though we (officially) know almost nothing about him.

Our brief encounter with the Goth Sisenath is fictional, but he is also historical, and will, within a few years of this story, take the throne of Spania.

Uti-Chan and Khak-Imish (their names simplified) are among the sixteen dynastic rulers of Xukpi/Copán. As our understanding of the Quiché Mayan dialect is still in its infancy, it will be some years before we know more of their reigns other than the monuments they left behind.

Breandan the Blessed (Saint Brendan) is claimed to have sailed from his Irish homeland far across the western sea, where he found a fruitful land and had grand adventures. Whether or not one of his brethren established a hermitage in the Azores is less certain.

Early in the 7th century CE, a volcanic eruption caused great flooding and destruction in Ha-Naab, what is today known as Quiriguá, Guatemala. That eruption ended this tale of Iudila and Chakin, but their adventures are just beginning.

Glossary of Principal Names and Places

AS MUCH AS POSSIBLE, I've tried to keep to place names as they would have been in the early seventh century CE. Similarly (and despite the suggestions of early readers), I've kept personal names as authentic as possible, though rendered into readable English without the diacritical marks. In rendering Mesoamerican names, I have generally replaced the Spanish *x* with the English *sh*, and *j* with *h*. I have relied heavily upon the historical, archaeological, and linguistic work of many experts, but any errors are my own.

Abul-Ghasem	Alternate form of Abu'l-Qasim, 7th-century Arabian merchant and religious leader.
Abyla	Southern Pillar of Hercules, present-day Jebel Musa, Morocco.
Aksum	Ancient empire comprised largely of present-day Ethiopia, Eritrea, Djibouti, Somalia, and Yemen.
Ali	Cousin and son-in-law of Abul-Ghasem.
Athanagild	Historical king of Visigothic Spain, reigned 554-567 CE.
Baetica	Roman (later, Visigothic) province of Spain, roughly equivalent to present-day Andalusia.
Balthi	Historical line of Visigothic nobility extending back at least to Alaric, who sacked Rome in 410 CE.

	Mythically descended from the Germanic solar deity Baldur.
Brehanu	Fictional sailor from present-day Ethiopia.
Breandan	Alternate form of Brendan, Abbot of Clonfert, Ireland, and Roman Catholic saint, c. 484-577 CE. Also called Brendan the Navigator, subject of *The Voyage of Saint Brendan the Abbot* (written c. 900 CE).
Britannia	Roman name for Great Britain.
Calpe	Northern Pillar of Hercules, present-day Rock of Gibraltar.
Chak-Ekh	*Rain Star.* Alternate rendering of Chak Ek', the planet Venus as the evening star.
Chakin	*Two Sun.* Alternate rendering of Cha' K'in, fictional Mayan princess of Shukpi. Daughter of Uti-Chan.
Chan-Kawak	*Jade Serpent.* Alternate rendering of Chan Kaywak, fictional ruler of Ha-Naab.
Constantinople	Capital of the Eastern (Byzantine) Roman Empire, present-day Istanbul, Turkey.
Corduba	Present-day Córdoba, Spain.
Dingha	Fictional sailor from present-day Mali.
Egyr	Also, Ægir. Germanic sea deity.
Eminio	Present-day Coimbra, Portugal.
Eneko	Fictional sailor from present-day Cantabria, Spain.
Fatima	Daughter of Abul-Ghasem.
Fu Sang	In Chinese legend, a mysterious land far across the eastern sea.
Gabriel	Judeo-Christian archangel associated with the West and travel.
Galicia	Roman (later, Visigothic) province of northern Spain, roughly equivalent to present-day Galicia, Asturias, Cantabria, La Rioja, Basque Country, and Navarro.
Goiswinth	Fictional noble of Visigothic Spain, son of historical Queen Goiswintha who was wife to Kings Athanagild and Liuvigild. Father of Iudila.

Gundemar	Historical Visigothic noble and king, reigned 610-612 CE.
Ha-Naab	*Broad Water*. Alternate rendering of Ha' Nab', speculative name of a 5th- through 9th-century Mayan city-state. Ruin located near present-day Quiriguá, Guatemala.
Hahkhan	*Yellow Water*. Alternate rendering of Ha' K'an, speculative name for the present-day Copán River or Xalagua River in Honduras.
Hahshuk	*Turning Water*. Alternate rendering of Ha' Xuk, speculative name for the present-day Motagua River in Guatemala.
Hibernia	Roman name for Ireland.
Hul-Balam	*Spear Jaguar*. Alternate rendering of Jul B'alam, fictional noble of Shukpi, half-brother of Uti-Chan. Speculatively associated with Ruler 5 of Ha-Naab (Quiriguá).
Hurakan	*Heart of the Sky*. Alternate rendering of Huracán, also known as U K'ux Kaj, Mayan creator and storm deity.
Isles of Atlas	Present-day Azores, Portugal.
Ispali	Also, Hispalis. Cathedral city and sometime capital of Visigothic Spain. Present-day Seville.
Iudila	Historical noble of Visigothic Spain.
Jasconius	Mythical living island mentioned in *The Voyage of Saint Brendan the Abbot*, thought to be a blue whale.
Kan-Tul	*Precious Rabbit*. Alternate rendering of K'an T'ul. Birth name of Chakin.
Keinan	Fictional noblewoman of Visigothic Spain.
Khak-Imish	*Smoke Jaguar*. Alternate rendering of Chan Imix K'awiil. Historical 12th dynastic ruler of Shukpi, reigned 628-695 CE.
Khal-Ayin	*Bound Crocodile*. Alternate rendering of K'al Ahin. Fictional ruler of Pah-Tullan.
Khu-Shul	*Owl Pillar*. Alternate rendering of Kuh Xol, fictional

noble and scribe of Shukpi.

Khuk-Moh   *Quetzal Macaw.* Alternate rendering of K'inich Yax K'uk' Mo' Ajaw, historical founder of a Classic period dynastic lineage of Shukpi, reigned 426-437 CE.

Kinich Ahaw   *Sun-faced Lord.* Alternate rendering of K'inich Ajaw, Mayan solar deity.

Kukulkan   *Feathered Serpent.* Also known as Q'uq'umatz, Gukumatz, and Waxaklajun Ubah Kan, mythical serpent-deity worshipped throughout the Mayan lands.

Lakam-Ha   *Great Water.* Alternate rendering of Lakam Ha', speculative ancient name of Calakmul, Mayan city-state located in present-day Campeche, Mexico.

Lemuel   Fictional Jewish scholar of Visigothic Spain.

Lusitania   Roman (later, Visigothic) province, roughly equivalent to present-day Portugal and Extremadura, Spain.

Malaca   Present-day Málaga, Spain.

Mauretania   Roman (later, Byzantine) province of northwestern Africa, roughly equivalent to present-day Algeria and Morocco.

Mika   Fictional sailor from present-day Egypt.

Milhma   Fictional sailor from present-day Spain.

Miriam   Aramaic rendering of Mary, 1st-century Judean noblewoman and wife of Yahshua.

Mutul   *Topknot.* Alternate rendering of Yax Mutal, ancient name of Mayan city-state of Tikal in present-day Petén, Guatemala.

Nak-Makah   *Covered Skin.* Alternate rendering of Nuk Makaj, fictional noble of Shukpi.

Niord   Germanic deity associated with the West and the sea.

Ocean Sea   Ancient theoretical body of water thought to surround the known continents of Europe, Africa, and Asia, and extending to the edge of the disk-like earth. Named for Oceanus.

Oceanus   Greco-Roman Titan associated with the seas, rivers, and lakes.

Oshlahun-Ak   *Thirteen Turtle*. Alternate rendering of Oxlajun Ak, fictional ruler of Wakhem.

Pah-Tullan   *Place of the Cattails*. Alternate rendering of Pat Tollan, speculative antenym of Teotihuacan, prominent Toltec city-state near present-day Mexico City, Mexico.

Pillars of Hercules   Greco-Roman name for the prominences of the Straits of Gibraltar, present-day Rock of Gibraltar (Gibraltar) and Jebel Musa (Morocco).

Popol Na   *Council House*. Alternate rendering of *Popol Nah*, speculative meeting place of Mayan city-states' rulers.

Reccared   Visigothic noble and king, reigned 586-601 CE.

Rusadir   Present-day Melilla, Spain.

Sakbe   *White Way*. Alternate rendering of Sak B'e, ceremonial limestone roadways found throughout Mesoamerica.

Sak-Chih   *White Deer*. Alternate rendering of Sak Chij, fictional wife of Uti-Chan.

Sak-Ishik   *White Woman*. Alternate rendering of Sak Ixik, Mayan lunar deity.

Sea of Atlas   Greco-Roman name for the Atlantic Ocean.

Septimania   Roman (later Visigoth and Frankish) province, and 7th- and 8th-century independent Jewish kingdom. Roughly equivalent to present-day Occitanie, France.

Seres   Greco-Roman name for the eastern extremity of the Silk Road trade route, part of present-day northern China.

Shan-Chitam   *Sky Peccary*. Alternate name form of Chan Chitam, fictional noble of Shukpi.

Shibalba   *Place of Fear*. Alternate rendering of Xibalba, mythical Mayan underworld.

Shmukaneh   Alternate rendering of Xmucane, Mayan ancestor-deity.

Shukpi   *Bright Corner*. Alternate rendering of Xukpi, 5th-

	through 9th-century Mayan city-state, also identified as Oxwitik. Ruins near present-day Copán, Honduras.
Sibolat	Conjectural endonym of the Maya civilization and associated lands.
Sisebut	Historical noble and king of Visigothic Spain, reigned 612-621 CE.
Sisenanth	Also, Sisenand. Historical noble and king of Visigothic Spain, reigned 631-636 CE.
Spania	Kingdom of the Visigoths on the Iberian peninsula, roughly equivalent to present-day Spain and Portugal.
Suinthila	Historical noble and king of Visigothic Spain, reigned 621-631 CE.
Tarracona	Roman (later, Visigothic) province of Spain, roughly equivalent to present-day Catalonia.
Tesfa	Fictional sailor from present-day Ethiopia.
Thanos	Fictional sailor from present-day Greece.
Tingis	Present-day Tangier, Morocco.
Tok-Ekh	*Black Cloud.* Alternate rendering of Tok Ik', fictional shaman of Shukpi, brother of Uti-Chan.
Tolupan	Indigenous tribes to the south of the Mayan lands.
Uti-Chan	*Smoke Serpent.* Alternate rendering of K'ahk' Uti' Chan Yopat, also known as K'ak' Chan Yopaat and B'utz' Chan. Historical 11th dynastic ruler of Shukpi, reigned 578-628 CE.
Wakhem	*Sign of descent.* Alternate rendering of Wo'j Emey, speculative ancient name for Kaminaljuyu, a major Mayan highlands city-state near present-day Guatemala City, Guatemala.
Witteric	Historical noble and king of Visigothic Spain, reigned 603-610 CE.
Wuk-Oh	*Moon Puma.* Alternate rendering of Uh Koj, fictional warrior of Shukpi.
Yahshua	Aramaic rendering of Jesus, 1st-century Judean religious and political figure.

Yahweh	Hebrew creator and storm deity.
Yash-Ahaw	*One Lord*. Alternate rendering of Yax Ajaw and Yahshua, conjectural founder of a Preclassic period dynastic lineage of Shukpi, c. 60 CE. Son of Yahshua.
Yashekh	*One Star*. Alternate rendering of Yax Ek', fictional queen of Shukpi, wife of Uti-Chan.
Yashwak	*One Hanged*. Alternate rendering of Yax Hek. Conjectural hypocoristic for Yahshua, referring to his having been hanged on a tree.
Zerah	Biblical son of the patriarch Judah, father of the Jewish people. Twin brother to Perez, with a disputed order of birth as described in Genesis 38.

Bibliography

WHILE THIS IS A WORK OF FICTION, I've done my best to set my story within the real world, as we understand it from 1400 years away. If you're interested in deepening your understanding of this long-lost world, I highly recommend the following works. Of course, all interpretations, conclusions, and errors in this book are my own.

Andrews, E. Wyllys, and William L. Fash, *Copan: The History of an Ancient Maya Kingdom*, SAR Press, 2005

Barney, Stephen A. (Tr.), W. J. Lewis, J. A. Beach, and Oliver Berghof, *The Etymologies of Isidore of Seville*, Cambridge University Press, 2006

Bell, Ellen E. (Ed.), Marcello A. Canuto, and Robert J. Sharer, *Understanding Early Classic Copan*, University of Pennsylvania Museum of Archaeology and Anthropology, 2004

Bradley, Henry, *The Goths from the Earliest Times to the End of the Gothic Dominion in Spain*, Kessinger Publishing, 2005

Carmack, Robert M., *The Quiche Mayas of Utatlan: The Evolution of a Highland Guatemala Kingdom*, University of Oklahoma Press, 2012

Coe, Michael D., *Breaking the Maya Code*, Thames & Hudson, 1999
— *The Maya*, Thames & Hudson, 2005

Collins, Roger, *Visigothic Spain 409-711*, Wiley-Blackwell, 2006

Fash, William L. Jr., William L. Fash, and Barbara W. Fash, *Scribes, Warriors, and Kings: The City of Copan and the Ancient Maya*, Thames & Hudson, 2001

Foster, Lynn V., *Handbook to Life in the Ancient Maya World*, Oxford University Press, 2005

Freidel, David, *Maya Cosmos: Three Thousand Years on the Shaman's Path*, William Morrow, 1995

Gardiner, Robert (Ed.), and John Morrison, *The Age of the Galley: Mediterranean Oared Vessels Since Pre-Classical Times*, Conway Maritime, 2004

Hapgood, Charles H., *Maps of the Ancient Sea Kings: Evidence of Advanced Civilizations in the Ice Age*, Adventures Unlimited Press, 1996

Heather, Peter, *The Visigoths from the Migration Period to the Seventh Century: An Ethnographic Perspective*, Boydell Press, 2003

Inomata, Takeshi, *Royal Courts of the Ancient Maya Vol.2: Data and Case Studies*, Perseus, 2001

Kulikowski, Michael, *Late Roman Spain and Its Cities*, Johns Hopkins University Press, 2004

Martin, Simon, and Nikolai Grube, *Chronicle of the Maya Kings and Queens: Deciphering the Dynasties of the Ancient Maya*, Thames & Hudson, 2000
McKillop, Heather, *In Search of Maya Sea Traders*, Texas A&M University Press, 2004
— *The Ancient Maya: New Perspectives*, W. W. Norton & Company, 2006

Milbrath, Susan, *Star Gods of the Maya: Astronomy in Art, Folklore, and Calendars*, University of Texas Press, 1999

Miller, Mary Ellen, and Karl Taube, *An Illustrated Dictionary of the Gods and Symbols of Ancient Mexico and the Maya*, Thames & Hudson, 1997

Montgomery, John, *Dictionary of Maya Hieroglyphs*, Hippocrene Books, 2002
— *How to Read Maya Hieroglyphs*, Hippocrene Books, 2004

Pate, Robert A., *Mapping the Book of Mormon*, Brigham Distributing, 2002

Richardson, John S., *The Romans in Spain*, Wiley-Blackwell, 1998

Schele, Linda, Peter Mathews, and Macduff Everton, *The Code of Kings: The Language of Seven Sacred Maya Temples and Tombs*, Scribner, 1999

Schele, Linda, and David Freidel, *A Forest of Kings: The Untold Story of the Ancient Maya*, William Morrow, 1992

Smith, Joseph Jr., *The Book of Mormon: Another Testament of Jesus Christ*, Church of Jesus Christ of Latter-Day Saints, 1981

Stocking, Rachel L., *Bishops, Councils, and Consensus in the Visigothic Kingdom, 589-633*, University of Michigan Press, 2001

Tedlock, Dennis, *Popol Vuh: The Definitive Edition of the Mayan Book of the Dawn of Life and the Glories of Gods and Kings*, Touchstone, 1996

Thompson, E. A., *The Goths in Spain*, Oxford University Press, 2000

Webster, David L., Ann Corinne Freter, and Nancy Gonlin, *Copan: The Rise and Fall of an Ancient Maya Kingdom*, Wadsworth Publishing, 1999

Acknowledgments

MANY HANDS AND HEARTS go into the making of a story. I'm grateful to all who had a hand in this.

My critters at Highlands Ranch Fiction Writers were Lynn Bisesi, Deirdre Byerly, Claire L. Fishback, Nicole Greene, Michael F. Haspil, LS Hawker, Laura Main, Chris Scena, and Vicki Pierce. Each of them played a role in making this a better story. Because magic.

Tracy Brogan and Jeanette Schneider are my touchstones of creativity, imagination, and getting-it-done-ness. See you at Arno's.

Of course, this book would not be in your hands without the faith and effort of my publishing and publicity teams. Kristy Makansi, Lisa Miller, and Laura Robinson believed in the work and brought it to fruition. Marissa DeCuir and Hannah Robertson believed I had something to say worth hearing. Thank you all.

And none of this means much of anything without Laura, my bride, to share it with. To many more grand adventures, my love.

About the Author

MARC GRAHAM STUDIED mechanical engineering at Rice University in Texas, but has been writing since his first attempt at science fiction penned when he was ten. From there, he graduated to knock-off political thrillers, all safely locked away to protect the public, before settling on historical fiction. His first novel, *Of Ashes and Dust*, was published in March 2017, followed by *Song of Songs: A Novel of the Queen of Sheba* and *Son of the Sea, Daughter of the Sun* in 2019.

He has won numerous writing contests including, the National Writers Assocation Manuscript Contest (*Of Ashes and Dust*), the Paul Gillette Memorial Writing Contest - Historical (*Of Ashes and Dust, Song of Songs*), and the Colorado Gold Writing Contest - Mainstream (*Son of the Sea, Daughter of the Sun*).

Marc lives in Colorado on the front range of the Rocky Mountains, and in addition to writing, he is an actor, narrator, speaker, story coach, shamanic practitioner, and whisky afficianado (Macallan 18, one ice cube). When not on stage or studio, in a pub, or bound to his computer, he can be found hiking with his wife and their Greater Swiss Mountain Dog.